REVENANT

STARWAYS
BOOK 4

ALEXIS GLYNN LATNER

AVENDIS
PRESS

Cover art and design by Adrian Doan Kim.

Copyediting and proofing by Terrance Grundy of Editerry (editerry.wixsite.com/proofreader).

Copyright © 2025 Alexis Glynn Latner
Published by Avendis Press, Houston, Texas
ISBN: 978-1-942686-34-7

All rights reserved. No part of this e-book may be reproduced, stored in a retrieval system or transmitted in any form or by any means, electronic, mechanical, photocopying, recording, or otherwise, without the prior written permission of the copyright holder, except for brief quotations used in a review.

This is a work of fiction. People, places and things mentioned in the story are either imaginary or used in a fictional manner.

To my lawyer friends, Chuck, Melissa, Pat, and Randall, and every other good lawyer out there.

ACKNOWLEDGMENTS

The Books on the Shelf writers' group, Bill, Gary, Kristin and Linda, gave me unstinting encouragement and good feedback all the way. Bethe Bugbee gave me very helpful feedback on the final draft.

Copyeditor Terry Grundy grappled with a long and complicated lexicon of names, places, and invented words, and reined in my penchant for too—many—em dashes. Thank you!

The Spiritual Direction Institute at Emmaus Spirituality Center in Houston was where I had a three-year training program to become a spiritual director, which is why I understand spiritual theology and Christian mysticism far better than ever before.

Several lawyer friends helped me get the legal angles right. But I alone am responsible for how I've represented law and being a lawyer in the far future.

CONTENTS

1. Messenger — 1
2. Journey — 11
3. Arrival — 23
4. Castle Courant — 35
5. Edvard — 47
6. Venture — 55
7. Reunion — 69
8. Star Bubbles — 81
9. Ghost Ship — 89
10. Lost Man Found — 99
11. The Hearth of Almaaz — 107
12. Martan Clark — 115
13. Val Savre — 127
14. Delilah of Dis — 137
15. The Wild Wife — 145
16. The Flame of Almaaz — 155
17. Mind Gate — 163
18. Memory — 173
19. Hall of Law — 181
20. Conspiracy — 195
21. Threshold — 205
22. Confession — 213
23. Atonement — 223
24. Green Holy Days — 233
25. Road to Hell — 245
26. Operation Inroad — 255
27. Legal Eagle — 265
28. Hellhole — 279
29. Nightwalkers — 289
30. Breaking Storm — 297
31. Exodus — 307
32. Storm Chase — 315

33. Safe Harbor	321
34. Destinies	329
More Adventures	337
About the Author	341
Also by Alexis Glynn Latner	342

1

MESSENGER

Looking like an unpotted houseplant, an innocent and untidy pile of leaves and tendrils, the hugwort retreated along the narrow hallway, staying just far enough away not to be caught. At present it was far from innocent, and Nia was in no mood for its games. "Stop right there!" she demanded in sheer frustration. It didn't have ears, though it could sense vibrations, possibly including the vibration of sound in air.

Its top leaves lifted, a movement that Nia recognized from previous experience as the hugwort feeling *enjoyment*. Then it ran away.

Nia raced after it.

The hugwort scrambled around the corner into the main hallway, darting between surprised students and professors. It headed for the open window at the end of the hall. If it got there, it could rappel down to the lawn—and elude her for hours. "Somebody shut that window!" she shouted, pointing.

An alert bystander did so.

Nia cornered the hugwort. "*You!*"

Bystanders laughed. This was Gembolt Hall, and as little as

she would have wanted the hugwort to be notorious, everybody who officed or attended classes in the building knew about it. That the university's interstellar lawyer, Nia Courant, had a misbehaving alien plant-animal for a pet was nothing if not entertaining—for everyone else.

She scooped it up into her arms. Sitting on the windowsill, she combed the hugwort's tendrils with her fingers. Its furry root mass purred. It somehow knew that when you misbehaved and got caught, it was a good tactic to show your most likeable behavior.

The student who'd been victimized by the hugwort caught up with her. Clutching his pilfered backpack, he stood there looking anxious and angry.

Nia's fingers found a cool, complex little shape. She teased it out of the hugwort's clutching tendrils. It was a stylized metal horse, the kind of talisman that was extremely important to tribal people from the planet Goya. "I apologize for my little green friend. It likes to investigate closed spaces, and it's attracted to things with interesting shapes and textures." She gave the talisman back to the student. "*Day'za tiljuege,*" she added, *may your name shine,* an appropriate thing to say to a tribal Goyan. She meant it. For him to belong to one of the upland tribes on imperfectly terraformed Goya, and make it all the way here, he had to have extraordinary intelligence and drive.

His expression morphed into a surprised smile.

One of the bystanders started telling everyone about the time the hugwort made off with Nia's identity bracelet, and her office practically had to turn Gembolt Hall inside out to recover it. Nia felt her face flush with embarrassment.

As though her bracelet impossibly knew it was being talked about, it trilled. The tone signaled that she had an interstellar messenger waiting for her. *Just wonderful,* she thought. It was probably a legal matter—an urgent and important one, if it warranted a messenger—and here she was, rumpled from the chase and with her hands full of the hugwort in a wild mood!

Even so, this was much better than how things had been a few months ago. A misbehaving hugwort was infinitely better than war in Wendis.

She'd long since adopted the Wendisan custom of keeping a carrycloth in her pocket. She wrapped the strong, thin cloth around the hugwort, firmly knotting the corners of the cloth together. The hugwort was very compressible. And when compressed, it quieted. She'd discovered that only a couple of weeks ago, by stuffing it into a desk drawer when it was running wild just before a sensitive meeting. Carrying the cloth by the tight knot, she set out across the campus to meet the messenger.

Outdoors there was the sky made of sea to remind her what a strange world the university existed in. Wendis was a spinning cylinder with a curved sea and three curling mountains; it was an interstellar city two thousand years old. It harbored the best interstellar university on this end of the long arc of human history. It could also be a very dangerous place. She'd come here four years ago as an exile, with her interstellar legal career derailed and her spirit in shambles. Since then, she'd done unremitting hard work punctuated by unexpected danger and, finally, the war. But she'd found success, a new home, and the love of her life.

Tonight she'd tell Martan about the hugwort's escapades. He'd understandingly laugh. He called it the weed, but he was fond of it, and it never fazed him. Her hugwort-related embarrassment and frustration would dissolve in his presence. Thinking about him made her smile.

The messenger portal was a small, dark room adjacent to the chancellor's office. Unlike her first years here, the chancellor's office was friendly territory now. The new chancellor was her trusted old boss, Minnie Toll. Minnie's assistant was the eminently trustworthy Hiro Low, who had been Nia's own assistant before the war. Hiro solemnly waved her into the portal.

Smoothing her hair, she faced the empty end of the narrow room. She steeled herself. Given Hiro's seriousness, this messenger could well be a lawyer speaking for the Faxen Union. And it was the Faxen Union that had made war on Wendis, unsuccessfully but very consequentially. Legal and diplomatic dominoes were still falling across the stars. Nia said, "Begin."

The portal's invisible message machines constructed a simulacrum—a likeness of whoever had sent the message. A man took shape in front of her, woven out of light, until he looked solid and recognizable. Very recognizable. The messenger wasn't from Faxe after all. It was from her home world, Azure. Tall and silver-haired, the simulacrum was Edvard Az-Courant, the New Catholic Orthodox archbishop of Azure-Tierre. Her father. The shock of seeing his image in front of her nearly made her knees buckle.

Years ago, he'd rejected the fateful choice she made in her early legal career. In so doing, he had truly rejected her. If he wasn't why her career on Azure derailed—the choice itself had done that—her father was why her spirit had been in shambles four years ago when she exiled herself to Wendis. How dare he send a messenger to her here? She felt anger so instant and intense that it had to come out somehow. She clenched her free hand into a fist.

The simulacrum made eye contact with her. Rendering her father's voice imperfectly—which was a relief: hearing a perfect rendition of his voice might have made her come unglued—it spoke. "Nia, your uncle is dead again."

That could only mean Uncle Val. Thick dismay layered on top of her hot anger. "How?"

The messenger had artificial intelligence. Edvard occasionally used interstellar messaging —he was important enough for that— so the messenger had learned to resemble him. It gave a faintly theatrical shrug. "Not explained except by a story so wild that we can't believe it."

Uncle Val had worked at a university research station on the moon of the planet Tellas before his first demise, which had actually been a staged disappearance. Nia had recently heard a rumor about that. The academic grapevine resembled the hugwort, every bit as curious and prehensile. It was rumored that Val had invented a stargate—a way to cross the stars without starships. That was something the Faxen secret intelligence agency would very much be interested in. But they wouldn't assassinate him for it. They'd capture him and put him in dark detention, with a believable cover story about his death. *So wild that we can't believe it* didn't sound like SECINTAG.

His first death had been plausible even without a dead body to prove it. Ostensibly he'd been vaporized by an alien artifact, something called a halo gate, which he was studying at the research station on Telmoon, the satellite of Tellas. It turned out that he'd run away with a beautiful girlfriend. The last Nia had heard, they were happily living on the free-trade moon called Stannto, in one of the shady interstices of the Faxen Union.

Edvard's messenger continued, "His separated wife on Albion, now his separated widow, is claiming his intellectual property for herself and their children."

Albion, where Val was from, had a perfectly legal marital status that amounted to *married but amicably separated*. Azure had the same thing. It was neither a sin nor a crime for someone like that to take a girlfriend. It didn't affect monetary or intellectual inheritance any more than it would have changed the heirs' genes. Nia pointed out, "That sounds like a matter for the minor Albion courts."

Any messenger was programmed to respond appropriately to any comments that the situation made likely. The messenger spread its elegant hands—a gesture so like her father that it made her dizzy. "It turns out he went to great lengths to transfer the inheritance of his intellectual property to his mother."

Better known to Nia as her redoubtable grandmother, Eirene, on Azure.

"In addition he changed his citizenship to Azurean. So it's headed for the courts here."

The messenger watched her. Fortunately Nia knew how not to let her feelings show, because her feelings were whirling now. Intellectual property and citizenship with interstellar ramifications could be complex legal issues. Stargates—if that was Val's intellectual property—would be catnip to SECINTAG. And the whole business landing on her family on Azure?!

Azure, unlike Albion, or for that matter, Tellas, was not an obedient client state in the Faxen Union: Azure was an independent world. She remembered Uncle Val as being pro-Unionist. But not a fool. If he'd made a star-shaking discovery, he wouldn't have wanted the Faxen Union to appropriate it. Moving it to Azure wasn't a bad idea. He'd just probably planned to stay alive and personally guard it.

She let out a long breath. Even apart from whatever circumstances he'd died in, this time for real, Uncle Val might have left a very loaded legacy.

The messenger said, "This needs a first-rate interstellar lawyer. Can you come home and help us deal with this?"

She wanted to say—or scream—*NO!* She wanted to continue her work in Wendis, not just her legal work, but repairing the damage caused by the war, and emotional work, since she was newly married to Martan. She did *NOT* want to tackle a messy and possibly dangerous legal challenge on Azure.

Least of all did she want to face her father. Or in truth she did want to face her father. Just not for it to damage her again.

Her emotions were layers of anger, dismay, and now consternation, all on top of old hurt. Didn't avalanches have layered falls of snow before the weight of it all made the oldest, bottom layer liquify? And when that happened, the side of the mountain came crashing down.

The messenger would record her expressions. She kept her feelings out of her face. "Well, what was the incredible story?"

"That something inside a halo gate killed him. A halo gate somewhere else," the messenger clarified. "Not the one that didn't kill him the first time."

Then she remembered the secret that Val had told her at least ten years ago, privately, asking for a promise to let it go no further. He was sure the gigantic alien artifacts called halo gates comprised a system, and that if humanity ever understood them, the gates would reveal how to go between them without starships.

She felt a sense of impending doom. Val would not have been able to resist investigating halo gates. In the same long-ago conversation, he'd said that his theories pointed to more halo gates than the known ones, some of them completely unsuspected on the colony worlds and planetary moons where they were dormant. Having faked his death and run off into the shadows of the Faxen Union, gaining anonymity that way, had he explored one or more of the unknown gates—and gotten inside long enough to see what was there? Had he left any scientific account, or notes about where the unknown halo gates were, or how the gates worked?

Legal proceedings bringing that out into the open could be bad in too many ways to count.

Her mind pivoted on the oiled axis of legal expertise. Given the nature of this mess, it could be made to look like a domestic matter, just a family feud. The domesticity of it could be emphasized and even exaggerated. That would keep SECINTAG away from her family out of pure disinterest. To create a charade like that would take great legal skill, considerable daring, and an intimate knowledge of Azurean law. All of which she had.

That approach would probably be anathema to Edvard, with his pride of being both a church leader and the scion of a prominent family. *Well, let him not like it,* she thought. He'd long since demonstrated that he didn't like *her.*

Edvard wouldn't crassly use a messenger for emotional leverage. But it could take initiative beyond its explicit programming. The messenger said, "Nia, half a year ago I got word from your colleagues in Wendis that you had disappeared, and they believed you were in deadly trouble. I was bitterly afraid for you. Soon I learned that you were alive, to my boundless relief. I considered contacting you but then came reports of war breaking out in Wendis, and only recently have we heard that it ended well for Wendis. Whether or not you wish to trouble yourself with Val's doings, please come home."

If the messenger had been Edvard, saying all of that would have cost him dearly. It wasn't Edvard. But it resonated with him, as it was designed to.

It expected an answer. That was the nature of messengers.

She heard herself say, "I will, as soon as I can arrange passage by starliner."

The messenger said, "Thank you. End of message." It vanished, the projection ended by the machines that created it.

Nia didn't move. She couldn't believe she had just promised —told a messenger, which was a duly recorded and legally binding promise—that she would return to Azure.

She would have to go alone. Martan, her new husband, favorite foil, and superbly effective protector when she needed protecting, was badly needed here. He should stay in Wendis. But the idea of going across the stars to Azure frightened her. It raised a wave of fear as cold and thick as the salt water of Azure. She tried to hold the fear off, but it built up. Too close—too inevitable—it towered over her.

A thin green tendril worked its way out of the carrycloth. It lightly touched her bracelet but then curled around her hand.

God only knew how an alien plant-animal was able to sense human emotion. But it could, and when she most needed comfort or reassurance, it did.

Behind her the portal's outer door opened. Martan's voice said, "Nia?"

She launched herself into his strong arms. He was solid bone and strong muscle, warm skin and brave heart—everything that a bloodless simulacrum wasn't. It felt incredibly good to have him hold her, with the cloth-wrapped hugwort pressed between them, purring.

"Hiro signaled me. He said you had a messenger that might have brought bad news. Did it?"

"Yes, and with hellacious knock-on consequences." She explained the messenger's request.

Martan's answer was, "I'll come with you."

She wanted to agree. That would serve Edvard right. It could also cause untold trouble, maybe even putting Martan and everyone else in danger if SECINTAG had gotten the faintest whiff that he was a renegade agent of theirs. It wasn't clear how much the Faxen secret intelligence agency had sifted out from the wreckage of the Union's plans to conquer Wendis. Assessing how much the agency knew, or guessed, about him was one of the things Martan was working on now. She said, "Not yet, unless I run out of ideas."

She felt as well as heard him chuckle. "You never run out of ideas, my love. But interstellar travel is hard for you. Will you be okay alone?"

Suddenly she decided, "I won't go alone."

He raised an eyebrow.

"The hugwort got into trouble again today. I apologized for my little green friend, but after that last growth spurt, it's not that little anymore. Instead of it being bored around here and getting smarter about undoing locks and fasteners, I'll take it to Azure and let it explore Castle Courant."

He said drily, "That should surprise your family."

Very likely. But not as much as if they knew what Martan really was.

He'd been a counterterrorism agent so effective and so deadly that they called his kind hellhounds. When he had been sent to assassinate a political figure who turned out to be honorable, though, he'd finally seen through SECINTAG's corruption and, under cover of a nearly fatal explosion, defected to Wendis. There, with the help of the doctor who pieced him back together, he had become a Wendisan hellhound. The distinction made all the difference in that little world. He'd done as much as anyone to win the war.

All of a sudden, it made her head spin in a good way to imagine bringing him home to Azure. Showing him her childhood home, the ancient, beam-carved, rambling stone edifice called Castle Courant. Exploring it together with him, including the high slippery places and the structurally unsound crannies where it was too dangerous to go—unless you had a companion with superhuman reflexes. Suddenly, she wanted all of that.

She took a deep breath. Someday, he *would* go home with her, she promised herself. This time, she had to go by herself, even if it meant fighting waves of fear as cold and thick as the seas of Azure.

2

JOURNEY

Robard Benedet's home was high up on the Wendisan mountain named Chance. Nia had been here a couple of times, but she'd never seen the sunroom before. The room had a wide window full of light from the sunspar with a view across the Celadon Sea to the mist-shrouded foothills of the mountains. The light made the room bright and warm, while the fresh spinwind, filtered through well-positioned screens, kept it from being stuffy.

This was a good place for an invalid to recover.

The two men here with Nia today were a visual contrast. Both were tall, slim, and attractive. Robard Benedet had the tawny Wendisan skin and dark hair, and an air of restless energy. Theo was Faxen in coloration, golden-haired and green-eyed, and he was obviously weak. Only a multi-jointed mobility chair kept him from collapsing onto the floor.

Edvard's messenger was well-intended, but it was wrong. The war had not ended well for everybody in Wendis. Theo was at least still alive, and the doctors had hope for his eventual recovery. Some people hadn't been so lucky.

Nia spoke slowly and clearly as she asked Theo, "You once said that when you spent a while at the university on Tellas, you heard a rumor that instead of dying, my Uncle Val—his real name was Vienradzis Al-Savre, but he usually went by Val Savre—had made a stargate. Can you tell me any more about that?"

"I'm not sure I remember."

She stayed sympathetically silent.

Theo spoke uncertainly, locating his memories like someone searching for their belongings in a house leveled by an earthquake. "His colleagues knew he really wasn't dead because he was subsequently seen in the research station and in the university. He'd disappeared from the Tellas moon along with a girl from bioscience. That had the whole university excited about their relationship, of course. The stargate rumor mixed into the gossip made it even more interesting."

Nia could imagine Theo in his previous life being a connoisseur of gossip. She nodded encouragingly.

Theo tilted his head, as though memory would spill out of his damaged brain. Maybe that worked. "But the people who'd been closest to him didn't say anything about stargates and didn't talk about him running off with the girl. I think he had loyal friends."

That squared with Nia's memories of her uncle. He'd been a student at the university on Tellas himself because it had the best halo gate research of any institution, anywhere. There he made lifelong friends. Subsequently he'd had colleagues whom he respected and who respected him in turn.

The previous Theo had been a mathematical genius. Nia asked him, "Did you wonder what was really possible about stargates?"

"Yes. Yes, I did." Remembering made him look, and sound, more lively. "Inventing a stargate would be a huge project. Impossible to hide—even if the theoretical underpinnings were completely understood, which they aren't. Val Savre had done real work with that, though—the theoretical underpinnings. I read his scientific papers. He hypothesized a localized kind of traversable interstellar connectivity."

"Local where?" Robard asked.

Theo looked up at him. "Across much of the Faxen Union."

Robard said, "The Faxen Union exists because starflight readily works between the stars of the Union."

Nia understood that much. Fast starflight didn't work everywhere. In fact, it worked hardly anywhere, but the galaxy was so vast that *hardly anywhere* amounted to millions of stars. The Faxen Union was founded on seven stars, each having a habitable planetary system, close together in realspace, and all accessible by starflight.

But Theo was shaking his head. "Not the same thing. Or...." He tilted his head the other way from the first time. "It might be different connectivity than realspace or fast starflight, a function of a deeper shape of spacetime, not understood yet."

Robard frowned. "Nia, I told you once before that there is an invisible net of intrigue across the stars, and the web is spun by the dark god called Shandy, who sends his Angels back and forth by strange and secretive routes to do his bidding."

Nia clearly remembered the day in a rose garden in Wendis when Robard had told her about Shandy's deadly web. She shivered.

He looked at her for a long moment, then continued. "In the Faxen Union, there are gaps in Shandy's web, places his Angels simply do not go. There's something there that the Angels avoid. Ordinary humans would be well advised to avoid it too."

Whatever it was, had her uncle found his way into it? "Thank you for the warning," she said grimly.

Theo said, "We have something for you better than a warning. The gift, Bard?"

Nia marveled at Theo calling Robard by a familiar name. The only nickname Robard had ever had before now was Bent, and it was not a compliment. In Wendis right now, the luckiest people were those who came out of the war with both life and love. She was one of them. Incredibly, so were these two.

Robard's set jaw softened. He told her, "This is for your wedding. We missed it because Theo was having a bad day." He handed Nia a carrycloth of first quality with something soft inside it. "Take this in case you need to make a formal appearance looking better than a threadbare academic."

Nia wasn't about to argue that academics, including herself, never looked threadbare, or that their appearances really didn't matter. She said, "Thank you."

How could the terribly bad turn to wonderfully good? Good may not erase bad; in her experience that happened seldom or never. Yet good could spring up out of death and desolation like flowers at the end of winter. She pondered that as the tube train took her back to the university.

She would leave for Azure tomorrow morning. She had today to get a great deal of work done, including tasking the junior lawyers in her office with responsibility to cover important work in her absence. But she'd taken time to visit Robard and Theo, because she wanted to know what Theo knew. Could it have been done by a vizcall? No, because that could have made Theo freeze up. A bloodless call wasn't in line with Wendisan propriety either.

By going to Robard's house and back, taking in the views from his high balcony and the tube train—maybe this was how she said goodbye-for-now to Wendis. It was a strange little spinning world. She had done all she could to set it right. And she had not failed. Wendis was better because of her, happier and more whole than it might have ended up after the war.

How was it that bad could turn out good? After everything that had happened to her in the war, she knew the answer to that now. *Christa Terra is present in everything.* Christa Terra was the holy home world destroyed by human greed and violence, resurrected on a dozen terraformed worlds, and just as miraculously restored in Wendis with its artificial but thriving ecosystem. Christa Terra was here.

From the inner pocket of her tunic, she took out her Christa Terra medal. It was made of metal cut from the starship that had made the long journey from Earth to Azure. It was intricately engraved with the outlines of the continents of the lost home world. She held it long enough for the star-traveled metal to warm slightly, then returned it to her pocket. More than ever, she did not want to leave Wendis, go back to Azure, and confront all that had turned bad there for her. And yet . . . and yet . . . Christa Terra would be with her there too.

It was evening before she could visit the other person she needed see today. Svetlana Tai was Nia's other enemy who—bad turning good yet again—had turned into a friend.

From talking to Robard high up in the Wendisan landscape, to talk to Lana, Nia went underground. Lana lived in a university apartment complex typically inhabited by graduate students and impecunious junior faculty. Her furnishings were battered, untidy, and unremarkable, except one of her walls was a vizscreen—a window to the universe as exquisite as that kind of window in a starship. Well she might have a vizscreen wall: She commanded the Wendisan research starship called *Pastfinder*. When not here at home, she and her daring crew pried at obscure corners of the stars, did field xenarchaeology in dismal and dangerous places, and whenever possible, made off with unattended prizes.

Lana obligingly served Nia hot tea in her best, only slightly chipped teacup. For herself Lana poured a shot of the Azurean liquor called Aquarel. It was pink. It was also potent, and not an option for Nia when she needed to think clearly.

In answer to Nia's question, Lana said, "The halo gates are the most profound mystery of the Star Age. They exist on a handful of moons and worlds. The civilization that made them, evolved on the super-earth world called Meridian." Lana waved her hand in a studied way. Her vizwall blurred into a swirling cataract of stars. When it stopped, it showed a wide Earthlike world. Meridian looked uninhabited, except for a faint stippling of light on the night side of a gray blotch on the terminator between day and night. "We have no idea what they called their one and only city. We call it Vere. Now it is an expanse of ruins so vast that you can see it from space."

The ruined city had to be the gray blotch on the terminator. Nia nodded.

"There are monitoring stations on the edges of it, but most of what they do is ecology in the wilderness around the ruins. The Vere ruins are very hostile to being pried into. So are all the halo gates that still work, anywhere they exist. If you poke them, they explode. Investigators have died that way."

"Is that why you never study them?" Typically, any artifact of alien origin fascinated Lana and her merry crew.

Lana pondered the clear pink Aquarel. "Thirty years ago there was a notorious incident on a rogue planet called Dhal. A research station had been built there near a dormant halo gate. One day something alien came out of the gate, butchering the staff and the resident families and then plundering the station. I do xenarchaeology only where the ruins are lifeless and likely to stay that way, thank you." She gave a short laugh. "I'm fairly xenophobic."

It made sense to Nia that Lana Tai, fearless and reckless, had to be afraid of something for her psyche to stay in balance. "My uncle wanted to get into halo gates. He may have succeeded, at least temporarily. Our family got word that he'd died somehow—inside a halo gate." Nia quickly explained why she was going home to Azure. Then she took a deep breath, knowing that what she could say next would matter to Lana very much. "He hypothesized that the halo gates may be a system of stargates."

"Stargates." Lana put the glass down. "That makes my antennae quiver."

"It should. Stargates are something you want very much."

"And so does the Faxen Union." Lana snapped her fingers in the air. The gesture that followed made her vizwall change again until it showed a section of the starry space around Wendis. Nia recognized the constellation that Wendisans called the Raptor, consisting of the seven stars of the Faxen Union. The Raptor's bright eye was the star of Albion. A dim star in its tail was the poor and backward world Estrella. Above the Raptor's shoulder was Azure's bright sun. That was the safest position so close to a raptor . . . but never truly safe. Point taken. Nia just nodded.

Lana said, "If you need help, milady, send me a bubble. Don't hesitate either. I think you could get into real danger with this."

Now that she'd finished her day and only had the journey across the stars ahead of her, Nia's dread and fear started building. The cold thick wave of it towered over her.

Lana's words rang in her ears. *I think you could get into real danger.* Unlike some people she knew—Martan, Robard, and Lana being three of them—Nia disliked danger. It never exhilarated her. But that wasn't why she dreaded going home to Azure, or not entirely. She was afraid of returning to the accusatory and angry emotional place with her father. She even felt afraid that the grandparents who'd always steadfastly supported her had changed their minds about that—even though they'd sent her a priceless bottle of Aquarel a year ago as a gift for Azure's Greening Day holidays.

Reminding of herself of that didn't fix her irrational fears. But it gave her a good idea about how to explain her sudden trip to Azure to everyone else here in Wendis.

After she got back to the apartment they shared, Martan made love to her and took her mind away from dread for a while. Then he held her for the rest of the night.

Morning came too soon.

When she'd first arrived, after her ambitious career on Azure foundered because of the ultimate repercussions of the early decision for which her father had never forgiven her, she knew no one in Wendis. She'd felt terribly alone, with the bridge back to her family scorched if not burned to ashes. Leaving Wendis today was diametrically different. Having announced that she was making a visit to her home world for its great holiday, Greening Day, she got plenty of good wishes from her colleagues, friends, and students. She also had the warmth of last night's love and comfort with Martan. She pulled that around her like a coat.

An uneventful space shuttle ride took her to the gateway of Wendis. During the war, Wendis had moved away from its gateway, making the Faxen Union's planned invasion much harder. After the war was over, Wendis had rejoined the gateway, and the gateway returned to the ordinary, vital business of interstellar travel.

Workers and pilots in the gateway waved at her. They knew who she was. She'd played a role at the end of the war—helping set the little world right—and there weren't many tall, slender, silver-haired Azurean women here to confuse her with. She waved back.

Boarding the starliner was hard anyway. That was when fear really hit her. Finding her assigned seat was like swimming in cold thick water too salty to freeze.

This was ridiculous, she thought. In the past year, she had faced danger more than once, not liking it one bit, but remaining able to function. Yet now, on a starliner—a technology so routine that ordinary people thought little of being whisked across the stars—she was a complete coward. Just wonderful.

As usual, she felt the transition into starflight space. It wasn't an objectionable sensation for her, just noticeable, a moment of dizziness.

On its way across the stars the starliner jumped through space from one turning point to another. Its computational intelligence painted its flight as a straight line on the visual screens that passengers either watched or ignored. Nia tried to concentrate on reading the library she'd taken with her, Azurean and Tellan law. The trip didn't last long, which was fortunate. Not so fortunate was the fact that it only got her a fraction of the way home. Azure not being a direct starliner destination from Wendis, her first stop was the interstellar way station called Starway.

The official in charge of the operations of the way station was a Wendisan named Rigel Keeper. They had met before. He warmly welcomed her at the threshold. Then he lowered his voice. "This time, do you have *It?*"

Once before when she came through Starway, there had been an extremely embarrassing incident involving the hugwort and a bowl of epicurean soup. She felt herself blush. "Yes, but in a special carrier. It won't get out."

He was visibly relieved. "Good, good, good. Now I have a room for you, one of our nicest!"

One of the nicest rooms in Starway would be very nice indeed. But fear returned. She shuddered. Without understanding why, she did not, not, *not* want such a room. It was as though something bad had happened to her somewhere like that, even though she could not remember it.

Fortunately she had an alternative. She gave Rigel Keeper a perfect Wendisan bow. "With the greatest appreciation for your hospitality, my legal assistant has a cousin here, and arranged for me to stay with him, in the comfort of a home."

"Yes, yes, of course!"

Nia wondered how Hiro had known that she wouldn't want

the Starway guest room. Hiro was amazingly astute. She easily found her way to the home of Hiro's cousin, Koi.

Koi lived in Starway's red-light district. His door had a color scheme that indicated what sexual services could be found within. He was a pleasant young man, more slender and pretty than Hiro. "I don't get many Azureans at my door," he said cheerfully.

Her mind slipped its gears just a bit. "You do understand I'm here just for somewhere to sleep tonight?"

"Of course, of course!" He fluidly bowed her in and directed her to his personal quarters. She immediately found the place comforting. It was a Wendisan home, with a few interstellar touches and a small, alert, fluffy white dog, a Wendisan Chivvier named Star.

"During the war, Star had a great adventure away with friends but is back home now," Koi said fondly. "As my honored guest, she will keep you company tonight."

Nia liked that idea. Seemingly Koi, like Hiro, knew something that she didn't. She wondered what it was. After spending last night almost sleepless, she was too tired to wonder for long. She was asleep almost as soon as she curled onto a cozy mat on the floor.

Later she jerked awake out of nameless fright to find the little dog pressed next to her, a warm presence with soft white fur. Cuddling the dog, which regally accepted the gesture, it occurred to her that whatever she'd been afraid of in the dream wasn't Azure. It was something else. Something nameless and interstellar.

She wished she could just stay here with Koi and Star. But by now the starliner to Azure was already berthed and undergoing nocturnal cleaning and maintenance operations that made it ready to cross the stars tomorrow. Like the shorter trip from Wendis, it would almost certainly be safe and comfortable. Why did the prospect make her shiver with fear?

The little dog yipped. In only a few minutes, Koi came in. He turned on soft lights and made her a cup of hot sweet tea, and they talked for a while.

Koi was very well informed about interstellar affairs, as well as the workings of Starway, in addition to news from Wendis. His intelligent, gentle manner made it easy to talk to him, and natural to discuss matters of a sensitive nature. Nia began to appreciate how he could be, as Hiro had once quietly and in confidence told her, an agent of Wendis. That spinning little world didn't have military might or great resources. It leveraged information. Guests of Koi's could easily become informants who came away as undamaged as they were unknowing.

The tea might have had a mild sedative in it. Nia became very sleepy, and when she curled back onto the mat, with Star at her side and Koi tucking a warm comforter around them, she slept dreamlessly until morning.

3

ARRIVAL

Koi walked Nia to the station's starport. He even settled her into her seat in the starliner. She was grateful. She wasn't sure if she could have forced herself there.

She stayed soaked with cold fear all the way to Azure. But for a starliner passenger, all that was necessary was to sit and be carried to a distant star. You could sleep or at least rest in the ship's night, when the seat turned into a narrow but comfortable curtained cot. This wasn't how her ancestors, the astronauts in their slower-than-light starship, had journeyed—braving the unknown, with the most primitive star-going technology, in search of a daunting new world to terraform and colonize in a frozen sleep that lasted centuries. And yet their bravery was enough to cross the stars that way. The comparison with herself did not feel flattering.

Her breath caught when she saw Azure in the starliner's vizscreen and knew that it wasn't a computer's simulation. It was real, that planetary globe of ice and sea, rock and air. Around the equator were traces of green—the recreated ecosystem of Earth.

Azure had its own gateway where starships came and went with flares of light. Azurean customs operated in the gateway. Nia having once been a citizen of Azure, and now being a citizen of Wendis with a high-level academic visa, put her into a short line at customs. Her name, though, was what got her a quick, cordial and private interview with a customs official. Her full name was Inanna Az-Courant. *Az* meant descended not just from colonists who came to Azure in the ancient starship, but also from the astronauts who piloted the ship here and first landed on the new world. She was a direct descendant of them. *Descendant being the operative word*, she thought ruefully. She wasn't made of the same brave stuff.

The hugwort easily made it through its own customs interview. Packed into a clear-sided box, it was motionless. Its paperwork declared it a demonstrably harmless alien species without venom, toxin, teeth, or claws. That put it into the same category as imported rocks. A pathogen-and-parasite test came out negative; it was clean.

Nia passed her own pathogen screening too. In the old days, humanity had been savaged by viruses repeatedly. Now there were preventions built into the genome, and precautions in place: genetic testing and screening for symptoms in every port of entry. Absent any ominous indicators, the screening was almost imperceptible.

The gateway was built into the transit ring. Like every other civilized world, Azure had a transit ring, linked to the planet's surface by space elevators anchored in transit towers. Safely seated in a descending module with other passengers, she fell down the space elevator like a falling star. She held the Christa Terra medal for the whole ride down. The medal made a difference. So did being married, having a husband and home she could return to in Wendis. Out of interstellar space and in the atmosphere of Azure, she wasn't as panicked as she'd expected to be.

The transit tower was on the edge of Denevez, the oldest and capital city of Azure, on the equator of the planet. In Denevez it was frigid midnight when she arrived. She remembered leaving Azure for the last time on just such a cold night. Her father had been even colder. And yet, in the greater scheme of things, it had turned out all right. She'd found a home in Wendis and done all she could to protect and make the spinning little world better. In an even bigger picture, the choice she'd made so long ago had proven beyond a shadow of a doubt to have been the right one. Christa was present in all things, not just human beings, but all living things and living genes of Earth; and not just life, but the metal of the ancient astronauts' starship, which her medal was made from. Like never before, Nia understood that Christa was everywhere—and with her here.

Not that Christa's presence made life any less hard for believers than for cynics. Nia's choice years ago, driven by her religious faith, had resulted in pain and estrangement that still might not end. Edvard might never forgive her, even though he was a New Catholic Orthodox Church leader and, as such, a theologian. A theologian who didn't want to forgive had a great deal of material at his disposal.

Yet he'd asked her to come home. He might not intend to resume their old conflict. Would he set aside his pride enough to be cordial to her and overlook the painful past? Maybe. The messenger had been a good sign. Would he ever admit that he had been wrong about her fateful and faithful choice so many years ago? That she did not know.

In Denevez she boarded the ice ferry, a jet-powered catamaran that glided across the frozen surface of Starfield Lake. She didn't want to be enclosed in metal cabins anymore, so she chose to ride abovedeck. Enough of the wind of the catamaran's speed eddied around the windscreen to ruffle her hair. Stars blazed overhead, more and brighter stars than the night sky of Earth had ever held. This was a different arm of the Galaxy than the environs of Earth, and the stars were closer together. A group of the brightest stars formed the constellation usually called the Astronaut. Those were the stars of the Faxen Union, as seen from here.

A lesser, lower and warmer star cluster on the shore of the frozen lake was the nighttime lights in the town called Arrival. The town was older than Denevez, but much smaller, constrained on a narrow isthmus between the lake and the sea.

It amazed her how easy it was to ride on the familiar catamaran, with the familiarity of the ferry crew, who as always were Arrivaltowners. She had only been gone for four years, she reminded herself. In her life, those were momentous years that changed everything. Evidently, not so, here.

Her destination was where the isthmus, Arrival Arc, was most narrow. There stood Castle Courant. It was called Castle not for how high it rose above the Arc—only the upper two stories were artificially built up—but because it was where the Arc itself rose in a high block of cliffs.

The lake gate under the cliff face was open, night-lights glowing. Someone at least leaving the lights on for her was a good sign. The catamaran throttled back and glided closer until it lightly connected to the dock.

Keyed up with tension, not waiting for the stairs to unfold, she jumped to the dock. It felt good to be in normal gravity. And Azure had her own childhood gravity—as familiar as her own body, though she'd never realized that until now.

The cheerful deckhand handed her bags over. Then the catamaran glided away. As the jet-powered purr of the engines ebbed, the silence of Azure reclaimed the night. Wendis, with its unceasing environmental machinery, was never as silent as this.

She turned, expecting an empty hall, the way it had been the night she left.

No. Edvard was there tonight. Every muscle in her body tensed. Every nerve tightened.

Edvard's face was lined in way it hadn't been four years ago. He said slowly, "When word came to me from your colleagues in Wendis that you were missing and in terrible danger, I was terrified. I've never prayed so hard in my life as I did then to ask Christa to take care of you."

Nia didn't remember ever being missing and in danger, although she clearly remembered being present for various unwelcome dangers in the last year. All she could say was, "She did."

To her astonishment, Edvard embraced her.

In her father's embrace, the tightly locked door in her mind suddenly swung open. She gasped. Then she spoke rapidly. "I usually can't talk about it, but I was a prisoner of the dark god called Shandy. He was taking a diabolical interest in interstellar politics and religion, and he intended to rid the stars of me. I talked to him and changed his mind about that and he gave me back to my friends. All of it was so terrible—and I found out such explosive secrets about Shandy's activities—that it's not safe for me to remember. So the memories are in a locked room in my mind. The door to the room only opens when it's very important. I won't remember saying this even five minutes from now. Being Shandy's prisoner was awful, but Christa was with me even there. What I said to Shandy may even turn the tide of interstellar affairs. Please pray about that. I can't."

Memory blurred like sugar stirred into water. Then she thought that she'd intended to tell Edvard something and not voiced it. It must not have been important. Why did he look troubled? Well, she could make a good guess about that. "Ah, did you hear about the election of the Old Cathor patriarch?"

"Yes, I heard from Adriance Vale as soon as she got back."

Nia remembered Adriance, there as an ecumenical observer, finding her in the midst of the council of the Old Catholic Orthodox Church on Goya. Nia had always liked Adriance, but encountering someone from home had been a shock at the time.

"She made sure I heard the news from her before it came from everyone else and blindsided me. That the man you legally defended as a very young lawyer, in such a way as to ruin your career and save his life, had just been elected patriarch of the Old Cathor Church."

"What do you think about it?" Wondering where she'd found the courage to ask this question, she held her breath.

Edvard said, "He's one of the few hopes of civilization, which, thanks to the Faxen Union, is in danger of collapse into autocracy or oblivion."

Too astonished to speak, she nodded.

"I was badly mistaken in my estimation of him. And of you."

Normal gravity or not, now she felt so stunned as to be dizzy. He steadied her. Then they walked into the hall behind the lake gate, arm in arm. It was a strange, distinctive progression, in which every step undid another old knot of estrangement.

Nia regretted Uncle Val's death, and yet she was grateful that it had made this reconciliation possible. As far as she was concerned, his legacy would never be all negative now.

Edvard's thoughts may have been running along the same lines. He sighed. "I do not understand how Val Savre, always an Albioni as hidebound as any of them, and a staunch Faxen Unionist, took such a midway turn in his life. He did it for love —you'll hear more about that tomorrow—but he's the last of whom I would have expected that."

"Love can make all the difference in a world." She knew that now as well as anybody.

She also knew that love might not be the whole story.

Sleeping in her own room—and in her own native gravity, and on a bed where she didn't have to line herself with spingravity to begin to relax—was an old experience that paradoxically felt new. It also felt very good. She slept dreamlessly, only waking up once, recognizing where she was, wondering why she wasn't still swimming in thick cold fear. She reached out to touch the Christa medal. *Thank you.* Then she fell asleep again.

The next morning Nia was the last person who made it to breakfast. The aroma greeted her first. It smelled like pot bread and iceberry jam, the smell of home. It almost made her cry. She tried to pull herself together and then entered the breakfast room.

"She's here!"

"Nia!"

"*Nia!*"

Before she knew it, she was buried in the embrace of her grandmother, Eirene, her grandfather, Vim, and her brother, Jon-Jon. Edvard was there too, gravely smiling. Then she did cry.

Also present was a younger man who strongly resembled Uncle Val. Eventually she was introduced to him and found out that his name was that of his father: Vienradzis Al-Savre. This was Val's son. Called Radzi, he was the vector through which the family had learned that Uncle Val had faked his death and was living with his beautiful lover on Stannto. Nia had heard about it in one of her grandparents' newsy bubbles.

In Nia's earlier life, Val Savre had visited Castle Courant many times. Today, with Radzi and all, Nia had a startling feeling of return to a whole family. Neither her mother nor her sister were here, but she'd never been close to either one of them. Eirene was her true mother figure.

Beneath her joy at seeing Nia, Eirene was grim with resigned grief for her son. "I only wish Val could be here—or anywhere else. Alive."

"He wasn't dead the last time," Jon said.

"There are worse things than being dead." Eirene was no fool.

The breakfast nook was the size of Nia's entire apartment in Wendis. Like most of Castle Courant, it had been beam-carved long ago out of the rock of Arrival Arc. Its long window was full of bright light. Sea fog filled the air outside.

Jon left to go back to Denevez, where he was working on an assignment in connection with his schooling at Azure's interstellar fleet academy. He gave Nia his wide warm smile over his shoulder.

Nia's genial grandfather, Vim, left too, with the same smile for her—Jon had inherited that smile. Grandda Vim was a scholar. Ensconced in his rooms in Castle Courant, he still wrote learned articles. Years ago, he'd written a magisterial book about the history of starflight. The book was famous across civilization on this end of history. Nia would have to tell him about her own adventures with his book.

Edvard, Eirene, and Radzi stayed around the table, drinking good strong Azurean kavva with Nia. The familiarity of it was a kind of shock, but a good one.

As the sea fog thinned, the view from the breakfast room gave Nia yet another shock of familiarity. There was the town of Arrival. Nia remembered the ancestral home of Adriance Vale, who was descended from some of the first colonists who settled there. Adriance had a nephew in Denevez who came on holidays to stay in their friendly, busy family compound in Arrival. His name was Daved, but his family and friends called him Taffy. He'd been Nia's closest childhood friend.

She remembered exploring Castle Courant with Taffy, taking berrying trips, and later, climbing glacier-draped mountains with him. She remembered her fondness for the dark-haired boy and his affection for her. Suddenly and sharply she missed her dark-haired man, Martan. *Someday he will be here*, she promised herself.

The conversation only lightly eddied around Nia's recent life and work, and completely avoided her old fateful choice and its consequences. It was easier to talk about Val's choices and consequences, especially with Radzi being an available and voluble informant.

Nia reminded herself that Radzi might be here because he was intent on getting the disputed inheritance for his mother, or for himself. She would have to find that out. To start with, she asked Radzi about what Edvard had said last night—that Val had taken his midlife turn out of love.

"Oh, yes. He loved his lady," said Radzi. "Her name is Lane, and she's really beautiful."

Beautiful was not something that could have been said of Radzi's mother, Val's separated wife, now separated widow. Val had married for more practical reasons, including having good Earth-original genes.

The inheritor of said genes added, "She's a Verian."

"Ah, what is that?" Edvard asked.

"A descendant of the colonists on a world called Meridian," Radzi answered. "There was a virus there that changed them. The colony was abandoned and the colonists scattered before it was understood that most of them were carriers of the virus. Their descendants turn up in different places, and either the virus is invisible, or they turn out to be somehow odd. Lane looks and acts like a normal human being. Their son is obviously Verian. He's quiet and dreamy, and either he'll never talk or it'll develop slowly."

Edvard digested this information about that young relative of the family.

Just before leaving Wendis, Nia had managed to contact Dr. Lila Tsuda to ask her about the Verian virus. Nia told her family, "A prominent doctor in Wendis told me that calling it a virus is a misunderstanding of the Verian syndrome, if not a coverup of it. Viruses don't do what causes Verians. There's a genetic vector with some viral traits, which raises the question of how the vector came to be. Genetic engineering on the part of the

Meridian colonists, perhaps, but only if there were first-rate genetic engineers among them, not just farmers shipped off to colonize Meridian. It's a biomedical mystery."

"So Verians are gene-changed." Edvard summarized, with obvious disapproval. Nia understood why. In his theology, Earth genes were sacrosanct. In this case, it might be his theology rallying in support of cultural prejudices. Azure and Albion, two worlds with many historical and cultural connections, both regarded unchanged Earth genes with an esteem that bordered on the idolatrous, in the opinion of Adriance Vale. Adriance had formed Nia's faith as much or more than Edvard had. Which had been fortunate for Nia.

In contrast to the Azurean/Albioni attitude, Wendisan law recognized the legal rights of Shades of Human—people mutated, genetically engineered, or evolved from humanity as it had existed on Earth. Nia knew a few of them personally. And in the war, she had learned that they were Christa's too.

This topic might make for an interesting discussion between her and Edvard. Or it might become a new bone of contention between them. If so, that would come later.

She extricated herself from the breakfast nook to let Edvard and Eirene talk about her in her absence. It was time for her to unpack, starting with her little green friend. She brought the hugwort, still in its container, to the sill of the widest and warmest window in Castle Courant, in a side room facing east. She took the hugwort out of its container. It unfurled one leaf after another. Then it explored the windowsill with the tips of its tendrils. Nia was alarmed to note that it could stretch from one end of the window to the other on the long sill. Its last growth spurt had really added to its reach. Maybe she'd gotten it out of Gembolt Hall just in time.

Radzi wandered into the room after her. "Is that a Wendisan house plant?"

"No, it's from farther away than that. Touch a tendril."

He did, and the tendril curled around his finger. "Am I shaking hands with a plant?" He sounded bemused.

"Well, an alien plant-animal." One that Nia had found to be a rather good judge of character, when it touched anyone. It wasn't pulling itself away or bunching itself up. Evidently it approved of Radzi. Interesting.

The hugwort expanded, overflowing the windowsill. It proceeded to anchor itself on the latch and rappel down to the floor.

Radzi's mouth dropped open.

There was no time like the present, especially if an informant was startled enough to be unguarded. "What do you think about your father's intellectual property going to our grandmother, Eirene?"

Radzi answered bluntly, "She's the only one smart enough to figure out what to do with it."

That was a fair assessment. "Tell me more. Have a seat." She waved at the room's furniture.

Radzi picked a comfortable chair in the window light. He readily explained that he didn't want the inheritance, the abstruse intellectual property of his father. He was a musician. A few months ago, after a private detective hired by Radzi's mother had ferreted out Uncle Val's whereabouts, Radzi had been delegated to go to Stannto to confront his father about faking his death and running off with a lover. But in the modest home Val and Lane and their little son shared on Stannto, Radzi had found himself made welcome. He'd felt accepted by Val in a way he'd never felt before. They'd even gone to a few live music venues that night, and Val, for the first time in Radzi's life, was proud of him as the musician he was.

Radzi bitterly disapproved of his mother and sister grasping at Val's inheritance. So much so that he'd spent a large fraction of his life savings to take a starliner to Azure. It seemed to him like it was time to take sides. And he knew what side he wanted to take—the one that followed his father's wishes.

It sounded like Val and Radzi had had an estrangement more lifelong than that between Nia and Edvard. Yet even Val had undergone a change of heart. Maybe the new love of his life, the Verian woman named Lane, had changed him that much. If so, Nia was glad.

The hugwort ventured away, rounding a corner. Nia let it. It was rather indestructible. And so was most of Castle Courant.

4

CASTLE COURANT

It hadn't been just a ruse that Nia was going to be on Azure for Greening Day. The holiday season extended before and after that day with all kinds of celebrations, the first of which would happen in just two days. Her family was expected to attend by reason of their prominence. Her being here put her on the guest list too.

With Eirene, she surveyed her closet. Her old dressy outfits—chosen with an eye to classic quality, not fashion—were still there. Eirene had brought her own best cape to find a good match for it in the closet. "There. This one will do just fine. Then you will need an escort. Jon will be happy to be escort you, or if he has a conflict, then one of his friends from the star academy."

What? That sounded so—very much like Azure. And so provincial.

"Chin up," Eirene said. "You'll make a good impression even in old clothes."

Nia remembered the Wendisan carrycloth with Robard's gift. She hadn't opened it yet. Now she did so.

The contents of the carrycloth were anything but provincial.

"I won't have to wear old clothes. A friend gave me this just before I left Wendis." She shook out a dress made of the distinctive, thick yet yielding fabric called opalweave. Nia had never owned anything made of that expensive material, but she'd seen it in Wendis. It softly reflected any light that fell on it. Its colors subtly changed to match anything held next to it—making a perfect match with Eirene's fir-green cape. The material could also be finger-tailored to fit perfectly. Nia demonstrated.

Eirene's eyes widened. "What kind of friendship?"

Nia thought about her dangerous borderline romance, then bitter enmity, then friendship with Robard. "A complicated one," she said softly.

Eirene cleared her throat. "The youth in the Courant family usually have an ugly duckling phase. Your mother met Edvard after his, and no one warned her. She thought you were doomed to remain an ugly duckling."

Nia remembered her mother, Suzana, using those exact words. Suzana had never reflected on how the old legend ended, with the duckling turning out to be a swan. She was not a particularly reflective woman. But she had been attractive and socially adept, a perfect foil for a rising churchman. With Suzana at his side, Edvard had climbed high.

Nia had never been close to Suzana. That wasn't how it usually worked on Azure anyway. For generation after generation, those in the prime of life had devoted themselves to building the world and its institutions. It was the elders who did most of the caring and nurturing of the rising generation. Some elders who were not very good parents turned out to be adequate grandparents. But Nia had been extremely fortunate to be grandmothered by Eirene and grandfathered by Vim.

During the travel here, in her swim-in-a-cold-thick-salt-sea mood, she had imagined Eirene rejecting her. That now seemed like a nightmare shredded by morning. Eirene had always been someone she could trust to be benevolent—as well as astute and honest. "Eirene, What happened to my father? He changed his mind about me. Why?"

Eirene said tartly, "What happened was that he had to admit that he'd misjudged you. Edvard being Edvard, he might have been able to polish up even that to make himself look good. But because of the news that rained out of that Old Cathor Church council, the truth that he'd made a terrible mistake came home to roost for all the world to see. And I'm glad it did."

With much to think about, Nia ventured around Castle Courant in the afternoon. She hadn't exactly forgotten what a large and loomingly quiet place it was—but after Wendis, that struck her as never before.

The first astronauts to land on Azure had begun by tossing down a clean bomb that flattened some ice-locked, hilly terrain to make a landing field. The astronauts soon hollowed out the high crest of Arrival Arc, beam-carving rooms and storerooms, to make a secure base that had geothermal heat to keep it warm. On this end of the centuries, that base was Castle Courant.

The old landing field filled with water as the early terraforming began to melt the equatorial glaciers. The landing field turned into Starfield Lake and froze over. Over time the astronauts and early colonists moved landing operations to the other side of the base, which bordered a bay of the sea. The bay made for a larger landing zone. So for that reason Castle Courant had an ancient sea gate, twice as large as the lake gate, and opening onto salt water rather than smooth ice.

She went down downstairs to see it again. The lowest level of Castle Courant was wide and high-ceilinged, with ranks of bracing pillars. It was called the Cistern because, centuries ago, it had held a reservoir of fresh water.

In the years since early colonization, the astronauts' descendants scattered across the equator of Azure as they labored to warm the world and seed it with an Earthlike ecosystem. The Az-Courant family had remained, promising to keep this, the first starbase on Azure, in good repair.

In case of emergency, Castle Courant could house a lot of people. Twice across the centuries, with the warming world's ocean currents changing, an enormous slab of sea ice had heaved toward Arrival. The first time, it flattened the town, but the population was safely sheltering in Castle Courant. The second time, strategic explosives reshaped the ocean floor and stopped the ice. But if anything like that ever happened again, Castle Courant would shelter many people again, with plenty of room to store their food supply, limitless geothermal heat, and the Cistern filled with fresh water tapped from Starfield Lake.

Today the sea gate was shut, but not sealed as tightly shut as she remembered from years ago. A thin line of daylight showed on one side of it. Maybe the frame of it had shifted. There were occasional tremors here, since this was a volcanically active part of Azure. Harnessing the volcanoes was part of the grand plan to terraform the planet. The price paid for that was frequent tremors and the occasional eruption of a volcano somewhere.

Entering the sea gate control room, she remembered Val Savre being here. He had been an energetic young man when she was an energetic child. They'd gotten along well. For some reason he'd liked the Cistern, explored it more thoroughly than probably anybody had for six centuries, and especially liked spending time in the control room which, when Val spent time there, was immaculately dusted. Today everything was dusty. There was a long wide crack in the floor . . . from the tremor that skewed the frame of the gate? Objects from an old shelf had fallen near the crack, if not into it.

The disrepair of the Cistern level disconcerted her. She went up to the utility level, where the Castle's energy, power, and water came from. The machinery was working—but she heard a few squeaks coming from the water wheel that dipped into the modern reservoir of melted lake water and carried it to the living level overhead. There was a legal agreement with the town of Arrival to keep Castle Courant in working order. Either the Arrivaltown effort had gotten slack, or likelier, the agreement needed updating. She would look into it. Some repair work was overdue in the bottom levels of Castle Courant.

She felt more at ease in the family residence, the top three floors of Castle Courant, and most comfortable of all in the greenhouse on top. She found Vim busily thinning and weeding his garden corner of the greenhouse. He smilingly welcomed her help. She sensed that his way of getting through grief for his stepson was to tend his plants.

While in the garden, she pondered her family history. The Courants, the last people to stay where people first landed on the new world, were either remarkably dutiful or dutifully staid. They had birthed generations of leaders of church and society, but not any interstellar troublemakers, until she came along. Well, Uncle Val had beaten her to it. But she and he didn't share any ancestors.

She visualized her family tree. It was complicated. She brushed a table clear and used some cut vines and leaves to map it out.

Edvard and Suzana were her biological parents. Vim was Edvard's father by an early marriage. That was a typical Azurean life pattern—marriage could be impermanent. The work of building a new world was the true constant.

Vim had atypically become an offworld scholar, spending much of his career on Albion, where he met Eirene, the true love of his life, and married her. She had a son of her own from an early arrangement on Albion. That was Val.

Further into the past, Grandda Vim's parentage was where a remarkable woman named Inanna Riga fit in. She'd been a

Wendisan citizen who visited Azure and liked it well enough to stay, marry an Azurean man, a dutiful Courant no less, and have a son—Vim.

Inanna Riga had been Earth-standard, genetically. Genes from Inanna Riga didn't explain Vim feeling the pull of the stars as a scholar or the starward turn in Nia's life. Much less did it explain the stargate fascination in Val's life, since he was unrelated to the Courant family.

Genes did not explain everything . . . but could point to something significant. And that, she realized, applied to the new Verian branch of the Courant family tree. Verian genes pointed back to something inexplicable on that mysterious planet called Meridian.

Genes pointing back to something inexplicable applied to the hugwort too. Professor Zeng, the xenecologist, had recently informed her that its species was a mixture of Earth genes: mainly domestic cats and the plants called morning glories, and genes of alien origin. It had originated on a failed colony planet, explaining the presence of both terrestrial and alien genes; but its genetic engineering was so superb as to have no explanation at all.

Nia introduced everyone to the hugwort so no one would have a rude surprise. It didn't bunch up suspiciously at meeting anyone. It did curl tendrils around all five of Vim's fingers and audibly purr. Afterward it harmlessly dozed away the afternoon in a west-facing window, worn out from travel and adventures. So far so good.

Supper was Azurean food and family, and Nia was glad to be there. Then she spent the long evening reading her law library in the small study attached to her bedroom. The night was dark and quiet. It got almost as late as when she had arrived last night. Since then, Azure had turned once on its axis. And her lost home had turned around completely in space and turned into home again. She felt ready, willing, and able to do the work needed here: sorting out Val's inheritance.

Suddenly she heard Edvard calling for her. He sounded alarmed. She ran down the hall.

Edvard's study was roomy, well-appointed, and where he kept his angelfish tank. He pointed at the tank. The hugwort had scrambled up onto the back of the armchair beside the tank and was dangling a tendril into the water.

Nia had no idea what a growing hugwort might decide to eat. "I think it's just curious. But you better count your fish."

He did so with alacrity. "They're all there."

"Do you still have a lid with a lock?" Years ago, there had been an unfortunate incident with a housecat that enjoyed fishing expeditions.

He nodded.

"Good, lock it and keep the key safe in your pocket."

"Keep. The. Key. Safe. Can it use a key?"

"Yes. It can also steal a key with intent to use it," she admitted.

Edvard looked stunned. "What is this thing?"

In a household where some people believed in the sanctity of Earth genes, it might be best to keep calling it an alien plant-animal. But Edvard had asked a question that deserved an honest answer. "Hugworts are a mix of Earth genes and genes not of Earth."

He frowned.

That wasn't all. "No one knows who did it. We haven't encountered a living alien civilization in all our centuries of star travel."

That statement bordered on untruth. Wendis, which had been collecting knowledge for thousands of years, and never forgot any of it, had ancient records of a brief encounter with birdlike starfarers in the Starcross Nebula. The Starbirds had been stranded, but with some help from a human expedition had found their way home never to be seen again. Nia had learned that in the secret history archive, which was crosslinked with a Shades of Human archive. A condition of her access to the secret history archive was that the information in it stay secret. She amended, "None that could have engaged in extensive genetic engineering with their genes and genes from Earth. The xenarchaeologists have only found the ruins of long-extinct alien civilizations. Including Vere." She crossed her arms. "We don't know who or what made the Vere vector either. That is a major mystery. A minor mystery is what would have designed a plant-animal so likeable and curious and indestructible that they are turning up, legally or not, in space places all across civilization."

She suddenly remembered something Martan had said months ago. Theatrically holding the hugwort up, he'd suggested that its species had been created by a reclusive and superhuman intelligence that wanted to understand humanity and the dangers posed by humanity, and had elected to do so by means of tactical infiltration. He'd rhetorically asked, *Salad—or spy?!* At the time, because they'd been having an argument, Nia had thought Martan was just trying to goad her. In retrospect, though, maybe he'd made a very good point. She asked her father, "Could there be designers much more grand than we are—beings so much more intelligent than humans that they are godlike with respect to us?"

Frowning, Edvard gave it real thought. "There's no theological reason why not. The ancients intuited it with their myths about gods and orders of angels and Satan."

From nowhere a cold wind blew through her. To her grateful surprise, Edvard held her until she stopped shivering. Thankfully he didn't ask what was wrong. Taking a steadying deep breath, she said, "We need to talk."

"Yes," he murmured. "You were in danger."

"Yes, there was a war in Wendis. Danger may hit closer to

home than that. Uncle Val's work may involve something the Faxen Union wants badly. We don't want their attention on this family. I have to prevent that."

His eyes went wide. "How?"

"I have an idea, but you won't like it." When she'd first thought about this, she'd shrugged it off, because she thought he disliked her more than any idea she might come up with. Now, though? She swallowed hard.

He gave a rueful laugh. "I am getting used to ideas that I don't like."

She took a deep breath. "I can make it out to be the banal kind of inheritance trouble, with family members squabbling and pulling in lawyers on every side. It's the only way I know to camouflage it all, so the Faxen Union doesn't see anything it needs to meddle with. Sorry about that."

He frowned while he thought. Finally he said, "Vienradzis al Savre, or when not wanting to look like Albion nobility and calling himself Val Savre, has certainly bequeathed us some trouble."

If it had been warmer in here, she would have had sweat to brush off her forehead. *Whew.* Edvard hadn't simply gotten over a monumental snit where she was concerned. He had truly changed. For that matter, maybe she had changed too. She was still his daughter—but she'd been shaped by influences that he had never met.

They talked for a while about what she could do to further her plan. Nia got the sense that Edvard disapproved of Uncle Val faking his death to run off to Stannto with a genetically compromised young woman, and finally getting into danger that killed him for real, leaving inheritance arrangements that entangled the Courants on Azure.

Nia didn't approve either. Still, she was sad that Uncle Val had died again. He'd always been one of her favorite relatives, the interesting young uncle. In death, he'd given Edvard a reason to ask her to come home. For that she was deeply grateful.

Much as they had done for most of her life, she and her father wished each other a good night. She gathered the wayward hugwort and carried it away with her.

Hearing music, she followed the sound of it into the sitting room where she'd introduced Radzi to the hugwort. He was there tonight, playing a stringed instrument with a long, slim neck and a bowl with a gracefully curved shape. The instrument had a prismatic, pleasant sound. The tune sounded sad.

"That's a beautiful instrument."

"It's one the ancients had," he told her. "A mandolin."

"Is your music saying you're sad about your father?"

He nodded.

She listened and let herself feel her own sadness for Val, gladness for Eirene's unwavering support, immense relief to be reconciled with Edvard, and liking for Vim.

The hugwort crawled out of her arms toward Radzi. It touched the bowl of the mandolin with a tendril.

"It can feel vibrations," Nia explained.

Still playing his mandolin, Radzi regarded the hugwort intently, Rather miraculously the tune he was playing changed, became sprightlier. It almost sounded *greener.*

The hugwort gathered itself next to Radzi. He said, "It seems a lot like a cat."

"It has Terran cat genes." She found its furry root mass. "If you hear it purring, you aren't imagining things." She recalled the Goyan boy's talisman that the hugwort had absconded with. The hugwort had always liked interesting metal shapes. But increasingly, it seemed drawn to things that were emotionally valuable to humans, like the talisman. The mandolin was another case in point. If the hugwort weren't so likeable, it would have been intolerably strange.

Radzi said, "You're an interstellar lawyer and you intend to sort the mess out."

"Yes."

"I'm going to trust you." His face hardened. "My sister's new boyfriend put her and my mother up to trying to get my father's inheritance. He's very interested in it. And I don't like him." With a swipe of the fingertips in which he held a flat metallic pick, then a twist of it, the notes turned discordant.

Nia had vaguely known that Radzi had a sister. This sounded like good material for her plan to make the whole matter look like a family feud. "Why?"

Strumming dissonant chords, Radzi described this new suitor making his sister's acquaintance, cultivating her a shade too deftly to be believable, proficiently ingratiating himself with their mother, asking questions about Val's inheritance that were too calculated, but only an almost unnoticeable fraction.

Radzi was very different from Val, but evidently, he'd inherited from Val the gift of being extraordinarily observant. What Radzi described gave Nia the unwelcome impression of a faint bad smell. Wendisans were hyperalert to bad smells, which, in that tightly contained environment, could mean death or disaster. Maybe she'd been there long enough to think like a Wendisan. In this case, it was not a happy thought.

She knew a great deal about the modus operandi of the secret intelligence agency of the Faxen Union, which Martan had described in exact detail to the interested Wendisan authorities, and to her. Martan loathed SECINTAG, but that didn't mean he underestimated them. He'd made it very clear that SECINTAG's operatives were highly trained in psychological manipulation as well as overt coercion. They were very good at what they did. Which was foul play.

With her heart sinking, Nia wondered if the new boyfriend was a SECINTAG operative. Asking a few more questions, she learned that he was from Faxe, and the right age to be a low-level SECINTAG operative. Maybe he was running an intelligence action, attracted by the stargate implications of Val's work. It was the kind of thing low-level operatives would try. If they succeeded, they'd become higher-level operatives.

Of course their success meant lives ruined, people hurt or killed, but it was just the cost of doing their business. And they weren't who paid the cost.

5

EDVARD

Edvard Az-Courant went to work the next morning, taking the ice catamaran to Denevez, as he had almost every day for decades. But this was a day more singular than any he could recall.

As the archbishop of Azure-Tierre, he had reached the pinnacle of his career. He commanded a complex of offices, archives and meeting facilities near the apex of one of the two city towers in Denevez. His personal office gave him a view of the Cathedral of St. Bonaventure. The cathedral was the masterwork of his life. Now it was almost finished, already in use, and only lacked its spire, which would be more slender, graceful, and taller than the city towers.

He was long since accustomed, with satisfaction, to the view from his offices. His life, on the other hand, had become very unaccustomed. Nia had an alien pet that looked like an animated plant and could filch keys and angle for angelfish. The hugwort disconcerted him as much as anything else at present, and that was saying quite a lot.

He remembered getting the bubble from Wendis, months

ago, in which her colleagues at the university there told him that Nia was missing, in terrible danger, and far beyond the reach of friends or friendly authorities. The Wendisans had suggested that, however his religious faith understood prayer, he should pray. The message frightened him. He did pray.

He also began to bitterly regret his estrangement from Nia. Shortsightedness or blind pride had made him never consider the possibility that she could die or disappear before he ever saw her again. He'd vaguely intended some kind of reconciliation after he retired from his active life to comfortable, grandfatherly retirement. The bubble from Wendis made him realize that he might never get that chance, no matter how fair and reasonable it seemed to him.

Better news came in a subsequent bubble. She was alive, in fragile mental and physical condition, but in the care of good doctors and good friends. That was followed by more praying on his part. He spent hours pacing in the nave of St. Bonaventure's under the great chandeliers that looked like clusters of bright stars and symbolized heaven. The cathedral was his favorite place. It had often given him comfort, perhaps in particular, comforting his pride. No more. Not after learning that he might have lost his daughter, then that she was still alive but somehow damaged.

Then came the day when Adriance Vale, a priest as well as a longtime family friend, rushed into his office when she had just returned from a church council on the distant planet Goya. She'd stepped off the space elevator less than an hour earlier. Communications skipped across the stars in bubbles, and bubbles flew no faster than starships, so Adriance had barely outpaced the general dissemination of the latest interstellar news. "Edvard, your daughter is alive and well and famous across the stars as a theological wonder-worker!"

Where Nia was concerned, his eloquence had never been infallible. This time it had fled. "What?"

Adriance had breathlessly explained how the man whose life Nia had saved, years ago when she was doing legal fieldwork on the Faxen Union's prison planet, Moira, had become famous; and Nia had become famous with him. That man, whose name was Olav Zakeri, had just been elected patriarch of the Old Catholic Orthodox Church.

Hearing that news from Adriance had hit Edvard hard. It was a body blow to his self-image.

Adriance added that hopes were high that Zakeri would be a vigorous, effective, even transformative patriarch. This at the very moment when the Old Cathor church had realized that it must either reinvigorate itself or wither into interstellar irrelevance. And now the news was radiating across the stars that Nia's old misadventure had turned into glory. Part and parcel of the story was that because of her courageous act on Moira she'd been disowned on Azure by a father who was a prejudiced and wrong-thinking high official of the *other* Cathor Church, the *New*.

Put in those terms, Edvard finally saw what he'd refused to see years ago. He'd long known the details of what had happened to Nia on Moira. Olav Zakeri had been a cleric who fought for the dignity and rights of the people on Moira. The planetary government had him out of the way and cooked up a crime whereby to accuse and convict him. Nia, defending him against the will of the planetary government, had been caught up in an unwinnable legal game. But on Moira, a backwater of civilization, the popular codes of law let a lawyer convinced of a client's innocence take punishment instead. What Nia took in Zakeri's place was thirteen lashes to the back with a whip. It wasn't technically capital punishment, but it would have killed Zakeri, who was in a sick and weakened state at the time. The planetary government knew and counted on that. Nia had foiled them.

Now it made Edvard wince to think about his daughter

taking physical hurt like that. Fortunately she'd been young and healthy and gotten good medical care on Moira. But her hurt had been compounded when she returned to Azure. How she'd saved Zakeri's life looked so disgraceful to the legal establishment on Azure that got her into trouble in her law school. It also presaged the dead end of any political career on Azure. And Edvard had thought it was an incredibly foolish if not masochistic expression of misguided idealism, or even falling in love with a disreputable client. She'd tried to tell him that her reason was her religious faith. But he hadn't seen it that way. His personal embarrassment had loomed too large, and so had his professional discomfiture. He'd rejected her reasoning in pride and anger and never reconsidered until Adriance brought the news from Goya.

Reactions to the news about the Council soon came at him from all directions, with far less kindness than Adriance had shown him. In particular, the Archbishop of Albion sent a bubble with a very pointed message. The Albion archbishop was the ceremonial head of the entire New Cathor Church. In his message, he pointed out that a person willingly taking undeserved punishment in the place of someone else, by divine providence and with significant religious repercussions, was no minor matter: Such a story was central to the theology of New Catholic Orthodoxy, Old Catholic Orthodoxy, and Old Catholicism. If Edvard Courant was blind to that foundational fact of the faith, perhaps he was unfit for his office.

That was when the edifice of righteous pride that Edvard had inhabited for years crumbled. His pride had been shaped like St. Bonaventure's, perhaps, expansive and vaulting, but made of weaker stuff than stone and steel.

Edvard finally had made his way to the church in Arrival where Adriance's father had been priest before her. This building was one-fourth of the size of St. Bonaventure's, with a history ten times longer. The chandeliers here had been rescued from the ice-heave of centuries ago, and the church laboriously rebuilt so that worshippers could return and the chandeliers again hang in its vaulted ceiling. This had been his home church as a child. He remembered having childlike faith, before ambition came into the religious picture for him.

In that small, old, familiar church, Edvard made the ritual of confession to Adriance. It lasted longer than the typical confession. He discovered that he had many excruciating details to confess. But he came out finally feeling slightly better. Adriance was a kinder priest than he had ever been. And, being a woman, with the feminine likeness to Christa Terra, she was naturally closer to God. That afternoon, he might have taken his first full breath since she told him what happened in the church council on Goya.

Then not long afterward the news came that war had broken out in the neutral city-state Wendis. The Faxen Union had brazenly attacked Wendis after having failed in a campaign of subversion. Such was typical of what the Faxen Union had become. It was a planetary federation metastasizing into an empire bent on conquest where co-optation and subversion failed.

War was never a safe place. And Nia was not the type to hide in a cellar until it blew over. When he eventually learned that Wendis had somehow repelled the attack, Edvard felt as relieved as anyone in a location other than Wendis possibly could have felt. That was what made him finally send the messenger to Nia, though his ostensible reason was an excellent one. By then the need for a first-rate interstellar lawyer in the wake of Val's death had become all too apparent.

But there was more to it than that. Edward now knew beyond a shadow of a doubt that he could have lost his daughter more than once. If so, the estrangement between them would never have been healed on this side of his own death—and the fault for that was his. The night she arrived, he had gone out onto the ice lake dock to meet her, steeling himself to ask her for forgiveness, though not sure that he would get the shameful words out past what was left of his pride. He'd been even less sure how she would react.

Instead, what she suddenly told him about in the hall the night she arrived, sounded like it could have been a fate worse than death. What she said and how she said it had unnerved him profoundly. Saints and prophets always made him uncomfortable, with their calm faces and long gaze, seeing beyond the mortal pale. He dealt with such people as seldom as possible. But that was who she was those few minutes, when the secrets in her mind permitted her to say them. He was still struggling to know how to think about her.

My daughter, estranged and exiled by my own fault.

My daughter the theological wonder-worker.

My daughter, a wrench thrown by God into the schemes of that counterfeit Satan called Shandy.

Another thought floated up out of the depths of his mind.

My attic child.

It was the Azurean expectation that for a marriage to be respectable and durable, the first sexual encounter should be in one of the couple's parental home. Most houses were big enough to comfortably accommodate that; rambling attics were ubiquitous. Typically, it happened before marriage. Edvard and Suzana had been very young when they made love in the empty upper corners of Castle Courant, conceived their first child, and then, protecting Edvard's reputation as a rising church leader, married in haste.

Had he ever mentioned that to Nia? Or had he assumed that bright as she was, she had figured it out? In any event, she might not be shocked. She'd become rather Wendisan, he thought. Something about her now distinctly reminded him of his own grandmother—Inanna Riga, the Wendisan actress who, while touring Azure, fell in love with a man and his planet and stayed. She was a remarkable old woman when Nia was born and named after her great-grandmother. It was customary in Wendis to name children after ancient heroes and gods. Inanna was an ancient goddess of love and war. Edvard's child quickly acquired the less portentous nickname, Nia.

Today, Edvard remembered what Grandmama Inanna had said many years ago, when she bequeathed her Wendisan citizenship to Nia, out of all the relatives she had acquired in a long stay on Azure. "That child has stars in her blood. I can tell."

When Edvard's clerk arrived for the day's work, Edvard intercepted him. "I need to provide someone a private space for communication and study."

Byron was a devout, even-tempered, well-intentioned man of young middle age. "A researcher?"

"My elder daughter." Edvard said it with a trace of pride. Just not the wrong kind of pride.

Byron was somewhat new in this position, since shortly after Nia had left Azure. The departure of Byron's predecessor had not *explicitly* been tied to how Edvard had treated Nia, but . . . now Edvard could see the connection. Yes, what he'd done then had lost him the respect of his clerk at the time. He sighed. *Pride comes before a fall.* A fall might take its own sweet time arriving. It certainly had in Edvard's case.

In Nia's youth, he had fantasized about his daughter becoming the prime minister of Azure and, by extension, *his* prime minister. That had been prideful folly. She was her own woman. He should have realized that. She had showed her daring young temperament clearly enough in escapades in which she field-marshalled adventures with that loyal and levelheaded local boy, Taffy.

And yet Edvard and Nia's mother, Suzana, and Vim and

Vim's Albioni wife, the redoubtable Eirene, along with Inanna Riga in Nia's early childhood, had shaped Nia into a remarkable human being. Even that rogue, Val, who despite his other faults had been an excellent teacher, had helped form Nia into who she was too.

And he should really reach out to Val Savre's other widow, the Verian woman named Lane. Edvard was surprised to hear himself thinking this, but the thought was loud and clear. Family was family after all.

Unusually, Byron interrupted his ruminations by entering his office. Byron's face looked troubled. "There's something I have to tell you about, but I hardly know how to say it."

"Try," Edvard prompted.

"In today's mail—no interstellar bubbles, mainly just communiques from church and political officials—there was an anonymous message that threatened your life! It said you should resign your position if you want to stay alive!"

"That's happened before, not often and not recently. It comes with holding a high office of almost any sort." With his mind absorbed in his personal matters, Edvard felt disinclined to take this threat seriously. It sounded outlandish to him. "Thank you, Byron."

The clerk exited the room, still looking troubled.

6

VENTURE

The space in her father's office complex in Denevez gave Nia the practical resources she needed to tackle the problem facing her. And if she just needed to see a long view while letting her mind shift into a neutral gear, she could look out toward the windswept park on the sea side of Denevez, and beyond the park to the bright blue sea and the icebergs on the southern horizon.

The second day she was there, while she was filling Edvard in on what she'd learned so far, his clerk Byron brought in two bubbles with messages from across the stars. A bubble for her came from Stannto. The bubble for Edvard was from Albion. "Open yours first," she suggested. "I'm sure it's the more important one."

Edvard opened the pearly bubble. He frowned as he scanned the message inside. "The Archbishop of Albion has come out with a statement in full support of the Faxen Union and its interstellar presence."

Nia frowned too. "Change of heart on his part?"

"No, completely in character, but poor timing, this soon after the Wendis war." He tossed the message onto his pile of items to deal with.

Church and state were closely intertwined on Albion. Ordinarily, that had no bad results. But the time of ordinary peace and stability might soon be over. Nia gave Uncle Val credit for moving his citizenship as well as his intellectual inheritance to Azure. People and institutions being manipulated by religious authorities who were tools of the interstellar state—that could only make a sad and sensitive situation after his death worse.

Nia's bubble from Stannto turned out to have been sent by Val's lover, Lane. Startled, Nia checked the date stamp on the message. It had been sent, at the slowest and most affordable interstellar rate, some days ago. She thought back over the years, matching her timeline and Val's. He had disappeared from the Tellas moon research station before she took refuge in Wendis. Maybe he never heard about that and assumed she'd been on Azure the whole time. That would be why Lane sent the bubble to Azure.

A bit of Albioni slang that Nia hadn't thought about in years floated up out of her mind. If one woman was the *separated wife*, another was called the *wild wife*. However, this woman did not come across as wild in any way in her message. She identified herself as Val Savre's life partner and the mother of his child, then said, *I know you are his niece and an interstellar lawyer. He once told me to reach out to you, personally, if ever in the future anything untoward happened to him. To prove to you that I really know him, he said to tell you that he once opened the sea gate for you at the wrong time and you both got soaked in salt water full of jellyfish.*

Nia nodded to herself. Oh yes, she remembered that episode. She'd been a young child, Val had been a teenager, and no one else found out about it because they'd spent most of a day drying out that end of the Cistern and throwing a hundred or so big, rust-colored, stinging jellyfish back into the sea.

Lane's message continued, *News of his death was sent to Azure and so I'm sure you know about it. But now I have reason to think he is alive. Unfortunately, my reason is not something that can be proven. It was an ESP experience. I don't know where he is. And he may be changed somehow.*

Nia felt astonished. Was it possible that Val wasn't dead—again?

Edvard was equally incredulous. "I assume a purported ESP experience wouldn't hold up in court?"

Nia answered, "That depends on the court. Wendisan law recognizes ways of knowing that aren't rational. Canon law in Old Cathorism has some parallel categories."

Edvard steepled his hands. "On Azure, I outrank such canon law as we practice. It would be a matter of ecclesiastical interpretation. I assume it could be introduced into court, if only to muddy the water the way you want to."

"Yes. Only if we must," she added. Inside, she felt amazed that Edvard was prepared to take her advice about a course of action that he disliked. "We would have to get a deposition from Lane."

He said slowly, "I was thinking of reaching out to her. As family. It's appropriate."

Nia agreed in surprise. She made a mental note not to automatically assume Edvard was the same man he used to be in his opinions about other people as well as herself.

She remembered her dread about traveling home, how hard it had been to make herself go through with that. Had the dread been pointless—so much agony for no reason? No, she thought. She was still puzzled by the intensity of her dread about star traveling, per se, but she'd had plenty of reason to feel apprehensive about seeing Edvard. The startling surprise was that he had changed in a way she would not have, could not have predicted.

And that means—? she asked herself, already knowing the answer.

St. Venture's Cathedral had unlocked doors, which was an ecclesiastical practice of great antiquity, wherever possible. It also had passageways and perches not well known to the public. Nia made her way to the small loft, higher than the galleries, right in front of the Christa Terra window. *This* was the right kind of Terra window, she thought, remembering a small static one in a grander cathedral on Goya. *This* window luminously showed the world created good, the matrix and mother of life, which had been destroyed by humankind, yet was resurrected on terraformed planets and in space places. Soft blue-green light from the window filled the loft. The image rotated so that all the continents of the world came into view, while the cloud patterns changed too. The beauty of it brought tears to her eyes.

She hadn't been here for painful years. Now, with her nerves tense and her heart beating fast because of how much it mattered to her, she thought, *Thank you, Christa, for the miraculous change in Edvard.*

She returned to Edvard's office with a lighter heart, pausing to appreciate the architecture of the tower in which the offices of the archbishopric were housed. Like Denevez One, the seat of city and planetary government, Denevez Two was a soaring but sturdy tower, built to withstand storms and even heaving ice. The lower levels had narrow deep windows, which would have meant deprivation of natural light except that the center of the tower was full of light from an enormous skylight at the top. Edvard officed high enough in the tower to have wide, clear windows, one of which framed the cathedral from which Nia had just returned. It was an imposing, symmetrical structure that seemed to radiate a different kind of purpose than the city towers. She wasn't sure it really needed the tall spire that Edvard planned for it.

Edvard's clerk, Byron, intercepted her. He urgently wanted to speak with her in private. "I need to tell you something important concerning Edvard."

Nia had a moment of mental dislocation. In Wendis, everyone referred to those who outranked them by complete names and titles, sometimes running to a twelve-word phrase. But this was Azure. Everyone from the prime minister down the social ladder to the iceberry pickers, and back up again, went by their first name. "Sure. What are you concerned about?"

"He's getting anonymous death threats." Evidently Byron was worried enough to be tactless. "He won't take them seriously."

Nia took a deep breath. "I will."

Theological heft was one thing. Politics was something else. There was always politics in a religious organization. At worst it could be murderous. The ancient saint whose name graced St. Venture's Cathedral had died during a church council, and was rumored to have been poisoned by his ecclesiastical enemies. And powers on the outside could reach into religion with deadly results. She asked Byron, "Have any senior church officials died suddenly and suspiciously?"

"No, but one suddenly resigned. Yesterday. The anonymous letters said that Edvard would die if he doesn't resign."

That put a different but still ominous cast on things. "If Edvard resigned, who would take his place? I've forgotten how the succession runs."

Byron blinked, taken aback by the question. "With

yesterday's resignation, and two bishops who are well known to be too old or complacent to aspire to the archbishopric, it would be the Bishop of Beyond." That was the nickname for Azure's transit ring, its space stations, and the habitats inside moons and asteroids in the Azure system. The Bishop's formal title included a long list of those places, often conveniently shortened to Beyond.

"Who would that make happy?"

Byron was a very qualified clerk—devout, diligent, and intelligent. "The Archbishop of Albion. And the Unionist faction of the Church on Azure."

Nia let out a long breath. That explained it. Somebody wanted the Bishop of Beyond elevated to the role of archbishop of Azure-Tierre. They wanted it badly enough to resort to threats. If they thought Edvard would knuckle under to clumsy threats, though, they were very much mistaken.

She frowned. This was a bad time and a bad way for things to get even more complicated.

The first and most formal festivity of the holiday season was held that night in the cathedral. Her brother Jon met her in the side hallway, ready to play dutiful escort. When she took off the borrowed green cape to hand to the cloakroom attendant, Jon's eyes widened slightly. "You look good."

"So do you." In his crisp starfleet academy dress uniform, he looked more mature than she'd ever seen him, and more polished.

Under the curved ceiling of the cathedral the chandeliers glittered like star clusters. For the holiday, lower strings of colored lights shone under the tall dark windows. Well-dressed people already stood in small groups scattered across the cathedral floor, even though it was still early in the evening. "Is Suzana here?"

Jon nodded toward the other side of the nave. Yes, there was Suzana. Being a lifelong social climber, of course she would be present. She stood near Edvard, at just the right distance from him to telegraph respectable separated marriage. Nia was struck by how young they were to be her parents. They were more the age to be Jon's parents.

Crossing the stars had made the human genome more fragile than it ever was on Earth. For most couples it took much more than the first sexual encounters to conceive a child viable enough to reach birth. That meant attic children were rare, not to mention, rather irregular. But attic children could happen. Could that have been how she began?

That wasn't important right now. With drinks on offer, soon to be followed by food, and the air filled with delicate music from a group of musicians, now was the time to make social connections, to network and trade confidences. Almost everyone present—and they included most of the Very Important People in Denevez—were intent on just that.

Since almost no one here knew her, she talked to Jon, learning about his academic work in the starfleet academy, how he had just finished an assignment in Denevez, and that he was scheduled for an expedition to the academy's training station at the nearest small red star. Like everyone else in his year at the academy, Jon was trying to decide between applying to join the starfleet of the Starmark Alliance, Azure's own small starfleet, or maybe the Tellas-Albion Consortium commercial fleet.

"Stay away from the Telal Consortium," she told him sharply. "Apply to the Alliance. I've traveled on the rangeship *Antares* and I know the captain and the crew. The Alliance rangefleet is a good organization."

He gave her a long look. "Nia, you're you, but you're

somebody new." With that he went to get her something to drink.

A minute later, Nia found the prime minister of Azure striking up a conversation with her. "Good Greening Day!"

Nia remembered Vidjas Finndur from when they both were students of law—fifteen Azurean years ago. On Azure, even the prime minister went by her first name. "I wish the same to you and your family, Vidjas."

"I'm glad to see you back on Azure. Is everything in good order on the Arc? Even your old sea gate? I remember a grade-school field trip years ago when we all saw it opened just for us. There've been some damaging volcanic tremors in the last few years in this region though."

After Nia returned from the disastrous fieldwork on Moira, Vidjas had never joined the chorus of criticism. She was a strictly fair and ethical person then, and by all accounts Nia had heard lately, now too. So Nia honestly answered, "I've seen signs of disrepair. I intend to review the legal agreement with the town of Arrival and see about firming it up."

"Good idea. Have you met Darko Thuler?" A man who looked Goyan had approached them. "Inanna Courant, this is the ambassador from the Alliance on Goya."

"My pleasure, Mr. Ambassador," Nia said.

"Please call me Darko," he said smoothly.

Jon reappeared, saw the company Nia was in, and evidently decided they outranked him. He deferentially handed her a long-stemmed glass of ice wine and angled away.

Both the prime minister and the ambassador wanted to know more about the war in Wendis. Nia knew enough to fill them in. She also knew the Wendisan ambassador to the Alliance, which had made a crucial difference. "Early on I sent him a confidential bubble describing our suspicions about what the Faxen Union was up to. He was able to inform the Alliance Command about it. Then when Wendis was attacked, a message immediately went to Goya to ask for help. The Alliance Command sent a tactical fleet to defend us, just in the nick of time. Otherwise Wendis would have lost the war."

"So I'd heard," Darko said gravely.

"In my ignorance I would not have expected that," said Vidjas.

"Something about a loophole in the interstellar treaties?" Darko asked.

"The message was a Mayday. The Chief Engineer of Wendis moved the city in its orbit, and so the situation fell squarely under the interstellar treaties about obligations to a vessel in distress."

Both of them nodded appreciatively.

Nia had not expected this conversation. It occurred to her that she might be coming across as an Important Person herself, because of the expensive Wendisan dress, the famous events at the Old Cathor Church council on Goya, her repaired relationship with Edvard, or all of it. She glanced away to see her father and mother both looking at her. Suzana looked visibly nonplussed. She'd never imagined her ugly duckling child turning out like this. Edvard's expression was harder to read.

Vidjas was someone who missed very little. "Your father is no Faxen Unionist. At least not publicly."

"Not privately either. His convictions about that are stronger than he lets on in public words and writings."

"His convictions may soon be tested." Made of sterner stuff than most people, Vidjas held a nearly drained glass of Aquarel with rock-solid fingers. "After Wendis, who will the Faxen Union attack next?"

The ambassador from Goya said, "Since the Faxen Union controls part of Goya already—in plain words, it owns our one large continent—there are fears that the Union may try to conquer the rest of Goya, the Archipelagoes."

Nia said, "The usual pattern is infiltration and subversion first."

"With the new leadership of the Old Cathor Church, that just got harder." Darko sounded grimly pleased. "Our patriarch is weeding the clerical ranks, relegating Faxen sympathizers to peripheral positions."

"He has no illusions about how Faxen authoritarianism works," Nia said.

The ambassador nodded, looking at Nia with thoughtful eyes.

After that conversation, Nia had to collect herself. She knew how to get into the galleries that ran along the walls high above the floor. From up there she watched the hall and twirled the stem of the ice-wine glass as her thoughts spun.

If she had become the prime minister, as her father had always wanted, she would have been her father's prime minister. After her misadventure on Moira she was an embarrassment to him—she was painted as an anti-Faxen political radical when her father's enemies seized on the truth and made it shrill.

But now? She was being taken for the *de facto* ambassador from Wendis. At a time of unprecedented peril.

No one had answered Vidjas' question, *After Wendis, who will the Faxen Union attack next?* There hadn't needed to be an answer made out loud. Vidjas and Darko knew. And now Nia knew too, even though it was a truth that she'd been trying not to face. Above the Raptor's shoulder as seen from Wendis, Azure was close enough to the Faxen Union to observe the unsavory workings of it. Azure was also close enough for infiltration, subversion—or invasion.

Azure was not a prize like Wendis with its ancient trove of

knowledge. Nor did Azure have the natural and economic resources of Goya. The fare tonight illustrated that well enough: The long table in the west end of the nave had platters of such food as could be afforded by the archbishopric and obtained locally. That meant thin slices of smoked fish, placed on small squares of bread, with a layer of savory seaweed or sweet iceberry jam. There were pickled eggs too.

Azure was not a rich world. But annexing Azure to the Faxen Union might be enough to salve Faxe's pride at having been repulsed by Wendis. Faxe didn't need to have a better reason than that. Earlier today, she'd thought that the time of ordinary peace and stability might soon be over. Wrong. It was already over, not just for Wendis, but for Azure too.

She paced along the gallery, intensely aware of the Christa Terra window when she stopped under it. Tonight the Christa Terra window was stardark—illumined not by the equatorial sun shining through it, as it had been earlier today, but by the stars that were thick in Azure's night sky and made the glass glimmer. She remembered how the Greening Eve Litany always reverberated through the cathedral, with her father's voice intoning a prayer for protection from a very long list of troubles. War was one of them.

Someone stood further along the gallery. His dark hair and his alert stance reminded her of Martan. She walked closer and recognized him. "Taffy!"

A smile lit up his face. "Nia! I saw you down there. I'm glad you came up here."

"Are you working security?"

"Yes. I'm a detective in the Denevez police force."

"You made it!" She'd known he meant to go into law enforcement. Glad to have her mind moved off the topic of interstellar war, and very glad to see him, she asked, "What else should I know about your life now?"

"I married a Denevez girl, a civil engineer, and we have two sons." He sounded happy.

Shortly before she left Azure, he'd admitted having been in love with her for years. Now he happily had a wife—by marrying up to a well-educated professional woman, very much in character for him—and children. Little Taffies? Things change and not always for the worse. *Thank you, Christa Terra,* she thought toward the stardark window. She told Taffy, "I'm married too. I haven't told my family. He's—"

Originally from the backward Faxen Union planet Estrella. Going by the name Martan, which sounds like he might be a gene-deranged descendant of Martians, but he's genetically Earth-standard. Just different from standard humanity in ways that were engineered to make him a hellhound of Faxe until he repented, and now he's the hellhound of Wendis . . .

She said, "Not what they expect, but they'll just have to deal with that."

He laughed softly, then scanned the floor below again. He moved along the gallery.

Walking with him, Nia recognized his actions. "You're protecting someone. Vidjas, I assume."

He looked into her face. "No, Nia, your father."

Nia frowned. "His clerk said he's gotten clumsy death threats."

Taffy seemed to weigh what he knew against whom he was talking to. Then he said, "The AI analysis flagged him as having a threat-risk level above that of the prime minister."

Oh, no, she thought in shocked dismay. "Thank you for protecting him," she whispered.

He tilted his head toward the stardark window. She knew what that gesture telegraphed: *With Christa's help.* He turned back to his work, with a little parting wave.

Nia remembered what the Wendisan ambassador to the Alliance, Elan Hazy, had told her eventful months ago. *The most dangerous game is one that plays out at the intersection of religion and politics.* But it wasn't supposed to be like that on Azure. Not in Denevez. Not during the Green Holy Days. And specifically, not for her father. Her throat felt dry. She drained the ice wine in her glass.

Even if the death threats were real, she knew Edvard would not back down. It wasn't in his temperament to do that. And if push came to shove, if he ever had to come out in favor of the Faxen Union or come out against it, she knew which way he would go. She uncomfortably remembered a few ancient saints who took a political stand out of a heartfelt conviction and then were martyred for it.

Now that she was letting herself face the truth, she made herself see all of it. The Bishop of Beyond, or his faction, actually might be quite innocent of scheming. The clumsy threats could be a prelude by SECINTAG, so there would be a red herring ready if something bad or even fatal happened to Edvard.

Even with policemen as good as Nia knew Taffy would be, law enforcement on Denevez was no match for SECINTAG.

Martan was. Suddenly and almost irresistibly, she wanted his help.

But that might be less important than the work he was doing in Wendis, picking up the pieces after the war, fitting together the picture of Faxen subversion there. She argued with herself, with the scales of decision trembling in perfect balance.

Then she remembered Vidjas asking about the sea gate. The small hairs on the back of her neck stood up in sudden dread.

A functional old space base, positioned by a bay of the sea on the world's equator, where ships from space could land on the water, with a big sea gate so that whatever landed could be brought into a fortress of a place—it was perfect for the first toehold of an invasion. That might be SECINTAG's real end game. Involuntarily she imagined Tellas-Albion Consortium mercenary soldiers stalking through Castle Courant with their metal boots, scarring the floors and vandalizing Grandda's greenhouse. They wouldn't mind killing anybody who got in their way either. The thought made her feel sick.

She left the party to return to Edvard's offices. There she sent a highest-priority bubble to Martan in Wendis. She phrased it indirectly, just in case the message fell under eyes it wasn't meant for. Martan would understand.

I need you to be you here.

7

REUNION

Two mornings later, she finally told her family about being married.

"When?" asked Grandda Vim.

"Where?" asked Eirene.

"How?" asked Edvard.

"In a civil ceremony in a rose garden in Wendis just a couple of months ago." She gave Edvard a long level look, implicitly daring him to challenge her marital decision, after he had exiled her from Azure.

Edvard just cleared his throat.

"How wonderful!" Grandda Vim beamed.

Eirene said, "Yes, you are married. I can tell. There's something more stable about you."

"Like an old married person?" Nia smiled ruefully. Already?

"More like a gyroscope," said Eirene.

The transit tower on the inland edge of Denevez, next to a mountain range, didn't resemble the city towers. It looked more like one of the mountains, more slender than any of them and so high that the top of it was invisible from the ground.

She did not need to meet Martan at the transit-tower terminal. He could find his way anywhere, even if he'd never been there. So she asked him to meet her in Memorial Park.

She had never looked forward to seeing anyone so much in her life. She got there early, standing near the rusted metal memorial in the center of the park. She tightened her coat against the wind. It was cold, and it would stay that way for another month, until the brief summer of Azure's perihelion in orbit around its sun warmed the world. Only then would the park be nice for playing games or lying on soft moss on the ground.

Play was not the real purpose of the park. The first colonists on Azure had cannibalized their starship to make their first compact city and sited it here. When the ice heaved five centuries later, it flattened the old city. Ice and rubble were eventually cleared away, but the metal ruins remained. They were a memorial to the bravery of the astronauts, the boldness of the colonists, the immensity of terraforming a world, and the tenacity of life from Earth as it found a foothold on Azure. The crushed and twisted metal girders whispered with the cold wind from the sea, *Never forget*.

I won't, Nia thought in reply.

The space elevator car came down to Denevez, decelerating with a thunderclap, right on time. Martan found her so quickly that it was obvious he hadn't taken a wrong turn or even hesitated. They kissed each other long and hard, his face warm against hers, his shoulders shielding her from the wind. He wore the unremarkable-looking coat he called the Turncoat, which happened to be loaded with protections and surprises. It was a familiar friend to her now.

Then she told him about the clumsy death threats to Edvard, and her wild guesswork about the sea gate.

"Your family home is a private spaceport?" He was surprised. "You never mentioned that."

"Growing up, it was just there. Am I being paranoid?"

He looked at her with the dark eyes that had seen many wonders and terrors across the stars. "No. You may be wrong about the Union's plans, but not paranoid. It's realistic."

She heaved a sigh against his chest. "Thank you for coming here. Ready to meet my father?"

"As ready as I'm going to be," he answered. Holding hands, they made their way to the offices of the archbishopric, high in the city tower called Denevez Two.

In the last hallway, the one that ended at Edvard's office door, Martan stopped her. "There's an argument going on in there. Somebody just said, 'Because now I'm getting death threats too!'"

Nia didn't need Martan's superhuman hearing to hear what came next. "I need your help for the Green Holy Days. I don't need your cowardice!" Her father's raised voice made her nerves go taut.

Martan whispered, "The younger man said, 'If you won't take this seriously, I quit!' Is he spineless?"

"He works for Edvard and has for several years. So no."

Martan murmured, "If low-level SECINTAG operators zeroed in on your uncle's family on Albion, they may be here too. Maybe they want to put a ringer into your father's inner circle."

Nia and Martan looked at each other.

She pointed at him.

He nodded.

Byron walked out, looking flushed and unhappy. Nia stopped him. "We couldn't help hearing you and Edvard airing out the problem you told me about, but don't leave yet. We have an idea."

"I happen to have the skill set to take your place, at least for the holidays," Martan said smoothly.

"He's my new husband." Nia took the surprised clerk's arm, turned him around, and steered him into Edvard's office.

Edvard looked up, unguarded, his face clouded with anger. Then he saw who besides Byron was with Nia.

"Father, this is Martan," Nia said lightly.

Martan said, "Sir, I can do clerical work. If your clerk will show me what to do, I can fill in for him during your holidays, and keep you safe too. I've had training in protecting dignitaries."

By assassinating their enemies. Nia almost laughed at that thought and because she had never seen her father at such a loss for words. Finally he managed to nod.

Byron brightened. For the next few hours Byron showed Martan the basics of the job. When Byron realized what a quick study Martan was, he became positively radiant. Byron finally left for the day with praise for holy Providence on his lips.

Nia thought, *Truly.*

On the way home across the ice lake, the catamaran crew noticed the difference between Nia's skin color and Martan's. The crew delivered the passengers and Martan's luggage to Castle Courant's lake gate. The catamaran then sped away in the direction of Arrival. Soon the news would be all over Arrival that Nia Courant had found herself a tall, brown Goyan man to bring home.

That night Nia's whole family was at Castle Courant to meet Martan. Even Suzana and Nia's younger sister Taylin were there. Suzana probably wanted to disapprove of Martan, but he gave her no traction. He effortlessly maintained his manufactured past as a former Goyan Guardsman who, when he got caught up in political trouble there, resorted to Wendis, finding a position at the university there as the proctor—the official in charge of student safety.

"You must have had your work cut out for you in the war," Eirene observed.

It was the understatement of the century. It was also true. Nia and Martan both nodded.

"He's the right escort for you," Jon told Nia in an approving undertone.

Grandda Vim was visibly pleased with Martan. Taylin, who strongly resembled Suzana in looks and temperament, seemed mildly impressed. Radzi, whose father had taken such an unconventional turn in midlife, was genuinely interested in meeting Martan.

The hugwort lifted its leaves when Martan grasped one of its tendrils. Then it stroked his hand with several more tendrils. "I'm happy to see you too, weed," Martan said.

The evening meal, attended by the whole family out of keen interest in Martan—and the prospect of the best food Castle Courant could offer—was synthmeat and potbread, vegetables and bread, icewine, glacier water, and a layer cake at the end. It was an Azurean feast graced by a vase of flowers from Vim's greenhouse.

Martan praised the flowers and the food, which was a relief to Vim and Eirene, who had prepared everything. Everyone had heard that long-colonized Goya had the best and most various food of anyplace. But Nia knew that Martan hadn't come from there at all. His home was a dusty village on Estrella, the poorest and most hardscrabble planet in the Faxen Union. Nia knew that he'd grown up eating corn, beans, squash, and fish from the muddy irrigation channels. His family worked hard to put food on the table, and it wasn't rich food any more than the meals on the average Azurean table. Even after so much had happened in their relationship, she felt reassured at another touchstone of how their backgrounds, though wildly dissimilar, were yet in many ways equal.

Throughout the evening, Martan, good looks aside, came across as pleasant and less ambitious and competitive than most of the men in Nia's old professional and personal circles. He really was all that, Nia realized, and that made him a good match for her.

But when he had to, he could switch-blade into the superhumanly capable hellhound made by Faxe, modified by Wendis, and dedicated to Wendis and to her. And that fascinated her and kept her madly in love with him.

When they finally had the privacy of her bedroom, they made love. Later, lying in bed with Martan, more satisfied and more relaxed than she could remember being here or anywhere else, Nia asked him, "What do you think of my family?"

"Eirene is the smartest one. I overheard her tell your grandfather, 'There must be more to him than meets the eye. We're seeing a presentable scabbard. What's inside is very, very sharp.'"

Nia laughed softly. "That is so true."

Then Martan surprised her by asking, "Someday soon, can we look for my Uncle Hazindo? He left our village before I did. So he wasn't there when SECINTAG bombed the base to blame the disunionists, with the village as collateral damage. He's all the family I have left."

Maybe it was no surprise that meeting her family made him think about his. She still had her home and her family too. He'd lost home, family, and everything else that had existed there. She tightened her embrace. "Of course we'll look for him." They lay twined together for a long, comfortable time. She ventured, "Someday can we have children?"

"I'd like that very much." Then he stroked her hair and her back, and she fell asleep.

She woke up, refreshed, at home in Castle Courant, in Azure's gravity, with Martan asleep beside her. It felt wonderful.

The skylight showed clear blue sky with a bright beam of light across it. The summer storms hadn't started yet: There hadn't been rain or snow since she got here. She remembered an early summer morning just like this one, most of her life ago. She said quietly, "Martan."

He woke up instantly and completely.

"There's something I want to show you. I don't think it will take more than half an hour—with you."

One of his expressive eyebrows arched.

They put on coats and went upstairs, through the level of empty bedrooms. Not needing heat in unoccupied spaces, the air in here was cold. It struck Nia how echoingly empty Castle Courant was, with so few people in residence. She and Jon, Suzana and Taylin, had all left, and their friends weren't here either.

She showed Martan the way outdoors, and then along the outside of Grandda Vim's greenhouse, to the base of the highest point on the Arc. The basaltic peak stood dark against the brightening sky. "That's the Gnomon. The word means the vertical piece in a sundial. The astronauts who discovered the Arc named it that when they saw the shape of its shadow. Think we can climb to the top?"

With a long look at the high, narrow peak, he said, "Sure."

The steep and little-used trail was coated with ice in shady spots. Even in the best of weather, like today, it was dangerous. A misstep could send a climber tumbling down into Grandda's greenhouse, and that was with luck. Luckless, a climber here would fall the other way and end up in the ice-cold sea below.

They had no ice axe, no ropes, no carabiners, no tools for climbing—just Martan's strength and lightning reflexes. And it was enough. Braced against the wind on top of the peak, he held her securely, taking in the full sky. The morning sun above the white mountains was surrounded with halos, arcs, and tangents of light across the sky.

"The light show is sunlight shining through ice crystals high in the atmosphere," she said into his ear.

He smiled. "You're giving me another wonder of the universe to see."

Back on the main floor of the Castle only a few minutes later, Nia laughed with relief and delight. "I did that climb once before. With a childhood friend of mine. We had ropes, crampons, plans, you name it. We inched up, and saw a halo display like that, but he slipped—I didn't arrest his fall skillfully enough—and he broke his ankle. I helped him back down. Whereupon we got into major trouble."

"How old were you?"

"Seven."

He chuckled.

He was browner than Taffy, and more handsome, but his dark hair and his build were much like Taffy's. Somehow this made her feel that she had just fulfilled an old wish for adventure. And that the universe offered many more opportunities like it.

Radzi was not at breakfast until he looked in and asked, "Has anyone seen that walking plant? I think it's got my mandolin pick."

Nia asked, "Did it have an opportunity to take it?"

"Last night it opened my mandolin case. I found it touching the strings, fingering the strings, making them vibrate. It seemed interested, if a plant can be interested."

"The weed can be interested, all right," Martan commented.

Everyone scattered to look for the hugwort. Edvard went to his study, more concerned about his angelfish than Radzi's mandolin pick. Grandda Vim went to check in his greenhouse. Suzana and Taylin were still asleep, but Eirene intended to quietly look through their rooms. Suzana's chest of unwanted old costume jewelry would be a hugwort magnet, if it discovered that.

"Show me your sea gate, and we can look for the weed there," Martan said to Nia.

They went down the Waydown Stairs into the Cistern. Martan took a long look at the fluted column near the stairs. "That was fancy work for a colony that was just starting out," he said, possibly thinking of the humble house on Estrella where his family had lived.

She said, "When they beam-carved tunnels, they made holes to outline the tunnel, and then took the rock cores out. And used the cores as building material."

When they reached the bottom of the stairs, he asked, "Besides your prime minister, who knows about the sea gate and that it still works?"

"A lot of people in Arrival and a few people in Denevez. If anything heavy needs to come here, it comes by sea, not on the ice lake. There's geothermal warmth and liquid water below the surface of the lake, and test beds for introduced organisms. Nobody wants a heavy load breaking through the ice."

Martan nodded.

The Cistern showed no sign of unaccountable green, nor was the hugwort anywhere near the sea gate. "You could get a huge load in this way, all right," Martan observed. "The high crane works?"

"It probably needs oiling, but yes, it should work."

She showed him the gate control room next. And there they found the hugwort. It had discovered the long crack in the floor. Anchored with tendrils wrapped around legs of a dusty desk and table, it was s-t-r-e-t-c-h-i-n-g itself down into the crevice.

"There's something interesting down there?" Martan asked.

"Its curiosity springs eternal."

"How much reach do you think it has?"

"Three meters, maybe more. Which is about how deep the crack is. Maybe it found something that fell in."

When it bunched itself back up, Nia gathered up the hugwort. It was clutching a dusty, battered small notebook. Since the hugwort did not want to let the notebook go, she bartered for it. Several days ago she herself had raided Suzana's cast-off costume jewelry for a few choice pieces in case of a situation like this. She offered the hugwort a shiny bracelet. It wrapped a tendril tip around the proffered bracelet and let go of the notebook.

She flipped through the notebook with Martan looking over her shoulder. "This is my Uncle Val's handwriting. It's a diary. The pages are dated. Years ago he was here exploring the Cistern and the control room." With an ache of grief, she remembered Val as an intense teenager, exactingly making notes, including the day he figured out how to override the lock mechanism and open the sea gate—at high tide. She remembered him holding the notebook above the flood of water and jellyfish. "The last time he left, he must have put his diary on that shelf, but the minor earthquake that opened the crack in the floor made everything on the shelf fall off." She looked at the last entries in the notebook. "There are sentences I can't read."

"Substitution code," Martan observed.

She found Radzi's smooth pick deep in the hugwort's tendrils, bartered a shiny earring to get the pick in return, and showed it to Martan. "Let's call off the search."

Radzi gratefully accepted his mandolin pick back. He looked at the diary with a kind of sad wonder. "It was my father's?" Settling into his favorite chair in the sun room, he used the pick to play soft, sweet, sad music on the mandolin.

Nia had thought about telling him that Lane had had an ESP experience that convinced her of Val being alive. Without meeting Lane, she had no idea how to estimate the truth of it, though, and it wasn't necessarily kind to undermine someone's grief with incalculable uncertainty. Finding Val's old diary was a real comfort to Radzi. Nia let that be that for now.

Martan leafed to the coded sentences in the diary. "This is fairly basic substitution code. I can decipher it. 'The gate was full of halos and arcs and then I saw the star man. Don't know if the star man is danger or opportunity. Must find out.' What does that mean?"

Nia thought hard. "The stars of the Faxen Union are all big and bright from here, and they make a constellation called the Astronaut—Star Voyager—that's bright enough to see even at dawn. It sounds like he saw that through the sea gate early on a halo day like today." If Val had ever opened the gate at low tide, he could have stepped out onto the sill and seen halos and arcs ringing the sun even with the stars of the Astronaut still shining in the sky.

And yes, the Star Voyager—the Faxen Union—had meant opportunity for him, with the education and the work he'd found on Tellas and the research station on the Tellas moon. The Faxen Union had meant danger as well. He was past all danger now.

Unless his wild wife was right about him being alive, somewhere and somehow. But that was sheer inference. The first thing Nia had learned in law school was the vital difference between inference and fact. With a lump of sadness in her throat, she felt glad Val had been at Castle Courant to visit his mother so often; that he'd found middle-of-life love with his wild wife, Lane, on Stannto; and that he'd had his reconciliation with Radzi, all before he died. Or—if his wild wife was right—before he stayed alive again but was somehow *changed*. God alone knew what *that* could mean.

And then there was the intellectual adventure of his lifetime, and his inheritance, the knowledge he'd surely intended for the good of humanity, not for the Faxen Union to exploit. Nia tensed, more in eagerness than anxiety. She would protect that legacy every way she could. And after last night's reunion with Martan, after the adventures they'd already had today, she felt energized and inspired to fight the legal fight—and win.

8

STAR BUBBLES

The next day Martan disappeared into Edvard's private office, which certain minor church officials, when they didn't expect to be quoted, called the Archbishop's Lair. Martan could handle working for Edvard and deal with potential assassins, if any. Meanwhile the AI report she'd ordered was ready. It distilled the case law of two centuries (since the last significant reworking of the Azurean legal codes about intellectual property and inheritance) into a single, succinct document. She was glad she didn't have to read all of that material herself, the way lawyers had needed to do in the ancient days on Earth.

The AI report also had weak points and false conclusions, but she could tell what they were, typical of non-sentient AI work. She missed the aid of Friday, the sentient AI in her office in Wendis. But she could work with this.

Then she went in to discuss it with Edvard. The good news was that she could build an airtight case for the inheritance of Val's intellectual property by his mother, Eirene. The better news was that any legal action instigated by Val's separated wife on Albion would presumably be done by lawyers less well-versed in Azurean law than Nia, and less expert in interstellar law relating to academic and scientific discoveries. It just so happened that she'd spent the last four years doing that kind of work in her role as a legal counsel for the university in Wendis.

Edvard readily agreed. It might have dawned on him that at this point he was much better advised by his daughter, the interstellar academic lawyer, than if she had been the prime minister of Azure, with her hands full of political crises and opportunities in the other high tower, Denevez One.

After a lunch in Denevez Two, Nia impulsively took Martan to the nearest ice cream shop on the street level. Along with almost everyone on Azure, she loved ice cream eaten Azure style: in bright sunlight while wearing warm outerwear, outdoors and out of the wind except for stray breezes that explored the street and blew a few strands of her hair across her face. The ice cream tasted cold, creamy, with subtle flavor. It tasted like the best memories of home, and she enjoyed every bite of it.

"I've usually had ice cream on other worlds in hot weather," Martan commented.

"That would be no fun, it would melt faster than I want to eat it!"

Their eyes met, he gave her his rare end-of-an-eclipse smile, and she laughed in delight.

The space elevator's afternoon car came down with messages from the stars. Martan instantly noticed the notification light. He left to go to the tower's message portal.

Edvard said, "He's very good at everything he's done so far."

Nia's imagination darted to their lovemaking last night. *Oh, yes.* She just smiled.

Martan reappeared, bringing three star bubbles. They were all for Nia. Edvard might have been a bit crestfallen.

One of the bubbles had been forwarded to her from Wendis. It was addressed to her in her official capacity at the university; it had originated on Tellas, coming from the legal counsel of the university—the lawyer there whose position was the equivalent of Nia's at her university in Wendis. Hiro had included in the bubble a note to tell her that the Tellan counsel was perfectly reputable, reportedly capable, but not as widely experienced as Nia herself.

The Tellan university counsel wrote that he faced an unprecedented situation involving interstellar law, ambiguous citizenship, and scientific and computational intellectual property. His wording walked all around the problem, without actually describing it. He only got specific with what he wanted from Nia: to set up a conference by simulacrum messenger.

"I think ripples from Uncle Val's death have gotten there," Nia said. "I'm not surprised. The university is a stakeholder in his intellectual property." She frowned. "Tellas is in the Faxen Union, but the university is insulated from the Union's control. There are sweeping legal and customary safeguards for academic freedom."

"What about religious freedom?" Edvard asked.

"There are guarantees of that," Nia said.

Martan told her, "There are sweeping guarantees of religious freedom all across the Faxen Union. But that can be undercut by infiltration, subversion, or what happened to your patriarch on Moira—unfounded accusation of committing a crime, followed by a rigged trial."

Edvard listened with a deep frown.

Another message came in a second bubble directly from Wendis. This one was keyed to Nia's fingerprint. Any other fingers would make the message disintegrate. It was from Lana Tai, and it was short and very much to the startling point.

Rumors are flying around the starways that your uncle died a hero in some kind of dustup against alien demons that live inside the halo gates because there's an undiscovered country in there.

Nia let out a curse. Both Edvard and Martan looked surprised at her reaction. But this was no mathematician's esoteric guess. It was a lurid rumor with long legs, and it would attract far too much attention if it floated into the ears of SECINTAG operatives. She explained, "The message is from a friend of ours, a xenarchaeologist who operates a university research vessel. She often skirts the edges of law and order—close enough to look over and see what's going on by way of lawbreaking and disorder." Nia read Lana's message aloud.

Edvard said tightly, "My deceased stepbrother doesn't need any more notoriety."

Alien demons. Hero. Dustup. Undiscovered country. Whatever all of that meant, it had the makings of notoriety, all right. Martan gave a slight, sure nod.

Nia eyed the last bubble. Looking pure as a giant pearl, it waited for her to open it. Surely it wouldn't top what she'd already seen, surely not. But she felt both curiosity and dread.

The date stamp that accompanied the bubble revealed that it had come from Tellas, only two days ago—a highest-priority bubble. It had skipped across the stars faster than a passenger starliner would have made the trip. Nia said, "Probably the Tellas university counsel learned that I'm here, not in Wendis. Maybe he's even learned something important." She took a deep breath and unfolded the message.

To her surprise, it came not from the university counsel, but from the academic department Val had belonged to—or probably still belonged to, since it wasn't as though he had officially resigned. The words of the message were even more unexpected. Stunned, Nia asked Martan, "Is it legitimate?"

He skimmed the authentication codes inside the bubble, looking for signs of counterfeiting or alteration. "Legit."

Nia handed the message itself to Edvard. Her hand shook slightly. "Please read it out loud and tell me I'm not imagining things."

"What do you mean? It says—" Edvard stared at the message. "I don't believe this. 'Your uncle is here at the university, alive and in good health.' He's not dead again?!"

Martan went as alert as a guard dog hearing something amiss.

Nia said, "If this is true, and I can't imagine his university department chair making it up, then Val's wild wife, Lane, was right—she said she thought he was alive." Inference had just morphed into fact, joltingly.

Edvard quoted the next part of the message. "'We don't know how he got here, he just reappeared, much as he briefly reappeared a few weeks ago, then disappeared.'" Edvard's forehead furrowed in deeper consternation as he continued. "'He doesn't know either. He has lost his memory of the last five years. We don't know how to keep him safe. He once told me you are his favorite niece, and one of the best interstellar lawyers anywhere. Please come help him.'"

With an incongruous spurt of happiness at the idea of Uncle Val having spoken well of her, Nia said, "It's signed by someone named Timothei Far. I remember Val talking about him years ago as his protégé, a brilliant scientist and potentially a first-rate administrator. Now he's the head of the department with a list of other credentials under his name."

"Val isn't dead again." Edvard sounded incredulous.

Nia was trying to get her bearings while it felt like Azure had just tilted on its axis and rotated in a new direction. Or maybe the universe had done so. "He's also not in the worst possible trouble. Not yet. Timothei Far is right. I've got to go there."

Edvard said, "Take the next starliner. I've already reactivated your access to the family bank account."

Martan shook his head slightly. Nia could guess what concerned him. "A Union starliner route would go through Union Central Station. My own notoriety could work against me there. An independent starliner would cost even more and take longer. No. I'll call in a favor. I'll tap the bank account to send a high-priority bubble back to our xenarchaeologist friend in Wendis. Her research ship can take me to Tellas directly and quickly," she told Edvard.

Edvard looked dumbfounded at the idea that his daughter could call in a favor of the order of magnitude of being whisked from Azure to Tellas.

There was a very great deal about her that she hadn't filled him in on. And she wouldn't get the chance very soon. She had to go to Tellas now.

That night in Castle Courant, she broke the news about Uncle Val being alive, but with a lot of missing memory, to Eirene and Radzi.

Vim and Eirene held each other. The hugwort crept into Radzi's lap and gently wrapped some of its tendrils around him, apparently realizing that he needed a hug too. Radzi asked, "Is the hugwort going to Tellas with you?"

Good question. Easy answer. "No. If I have any occasion to go through Faxen Union security, it might be confiscated."

"We'll take good care of it," Radzi promised.

"When does the Wendisan ship come for you?" Edvard asked.

"I'll know when I get a bubble back, but it may only take a day or two."

Nia felt sure that Lana could and would come for her. But

operating even a small starship like *Pastfinder* could be expensive, with the costs for esoteric fuel as well as docking fees adding up. In the aftermath of the war, it might be an expense that Lana could ill afford. Nia had an idea, though, which she'd already proposed in her bubble to Lana.

Now she made a vizcall to Jon-Jon. Calling the academy involved an atmospheric communication link, so she was glad of clear skies tonight. "You told me about the upcoming Academy expedition, that you need passage to that red star for an important training stint there, and you and your classmates have saved up money for it. Is it still on?"

The academy was on the other edge of this continent, where it was so late that the terminator had almost brought dawn there. Jon looked sleep-rumpled but alert. That was good. Starfleet crew needed to be able to cope with losing sleep. Sounding coherent, he said, "Some of my classmates have well-heeled parents paying for their passage to the red star, but the rest of us are on our own. Edvard doesn't have that kind of spare money and neither do their families. We're going to pool our funds to hire a freighter to get us there."

A freighter might stop at several asteroids and as many moons to deliver or pick up freight, and then it would make a large number of low-energy starjumps to its final destination if that was the red star. It could take days. Jon's classmates who had speedier transportation bought for them would already be there, soaking up the special training. That might even be the advantage they needed to qualify for better early postings in their starfleet careers, leaving Jon and his friends to qualify for the dregs.

Money buying privilege was the long shadow of Faxe, Nia thought. It might be euphemistically called "training in resourcefulness" to require academy cadets to pay their own way to the training star. *But if you want resourcefulness*, she thought, *look to Wendis!*

The atmospheric communication link meant that this call could be overheard. So she chose her words carefully. "I just learned that a Wendisan research ship will soon briefly stop by Azure." *Because the captain is a good friend of mine.* "You can pay for passage to the red star on the ship on its way out of the Azure system." *It'll sweeten the deal for Lana to get some recompense without even having to bend any laws or make off with any unattended artifacts.* "Wendisans always appreciate a fair trade of money for services." *That at least is the literal truth.* "It will get you there faster than a freighter." *Oh yes.*

9
GHOST SHIP

Sipping strong Azurean kavva—both because this would be her last chance to have any for a while, and to stay alert because she hadn't had much sleep—Nia watched the view window in the section of Azure's transit ring called Denevez Up. The window was full of stars. Some of the stars winked in and out. The brief stars were starships and message bubbles, coming and going. Most of them were dim as fireflies, or even dimmer, like the brief gleam of a tumbling snowflake at night.

Jon sat beside her. "Why do you need to go to Tellas in a hurry?"

He was too young to remember very much about Val, or to have mourned at the news of Val's deaths. "It has to do with our Uncle Val's legacy. Is everyone here?"

"They are now." He pointed at a group of mostly young, straight-spined people, with another one quickly walking over to join them.

"Everybody paid up?"

Jon checked his tablet. "Yes. Not everybody can pay as much as everybody else. That's okay." He indicated a man in the group who looked older than the rest of the academy students. "Axel has more money because of his first career in the import business. He's subsidizing the rest of us." Jon's eyebrows went up. "Edvard sent in some money too!"

"He wants me to get to Tellas. And you to get to the red star for the training there." As Nia understood it, the students, soon to be called *cadets*, were in for real-life training in starflight, systems, and tactics at the red dwarf star. The more of all that they could get, the better for their futures.

Jon's classmates gravitated closer. One of them asked, "Are we going in a Wendisan freighter?"

Nia answered, "No, a Wendisan research vessel, though not originally designed as such. I understand it was salvaged from some old war. Wendis is good at salvage."

Wendis sometimes salvaged people too. Martan was a case in point. He'd been a badly damaged Faxen hellhound when he defected to Wendis under the cover of an explosion that should have killed him. In Wendis, he'd been physically rebuilt. There was psychological rebuilding too. He was no longer what Faxe had made. He was better than that, and he was free. Just before she boarded the space elevator in Denevez Down, they'd shared a fierce kiss. She'd told him "Take care of Edvard—and everybody." He'd said, "I will." And they'd kissed again, longer and harder, until they had to let each other go.

Bringing Nia back to the here-and-now, another cadet asked, "Is it a star-survey ship?"

Nia said, "Good guess, but no. Xenarchaeology. Alien ruins. There are some on Tellas." Not that Lana and her merry crew were going anywhere near those sites this time. Not after their last, highly irregular and even more highly rewarding, fieldwork on Tellas a few years back.

A new star shone brighter than any of the fireflies and snowflakes. "If I'm not mistaken, there it is."

The light illuminated surprised faces. "The brighter the light, the faster the ship," one of the cadets murmured.

Still shedding light, the shining metallic spindle drifted toward the nearest dock in the transit ring. Sections of the spindle were slightly different shades of pale gold, subtle evidence of major repair work. Nia said, "That's it, all right."

Jon stood up with a sweeping gesture. "Ladies and gentlemen, here is our transportation."

Lana personally welcomed them aboard. Dressed as the star captain she truly was on this ship, she reminded Nia of a falcon that ruled its own aerie. Lana's tablet had the same information Jon's did, and she checked each of their identities—and payments for passage—as the cadets filed in. "I see you're a second-career academy student," she told Axel. "Excellent. Prior vocational experience is always good in star service. Everybody accounted for? Good. My name is Svetlana Tai, and *Pastfinder* is my ship. I understand that paying for this passage is a significant expense for you. So I'll get you to your red star with value added." Lana gave a slow smile. "I have Alliant starfleet instructor qualifications, which are recognized by your academy as valid. This will be an instructional flight for you. *Pastfinder* was a warship in its previous life, and much about it is still illustrative."

Jon and his friends looked more delighted with every word Lana said.

"I welcome you aboard as well, Nia Inanna Courant," Lana said with impeccable Wendisan courtesy, and a wink.

The entrance passageway was narrow and twisting, obstructed by conduits crammed under the ceiling. Nia had never seen a starship that struck her as roomy, and this one was no exception. One of the cadets—the tallest and thinnest—craned his neck to look past the conduits.

"Looking for the nameplate?" Lana pointed.

Startled, the cadet hit his head on a conduit. "Ouch—it says *Galant!*" His friends crowded closer. "We studied the Goya-Whimbrel war and how the fast attack ship *Galant* helped win the war. But *Galant* was destroyed."

"Not destroyed," Lana said smugly. "Just totaled by the Goyan shipyard. It was salvaged by Wendis. Complete with many of its original features." Deeper into the ship, where the passageway straightened out, Lana touched a switchplate on the wall. A long narrow section of the wall instantly rotated, bringing a row of beam rifles out of the wall. "I've scheduled a rifle drill for tomorrow morning. You'll learn how to be part of a crew repelling hostile forces attempting to board the ship."

Nia slept most of the way to the red dwarf star. By the time she woke up, the academy students were all busy and clearly feeling at home on *Pastfinder*.

Lana said, "That's a good bunch of cadets. Now, what didn't you say in your bubble to me?"

They were in what Lana called her war room. A computer-synthesized picture of the universe filled the vizwall that wrapped all the way around the central chairs and consoles. Azure's sun had become a point of brilliant yellow-white light. The red star was a brightening ember. Of course, that picture wasn't true, or not the whole truth. Getting to the red star required a ladder of starjumps to turning points. Today the cadets were learning about that in practice, and not just in theory.

Nia said, "I think my uncle really did discover stargates."

"And what in nine hells makes you think that?"

"He dedicated his career to understanding the halo gates. He called them that because the gates, if they're active, emanate bands of colored light that may have reminded him of the solar halos and arcs in the skies of Azure that he saw when he visited while he was growing up. Once he told me that he was convinced the gates are a system, all connected. Your rumor about him even implies as much, with the part about undiscovered country. Maybe he discovered it."

"Damned impressive if so. But why do you need to go to Tellas in a fluttering hurry?"

"To keep Faxe from getting the secret of the stargates out of him."

"He's dead," Lana pointed out.

"No, he's not. He's reappeared at his university on Tellas. But his memory has a major hole in it. He can't remember the last five years."

Lana tilted her head. At that moment, she looked more like an alert falcon than ever. "Some kinds of memory loss can happen by design—to protect the rememberer, or to protect the secrets they know. Or both."

That sounded plausible, or maybe familiar—Nia wasn't sure which—so she just said, "I believe you. Then there's one other thing. How he keeps disappearing and reappearing. He vanished from the Tellas moon. Now he's turned up at the university for what my informant there says is the second time—that he appeared and soon disappeared there not long ago."

Lana processed this information so intently that Nia could almost hear her mental abacus clicking. Finally Lana said, "I've always thought a stargate would be big enough to fly a ship through."

Nia answered, "What if you just *walk* through it?"

Lana gave her a wry grin. "That would fluttering well sink half of my stargate dreams. But the other half would come alive like never before."

At the red star, the academy students disembarked with proud faces, good-luck wishes from *Pastfinder*'s crew, and fresh starship-qualification signoffs in their official tablets. Their wealthier classmates had not even arrived yet.

Nia hugged Jon goodbye. She suspected that the next time she saw him he'd be a full-grown man, one of what Azureans called the rising generation.

He told her, "I never thought I'd have a Wendisan sister. But I'm glad I do! Godspeed!"

Speed. There was certainly going to be that. Nia made her way to *Pastfinder*'s war room and summoned a chair up out of the floor. It was a wraparound chair designed to hold a person securely. She was probably going to need it soon. Until then, she watched the realspace view shown by the vizwall.

The red star dully illuminated the angular academy training station that orbited it. *Pastfinder*, pulled by a sturdy space tug, slowly withdrew from the academy training station. *Pastfinder* could have left from its original position, since the starjump "point" was really a complex and extensive shape in realspace. But that would not have set a good example of responsible star navigation: It would have oversaturated and damaged the station's light sensors, not to mention the eyes of anyone looking at it.

Nia imagined the cadets inside the station dashing to find a view window to watch *Pastfinder* depart. They'd see the ship tugged to a safe distance away from the station, until the tug released it and retreated. Then *Pastfinder* would flare like a nova. The cadets, and possibly even the station administrators, would have never seen a starjump flare like that.

She could already feel the ship's energy building toward the starjump. It gave her goosebumps.

When the jump came, the wall all around her blurred into a

maelstrom of star trails. Feeling faint, she put her head on her knees. She struggled back to full consciousness with Lana's hands on her shoulders. "Are you okay, milady?"

Nia managed to sit up. "As you once observed, I am sensitive to starjumps, and the higher-energy the jump, the harder it hits me." The vizwall showed stars streaming around them like a river. She could already identify the sun of Tellas—the one unmoving star in the visualized universe. "Will you and your crew be safe going to Tellas?"

"Not really. We had a dustup there a few years ago."

"The one that got you the alien robot warhorse."

"Right. Sleipnir is decidedly not aboard. We won't be *Pastfinder* from Wendis either We'll be the tradeship *Gallant*, duly registered to a mercantile syndicate in the Goyan outsystem. We'll arrive at an obscure point behind the moon, so our arrival light doesn't attract undue attention. Then we'll make an inconspicuous hop to the free trade ring at the moon. There's a shuttle from there to the transit ring. Your academic visa should get you into the space elevator and you'll be at the university by local morning."

Nia wondered if Lana had any special activities planned at the free trade ring for the next few days. But if said activities were illegal, Nia didn't want to know. So she asked, "What do you think about the cadets?"

"Qualified, talented, and motivated," Lana answered. "That girl Kandas has the mind of a first-rate astrogator. The others each have a distinct bent toward engineering, diplomacy, military tactics, or command."

"Which one—?"

"Is the potential commander? Your brother. His father—and yours—has the mettle to command an organization that extends across the face of Azure and to the ends of that solar system. So I'm not surprised."

Nia *was* surprised. But that was only because she'd never thought about it that way.

The yellow sun of Tellas brightened in the field of stars. *Pastfinder* returned to realspace camouflaged by the glare of sunlight shining behind the moon.

Earth's moon had had dark basins from ancient asteroid impacts that released lava flows. This moon looked roughed up in a different way, its skin long since broken, but never bleeding.

Pastfinder hopped to the moon's free trade ring, causing no stir there in its guise of a trader named *Gallant*. Starships did all look alike, although Martan could see structures in their starjump light that gave him a great deal of information.

Buoyed by goodbyes from Lana and her crew, Nia easily found the shuttle to the transit ring. Even better, she found it affordable.

The automated screening to enter the transit ring went without a hitch. Nia had a top-level academic visa, which conferred a high level of privilege. In addition, the academic visa overshadowed the bigger picture. The screening AI failed to add up the scattered clues to her past, distinctly nonacademic, role in interstellar affairs. A sentient AI might have added it all up. Wendis knew how to construct sentient AI's which were also sane. But Wendis did not freely share that knowledge, or its AI's either.

In the space elevator, she fell like a star again, this time into a seaside city warmer than Denevez. This city was called Tellas Prime. The university was on the other side of it, where the well-terraformed, green coastal terrain buckled into a barren low mountain range.

She'd never been on Tellas before. Six years ago on Azure, when it was becoming clear that her misadventure on Moira had been dredged up again and would doom her career there, Val had suggested she look for work on Tellas. Certainly there were Tellan organizations with interstellar affairs that needed qualified lawyers. But Tellas was one of the anchor points of the Tellas-Albion Consortium. Even then, long before Martan told her that the Consortium was also called the Telal Cartel and why he hated it, she knew it had its fingers in many interstellar pies, and not in a good way. Avoiding the Telal Cartel was a good idea then—and now.

Walking out of the transit tower, she tested the gravity. It was a little more than Azure's, but it was normal planetary gravity. It felt right.

With a warm sea breeze in her hair and soft morning sunlight on her face, she wondered if Val would remember suggesting that she come here. His memories from his earlier life, before five years ago, might be clear. Or might be ghostly and unconvincing. Or even effectively gone.

It would be truly awkward if she'd come here to be his lawyer and he didn't know who she was.

10

LOST MAN FOUND

This was unmistakably a university, made in the mold of the schools that had existed since the Middle Ages on ancient Earth. The lawns had colorful flower-bed fringes. The buildings had colonnaded cloisters, steep roofs, and decorative carvings ranging from ponderous to whimsical. Nia easily found her way to the right building and the right wing, and then she was led to the right door by a student assistant from the departmental office. The student assistant knocked, then opened the door to announce, "Dr. Far, you have a visitor."

There were several people in the office. The man who stood up was trim, dark-haired, and immaculately dressed. His eyes widened when he saw Nia. There weren't many tall, silver-haired, blue-eyed Azureans on Tellas, much less coming to his office unannounced in the middle of a crisis. "Are you Nia Courant?"

"You sent a bubble to Azure," she answered. "I was there because the family asked me to come help sort out the legal complications of my uncle's reported death. After I read your message I found a fast way to Tellas. Yes, I'm his niece, he's my favorite uncle, and I will do everything I can to help him."

Timothei Far smiled radiantly.

Nia looked around the office. There were four people here besides her, and none of them was Val. "Where is he?"

"In detention in the Union Authority Liaison office, because he's about to be extradited to Faxe."

Nine hells! Nia thought and felt intensely grateful to Lana for getting her here fast. "I need to know the legal side of what's going on."

One of the others present turned out to be the university counsel, the same person who'd sent the message to her on Wendis, from where it had been forwarded to her on Azure a few days ago. He'd been hoping for a meeting by simulacrum. He looked just as overjoyed as Timothei Far to see her in person. He rushed away to prepare a data download to send her.

Timothei said significantly, "Everyone still here is a good friend of Val's."

"Introduce me."

The middle-aged, fit-looking man with sandy hair was Gered tel Brithold. The scion of an old family on Tellas, he taught geology here at the university now. Gerry had been Val's friend since their first student days. Nia remembered Val talking about rock-climbing expeditions they'd taken together with a third friend, an Almaazan named Jack.

Jack wasn't here, but an older Almaazan woman named Idris was. Her name rang a bell for Nia too. She was the colleague whom Val called Idris the Unimpeachable. He and she differed in many of their opinions, but he respected her integrity and intelligence. Almaaz had significantly less gravity than Tellas. Very tall and slender, Idris wore gravity braces. She had dark skin, gray hair, and keen black eyes. Without saying more than a few words, Idris gave Nia the sense of being sized up as accurately as though she were standing next to a measuring stick.

As to Timothei Far, Val had more than once mentioned that Timm was a Sleighter, meaning that his people were shabby interstellar riffraff. The polished man in front of her had zero resemblance to that description. She'd figure it out later. "I can't afford to know too little, not about the legal situation—I'm glad your legal counsel is working on that—and not about the facts either. Will someone please fill me in on whatever is known about how Val got back here?"

Timm said, "I can't explain more than anyone else, but I can tell you how he was found, because I became involved very soon."

"Please do," she told him.

As he described what he'd heard and seen, his story took shape.

It happened on the hills inland of the university, during a wargame.

Wendis had an elaborate culture of reenacting ancient battles with archaic weapons, and Wendisans turned up on colonized planets and in various moonbases and space stations everywhere. Between the Wendisan wargame hobbyists and countless tourists who'd been introduced to the games when they visited Wendis and become aficionados, wargames were a popular pastime in many places. The university on Tellas was one of them.

It had been twilight, with the game still going strong even as the last daylight faded. Two of the gamers were hiding just inside one of the many fissures in the cliffs. Expecting a war party from the other side to run by, they planned to hit them with paintlight-gun sniper fire. But the wargamers suddenly became aware of colored light coming from deeper in their hiding place. One of them warily investigated. Deep inside the fissure, she couldn't see what caused the light. But she found someone lying on the ground. She called for her friend. The urgency in her voice told him reality had somehow intruded into their game. She said, "He's got war paint on his face, so he must be a wargamer too, from the other side. I think he's a casualty. Maybe even a real one!"

Her friend bent down and checked the casualty's pulse. "He's cold."

The girl gamer gasped. "Oh no, dead?"

"Colder than that! But he's got a pulse anyway!"

They signaled an emergency stop to the game. Within minutes, the other side's war party ran into the fissure. Everyone who had a flashlight or firestick turned them on.

The girl said, "We don't recognize him. He must be one of yours."

The new people shook their heads.

She was baffled. "Wait, how can he be not ours and not yours either?"

They weren't enemy warriors now. They were all university students and staff united in dealing with an emergency. One of the new people, sporting the garb and the weapon of an ancient archer, looked closely at the pale, prone, cold man with the painted face. "I know who he is! I was in a class he taught five years ago. Before he disappeared."

Everyone else blurted out something to the effect of, *How can he be here?* They also called for the university emergency medics. The archer contacted Timothei, who was the head of his academic department and, the archer remembered, had been the protégé of the missing man.

At a run, Timothei reached the university hospital minutes after the medics brought the found man in with the wargame archer running in too. The emergency physician was someone Timm knew quite well: his cousin Kameron. Timothei shakenly assured Kam that this man was Val Savre, the notoriously missing university researcher.

Kam informed Timm, "When they found him, he was as cold as though he'd just come out of a blizzard. We're carefully warming him. He'll live. But he came close to his show folding." That was a Sleighter expression that they both knew, and it meant death. "Something smashed through his chest at the solar plexus not long ago. The wound was repaired with techniques I don't recognize. He'll have a star-shaped scar there for the rest of his life."

Timm and Kam shared the Sleighter appreciation for scars as testimonials to adventure. But what Kam had just described was extraordinary.

Kam traced the pattern of paint on the man's face. "I don't think that's a pattern anybody in your games uses," he told the archer, who shook his head. "Does it look familiar to you?" Kam asked his cousin.

It looked like something from the legends of their people, the Sleighters. And Timm could not imagine an explanation for that.

When the found man came back to consciousness in the hospital several days later, the first thing he saw when he opened his eyes was Kam in his doctor's coat, and behind Kam, his concerned friends along the wall: Gerry, Timm, and Idris, as well as the archer reenactor who'd recognized him from a class five years in the past.

"What happened?" Val Savre asked, faintly but clearly.

Hugely relieved that Val was coherent, Timm waved at the archer, Val's onetime student, now a full researcher. "You had some kind of accident. The wargamers found you on the mountain, and Donalt recognized you."

"That can't be. I didn't do any rock climbing today."

His friends looked at him, puzzled.

Val asked, "What time is it?"

"Two in the afternoon," Kam answered.

"I have to teach class in an hour." He tried to sit up. "Ow!"

"Lie down. You got hurt." Kam pressed him back onto the pillow.

"Ow! I must have." Val waved at Timm. "Will you teach the class for me?" He rapidly specified a complex topic, along with how the class he'd taught the previous week was a carefully tailored prelude to it, and how he meant it to prime the class for the topic of the next class. He added that Donalt was sharp enough to fill Timm in on anything else.

Amazed, Donalt whispered, "That was years ago."

Kam asked Val, "What is today's date?"

Val Savre specified an exact day, month, and year— five years in the past.

Kam asked, "What did you have for supper last night?"

"I'm a bachelor. I don't pay attention," Val said impatiently. Then he recalled a meal complete with the flavor of the sauce he'd used on the synthmeat.

It turned out that Val Savre remembered all the significant details of his career, most of the interstellar news from the week of his disappearance, the last rock-climbing expedition he'd taken with Gerry—everything, with clarity and accuracy, until a point in time five years ago. And nothing since.

Whew. Nia was glad to feel some real relief amid all this. Given the clarity of Val's earlier memories, it was likely that he would remember *her*. Of course that still left far more questions than answers. "Is he changed in any way, besides the lost part of his memory?"

Val's friends reflected. Gerry finally said, "No and yes. I don't think I'm being unfair to say that in the last years before he disappeared, he was getting rigid in some of his opinions."

Nia nodded. She'd seen that too. As he aged, some of Val's attitudes, and not the most charitable and openminded of them, had hardened.

Gerry said, "As a younger man, he used to be more fun. Spirited." That was the Val whom Nia remembered. Gerry said, "He's more like that again."

Timm said, "He didn't care for my people. We're Sleighters."

"He was quite prejudiced," Idris said precisely.

"But just yesterday, he told me that everything he's heard about Sleighters can't be true any more than everything people and authorities are saying about him. I almost couldn't believe it," Timm finished.

Nia heard between the lines, *I always yearned for my mentor to drop the prejudice and relate to me as who I am and since he has, I too will do anything I can to save him.*

Gerry said, "But for some reason, he's become afraid of slender blonde girls. Even my daughter. It's a reflex he can't explain. And he's afraid of red light. The detention center has red night lights, and that gave him a bad night last night."

Nia knew how to read a room. What she read here were genuine concern and good intentions. There was power in this room too. Timm had authority as university department head. Gerry, in his good-academic-natured way, had definite standing as both a full faculty member and a descendant of an old Tellas family. And Nia suspected considerable power on the part of Idris. She turned to the Almaazan woman. "Do I have the singular honor to address an emissary of Almaaz?"

Idris smiled slightly. "I see you've done your homework. There's no need to be flowery about it, but yes."

"Because of that, your hearth is sacrosanct. If you will let us move this meeting there—and I know that this is an unheard-of imposition, and I deeply apologize—we can all speak freely. We cannot be compelled to testify in court about what is said beside an Almaazan emissary's hearth. And I need to ask some incredibly loaded questions."

11

THE HEARTH OF ALMAAZ

Idris' cottage in the University Village was modest enough, looking like where any other academic might live. Except it had a hearth. Since Idris was far from home, this was a portable hearth—a gracefully shaped metal box on a low platform. When the box was open, a small flame would burn.

In the outside world, Almaazans were famously abstemious of mind-altering chemicals. But in their own homes, they could partake of such, and they were generous hosts, according to the rare reports of outsiders who had ever been in that situation. Apparently, those reports had been accurate. Nia was profoundly grateful when Idris made strong kavva for her. It had a note of a spice she didn't recognize, but it was very good.

She took a longer sip and considered the small group that had relocated from the department office. Academics all, they looked at home here in a university residence, and expectant. "Okay. Here's what I need to ask you. This discussion must not be repeated outside this room. But no court anywhere can force any of us to relate it. Now, rumors went all the way to Wendis that Val was making a stargate. That's outlandish. But can he have discovered something about the halo gates? Something, well, stargate-ish?"

Gerry looked surprised. The other two didn't. Timm said, "When he came back a few weeks ago and disappeared again, he worked on a computer model of the halo gates that he'd created years ago and that had been running ever since. He spent hours with it, we later discovered."

Idris said, "In the early morning he came to me to warn me that there might be a halo gate on the island we call Toliman's Hearth on Almaaz. He said the same thing could happen there that happened on a rogue planet named Dhal, where an unsuspected halo gate opened and let loose alien attackers who massacred almost the whole research station there. I already knew about that disaster from one of our university colleagues. Her family was at the research station. Everyone except her son and two other people were murdered. What the traumatized survivors remembered was so awful that they called the attackers demons."

Nia had a headache trying to happen. The kavva valiantly fended it off. "A well-star-traveled associate of mine picked up a rumor that Val recently died a hero's death battling alien demons in an unknown country, inside a stargate. Maybe it was the same enemy. Maybe he was wounded and presumed dead." She took a long swallow of the kavva. "The Faxen Union will do anything for stargates. And I do mean anything. What my Uncle Val has gotten involved with may be very, very dangerous to anyone who helps him—or even makes the attempt. If a huge risk is not acceptable to any of you, you'd better get out now, and get far away too."

Idris and Timm just looked grim and unsurprised. Gerry visibly wavered. Then he firmly put down the cup from which he had been drinking tea. "I won't desert my oldest friend," he said resolutely.

Nia nodded. "First we have to get Val out of detention. In the

Faxen Union, one detention sometimes leads to another, and the end of the line is black detention, where somebody disappears never to be seen again. I can't let that happen to him." She tapped her identity bracelet. "I have the legal download from your university counsel in my data pod, and I've looked at it. I think I know what will work."

Situated at the interface of town and gown, on the city edge of the university, it was a backwater Faxen Authority detention center. And she was a frontwater interstellar lawyer. She'd dealt with situations like this before, usually not in person, but the same kind of thing: a researcher landing trouble in some remote corner of the Faxen Union and now languishing in some kind of jail, detention facility, or under house arrest.

The trick was to turn the situation into a vivid story. This time around she had a handy embellishment. She presented herself as an agent of Val's family on Azure. Emphasizing that theirs was a prominent family, full of indignation at Val's misdeeds, intent on dealing with him according to the family's sense of affronted honor, she granted that Val Savre needed to be reined in, but insisted that he not be detained like a common criminal. She proposed that Val be required to wear a locator if he left the university. That being provided for, there was no practical reason for him to remain in detention. And, as she demonstrated with a spate of legal filings, declarations, and formal protests, there was no legal justification for it either.

Her mix of looks, attitude, and legal firepower, along with Timm backing her in his official capacity and immaculate attire, worked. Glad to get Val off their hands, the detention center officials released him into the custody of his department in the person of Timm.

Val was thinner and paler than Nia remembered, and he

seemed shaken and wary, including wary of Nia. He hardly said anything as she and Timm escorted him to across the campus to their destination. "This is Idris' house," he said when they got there. "Does she have a bone to pick with me too?"

"You'll see." Nia steered him into the hearth room. Idris and Gerry were waiting there.

"She did it!" Timm announced. "She's good!"

Gerry leaped to his feet and applauded.

Val looked confused. "What?"

Nia threw her arms around him. "Uncle Val—you're alive! I'm so glad!"

"What? You're not just your father's agent?"

"I was pretending. I really came here to rescue you. With Edvard's blessing."

He started looking less crushed, like a plant out from under careless footsteps. "Thank you, Nia, thank you all."

Idris said, "We understand you had a bad night. What would help?"

"Whiskey is good medicine for him, after a bad shakeup," Gerry suggested.

"I do have that."

Val said, "Oh. Yes, that would help."

He gratefully sipped the strong, golden liquid. Everyone else had coffee or tea and conversation that Nia kept light, while she gauged Val's condition. They had all agreed beforehand to do it this way, not hitting him with questions or demands before establishing a sense of normalcy. He looked careworn and even frail. But his body language and his eyes were the uncle she remembered.

To Nia's surprise, a large, brindled cat materialized from a back room. Nia had never seen a housecat that big. It looked around with a narrow-irised stare.

"What's that?" Gerry asked.

Idris answered, "Her name is Tsaalith, but foreigners may

call her Sally. She is a dhalcat, meaning a predator of dhalrats, a plague species that originated on Dhal, of which some of us were speaking earlier. The dhalrats are widespread across the stars. On Almaaz they infest the island we call Toliman's Hearth. And they can swim. Our people in the lands across the channels from Toliman's Hearth bred the dhalcats for protection."

Listening to Idris calmly explaining her pet, Val rubbed his right forearm under his shirtsleeve. That caught Nia's attention. So she saw a change come over him, a hardening of his facial muscles and a more taut stance. Speaking more forcefully than he had all afternoon, he said, "Timm, you'd best check the computer model. When I looked at it last, instabilities were sweeping across it, pointing to where halo gates may exist and potentially come back to life. Toliman's Hearth on Almaaz is one of those places, as I warned you, Idris."

"I took it seriously," she said, unfazed.

"The instabilities may have crystallized in more places by now. Timm, you helped me make the model, you can understand it, first-son-mine."

Then, just as subtly yet completely as it had happened in the first place, he shifted back to his previous expression, stance, and voice. "Why is everyone looking at me?"

Even the dhalcat was staring fixedly at him.

Nia gestured to everyone else to keep quiet. She moved to sit beside Val on a low divan. "Does your arm hurt?"

He rolled up his sleeve, revealing a set of thin scars that looked like having been clawed by something vicious. "No. I don't even remember how I got this. Or how I got the scar in my midsection. Which still hurts." He gingerly put his hand there.

Nia said softly, "Val, I don't think your memory is lost. Can you trust me?"

He told her unhappily, "For reasons I don't understand, I am in truly hot water. Why are you getting involved?"

"Years ago after what I did on Moira, when you heard about

it, you stood by me." She remembered that with sudden clarity and gratitude. "That's why. Will you trust me?"

"Do I have a choice?" He answered himself. "Of course I do, but I've known you since you were a free-spirited girl. I trust you."

Impulsively, she put her arm around his shoulders. He put his around hers with a crooked grin she recognized from decades ago. *He's back, oh yes, my Uncle Val is back.* "You should get some sleep. Where are you living?"

"My residence, back room," Gerry supplied.

Val sighed. "I may not be able to sleep. The red light in that detention cell last night tapped into my nightmare stuff. Your daughter has that effect on me too," he told Gerry. "I don't know why."

Surprisingly, Idris said. "I have a guest room. Stay here."

Val still looked disconsolate.

Nia remembered her night in Starway, and how the alert little dog, Star, had been a comfort to her. Tsaalith the dhalcat could probably disembowel anything that posed a threat, having sensed it long before humans would have. "Idris, with your dhalcat here, can anything really get in to hurt Val?"

"Certainly not." Then Idris spoke to the cat in Almaazan. That was not a language Nia understood, not even the usual casual phrases that were handy in interstellar negotiations. Almaazans kept their language to themselves, to the frustration of linguists everywhere. The cat apparently understood Almaazan. It lifted its tufted ears. When Idris finished speaking, the cat nodded. Idris told Val, in a kind voice, "Have no fear. Tsaalith will guard you while you sleep."

Val's relief was all but palpable. Pointed toward the guest room, he went that way, staggering from fatigue and the shot of whiskey. The cat paced beside him. He shut the door behind the two of them.

"That was an excellent idea," Idris told Nia. "Now what happened here a few minutes ago?"

Val didn't need to hear this, but he was already half unconscious, and the door to the guestroom was thick. Nia spoke quietly. "I don't think his memory is lost. I think it's in safekeeping behind a locked door in his mind. At need, the door can briefly open. We just saw that. It's not an unreliable fugue state. It's an engineered amnesia that can keep explosive secrets secret." She'd heard about such things. Hearsay didn't justify how absolutely certain she felt that she knew what she was talking about, but she did.

Everyone looked startled but they nodded. So far so good.

"Now, I know he turned up here a few weeks ago and vanished again. We can spin it as a sneaky academic in pursuit of some foible and well aware that the security here—if it's like most universities—has holes in it. But there's another explanation. A possible reason for somebody magically coming and going, being here, then not here, then here again." Following this to the logical end made her head spin. "Halo gates generate light, and there were mysterious lights in the fissure just before the wargamers found him. Suppose Val learned how to use the stargates."

Gerry and Timm stared at her like she might be out of her mind.

Idris said, "He did. Our colleague Meredet, who works in the research station on the Tellus moon, saw him there several time since he disappeared. He came and went through the halo gate at the research station. Finally, though, because the Faxen Union put agents into the station, he turned that gate off."

Gerry and Timm looked thunderstruck. Nia's head was spinning. "Suppose there's one here too—in that fissure. Timm, you better look at the model. What did he mean by 'You helped make it, you can understand it?'"

"The model was a post-graduate project for me. Val helped me refine it then showed me how to take it to the next level."

"What about him saying, 'First-son-mine'?"

Timm said, "My people, the Sleighters, refer to an eldest son that way, or to someone considered like that."

She nodded. It was nice to have something—anything whatsoever—making sense in all this. "He has an adult son presently on Azure and a much younger boy on Stannto. You're the oldest."

Timm's shoulders got even straighter than usual. Between the lines, Nia read, *I will do absolutely everything in my power to save Val.* And besides academic authority, he might have some kind of power as a Sleighter too—practical knowledge, personal connections, maybe even racial talents. She should find out about that, and what kind of difference it could make.

Over the last few years she'd learned not to underestimate anyone's power to change things. Not even a hugwort's.

12

MARTAN CLARK

The ice catamaran approached Castle Courant, the thrust reversers on its jet engine smoothly slowing it to a full stop at the lake dock. Jet engines were a simple, ancient, and competent technology. Martan approved.

Edvard Courant stepped aboard after Martan. The ice cat accelerated toward Denevez and what would be Martan's longest day as Edvard's clerk so far. Their work would stretch long into the evening. They stood behind the windscreen instead of going belowdeck to find a seat. Martan welcomed the bracing cold air to start the day with.

Edvard said, "I didn't see the hugwort this morning. I hope it's not getting into more trouble."

"The weed has been in the greenhouse fraternizing with Vim's plants," Martan told him.

Edvard looked up at the sky. Martan recognized the gesture. Like his daughter, Edvard looked up and away when seeing an idea. Edvard said, "I've been reading the work of Olav Zakeri, the Old Cathor's new patriarch. He extolls weeds for their role in terraforming on Goya."

"When I was in military service there"—Martan didn't specify that it had been the Faxen military; for once, that detail was irrelevant—"I saw a shrine to tumbleweeds."

"Zakeri sees weeds as mortal, terrestrial beings that can find a foothold in a barren place on a new world. *Weeds like us*, he says more than once in his writings, because we too—the strains of humanity that reached the stars—have determinedly taken root in barren places."

Martan had the duration of the ferry ride to transition out of being Edvard's son-in-law and into being Edvard's dutiful clerk. Dutiful yes, mute no. "I'm a bit surprised that you've read Zakeri's work."

Edvard half smiled. "It was required reading given me by Adriance Vale as penance for my sins. Then I found it rewarding. The man is a good theologian."

Martan guessed that the clerk should be not mute, but not verbally assertive either. He should have more questions than assertions. "As a New Cathor Church leader, don't you disagree with his theology?"

"That's not how good theology works. Agreement on doctrinal specifics across a hundred stars is not the metric. Rather, is it consistent and humane, informed by reason, history and sacred writings, and intelligible in the community where it is articulated and received? Zakeri meets that benchmark."

Nia had once said Edvard was no great theologian but didn't have to be. As an archbishop, he was a politician, a compromiser, and a defender of New Cathor theology more than an originator of it. Nia would have given him bonus points for informing himself about Old Cathor theology.

Edvard seemed to be in a mood to reflect about the varieties of faith. "The Old Catholic and Old Protestant Church bodies reunited at the beginning of the Star Age, with the long-awaited reunion with Old Orthodoxy coming not long after. In those desperate times of civilization breaking apart at the seams, it seemed ludicrous to hold on to the old divisions. But after we crossed the stars in slow ships and began to terraform new worlds, New Catholic Orthodoxy split from the Old. They haven't forgiven us for that, but the difference is fundamental. We worship God in the form of Christa Terra. Old Cathorism still worships God in human form. That can shift into the idolatry of overvaluing human biology as it did on Old Catholicism, resulting in the prohibition against birth control. Overpopulation was part of what shattered Earth's ecosystems."

Not for the first time, Martan realized how being a friend, a lover, and a husband let you hear your partner thinking in your head. At this point, Nia would have had something to say about idolizing the unmutated human genome. New Cathorism, and Edvard specifically, certainly leaned that way. Martan kept the observation to himself as they quickly walked from the quay to Denevez Two. Edvard may have heard a faint echo, though, because Edvard asked, "I assume you have some kind of faith or religious background?"

Faith? Martan wasn't sure. His faith, if indeed he had any, might be a work in progress. Background? In his distant childhood in the village of Delagua on Estrella, yes. "I was born Old Catholic."

"Then I apologize if I've just belittled your faith." Edvard might be treading more lightly on other people's religious convictions than years ago when Nia acted out her convictions on Moira. With her, then, he'd been brutally rejecting. In Martan's opinion, whatever penance he'd done because of how much he'd hurt Nia had been well deserved.

Martan said, "I left it behind." What took the place of his childhood religion was revenge against the disunion terrorists who destroyed his home. He'd been so zealous that it had probably amounted to religion. It had not ended well, because it was built on a lie.

"Many do leave an outgrown or inconvenient faith behind."

For some reason—an impulse he didn't need to analyze; it wasn't risky, just insistent—Martan needed to say something to take Nia's side. She was his wife and his lover, and years ago Edvard had used religious reasoning to wound her, only because her decisions had injured his pride. "Nia couldn't. Her faith really matters to her."

"I think faith matters more to her than to me." Edvard looked up into the clear blue sky. Sometimes when Nia did that, she wasn't seeing a random interesting idea, but rather something that struck her as truth, whether welcome or not.

The day consisted of the everyday business of the archbishopric. There were details to deal with, negotiations to navigate, and meetings at which to appear. Martan noted how Edvard, a competent but not compelling conversationalist in a one-on-one setting like on the ice catamaran this morning, came into his element when in a room with many other people. Then he was nothing less than charming, compelling, and exquisitely sensitive to how to capitalize on the moment.

Playing the part of Edvard's clerical satellite, Martan carefully, subtly reflected his radiance. To the limited extent that he needed to be introduced to anyone, Edvard called him Martan Clark. *Clark* was an ancient word for *clerk*. It made a serviceable alias. That he was also Edvard's son-in-law was not something either of them mentioned to anyone. Martan had been on Azure so briefly before Nia had left, that the usual introductions in Edvard's ecclesiastical circles had not been made.

In the third meeting of the day, Edvard described the near completion of the cathedral. At this point it only lacked a planned spire taller than any other building in Denevez. He had most of his hearers in the palm of his hand. But a church official protested on the grounds of expense. Edvard smoothly explained how it could be folded into the financial planning that he'd long since arranged. A city official objected on the grounds of building codes: New buildings had to conform to codes to withstand ice-heave. Yes, the spire could be made resistant to that—but at greatly increased expense. No real consensus was reached despite Edvard's best charm and effort.

Afterward, Edvard asked Martan, "How did that seem to you?"

"They shouldn't have objected to your plan, because it's for the glory of God."

Edvard rolled his eyes. "You're overdoing it. No one I'd have working for me would be so sanctimonious."

Martan immediately adjusted his body language and tone. "You missed an opportunity. Somebody brought up lighthouses and got talked around, but it really could be a lever. Every famous coastal location in ancient history had a lighthouse. You could enlist the glorious history of lighthouses."

Not a man who welcomed criticism, even when he'd invited it, Edvard almost snapped a retort. Then he just cleared his throat. "Good idea."

At the end of the day, he asked Martan to review a letter. It was at least the eighth communication Edvard sent that day. This one, though, was destined to travel by star bubble to Goya. Edvard had written a letter to the patriarch of the Old Cathor Church.

Martan skimmed it. Then he read it closely. Evidently, it wasn't the first letter to go from Edvard to Zakeri. They'd been having an exchange.

"And what you really think, is . . .?" Edvard prompted.

Martan stepped out of his role as clerk, into blunt truth. "This could get you into trouble if it gets intercepted. You could be taken for an enemy of the Faxen Union."

Edvard looked up into the air. "I know."

"Does historical accuracy matter in the discussion you're having with him?"

Edvard came back to the here and now. "Absolutely."

"It's not hypothetical that the Faxen Union would choose calculated losses to consolidate its power, as though it were all a chess game in which a player sacrifices pieces to win the game. There's an academic in Wendis, one with a distinguished career in the study of interstellar politics, who's certain that when an atomic bomb went off years ago at the military base at Delagua, on Estrella—which was blamed on disunionists—it wasn't disunionists who did it. It was the Faxen secret intelligence agency. They did it to fire up sentiment across the Union against Disunionism, and a remote military base was an acceptable loss. So was the nearby village of colonists, and fifty square miles of terraformed desert. Fifty square miles of your resurrected Christa."

Edvard looked appalled. "Are you certain?"

"I saw it before the bomb." Martan described the small river streaming out of the hills, with fish and frogs in the cooler spots shaded by trees. There had been grassland spreading toward the hills, populations of busy rodents that softened the barren dirt, and a small herd of antelopes. Martan had never told anyone about his childhood home in such detail. Something in how he told it must have been convincing. Martan could see his words connecting with Edvard's imagination.

"Go on," Edvard said, almost in a whisper.

"It wasn't ever a paradise. But the people who lived in the village loved it. Even the soldiers in the base liked it. They helped with community work like clearing the irrigation ditches and came to dance with everyone on the town square on the holidays."

"You've described a web of resilient life, with humans part of it, lovingly tending it. I would not call it paradise. I would call it Christa." Edvard made a reverent movement with his hand.

"Earth was the material revelation of the transcendent God. A terraformed ecosystem on Goya or Estrella is Christa resurrected. To destroy it as a political machination is an abomination."

Martan said, "You hint at something like that in your letter. You can state it. Zakeri knows the rules of engagement for the Faxen Union turning into an empire. Ecosystems are disposable, whether it's the native ecosystem on Faxe itself, or your resurrected Christa, anywhere."

Edvard rubbed his face. He looked drained. "I was afraid of that, but I still hoped that it was more like a nightmare that dissolves upon awakening in the morning."

"Spiders and fish, villagers and soldiers, the corn and the grass at Delagua met a nightmare from which they will never wake up again," Martan said harshly. He felt the loss more deeply than he had in years, in grief mixed with anger.

The feelings Martan had shared with Edvard stayed with him. In the middle of the afternoon, with a long evening ahead, he took a break by walking to the Memorial Park where Nia had met him only a few days ago. The high, twisted metal ruin of the first structure on this planet had wind blowing through it with whistles, sighs, and moans. He touched it. To his surprise, he found himself asking the ruin to include Delagua and Estrella in its long lament too.

For the rest of the day he felt better. Still sad, but not as bitter and burdened.

Martan's Old Catholic upbringing had not involved a holiday like Greening Day. Ahead of it, there would be religious services each of several evenings, to be crowned by a celebratory service on the Day itself, with a large part of the population of Denevez in attendance. A great deal of the work this week involved readying the cathedral. This would be a shakedown cruise for the newest, just completed, phase of the building's construction.

By now, Martan had realized that the cathedral was the main and most prized achievement of Edvard's entire career. It had been started decades ago, and then long stalled, until Edvard became the bishop of Denevez. In that role and then as the archbishop of Azure-Tierre, he'd advocated for the cathedral, redesigned it, and made the building one that could take its prominent place in the city. The planned spire would complete the cathedral. It would be the crowning glory of Edvard's longest and most determined passion too.

That could happen with high achievers, people who were married to a mission, a building, an idea, or a movement, far more truly than they had ever been married to another person. Suzana might be his long-standing wife, and Nia's mother, but she didn't seem to be the love of Edvard's life. Not like his own parents, Martan thought, with a new pang of old grief. They'd loved each other deeply. Because the bomb went off at suppertime in Delagua, they'd almost certainly died together. For that, Martan thought, he should thank God, however belated it was to do so now.

The earliest of the evening services leading up to Greening Day were lightly attended by the more devout of Denevezans. A few people in the back were more interested in warm shelter than the religious message. Under the watchful eyes of the vergers, they made no trouble, and there were no objections to their presence.

Again tonight Martan saw Edvard's magnetic charm in front of a crowd. Here, his charisma was amplified by religious regalia. No wonder Nia had always been in love with her father. No wonder his rejection had wounded her so deeply.

In his homily, Edvard quoted the patriarch of the Old Cathor Church. That caused surprise to shiver through the congregation. Martan guessed that Edvard had never done that before. Here and there, the surprise turned into disapproval. More generally it shaded into enthused approval. These congregants had evidently been paying attention to religious developments on the other side of the stars.

Afterward he and Edvard hurried toward the quay. The ice cat crew earned extra pay past a certain hour of the night, and certainly deserved it, but Edvard wanted to avoid the extra expense. He nodded toward a poorly lit side street. "Shortcut that way. By myself, I wouldn't take it. But two men are unlikely to be waylaid by thieves."

So Denevez had a dark, poor side near the waterfront. In this case it might be more of a dark, poor rim. Martan had seen much more extensively seamy cities than this one. Nonetheless, he looked and listened, assessing hiding places for a thief—or an assassin, for that matter—not that he expected any.

Martan could see in the dark and hear sounds only a trace louder than silence. In a deeply set, unmarked doorway, a shadow shifted in a predatory way. Moving with the speed he'd been given by the makers of hellhounds, Martan knocked the hand holding a small gun up, a fraction of a second before the gun went off. With the shot still reverberating, he knocked the gunman out with a bonemetal-knuckled punch.

"What! What did—what was that?" Edvard asked, turning around.

Distantly, Martan heard the cries of citizens who'd heard the gunshot, and a police officer responding. The policeman started running to the scene. There wasn't time for Martan to telepathically interrogate the attacker. It didn't seem necessary anyway. Rifling the pockets of the man's coat, he found an envelope and assessed the contents of it. "This is paper money—the kind of currency that works on the seamy side of a city. He wasn't trying to rob you. It was a hit, meaning somebody paid him to shoot you. Maybe not fatally. I don't think this was enough money for that."

Edvard shakenly contemplated his unconscious assailant. "You said you had experience protecting dignitaries. I never thought I'd need protection like that."

The policeman was shocked too. He took their statements and the envelope, while more police arrived to arrest the still-unconscious attacker. Martan knew how to knock somebody out so they stayed out.

Edvard and Martan continued to the quay, not bothering to hurry. By now the ice cat crew was already on overtime pay. "Interesting timing for that incident," Martan said. "Right after your homily tonight."

"I knew that might displease some."

"It stirred a few people up. But a natural stir has to percolate for anything to come of it, and that takes time. A staged reaction to something doesn't have to take time."

"Staged? What do you mean?"

"Your enemies may have been waiting for you to do or say something controversial. They may also have known you'd take this route to the quay tonight, if they've been watching you." Edvard was a creature of habit. Which would have to change. "Most likely the idea was to hurt and scare you, not kill you."

"So Byron was right?"

"Yes, sir, I believe so." Martan didn't think he was overdoing the act of being a polite son-in-law. In fact, it didn't feel like an act at all. After today, he had begun to feel some real respect for Edvard Courant.

When they reached the ice cat, Martan slipped the crew several of the bills that had been in the envelope. "Thanks for the late transport. Good Greening Day to you!"

That should guarantee that whatever trouble Edvard's assailant got into with the police here, whoever hired him would note a certain amount of the money unaccounted for. An honest policeman wouldn't have taken it. A high-ranking clergyman and his clerk couldn't conceivably have done so. That meant additional trouble for the attacker. A good night's work, Martan thought, feeling the clarity and energy of increased adrenaline.

Smiling at their reward, the ice cat crew steered the swiftly gliding ferry toward Castle Courant. Edvard brooded, silent.

Martan looked up at the stars, identifying which one was the sun of Tellas, brilliant in the night sky. It was supposed to be the beacon on the helmet of the constellation called the Astronaut. Tellasun, as it was known in the Faxen Union, was not far away in realspace. It was a much longer and more convoluted course away in starjump space. But the starjumping still only took days, where crossing realspace took centuries.

Seeing the bright star, Martan felt close to Nia. Haltingly, he prayed for her safety and success.

13

VAL SAVRE

The next day, Val's friends relocated him back into his old friend Gerry's guest room. They had located as many of his old belongings as they could, so he had some familiar furniture and utensils. Gerry and his wife provided a room for Nia, too, by displacing the family's possessions from a long closet. Val told Nia, "I feel better with you here."

"I'll guard you the best I can." She smiled. "I'm no dhalcat though."

"Don't be so sure," he answered, with a glint in his eyes. "But will you be comfortable? Your room is tiny."

She shrugged. "I've lived in Wendis for the last four years, so I'm used to small living quarters."

"Wendis? Why are you living in Wendis, of all places?"

Even if he'd still had his memory, he might have never heard about her move to Wendis. "What I did in legal fieldwork on Moira early on, later compromised my career on Azure." *Enemies of my father dredged it back up to kill my career* would be more accurate, but she wanted to avoid naming once and future battle lines.

"I remember when things started going downhill with that. I suggested that you find work here on Tellas. Until just now, as a matter of fact, I thought you'd done so, so I wasn't surprised to see you here."

"My career did go downhill on Azure, all the way to a dead end. And I didn't have undiluted family support." More accurately, *Edvard never forgave me, and we argued until I was sick of that and of him.* Too much information was very likely a bad idea, though, given the mysterious absence of Val's memory.

On the other hand, she wondered what could make the locked room in Val's mind open again, the way it had at Idris' hearth. Could she say anything to have that effect? Not random information—maybe something with an edge? "It's not that the Courant family has no tolerance for irregularity, but your adventures used it up."

He listened intently. "Whether or not I had good reason for doing what I did, the last thing in the universe I'd want then—or now—is to cause trouble for you. I'm sorry."

The door in his mind stayed firmly shut. Still, what he'd said was good to hear. "It worked out for the best, by the grace of Christa."

He'd been a staunch atheist in the past, always eager to argue about that. He opened his mouth. Then he murmured, "Odd. My mind just went to a criticism of your religion, but my heart isn't in it." He tilted his head. "And I have found that I can't praise the Faxen Union anymore. The reasons are there, as always, but they feel flimsy." He shook his head. "I wish I could remember the last five years. It seems like only a week, just the week since I woke up in the hospital, since the last day I remember. I'm changed, yet I don't even feel older."

He didn't look older either. But Albionis were famous for having long midlives. From age forty to sixty or even longer, they usually looked the same. And typically stayed firmly set in their ways. In that respect, Val had truly deviated from the stereotype. "Your friends say you changed for the better," she said, still hoping that the locked door would open.

"I don't know." He sounded skeptical. "Blonde girls terrify me. Gerry's daughter is a fine young lady, but any time she looks at me, my blood runs cold. That's not good. On the other hand, I've discovered that I can expertly mend children's clothes. Gerry's boy had a misadventure climbing trees and came home with his shirt ripped. I mended it so neatly his mother didn't notice at first. I've made a friend of that lad."

That gave Nia an idea. "Is Gerry here?"

"Yes, his study is the third door in the hallway, and I believe there was something he wanted to ask you."

Gerry was a geologist. Unsurprisingly, his house had rocks in odd corners. His wife may have set rules about the placement of rocks in the main part of the house, but his study was packed with rocks. She asked him, "You had a question?"

"Can I contact our other old friend on Stannto? Give him the good news that Val is alive?"

Wait—what? "Your other old university friend is on Stannto?" That was where Val had been the whole time, or most of it. "That's Jack, right?"

Gerry nodded.

Nia couldn't imagine Val living on Stannto without having been in touch with Jack. So Jack might be someone who knew how to keep a secret. "Let me see your message before you send it. It has to be something that would not be understood if intercepted."

Gerry readily agreed to that condition. Beyond his window, children were playing in the University Village trees, tumbling, climbing, even swinging on some of the branches. Nia could understand how Gerry's son came home with a ripped shirt.

The children ranged from adolescents down to a baby in the arms of an older sibling. They were the nestlings of the university. Nia said, "Can we borrow a child? I'd like to see if that makes Val remember his youngest son."

"What kind of child?"

"A boy, quiet, two or three years old, or older but small for his age. Maybe that one in the corner of a flower bed, there. Does he know you?"

"All the university children know all of the other children's parents." Gerry left and soon returned to Val's room with the child. Because he had never met an Azurean before, her silver hair and blue eyes dazzled the little boy. He hadn't been born yet when Val disappeared, so, without any surprise, he let himself be introduced to Val too and solemnly shook Val's hand. A strange look came over Val's face.

While Gerry took the little boy back outside, Nia asked, "Did that make you remember anything?"

Val absently put his hand on his solar plexus. "Nothing I can describe, but the feeling was very strong. There's something important, very important, and I'm missing it."

"Not forever," she told Val. "Rest for a while. You need to conserve energy for healing."

"High bright day, no red lights," he murmured. "I think I can."

Nia felt a bit starlagged, but it was a pleasant day, summer at a location between a cold sea and a hot continental interior. Fog lay just offshore. A breeze from that direction softened the summer heat. The campus felt like a safe and interesting bubble, set apart from the outside world, and shielded from politics.

To a degree that impression was accurate. A set of interstellar legal agreements in the interests of research, education, and the preservation of knowledge insulated this institution. Neither the government of Tellas nor that of the Faxen Union dictated what went on here. Institutions on other worlds, even outside the Faxen Union, knew they could trust the research done here, and so knowledge flowed without onerous barriers.

It was still far safer to discuss sensitive topics beside Idris' hearth. Idris came home with her tablet in one hand and a thick sheaf of printcopy paperwork in the other hand. "The work around here wouldn't stop even for a tear in the fabric of the universe," she said drily.

Nia remembered how the faculty, administrators, and students at the university in Wendis had doggedly kept working even with a war going on. "I understand."

Timm arrived looking rumpled. He sagged into one of Idris' chairs.

Idris asked, "Kavva? Tea?"

"Food?" Timm asked hopefully. "I haven't eaten since yesterday morning."

While Idris rummaged in her kitchen, her dhalcat emerged from another room. The dhalcat sat down beside Idris' favorite chair, wrapping her tail around her forepaws, just like any house cat.

Idris came back with a plate of rich thick cookies. Timm wolfed two of the cookies down. "I studied the model all night. He was right. Besides him, I'm the only one who could make much sense of it. And it is awesome. It predicts the halo gate at Dhal, in a way inherent from the model's properties, not because it was entered as an initial variable. There's a halo gate here too, all right, in the hills, with a sixty-two percent probability. When I adjusted the model to set that probability at one hundred, and narrowed the location to the exact coordinates of where the wargamers found Val, values all over the model solidified. Including"—he held up a finger, as if to signal an important announcement—"the gate at Toliman's Hearth on your world,

Idris, and another gate at the nearest other star, on the planet called Hades orbiting the red dwarf star named Algol. Then I did some research and learned that there was a science station on Hades years ago, but it met the same fate as the station on Dhal. Overrun by alien marauders, destroyed, never reoccupied."

He devoured two more cookies while Nia and Idris shared a look of apprehension. Increasing certainty was not good news when it concerned danger too close to home.

Timm went on, "Then this morning I took a quick trip to the free trade ring, too, to talk to my godfather, Emir. He's a wilder Sleighter than I am and better connected to our people. I described Val's condition. Emir told me it sounds like he's hell-shocked. You see, there's a fight going on, a kind of forever war, Sleighters against the same aliens that overran the stations on Dhal and Hades." He watched Nia's face for how she reacted to that statement.

She remembered Lana's rumors that that Val died a hero's death battling alien demons in an unknown country, inside a stargate. "Through my Wendisan connections, I heard something about that."

Encouraged, Timm said, "The Dhal demons haunt the fringes of the Faxon Union, which happens to be where most of the Sleighters are trying to eke out an existence. They attack us. We attack them back. We call it the Unspeakable War. People sometimes come out of it like Val—afraid of things they'd never feared before, refusing to describe what happened, even with medically induced amnesia for intolerable memories. That's what hell-shocked means."

Hell-shocked had a genuinely ominous ring to it. Nia asked him, "You're saying Val took part in the Unspeakable War?"

He swallowed the last half of the last cookie with a sigh of contentment. "For the record, I'm *not* saying that, because it's a secret. If the government of the Faxen Union knew about the

Unspeakable War, not only would they not protect us all from it, they'd take everything to the weapons lab to make better and more terrifying weapons."

Nia shivered, knowing how true that was.

Idris said, "Val certainly did become a Sleighter. I've been in contact with the son of our colleague Meredet, and Meredet herself. They assure me that Val became both a Sleighter and a demon hunter, operating in secret for the reasons you say, Timm."

Timm said, "The way his face was painted when the wargamers found him—I and my cousin Kam both recognized the pattern. Fighters in the Unspeakable War have their faces painted like that for courage. Then this morning I took a long shot and asked Emir if our side of the Unspeakable War is missing a fighter, any recent casualty. And he said, '"Yes! We're missing our mage!"'"

Timm's intense tone made the dhalcat raise its tufted ears and stare at him.

Nia felt a tension headache start spooling up. "Mage?"

Timm spread his hands. "Sleighters prize magic. Magic tricks, magic lore, sleight of hand, secret passwords. Unlike most of us, I never liked all of that more than anything else. Well, I don't have talent for it either. A mage is someone who can do the hardest magic and the most spectacular tricks."

Nia remembered how Edvard, approximately a week and a hundred stars ago, had referred to *Vienradzis al Savre or, when not wanting to look like Albioni nobility, calling himself Val Savre.* It sounded as though being Albion nobility was the least of what Val had managed to downplay to date. "My uncle is a man with three lives. Scientist, Sleighter, and mage. Or more lives than that. He was supposed to have died twice, so he's on his third literal life. But three times three is nine. He may be on his ninth life and may not have any more. I've got to figure out how to save him. Sorry, I'm rambling," Nia admitted. "Watching the cat made me think of nine lives."

She had never felt this perplexed. She remembered the challenge of sorting out the legal issues underlying the Faxen Union's attack on Wendis. As monumental as that challenge was, she'd had plenty of well-honed tools to use. She also remembered the time on Moira when she only had one legal tool to use and had to work up her courage to use it. But she couldn't even imagine how to grapple with Uncle Val's predicament. "If *mage* means he knows how to use stargates, and if the Faxen Union's secret intelligence agency finds out, they'll scheme to disappear him into detention so dark no one will ever know what happened to him. We've got to find out more before the intelligence agency does. We may not have much time."

Nodding agreement, Idris said, "I have arranged for Val's life partner to return here. She is a biological scientist, and five years ago she had a research appointment under my supervision. That appointment was never completed. Nor was it canceled. She may be able to tell us what we need to know in shortest order."

Lane coming here sounded like a good idea. Nia asked, "How long was Val her lover before they disappeared together?"

Timm shook his head. "They never knew each other while he was still here."

Idris said, "He met her in the station on Telmoon only a few days before he disappeared. Meredet's son told her that the two of them were equally obsessed with the gate, and when an opportunity became apparent, they combined their intellects and courage to get through the halo gate alive and explore what was behind it. Love came later."

That sounded just like Val. There could be reasons for a very different story having been disseminated—and keeping enemies away from his trail was one of them. But Nia saw where this new information was going. "Oh, no. That means he won't remember her."

14

DELILAH OF DIS

In her little bedroom, the gravity was normal. The open window let in fresh mild air. Nia felt so comfortable that she was sound asleep, until the small vizcall unit trilled. The caller was Val. "Sorry to bother you so late, but I've had a bit of trouble. Can you come to the clinic at the university hospital?"

She was already throwing off the covers and reaching for her day clothes. Earlier today, he'd told her that he was going to the university library. He had a favorite nook there, a spot that had not changed at all in five years. She could imagine why he liked his nook. But not how his evening could have taken him from there to the university hospital.

She found him in the care of a doctor who looked like Timm, for the understandable reason that he was Timm's cousin, who was named Kameron Far. As much as they looked like each other, Kam seemed to have a less sunny temperament than Timm. He scowled at Val and waved a tablet with fresh images. "You're tougher inside than you have any right to be. Taking a punch to the middle tonight should have damaged your recovered tissues. It didn't, but you're lucky you didn't get any more hits!"

Nia glanced at Val's bare chest. There was the star-shaped scar. She'd never seen anything like it.

Val shrugged into his shirt.

Nia asked, "What happened?"

The doctor snapped, "Your uncle got into a fight at a tavern on the edge of campus."

"Calmed the fight, actually," Val said diffidently.

"Explain," said Nia, curt because this sounded like a complication she didn't need. As Val unfolded his story, she saw just how complicating it might be.

Many of Val's former students were quite fond of him. Unlike everything more recent, he remembered them, and took a keen interest in how their lives had gone. Some had graduated and found jobs and marriages in the city. A few had stayed at the university as researchers. So this evening, he'd gone with a group of them to a favorite tavern on the edge of the campus. It wasn't actually leaving the campus, but very nearly doing so, without asking his lawyer how advisable that might be.

Halfway through the one and only beer he intended to enjoy, he became aware of a disturbance on the other side of the tavern. "What's that?"

Donalt, the wargame archer, listened and frowned. "An argument? No, somebody's getting beaten up! And it's a university student. They called him—a slur!"

Val pushed his chair back. "Come on, Donalt. Cindi and Jerad, you too. You wargamers know what to do in a fight."

They only hesitated for a moment. They didn't have weapons, but they had each other and a leader in the unexpected form of Val. He waded into the ugly scene, where a brawny youngish man had already punched a slender university student, whose face was bleeding. Cheered on by several loutish friends, the bully had his fist pulled back for another blow.

Val quickly stepped in front of the victim. He got a punch to the middle for his trouble.

A faculty member doubling over in pain gave the bully pause. The wargamers pushed his friends away, easily ducking a couple of drunken blows. Then the campus police arrived. Val's young friends spirited him out the tavern's back door. That maneuver was well known to them, because they were regulars here, fights did sometimes break out, and in that case it was wise to depart unobtrusively.

Nia irritably reflected that Val might be more difficult as a living client than as a dead one. "Did you tell anyone at the scene your name?"

"No."

"Good. If questions are raised, we'll spin it as mistaken identity, because you look like half the middle-aged male faculty and researchers at this university."

The ill-tempered doctor looked mildly entertained. "For a nice night out, you should have gone to the other side of the street, the dancing venue there. You'd have been in a more sophisticated and less intoxicated crowd with better music."

"I don't dance," Val said primly.

"Dancing venue?" Nia acutely needed a break from the tension of the past days. "A good one? I'd like to go there myself."

"That's right, you always were a wonderful dancer," Val encouraged.

Nia asked the doctor, "Can you set me up with someone respectable who dances?"

Crossing his arms, he said, "Sure. Me. I'll be off tomorrow night."

She had a satisfactory temporary office. So she was literally comfortable. Figuratively, she spent the day beating her head against the wall. She saw no way to protect Val's intellectual property, particularly not the part of it that might be in his head behind a locked door. His Azurean citizenship was an asset. His status wasn't clouded by citizenship in a world in the Faxen Union, which in recent months had shown tendencies to redefine citizenship to suit the state's interests rather than the citizens'. Azurean citizenship wasn't enough to protect him though.

Worse yet for him personally, there was no way to keep him safe if he ever left the university. The vague charges for which he'd been detained a few days ago could get him detained again.

When evening came, she was glad to meet the doctor on the doorstep of Gerry's house. He had his habitual frown, until he looked at her. "You look different."

"I'm not going dancing while looking like an interstellar lawyer," she pointed out. Gerry's wife and daughter, who had been instrumental in finding her the right clothes and makeup, smiled and giggled behind her.

"You look younger and artsier." As they walked across the campus, he asked, "Can you act differently too?"

"You'll see," she told him impishly. "By the way, I'm a native Wendisan visiting a friend who teaches at the university. My name is Delilah of Dis, with Dis being a nickname for Wendis, and the silver color of my hair is artificial, like one of trendy young women who call Wendis, Dis."

"Right." He sounded bemused, but the frown lines on his face had softened, hopefully for the duration of the evening. He seemed like a nice man, when not habitually frowning.

His description of the venue had been accurate. What he hadn't mentioned was that he, himself, was an excellent dancer —good enough to comprehend just how good she was. With that, he proceeded to enjoy himself. Kam wasn't the impossibly coordinated dancer Martan was, but on the other hand, in regular planetary gravity, she didn't need a partner like Martan to keep from tripping over her feet or his. She found it exhilarating.

At one point, Kam asked rather shyly, "Are you single, or—?"

"Happily married, but he wouldn't be jealous of this."

Kam decided to say, "Thank you for going out with me, thank him too. I don't have too many chances to relax, and some girls won't—I'm a Sleighter even if I try not to look like it."

"From what I've seen, Sleighters are an asset to the human race," she answered, and meant it.

But soon there were disturbing signs of town-gown conflict here too. "Who's who?" she whispered to Kam.

He muttered back, "You can tell the university people, assorted races and clothes, intelligent faces. The people with working-class clothes are town people. They don't usually come here. If they do, they don't cause trouble, usually."

She watched the town people closely. Their clothing looked vaguely working-class, but too cheap and flimsy to withstand any actual work. "Whether they're who they're pretending to be is another question."

She was angry to have her evening polluted like this. When one of the louts accosted her, she channeled her anger into a one-handed blow, driving the heel of her hand into his solar plexus. It made him collapse like a rag doll. She glared at him for an instant, then grabbed Kam's arm. "Val's friends had the right idea last night. Let's get out of here but not through the front door."

Pushing past surprised bystanders into a service hallway, they found an open window and departed the building that way.

Nia dusted off her borrowed dress.

"How did you do that?" Kam asked.

"My husband taught me self-defense." Never before had she struck anyone in angry self-defense. But Martan had been a very good teacher.

Kam was apologetic. "Trouble like that never happens in there. I am so sorry."

"Don't be. Between last night at the tavern and now this, I don't think it was random. Somebody is turning up the heat."

Was it just because of the political climate across the Faxen Union getting tense? Was it because vested interests wanted the university to be a more permeable bubble? The working-class-looking troublemakers were the age and probably the temperament to be new recruits to the Telal Consortium, which had a sprawling base inland of here. In many places, Telal was an employer of last resort, meaning its recruits were the dregs of their generation. In some places, Telal sent new recruits out to do its dirty work.

Did the trouble have everything to do with Val, or nothing at all? God only knew. But from now on Val would have to stay well away from the edges of the campus.

Val had waited up for her. He asked how it went, and she gave him an upbeat account. She didn't mention the trouble. Important as it was, it could wait, because she didn't want anything distracting on his mind tomorrow.

Tomorrow his wild wife, Lane, would be here.

The dancing had cleared her head. The unpleasantness at the end of it might have even helped. Now she felt cooly certain that the arena of her real fight was not interstellar law. It was interstellar politics. Interstellar law was her familiar, well-stocked and well-used toolbox. But she was going to have to reach outside the box. And she should take better advantage of her connection to Wendis than just pretending to be a Wendisan tourist.

Wendis, the spinning star city, was the ancient hinge of interstellar affairs. Wendisan institutions had been amassing knowledge and collecting secrets for centuries. Agents of Wendis were still everywhere doing exactly that. So the prime secret databases of Wendis included vast amounts of information.

Not that she had access to the prime secret databases, or would have been able to do much with them if she had, because of the sheer volume of data. But Friday, the sentient AI, did have such access. She collected all that she knew about Val's predicament and everything connected to it, saved it all in a data seed, and sent the seed to Wendis in a highly secured bubble addressed to Friday. As with a top-level academic visa, so with a top-level academic priority for a message bubble. Not only would the bubble go as fast as a starship, but it had immunity from inspection thanks to interstellar legal agreements. The history of humankind had shown the importance of shielding knowledge from the machinations of politics, and that kind of shielding was foundational to civilization. The Faxen Union had never contravened that. Not yet.

15

THE WILD WIFE

Lane was a Verian, with subtle genetic changes wrought by the mysterious vector that had touched the human race at the abortive colony on the world called Meridian. She was also a beautiful woman. She had the kind of tempered beauty that came from the combination of attractive features and a history of painful life experience.

Today might be as painful as anything in her life.

Sitting with Lane in the small but adequate temporary office, Nia explained what she could expect.

Lane repeated, "He doesn't remember the last five years. I understand."

Nia said gently, "No, you don't understand. It's just a concept until you see it. Seeing him, and him not recognizing you, may hurt like hell." Nia hoped that seeing Lane might open the door to Val's memory. But she wasn't going to talk about that openly, much less raise Lane's hopes in vain.

Lane buried her face in her hands. Then she raised her head and said resolutely, "He's alive. That's what's most important for me, and for our son."

"Where is your son?"

"He's with friends on Stannto. I didn't dare bring him. Dikk is an obvious Verian. I was afraid of trouble."

That was a wise choice, and one that left her bereft of her beloved child. Nia told her, "Work with me on that. My main legal authority and experience is Wendisan law, which has an area called Shades of Human. That means legal protections, including rights to interstellar travel without interference, for people who aren't baseline human. Meanwhile, do you have the right kind of support here—housing, research equipment, database access?"

Lane had lifted her head with hope flaring at the prospect of being reunited with her son. She answered Nia's question offhandedly. "Good enough."

Nia checked the time. They still had time to spare. "Can you explain the research you'll do here, in terms a nonscientist like me will understand?"

"Easy. You won't believe me though."

"Try me."

"My previous work here was on viral vectors of genetic change. I need to continue that, but with a different focus. You see, there is an alien life form that's so relentlessly destructive that they're called demons. That means—"

"I know about Dhal demons."

Lane looked relieved. "In a series of dreams, I saw how the Dhal demons were created thousands of years ago by the civilization that existed then on Meridian. They were genetically uplifted from an intelligent but primitive species on the rogue planet we call Dhal. It was a bad idea. But the final dream told me how it was done, in genetic detail." She watched Nia closely, probably expecting skepticism if not scorn.

Nia was connecting the dots of everything she knew about all of this. "Is that more of what you called ESP, in your message to me?" It sounded more powerful than any kind of extrasensory perception that Nia had ever heard about.

"Yes, but ESP isn't what it really was. I dreamed while I was asleep in the Vere system that's inside the halo gates. The system is an extensive network of passageways and doorways built by the same Meridian technology that built the ruined city called Vere on Meridian," Lane said helpfully.

A network connecting gates across stars? Suddenly Nia felt like she was standing at the edge of an unexpected precipice, higher than the crest of Arrival Arc at home, seeing a vast landscape of cosmic mystery. The edge of the precipice was the end of everything certain, and it was unstable, crumbling. Nia managed to ask, "The dream gave you genetic detail?"

Lane nodded. "Here, I can use the computational power that I need to create a viral vector to undo the uplift. If my virus infects their companion species, something called dhalrats, it can jump to the Dhal demons and neutralize them. In other words, to destroy the demons without war."

With a crumbling edge of knowledge right in front of them all, Lane meant to stabilize the part of it she could for the sake of everyone and everything. That this woman had thrown her intellect and courage in with Val's to challenge the mystery of the halo gates now made perfect sense to Nia. It was no wonder that later, love came. They were kindred spirits.

Lane said, "The last dream I had was the one that made me send you a message. In the dream, I saw Val alive. He told me he would be somewhere safe, but that he might be changed." She shakily stood up. "I'm ready."

Nia believed her.

It was as casual as it could be arranged to appear. Nia and Lane walked a university pathway, winding down toward the small stream in the center of the campus. Gerry and Val came the other way. They passed Nia and Lane with no sign of recognition on Val's part. Nia saw how a quiver ran through Lane. But she didn't fall apart. She just stopped short and looked back at her oblivious lover.

Val abruptly turned and walked back to them. He asked Lane, "Do I know you?"

She looked at him mutely. In that position, Nia would have been at a loss for words too. She put an arm around Lane's shoulders.

Then Val said "I don't remember you. But I know you. My body knows you."

That got to her. She folded into Nia's arms and started crying, hands over her face.

Val looked from Lane to Nia, then to Gerry. "Was this a setup?"

Gerry nodded. Nia guided Lane to the nearest shady bench and helped her sit down.

Val knelt in front of his wild wife. He took her hand and kissed it.

She ran her other hand through his hair.

Nia quietly told Gerry, "Don't intrude, but stay around, in case something goes wrong."

Gerry murmured back, "She really loves him. *She* may be what changed him."

Gerry later reported that Lane and Val had talked for a little while, until Val was overcome with fatigue, and Gerry walked him to his room at Gerry's house. They weren't going to let Val and Lane be alone without a chaperone for a while. But their first encounter could have gone much, much worse.

When the sun was setting over the ocean in the west, Lane

met Gerry and Nia on the inland edge of the campus. They intended to visit the fissure in the cliffs. "Are you okay?" Nia asked Lane.

"It was hard. But I'm okay."

Lane was a brave and resilient woman who loved Val dearly. Nia hoped—and prayed—that the locked room in Val's mind would open, at the right time, whenever that was, and that he would remember all the days and hours he'd known Lane and their son. With luck, they could share their life and their love for decades to come. Val was much older than Lane, but he was aging more slowly. The difference in their ages was at least twenty years, but it already looked more like ten.

Val wasn't going with them on this expedition. He couldn't have handled the exertion of the climb. And he had to stay not just technically inside the university, but well inside the university, on Nia's orders. The hills and cliffs were only tenuously university grounds.

Nia asked Lane, "How does he seem to you?"

"He's like he was when I first met him. Except since I've known him, he's gotten less rigid and harsh, more playful and forgiving, and that's what he's like now around the edges. He's still as mannerly as ever though. Today he apologized for getting tired and needing to rest."

Gerry said, "He needs rest and recuperation, so he's been taking a long nap every day."

Nia said, "Then he stays up late in his favorite nook in the library, reading and thinking."

Lane actually smiled. "That sounds like him."

Nia had borrowed hiking shoes from Gerry's generous wife, and it was a good thing she had. The terrain was increasingly uneven as they climbed a high rough hill. Nia wanted to see the fissure with Lane there, because Lane might know something about halo gates that no one else did, except Val—who *didn't* know, until further notice.

Gerry was more than willing to show them the way. It all had to do with rocks, and his professional interest was intense.

It was a hard climb, especially in higher gravity than Azure. When they got to a flatter part of the terrain and Nia had caught her breath, she said, "Lane, if I may ask, what made you every bit as determined to investigate the halo gates as my uncle was?"

"More like fixated." Lane said. "I had—it comes with being Verian—I had an irresistible compulsion to find more halo gates. We discovered that together, we could open the gate at the Telmoon station. Each by ourselves, we would have died. Together we made it through the gate and found a whole network of passages and gates. That was how we got to Stannto, because there's a gate there too. Oh! I just remembered, Jack says hello," she told Gerry. "He and his wife are good friends of ours on Stannto, so I've heard about you, and I know to trust you."

That confirmed Nia's guess that Val had contacted Jack and that Jack was one who knew how to keep a secret. It might come more naturally to Almaazans than to most people.

They crossed a small, grassy meadow, a pleasant place. Nia glanced back at the university. She reflected how humankind had ventured out into the stars, and on other worlds and in Wendis, duplicated ways of living that now dated back thousands of years—everything from the horse nomads on Goya, to the dusty agricultural villages on Estrella, to the farms on Agraria that fed the population of Faxe's star system. And human cities existed on various worlds and inside Wendis. There were also the ancient societal structures that went with cities, like having apartment buildings and working in offices. And universities like the one Nia saw below her in late afternoon sunlight.

But across the stars, other intelligent races had existed long before humanity. They'd had their own planets and other places. All or most of them had died out, leaving the ruins that were so interesting to Lana and her xenarchaeologist colleagues. The halo gates might be the most mysterious and dangerous of any such ruins. The idea of a halo gate here, just outside the perimeter of a university, even one with a strong program of studies about halo gates because of the halo gate on the world's moon, made Nia feel the crumbling edge of certainty right under her feet.

Not far past the nice little meadow, they found the fissure. The wide rough trail they were following passed near it. Nia imagined the wargamers excitedly running back and forth a few weeks ago, and the two who'd hidden inside the fissure hoping to get an advantage over the other side. Instead they'd gotten a stunning surprise.

The fissure was twice as tall as a person, wide enough that the three of them could have touched outstretched hands and barely spanned it. There was a high pile of rubble inside. Behind that, the fissure ended in a flat rock face. Gerry said, "I've been in here before—even camped in here." With a flashlight, he peered closely at the rock face. "Nothing looks unusual or I'd have investigated it before now."

Lane said, "When the gates are closed, turned off, they look like the surrounding rock. It's an illusion."

Gerry looked at her sharply. "Illusory basalt?" His hand went toward the geologist's pick on his belt.

"I'd rather you didn't use that here!" Nia said quickly. "Lane, can you tell if this really is a halo gate?"

Lane put her hands on the rock face, and her forehead against it. She stayed motionless for a while. Nia remembered what she'd about her dreams, but she was wide awake now. She stood back from the rock. "Yes. I can feel it. It's turned off."

Gerry paraphrased incredulously, "This rock, looking just like a thousand rock faces within a hundred kilometers of here, out of all of them, this is rock can that turn into a stargate."

"You better believe it," Lane said firmly.

They backed away from the gate. Gerry paused at the pile of rubble. "This, I don't remember." He shone his flashlight at the walls and ceiling of the fissure and then looked closely at the rubble. "There's some fresh cleavage that doesn't match the planes I'd expect. This isn't seismic country. There's never been any blasting up here. This rockfall shouldn't have happened." He selected several small rocks to take home and study.

They started back down the mountain to get back before full dark. "Do you know how Val got hurt?" Nia asked Lane. "Was it in something called the Unspeakable War?"

Lane nodded. "Not just hurt. He died."

That could certainly account for missing memory. But not for memory behind a locked door that she'd seen open once. Much less did it explain why he didn't stay dead. "I'm very happy about it, but why is he alive?"

"You won't believe me."

"At the rate things are going, we probably will," Gerry pointed out.

"Okay. The halo gates are all one system, not just a scattered collection of artifacts. The system was created by scientists in the ancient civilization on Meridian. It was their way of crossing the stars."

"Stargates by stepping through doorways." Nia remembered what Lana Tai had said. "It sounds like something that no credible scientists on Earth would have ever pursued. They developed rockets instead."

"Meridian is a super-earth. The gravity well is very deep and hard to get out of. So they invented stargates. I don't know how long their star age lasted. It may have been a very long time." Lane sighed. "The Meridianers are long gone. Their world had a close encounter with the rogue planet Dhal, and it destabilized the ecosystem of the planet. They tried to recruit the apex species on Dhal to help them, by uplifting its intelligence, hoping the species could help them construct engines to move

Dhal away from the path it was on. But the uplift turned out badly. The species gained intelligence, but not conscience. It became the demons, and the Dhal demons turned on their makers and destroyed them. The halo gate network fell into disrepair. From the beginning it comprised one, distributed, and sentient artificial intelligence. That still exists. It can manifest itself, maybe like how our simulacra work. In that case it takes the dark shape of a man, full of stars; Val saw it in dreams."

Nia's neck hairs stood up. This conversation had just vectored toward an artificially created intelligence—an alien sentience of utterly unknown intentions. A door in her mind swung open, briefly, to give her a glimpse of something frightening. "Artificial intelligence can go very wrong, and if it's immensely powerful, it can meddle like nothing else. Does the star man have good intentions?"

"Oh, yes. The Meridianers knew how to make artificial intelligence benign," Lane answered. She sounded unworried.

"Val is alive because?" Gerry prompted.

"The gate system was in disrepair and infested with dhalrats and demons. Val has been repairing it. Meanwhile some of our friends have been fighting the rats and demons, and Val joined them. In the last battle he took a spear through his chest—" Lane broke off. It had to be upsetting for her to think about. "A young woman fighter picked him up to take back to me. He was far gone, dying, but she didn't want the demons to feed his body to their pet rats. But the star man appeared, and asked for Val, and she gave him to him. I'm sure the star man healed him."

Nia definitely sensed herself on the crumbling ledge of a cosmic overlook like never before.

Gerry hazarded, "Val repairs the system, its intelligence repairs Val?"

"Something like that," Lane said. "Finally he brought Val here through the gate, to friends and a safe place. In the dream, Val told me that would happen. He didn't know exactly what safe place it would be, but it was true. He's here, and all of you are protecting him."

She sounded tranquil. She might be a naturally good-natured, unruffled person, more like Gerry than Val—or Nia. Nia's nerves were still ringing like a fire alarm. She didn't understand why the idea of an old and viable artificial intelligence, with a simulacrum looking like a star man, disturbed her more than anything else, when there was so much else to be at least as disturbed about. But it did.

At least she now had an explanation for the neatly locked room in Val's mind: It had been constructed by an alien agent with an unknowably high degree of intelligence, capability, and sentience.

Which might mean that no human agency could open it.

16

THE FLAME OF ALMAAZ

An academic priority bubble skipped across the stars to bring her Friday's analysis of the data she'd sent. She put the data seed in her bracelet, connected it to a display in her temporary office, and skimmed it eagerly.

Then she was interrupted by late-night vizcall, again. It was Val, again. He said, "I'm afraid I had another bit of trouble."

She briefly gritted her teeth. "Where are you?" *Please let him not be in detention again!*

"Oh, in the library. Yes."

"Alone?"

He paused before answering, "Yes. Effectively alone. It's very quiet."

"I'm on my way." He was definitely more trouble alive than dead, she thought in utter exasperation. If he had stayed dead, she wouldn't be trying to figure out how to cut through a Gordian knot of legal and political complexity in order to keep him alive.

This late, the library was almost deserted. She'd been issued a temporary ID, one with a high enough level of permissions to get her into the building through the autoscanning door. She found the arched entryway to the Sciences wing of the library only to meet Kam the doctor arriving there at the same time. This struck Nia as a bad sign. She asked him, "What's happened?"

"I don't know. Where is he in here?"

"This way."

Seated at his usual big table, with his back to a corner of the building's wall, Val looked fine. He wasn't in his usual chair at the table, but he sat up very straight with his tablet neatly positioned in front of him. He was pale, but he probably hadn't been getting enough sun not to be.

While Kam glowered, Nia crossed her arms and prompted, "We're here because?"

"I was in my accustomed chair." Unnecessarily, he pointed at it. "A fellow I've seen in here a time or two before walked toward me. A visiting researcher, I believe."

Nia tensed up. "Did he ask a compromising question? Threaten you?"

Val said, "Moving unbelievably fast, he grabbed me by the throat and slammed me against the wall. And then I felt a compulsion to tell him everything about the halo gates."

Nia felt so shocked that it was like the floor dropping out from under her. This was inexpressibly bad. She made her voice even. "Did you?"

"Before I could form any words, I remembered the lights of the halo gates. The lights are a mind field, you know. Get too close, and your mind will be wrecked, followed by death, because the brain will no longer be able to regulate the bodily functions." He swallowed hard. His throat probably hurt. "It was a more vivid memory than typical for me."

Kam listened with narrowed eyes, probably understanding little of this but registering that Nia was very alarmed.

She asked, "What happened to you then?"

"Nothing as far as I can tell. But something happened to him." Val pointed under the table.

Beneath the wide table, a man lay curled up on the floor in a fetal position. His face was a frozen spasm of pain or fear.

Kam dove down to check his vital signs.

Nia heard herself say, "This was a hellhound attack. The secret intelligence agency of the Faxen Union has agents that can telepathically attack someone and compel them to answer questions and confess guilt or conspiracy. They're almost invincible. I can't imagine why it didn't work."

Val said, "He looks exactly like a man who tried to get through a halo gate and failed."

A hellhound would have tried to telepathically force his way into the locked room in Val's mind. Maybe it was—protected. After what she'd heard from Lane about the star man, Nia could guess who designed it that way. It was almost unbelievable. But so was everything else.

Kam punched his identity cuff, calling for medical backup. He told them to bring a body bag.

Nia told Val, "A medical body bag will contain him. It will also keep him alive—if you call how he is right now alive."

"Not very," Kam said grimly.

Adrenaline galvanized her nervous system. Her thoughts raced. Thanks to the unsuspected minefield—*mind field*—in Val's mind, Val was okay. But the coefficient of danger for him and everyone else had just gone up a hundredfold.

They quickly invented a story that Val had stepped away to look something up and returned to his favorite spot to discover an unconscious man. Kam said it looked enough like a brain aneurism—sudden and disastrous rupture of the arteries in the brain—to announce that as his diagnosis, tipping the scales away from medical fact-finding that might reach another conclusion.

The medics arrived. They lost no time folding Val's attacker into a body bag, which would sustain his vital functions, if his brain couldn't manage that.

Meanwhile in the back of Nia's mind, the information she'd gotten from Friday was trying to tell her something. She finally gotten back to it in the middle of the night. Now she knew that she couldn't be a defensive strategist in this any longer. She had to make a countermove, and it had to be very effective and very soon.

Friday had suggested just such a move.

It had to do with citizenship. Most civilized places weren't like Wendis, so self-contained that population growth wasn't allowed and citizenship was hereditary. Azure, which could always use more inhabitants, had much more relaxed criteria for citizenship. Val had petitioned for that. Val being Val, he had correctly filled out every clause of the petition. Given his family ties and his professional distinction, it had been granted automatically.

Azure was independent. Val's native world, Albion, wasn't under the Union's bootheel either—the world in that unhappy position was Moira—but under its prying thumb. That was not a safe place for Val's intellectual property to have remained, and he'd known it.

The colonized world called Almaaz had very different ideas about citizenship. The Almaazans kept their criteria for citizenship secret. But not so secret that Wendis hadn't found out about it.

They soon discovered who the researcher the hellhound had been impersonating was. Or rather who he *wasn't*. He had believable identification as an academic visitor from Faxe, under the auspices of the university's political science department. But that department could not account for him. They had on file his request to do research here, along with his academic credentials, all looking in order. But the department official whose name was on file as approving the request knew nothing about it. The approval had been faked well enough that all of the automated visitor processes accepted it.

In other words, the university's bubble of protection from Faxen Union politics was permeable. A sophisticated attempt to pierce the bubble could succeed and had. This would justify a long, involved investigation which might go somewhere. Or with enough Faxen roadblocking, it would go nowhere. Nia didn't have time for that. She had to find a swift, effective, and above all, unexpected tactic. And Friday had described one.

Idris was an early riser, usually in her office by dawn. Nia went to her cottage even earlier. Cool night fog still lay thick in University Village, with cold water condensing on the bark of the trees and trickling down. Idris was wide awake and surprised to find Nia on her doorstep.

Nia was blunt, because she was too tired to be anything else. "I need a word with you, at your hearth."

Idris gave Nia a searching look. She probably observed that Nia had the same clothing as yesterday, except more rumpled, and a tense face. "Come in."

Idris seated herself in her favorite chair with a grateful sigh. The chair was sized for her, with support for her back. The gravity here had to be always hard on her. She waved Nia into another chair. The dhalcat, napping near the hearth box, woke up and stared at Nia.

She asked, "I need to know if Val was right about the gate on Toliman's Hearth. If you somehow have proof of it now."

Idris' gaze seemed to sharpen even more. "Not long ago, at my behest, a team of military rangers went to Toliman's Hearth to see if anything was amiss there. They had firearms and four dhalcats. They found a nest of Dhal demons, and there was a fight, but they killed the demons, although a soldier and a dhalcat perished. The rest made it home to testify to what they'd run into. It seemed the demons were preparing an invasion. They had boats. They could have fallen on the nearest unsuspecting town and done murder and plunder before running back into their gate. Oh yes, there was a halo gate. It seemed to be frozen open. It doesn't make the famous lights, but it goes—somewhere. There are armed guards in front of it now."

"Then Val's information saved the town."

"That and more." Idris sounded certain. "He may have saved my world."

That confirmed the slender strand of hope that had brought her here. With a deep breath, Nia said, "Your Excellency, in return for the service he did in a lifesaving warning for Almaaz, by the flame of your hearth, I ask you to bestow Almaazan citizenship on him."

"I cannot do that on my own authority," Idris said.

Nia's heart sank.

Idris said softly, "How you have come to know of our criteria for citizenship I do not know. Then again, it seems you are the individual who caused a landslide in that religion called Old Catholic Orthodox, and it started with what you did on Moira—an amazingly foolish, brave, and consequential act."

So Idris had followed up on references to Moira that she'd heard in Nia's presence. Well, it wasn't surprising for a scholar to do research and do it quickly and accurately.

Nia was almost shaking with fatigue. She might be feeling the effects of the unaccustomed gravity over the time she'd been here, too, plus a long hard night. "If you requested citizenship for him on Almaaz, would Val have to remember what he did?"

"I think not. My part would be to send the request to

Almaaz. But for me to do that, *you* will have to swear to the truth of what you have to say. Will you?"

"Yes."

"Kneel in front of the hearth."

Nia did.

With an effort, Idris stood up. She tipped the top of the box back. An artificial ember glowed inside the box. Exposed to more air, it generated a globular golden flame.

Idris said, "You say that Val Savre merits the bestowal of Almaazan herebelonging, what you call citizenship. In truth, why do you wish it for him?"

"It will give him ironclad diplomatic immunity. There are machinations going on to get his intellectual property, if he's dead. Alive, the Faxen Union's intelligence agency can gin something up to justify arresting him, or kidnapping him, and he'd go into dark detention. They don't dare do that to an Almaazan. Your world has been very strategic in making protective legal arrangements, on the level of fundamental interstellar law. To violate law like that would be a startling declaration of lawlessness on the part of the Faxen Union. The Union is willing to be lawless. The war on Wendis proved that. But they will still be reluctant to violate the diplomatic safeguards of Almaaz."

"Is using that diplomatic immunity to protect Val and his knowledge what you intend to do—nothing for your own personal gain or good fortune? Say 'in truth,' if you really mean it."

If this legal gambit succeeded, it wouldn't lead directly to gain or good fortune for Nia. Win or lose, it might earn her new notoriety. She knew how dangerous that was. She was too tired to parse it through any more thoroughly than that. She was too certain that it represented the only thin hope she had left not to try it. "I intend to do that in truth."

The flame blazed higher and brighter.

"Then I will do as you request. An attestation of citizenship, if it comes in answer, will come from Almaaz."

"It needs to go to Azure. I intend to be back there soon, to finish the legal work there." *Pastfinder* was still at the free trade ring, Lana Tai and her crew having doubtless found profitable ways to spend their time there.

"I see why you find it necessary, but I am uneasy that you will leave Val unprotected. The rest of us can't protect him very well."

"I can't either. Last night, he was set upon by a hellhound. That memory block in his mind turned it away and incapacitated the hellhound, which is in a body bag at the hospital now."

Idris looked shocked. "I've heard rumors of that damnable abomination, the hellhounds of Faxe. Are the authorities sure of it?"

At this point, Nia could not possibly have told a lie or even shaded the truth. She was too exhausted. "Yes, I am sure. I know a lot about hellhounds. Exactly once that anyone knows about, a hellhound of Faxe repented of what he was, defected to Wendis, divulged all he knew about the secrets of the hellhounds, and turned his life and his soul to the better. And I married him."

Again the flame rose and brightened.

17

MIND GATE

Martan hadn't expected what the bubble from Nia told him. She'd phrased it in an oblique, heavily coded way that made the meaning crystal-clear to him. It was also electrifyingly urgent. He left Denevez the same afternoon to take the space elevator up to the transit ring.

He didn't leave Edvard unprotected. The Church had assigned security guards to protect him. Martan had interviewed them and found them to be tactful, loyal and competent.

The journey to Tellas was like his old days of being a wide-ranging assassin. He transferred from a freighter to a starliner to another freighter, slipping through scanners that did not know what to look for about him, hiring onto the freighters for temporary jobs, leaving only ghostly traces of a trail. All the way he thought about the message in Nia's bubble. In his mind he called it *the dire bubble*. He couldn't imagine anything worse than what she described happening to her uncle. Except for how it had ended.

He reached the free trade ring at the Tellas moon a few hours before the next shuttle to the Tellas transit ring. Since Nia had given him enough information to go on, he located *Pastfinder*, pretending to be the ordinary tradeship *Gallant*, in the trade ring's shipdock. There he had a long conversation with Svetlana Tai. He told Tai, "Good thing you were able to wait here. Nia may need to go back to Azure very soon. At least if things go better than there's any reason to expect."

"Good luck," was Tai's response. "You two have everything else—talent, skills, drive, love. What you don't have, which nobody can arrange ahead of time, is luck."

Martan couldn't argue with that.

He asked her what she knew about halo gates. Nia's uncle was the real expert in that but, given his amnesia, Tai was the best available informant. He was curious about why she'd never investigated the Vere ruins and gates.

For one thing, the gates had poorly understood but devastating protective mechanisms, activated when anyone meddled with them. Furthermore, unpleasant alien creatures had long and insistently been rumored to live inside the halo gates. Tai had a strong aversion to encountering aliens in alien ruins, because more than one xenarchaeologist had died that way, sometimes very unpleasantly. That Nia's Uncle Val had actively explored halo gates, and possibly gotten inside one, struck Tai as spectacularly suicidal.

Martan mentioned discovering Val's diary. Tai wondered if the diary said anything about halo gates. If it did, Martan hadn't gotten that far in the diary when he decoded passages for Nia and Radzi. However, he'd leafed through it. And he had a photographic memory. He recalled and reviewed the later pages. The last entry seemed to be from a visit Val had made to Azure not too many years earlier, when he was already a notable halo gate researcher. Val had adopted a more sophisticated substitution code by then. With real effort, Martan decoded the last entry in his mind's eye: *I believe the gates to be a system coterminous with the Faxen Union in realspace. If so, any planet or moon inside the REALSPACE extent of the Faxen Union could have an inactive halo gate. Must investigate further.*

Tai took that in. Then she cursed, long and colorfully, about the universe having an objectionable sense of humor. To that commentary, she added, "For the record, it's a long way from here to Meridian, which is practically on the other side of known starspace. But would you like to guess where Meridian is relative to the Faxen union, in oh-so-impractical, because it takes a spaceship centuries to cross, realspace?"

Martan took the hint. "Dead center."

"Fluttering close to dead center," she said, "As you might well expect of a gate system that seems to have been invented there."

Finally, Tai gave Martan a summons chip. "There are nine ways in hell this business could explode around you and Nia. If you need a hand, an armed rescue team, space artillery—whatever *Pastfinder* can do, if you need it, send the chip. It'll tell me where you sent it from."

He fitted the chip into his identity cuff. "Where do I send it to? Are you going back to Wendis?"

She laughed. "I got an invitation to teach an intensive session at the Azurean star fleet academy's starspace training center, at the nearest red dwarf star to Azure. Evidently, the training I gave Nia's brother and his friends impressed them. That's where I'll go after I take her home." Then she added, "It occurs to me to leave two of my crew in case you need help in a firefight. The two I have in mind will be bored witless at the academy, because they love violent trouble a little too much."

Martan easily found the university hospital. Nia met him at a side door. They held and kissed each other for a few priceless moments. Then she led the way to an isolated morgue where bagged bodies were preserved. For the most part, these were donations to the medical school, research-spirited people who'd given their bodies to medical science after natural death. Only the most recent addition to the collection hadn't donated his body. He hadn't completely died either.

On the way to the morgue, Nia explained the little they knew about the bagged patient—that he had been in the university with a false identity, what her uncle had said about the attack, and how in the end the supposed hellhound's condition superficially resembled catastrophic brain aneurism. Because of his false identity, there were no friends or relatives or even university contacts to update. He'd been added to the hospital patient census, his condition carefully assessed each morning for any changes, but there were none. He was basically being ignored. It was late afternoon here, with hospital shifts changing, the daily tempo sliding toward the slow pace of night. A good time for this mission.

A doctor met them in the morgue. "This is Dr. Kam Far," Nia said. "Kam, this is my husband, Martan. Among other skills, he's a telepathic specialist. He may be able to learn what your patient had in his mind."

Kam Far gave Martan a long, interested look. Then Far opened the body bag to show him the man inside it. "Same coloration as you, skin and hair," Far observed. "Same kind of build too."

"The most common across the human race," Martan said offhandedly. Oh yes, the more recent hellhounds were chosen, or remade, to look like generic human beings, not memorably tall or short, skinny or fat. It made it easier for them to be invisible.

But looking generically human didn't make someone a hellhound. It was Nia's uncle's account of what happened that had made her conclude that the man was a hellhound. The uncle, with an amnesiac hole in his head, couldn't be the most reliable witness. Nia might be mistaken about the bagged attacker. If so, that would be interesting enough. Anybody with a carefully constructed false identity as a researcher had to have been up to something illicit.

If Nia had *not* been mistaken about what he was—that would be even more interesting and an order of magnitude worse.

The body bag had tapped into the patient's skin and organs to sustain him. It had also chilled him to drop his bodily functions down to the most minimum level. With hands that had sensitive neonerves in his fingertips, Martan touched the man's temples.

Immediately, he could tell that the electrical action of the man's brain had been catastrophically disrupted. His memories were shattered. Martan studied the pieces to understand how they might fit together. He found several names the man had gone by. It was too hard to tell which was the earliest and presumably authentic, but the easiest to find matched his latest false identity as a researcher.

Even easier to find were splintered memories of at least a dozen interrogations and or kills he'd made as the hellhound he truly was. Under those more identifiable memories were shards of something deeper and darker. Its name was Varry: the moon of Faxe that harbored the nursery of hellhounds. What this hellhound remembered of Varry seemed much worse than Martan's own memories.

More important right now was why this hellhound had been sent here to interrogate Val Savre. Martan gleaned as much of that as he could.

Enough. Martan pulled away. Nia grasped his arms to steady him. She understood that he could be disoriented, dazed after a telepathic investigation. He told her, "It's what you thought."

After a sharp intake of breath, Nia said, "Kam's on our side.

We can say the truth. You mean this really is a hellhound. Or was."

"Was. Zip it up," Martan told the doctor. "I don't think there's enough coherence left in his brain for him to ever regain consciousness."

Nia said, "Val says that's what halo gates do to people who force their way in."

No wonder Svetlana Tai didn't want to go near a thing like that.

Nia said, "But it wasn't a literal halo gate. It was something in Val's mind. Something that retaliated against telepathic intrusion."

Martan said, "If it came with any kind of warning, he ignored that or maybe misread it." He reviewed what he'd learned. "He may have thought it was some kind of atypical psychological resistance to interrogation. But yes, he was after what your uncle knows about halo gates. After that the idea was to get him extradited on the grounds of disunionism. That's the trump card they always play against somebody hard to get, but valuable." He grimaced. "Being a disunionist."

That wasn't all he'd learned from the hellhound in the body bag. Some of it was important to him personally, and he was still trying to comprehend it.

The doctor, having sealed the body bag, checked the readouts. The bag would quickly compensate for the brief influx of warmer air, and diligently return the patient to the cold stasis it had created for him. The doctor said, "Now what?"

Martan felt steadier, because some time had passed, but most of all because Nia steadied him. "I want to meet your uncle, Nia, and read his mind. Very carefully."

Nia was as focused as an arrow in flight. He loved her for it.

She led Martan and the doctor across the campus to a cluster of houses in a grove of trees. At one of the houses, an Almaazan woman met them at the front door. The woman recognized the doctor and gave him a grave nod. Nia told her, "Idris, this is Martan. He just confirmed that it was what I thought it was."

Idris said, "Go around to the back porch if you would. That's where I have room for more people. It's screened and I don't just mean netting. It's electronically screened. We of Almaaz take our privacy seriously."

They did what she asked. "You told her about me?" Martan asked.

"Yes. At the time I was in her house, and in an Almaazan's house, lying is a bad idea. Even lying by omission."

The planet Almaaz, thinly populated and reclusive, stayed out of politics in the Faxen Union. But Martan remembered that for the secret intelligence agency of the Union, Almaaz was forbidden territory. For some reason, SECINTAG had found it worse than futile to operate there.

The back porch looked like any unassuming back porch might be expected to look, with assorted chairs and crates for people to sit on. But Martan could hear the active security screen. Nobody outside was going to hear or see what went on here, no matter how hard they tried.

Inside the porch, Idris told Martan, "You are better-looking than I expected. Not thick and burly."

"That was the early generations of hellhound," he said.

"What do you want to do here?" Idris asked Nia.

Nia said, "Martan has neonerves in his hands, sensitivity to electric signals in the human brain. One of his hands has Wendisan biotechnology mirroring the Faxen neonerves in the other hand. That was because he defected to Wendis under an explosion and one hand was mangled until it was rebuilt in Wendis. The Wendisan biotech ended up being better. It had the effect of amplifying his sensitivity. He doesn't have to bludgeon to get the truth out of anyone. He may be able to simply see it. So we want to let Martan just take a look into Val's mind."

That was surprisingly more detail than she'd given the doctor. But she was taking the stricture against lying seriously. So would he.

Idris said, "Since this doctor is with you, with a medical kit on his shoulder, I assume you anticipate risk in this."

Nia said, "Nothing is not risky now." She pivoted, telling Kam Far, "That includes you being involved in all this. You might need a faraway place to go just to stay alive and free much longer."

The doctor gave an offhanded shrug. "I don't really like it here, and my medical training would be welcome if I go back to my people."

Nia had told him that Kam was a Sleighter. Martan had known that the Sleighters were a disrespected class on the ragged edges of the Faxen Union. He'd never met any.

Idris gave Kam a slight, wry smile. "Well, Doctor, you'd best keep a small bag packed with necessities with you at all times. Things are happening fast."

Martan couldn't argue with that.

A few minutes later, three more people came running to the door of the porch. Nia had contacted them, asking them to come here as fast as they possibly could. She spoke quickly. "Martan, this is Gerry, an old friend of Val's, and Lane, Val's wife. And my uncle, Val Savre."

Val Savre was a lean middle-aged man with graying hair. He was panting too hard to talk, and holding hands with his wife. His friend Gerry asked, "What's up?"

Nia said bluntly, "This is my husband Martan. Among other things, he is a telepathic specialist with a light touch. He assessed the man who attacked you in the library, Val, and pulled out information that squares with what we knew. It was a hellhound attack that failed. The Faxen Union's secret intelligence agency has you in its sights. If anybody can touch your memory and give it back to you, Martan can. But it will be risky. He hopes not to turn out like the attacker in the body bag."

Val objected, "But if he's your husband, Nia, I don't want him risking that!"

Martan didn't either. Unfortunately, he couldn't assure Val Savre, or himself, that it would go otherwise.

Nia looked at the sky above them. Martan recognized the onset of an idea. She said, "Lane, if it really is like the destructive halo in a halo gate, you might be able to help Martan go through it, because you're Verian."

Lane just nodded. She took both of Val's hands, and Martan stood behind Val, ready to touch his temples. Nia positioned the doctor on one side of them, and she stood on the other side. "If anybody is in distress, we'll separate you," she said grimly.

Martan had never done anything like this. There was a first time for everything, he thought. Of course, the first occasion for something would also be the last occasion, if it turned out fatally. The expression on the bagged hellhound's face had been a disfigured mask of fear that the body bag hadn't been able to smooth out.

Taking a deep breath, Martan lightly touched Val's temples, sought the whispered electrical signals of thought, and found them.

Yes. There was a blank place in Val's memory. To Martan's hellhound training and instinct, it was almost irresistible. *Something hidden here.* He telepathically focused on it. That was when he had a sense of colored light. It might be a kind of synesthesia, inexplicable in terms of anything else he had ever experienced telepathically. It didn't advertise danger and death. But that could be only because it was a code he didn't know. With an effort, he said aloud, "I see it. Like a blank space full of patterned light."

Suddenly the colored light exploded around Martan's awareness, impulses hammered through his reflexes, and he staggered backward.

Nia caught him. "*Martan!*"

Dazed, he mumbled, "M'm all right. It just threw me out."

Lane said, "After a halo gate repels, it ebbs back, and that's when it can open." She stepped in front of Val, took him by the shoulders, and said, "Open! Val needs to remember everything and he's strong enough now. Open like the gate you are!"

Val Savre shook himself. He stared at Lane. Then he said wonderingly. "You. Only you. Oh, I remember you!"

Lane's face lit with joy like a nova.

Val threw himself at her so hard that Kam caught them to keep them both from falling down. Steadied by Kam, they clung to each other, laughing and crying.

18

MEMORY

Val Savre felt like a man awakening from a dream. In dreams, you never seem to have all of who you are or what you know in the usual memory bank. Get woken up from the dream and you remember everything again.

He remembered going through the Tellas moon halo gate with Lane, exploring the tunnels behind the gate, and getting his arm slashed by an attacking dhalrat . . . staggering to the gate on Stannto, finding his old friend Jack there, and being treated for the dhalrat injury by Jack's physician wife Jill . . . joining the Sleighters and becoming one of them . . . repairing the Vere system—everything, all the way to the battle on Hades. Above all, he remembered Lane.

Idris was good enough to let them talk in private beside the firebox she called a hearth. Val and Lane held each other like lovers who'd just found each other after they separately survived a shipwreck.

"What happened after the last battle?" she whispered.

"Vere healed me," he told her.

She nodded against his shoulder. "I dreamed that you came

to me and told me that he'd take you to a safe place, but you might be changed."

"Where is Dikky?" He remembered his son too, easily visualizing the little boy with his dreamy eyes and uncanny skill at art.

"On Stannto with Jack and Jill."

That was a relief. Dikk was in good hands. Val could visualize how Dikk looked up at him with solemn eyes. This was what had made him feel strange the other day when Gerry introduced him to that university child about the age and size of Dikk—at Nia's behest, he suspected. She'd always been a smart one. By this point in her life, her native intelligence was honed to a shining edge. "Well, I can't stay here without endangering friends, and relatives too, Nia and her husband, and most important to me, you. We could go back to Stannto through the gate. I remember how."

But she shook her head sharply. "I want to stay here to create a virus to defeat the Dhal demons. I saw how in the dream. The star man gave me the dream. There was a lot of genetic detail. And it's workable. Here, I can make a virus that will undo the genetic engineering that created the demons. They can be infected with it by using the dhalrats as a vector."

It was a dazzling idea. Here was another brilliant woman. And this one was his wife. Her plan made him proud and sad at the same time. "All right. Just so I remember you even though we're apart. And now I do."

Idris' dhalcat had come out of its lair in the back bedroom. Val appreciatively scratched behind its tufted ears. The dhalrat attack that scarred his arm was something he recalled with great clarity and equally great dislike. The dhalcat, bred to prey on dhalrats, was a friend indeed.

The dhalcat padded along with them when Val and Lane rejoined everyone else on Idris' porch. Nia, Martan, Idris, Gerry, and Kam Far all looked at him with questions in their eyes.

First things first. "I know why your daughter scares me," Val told Gerry. "I got into a battle with the murderous aliens called Dhal demons. They're shape-shifters. The queen of them had taken the form of a young, blonde woman—probably someone she murdered. The queen was inhuman, and she had me run through with a spear. Remembering her makes my blood run cold."

Gerry managed to say, "That would explain it, all right."

"What about red light?" Nia asked.

"The battle was on the planet called Hades, one of the worlds in orbit around the red star Algol, in your star system, Idris. The sunlight was very red." He turned to Lane and urgently asked her, "How did the fight turn out?"

Lane said, "At the end, our last fighters made it to Hades, they came through the gate and turned the tide. Spark was one of them. She found you dying and picked you up to bring home so dhalrats wouldn't eat you. But a star man, a man made of darkness full of stars, stepped in front of her. He asked for you. She put you into his arms. He wasn't exactly solid, she said, but solid enough to carry you."

Val didn't remember seeing a dark man full of stars, just darkness deeper than anything he'd ever seen. In dreams, yes, he'd seen the star man in dreams when he was sleeping inside the Vere system.

But wait. His memory ricocheted back through decades. He *had* seen the star man, once, long ago and far from here. That time the star man hadn't been any more solid than smoke. But for the past five years, Val and his Sleighter friends and Verian helpers had busily repaired the network that was Vere. The artificial intelligence must be in much better shape by now, its simulacrum stronger. Even able to carry a dying man.

Nia looked shaken. Her husband looked at least as much so. *Finish the first things,* Val told himself. To Martan, he said, "Thank you for coming into my mind, at risk to yourself. You helped me get my memory back, and I am profoundly grateful. I hope that didn't injure you."

Martan said slowly, "It threw me out, but no harm done."

"Well, I'm glad of nothing worse coming of this for you than being shaken up."

Martan looked around at his wife, Val's friends, the dhalcat, and the doctor. Evidently, he decided that he could say something pressing on his mind. "I'm more shaken up by what I found in the hellhound's mind, when the doctor opened the body bag for me to touch him. I learned how he was made into a hellhound. It was a lot worse than what I remember when I went through it. Worse and more immoral."

"In what way?" asked Idris.

"They're stripping agency and initiative out of them and leaving almost nothing but ruthless obedience. It's as though they're trying to make hellhounds soulless. Maybe my defection made them want hellhounds that can't defect."

Nia quickly said, "There may have been other defectors. Anybody with a soul can't be a perfect tool."

Looking truly offended, Idris said, "It's bad enough that we have the Dhal demons to deal with. If I understand Lane correctly, they were accidentally created by alien scientists on Meridian—a terrible mistake, but a mistake nonetheless. If I understand what Martan means, though, the Faxen secret intelligence agency is making human demons." Idris the Unimpeachable took a very dim view of immoral and exploitative activities. Val's sentiments lay in the same direction.

"Genetically?" Lane asked. That brilliant, bold mind of hers might already be running toward undoing the human demons, after she invented a way to undo the alien ones.

Martan shook his head. "It's not genetic, not primarily, although in my day, there was gene therapy around the edges. It's more like brainwashing and brutal reprogramming. The program operates in the smaller moon of Faxe, the moon named

Veritas and known as Varry. It's now the headquarters of the secret intelligence agency. And their blackest detention center too. It didn't used to be all of that."

Gerry said caustically, "That has to be one place that would be improved by an influx of Dhal demons."

Nia said, "We might wish! Realistically, we now have hellhounds to deal with, and not just the one who's incapacitated." She told Kam Far, "If you can scan that one's body in detail, looking for what you don't expect, we might learn about any physical modifications they've come up with recently. That may be important for somebody, maybe even us, to better understand what they're dealing with."

Kam Far nodded.

Nia said, "Then you and anybody else involved with the fate of that hellhound of Faxe had better go far away. This includes me. I'm going back to Azure. I hope I have what I need to resolve the issues of your intellectual property, Uncle Val."

Her redoubtable husband shook off his gloom, or maybe stuffed it into an inside pocket in his mind. "Val, you are not safe here anymore. You better go somewhere—not easily traceable. And Nia does not need to know where it is."

Nia narrowed her eyes, doubtless disliking the idea of not knowing where a legal client was. Once a lawyer, always a lawyer, even in dealing with hounds of hell.

Val said, "I can manage going elsewhere. I remember how." Suddenly his tiredness felt like a wave, threatening to pull him under. "Unfortunately, I'm not recovered. I may not have the fortitude to go anywhere for a while yet."

Martan said, "I'll stay here with you in case they send another one. I've defeated hellhounds before," he said, with a predatory gleam in his eyes.

The dhalcat lifted its head and gave him a long stare. Maybe it sensed an apex predator much like itself.

"Very good," said Idris. She was not easily rattled, even by an interstellar conspiracy brewing on her back porch. Val's opinion of her, already at an all-time high, rose higher still.

Val remembered too his life before entering the halo gate, his early years, his education on Tellas, his work of research and teaching, his family on Albion, and his relatives on Azure, including his remarkable niece, Nia. Not that he'd ever forgotten any of that; but the last five years, remembered, put everything in a different light. Especially Nia.

That evening, the two of them conferred privately in the room Gerry had given him, sitting on Val's own, old, familiar couch. Nia wanted to know in detail about how he'd gotten into the halo gate and what he'd found there. Maybe she feared that his memories would develop the gap again. He doubted that, but he could understand why as his lawyer, she needed to know. He had the impression that what he said was reviewed by a keen, versatile intellect on its way to being filed away in her mind.

He had an old habit of touching his dhalrat scars when he thought about how he got them. She noticed. "If they bother you, could have those erased."

"Sleighters wouldn't. I won't," he answered. "They treasure their scars."

That seemed to surprise her. "As signs of honor or proof of victories won?"

"I'd say souvenirs, as likely due to misadventure as victory. What matters is not so much winning as having lived and dared." He recalled something about her that was very important. "You had an adventure when you were young that left you with scars on your back, as I recall, to the consternation of your mother and father."

"Yes," she said evenly.

"Sleighters wouldn't have minded," he told her. "Sleighters would just admire you for having had the adventure."

And so did he.

That night Lane slept with him. This was a place, the university on Tellas, that he remembered from before her. She was the companion he remembered from more recent years. Her warmth, her breathing, her presence reassured him at a level too deep for words.

Teetering on the edge of sleep, slightly anxious that if he slept, he might lose his memory again, he found his mind repeating the words very, Vere, and Varry, as though they formed a small but significant constellation. What was it Gerry had said with black humor earlier today? *That has to be one place that would be improved by an influx of Dhal demons.*

Val remembered the long night of running his computer model, here at his university, only a few weeks ago. He'd seen potential gates flicker into probability in places he expected and places he didn't. He'd not identified all of them. It was astoundingly hard to correlate otherwise unidentified locations in realspace with the starjump maps. Civilization had long favored and elaborated the starspace maps, almost forgetting about realspace except at the most local level.

But he'd long suspected that the halo gate system was more or less coterminous with the extent of the Faxen Union. That put a few welcome limits on the problem. Wide awake now, just careful not to register enough surprise to wake Lane, he realized that one place firmly inside the Faxen Union was Varry, the moon of Faxe.

Must investigate further, he thought. Then he fell into a deep dreamless sleep.

19

HALL OF LAW

Nia returned to Azure on *Pastfinder*. It was strange how traveling that way didn't awaken the terror she'd felt going home to Azure in the first place. That had been in perfectly ordinary commercial starliners. *Pastfinder*, on the other hand, thanks to Lana Tai and her redoubtable crew, would gravitate to any attractive trouble that crossed its path. Her fear had been irrational and inexplicable, and good riddance to it, Nia thought. Then she slept most of the way home.

To her surprise, Lana wanted to see Castle Courant. Lana had a top-level academic visa too. So it was easily arranged for her to descend the space elevator to Denevez. But Nia wondered what her motivation might be.

"Martan told me that in any Faxen invasion, they'd try to first take your Castle as a handy base from which to conquer Azure," Lana told her bluntly.

Oh. True to form, Lana was interested in where interstellar trouble could strike. And this time, it was Nia's home. Not just her home world, which was bad enough. Her home. Only a few weeks ago, Nia had returned and in effect gotten her home back.

It felt deeply unfair for any kind of danger to threaten it now. It made her angry deep down.

They arrived in the middle of the night, in the same scheduled space elevator descent that had brought Nia here weeks ago. The next morning, Lana breakfasted with Nia, Eirene and Vim. Edvard had already left for Denevez.

Maybe because of her likely motives—checking out Castle Courant's likelihood to be a battleground—Lana struck Nia as being like a falcon in the breakfast nook. Only there was no prey for her here at present. If the Courants were lucky, there would never be any. Not here.

Eirene and Vim were interested to meet Lana. Both were scholars too; not knowing about Lana's troublemaking side, they simply approved of Nia bringing home a xenarchaeologist. And Lana had plenty of solid knowledge to share with them.

Eirene asked, "What kind of artifact is the most commonly found?"

Knowing a good question when she heard one, Lana smiled. "Every species with intelligence and constructed habitats has a need to clean the floor, because dirt and crumbs happen. The most common artifact found at our sites is brooms."

Nia remembered watching one of Lana's crew—a graduate student in xenarchaeology—methodically sweeping a corridor floor in the starship. She nodded.

"Sweeping is a good exercise for contemplatives," Vim pointed out. "It always needs doing anyway, and there are those who can't sit still long enough to contemplate in sitting silence."

"You've done that since you retired, haven't you?" Nia asked. Vim was older than Eirene, who stayed busy with scholarly research as well as running the household. Contemplation was exactly what the eldest generation was supposed to do after building the world and raising the grandchildren—devote time and energy to contemplative practices and develop their spiritual faculties.

"And so my greenhouse floor stays clean." Vim grinned. "And your hugwort enjoys riding the broom!"

Lana, who knew the hugwort well, laughed. Then she asked to see the famous sea gate.

"Famous?" Nia asked, as they went toward the lowest level of Castle Courant. Nia led Lana to the Waydown Stairs—the way down that didn't involve an elevator. Not having been built up out of blocks, but carved out by programmed beam-carving equipment, by a technology with which beauty was as easy to program as utilitarian bulk, the stairway spiraled with geometric flourishes. The footfalls of generations before her had worn hollows in the beam-carved steps. "I hope our sea gate isn't so famous that the Telal Cartel knows about it to plan an invasion."

"Maybe and maybe not. I just know about it because Martan described it to me."

Evidently Martan had had Castle Courant on his mind when he arrived at Tellas and spent a couple of hours talking to Lana while awaiting the space elevator ride down. That reassured Nia that Castle Courant—her home—was real to him. He didn't have a childhood home anymore, just the radioactive desolation that had been Delagua on Estrella. Maybe some peaceful day he'd feel at home here. She hoped so.

Descending the Waydown Stairs, they could hear activity below in the Cistern. Thuds, scraping sounds, tapping chisels, and conversation echoed in the huge empty space. "This region has earth tremors," Nia explained. "Over the years, that caused some minor damage, especially a crack in the floor of the control room. When I was here last, I also discovered that the sea gate mechanism was out of alignment. I arranged for teams of townspeople to come in and make repairs." Nia frowned. "Under the circumstances I hope that was a good idea."

"It was. A Telal Cartel expeditionary force would have it repaired in two days anyway. Your locals are doing it slower, but more painstakingly than what Telal would do," Lana observed. Then, with a laugh, she pointed toward a young Arrivaltowner pushing a broom across the floor behind the barrow full of larger debris his team had just cleaned up.

Nia realized that she liked having Lana's company here—although Lana staying long enough to meet Edvard and talk to him at any length was a certain recipe for conflict. Lana getting along with Edvard was about as likely as nitro and glycerin combining without explosive potential.

She wished Lana a good starflight back to Wendis.

To her surprise, Lana said she wasn't planning to return to Wendis right away. It was still the summer session for the university there, with no regular classes, and no need for her to go back immediately. She had an invitation to teach a special session at Jon's academy field station at the red star. Evidently, her training starflight with Jon and his friends had impressed the administration of the academy. "So we'll be close by for a while," Lana added. "Send a bubble if you need me."

Nia sincerely thanked her and hoped not to have any such need. Not here. Not at her home.

That Val was alive, not dead, made the legal challenges for Nia an order of magnitude more difficult, dangerous, and urgent. So she got to work.

The new dean of Nia's old law school in Denevez, Basil Al-Hurni, was an Albioni, and no party to past law school politics. Even better, he was neither a fool and nor a Faxen loyalist. As far as anyone could see from the public record, he didn't automatically take the Faxen Union's side in interstellar politics. After hearing Nia's request to use the resources of the library, and her explanation of why she needed to do so, he reviewed her professional resume, noting the details that substantiated the high level of her academic visa.

"Few travelers have such a high level of visa, of the academic or any of the other variety." With that comment, Dean Hurni gave her faculty-level privilege to use the library and its extensive legal database.

It had been a surprisingly good interview. Nia remembered her highly conflicted relationship with the law school after her misadventure on Moira years ago. Politics aside—

and off to the side was exactly where politics should be in the affairs of a law school—Dean Hurni understood that the key component in her visa was *top-level*; academic was a relative detail, a subtype.

Soon she was surprised to see that, compared to her time here as a student, the library's collection and legal database had a great deal more substance in the area of interstellar law. In her student days, that area had been one-sided in favor of material about the Faxe and the Faxen Union. She'd always sought a wider horizon than that. Moira had been a wider horizon to a disastrous degree. In Wendis, she'd positioned herself in the widest possible horizon of interstellar law. In the meantime, her law school had at least caught on that such horizons existed. That was encouraging.

On the other hand, the Azurean legal establishment remained provincial. Almost no Azurean interstellar legalists specialized in anything other than Faxen contract law, tariffs and trade regulations. As a result, the legal establishment here was likely to underestimate her.

Since she would soon face off with a legal adversary from within that establishment, being underestimated was all to the good. She could even help it along. Inspired by her recent disguise as free-spirited Delilah of Dis, she tweaked her looks the opposite way, to look older and more conventional. The old clothes from her bedroom in Castle Courant worked fine for that purpose. A few of Suzana's less ostentatious pieces of cast-off costume jewelry completed the costume, with the curious hugwort helping her make the selection.

Azure might be the only planet in known space she could easily understate herself. At least a fourth of the population had her same general looks. She crafted the persona of a hardworking lawyer, accustomed to the narrow specialty of academic interstellar law, on unfamiliar ground in Azurean inheritance law. Most busy legalists would, unlike the astute Dean Hurni, take *academic* to be the primary nature of her visa and her career, and suppose it to be a narrow field. What was it Robard had said when giving her the opal dress—that it was an alternative to looking like a threadbare academic? Well, for now a threadbare academic look would be just fine.

Her first order of legal business was to petition the courts to hear the case regarding Val's inheritance. For that, she had to talk to three different clerks, providing increasingly detailed documents. As she went in and out of the Hall of Law on the first floors of the tower called Denevez One, she saw people she recognized from law school. They had been fellow students at the time, or adjunct lecturers. Most of them did not recognize her. Those who did, and were friendly, had the impression she'd found an academic law position offworld somewhere. Several of them who'd heard that her work was in Wendis had also heard of the trouble there—the attack from the Telal Consortium. It was easy for them to surmise that with Wendis in turmoil, she had retreated to Azure to work on her uncle's estate. Her qualifications to represent that kind of work would of course be a secondary consideration. She did not correct that misapprehension. But it mattered to her that these people had no ill will toward her.

By midday, a formal court date had been set. It fell two weeks in the future. That struck her as a longish time considering the importance of this matter—and the unimportance of a great deal else in the court dockets—until she realized that Greening Eve and Day fell right in the middle of the two weeks. Then she thanked Christa for the extra time, which made it more likely that a bubble from Almaaz would arrive before the court date.

She would have wished to have that bubble already. And know what it said. The best she could do was to make very sure that she would quickly and securely receive a bubble from Almaaz

If any.

Vidjas officed at the apex of Denevez One. As the prime minister of Azure, she had windows in four directions, a devoted staff, an AI that was state-of-the-art although not sentient, and plenty to do. Nonetheless she made time to see Nia the same day, and her personal secretary served them sweet cakes and tea.

"You look like a vagabond lawyer," Vidjas observed shrewdly. "Having seen you that night in the cathedral, I know better."

"Am I overdoing it?"

"Not at all, if, as I suspect, this is *not* the time to come off as the highflying interstellar lawyer you are."

Evidently Vidjas had investigated Nia's work and reputation. Much of it was public, so anyone could do that. Whether they *would* was another matter.

"Just sharpen up your look when you formally appear in court downstairs."

"I plan to."

"How can I help?"

Tears pricked the corners of Nia's eyes at the sign that their old friendship was still in force. Coming home had been a good idea on so many levels. "I'm expecting a diplomatic bubble. I'd rather it not be relayed through the usual routing procedures. If it comes, it will be extremely urgent. I trust your office more than the usual routes not to misplace it, embargo it, or let it be pilfered," she added.

Vidjas looked surprised. "Where will your bubble come from?"

"Almaaz."

Vidjas' surprise sharpened into keen interest. "Late in law school, I did a special study of Almaaz, for extra credit. No one thought anything having to do with Almaaz would ever touch Azurean law. But it was a fascinating study. Almaaz is part of the Faxen Union—and a vital part, with the intellectual and scientific work it contributes—yet Almaaz has managed to hedge itself with nearly ironclad legal agreements that protect its citizens from interference. And it's a place, perhaps the only place in the Faxen Union, where infiltration by outside agencies would be impossible, and so would the imposition of martial law if Faxe ever tried to take control. The line between Almaazans and foreigners on Almaaz is brightly drawn."

Evidently Vidjas had done that school study with her usual thoroughness. Nia said, "Nonetheless, their citizens turn up on other worlds and moons, blending in with whatever organization they've attached themselves to, and using special names for the purpose. Their real names are kept secret. I know of an Almaazan couple who call themselves Jack and Jill from an ancient nursery rhyme on Earth. Some of the dispersed citizens of Almaaz are special emissaries, not that they draw attention to that. The emissaries have extraordinary diplomatic authority. One of them is a colleague of my uncle on Tellas. She goes by the name Idris. That might be the identifier on the bubble."

Vidjas contemplated a pepper cookie. "It sounds like a consequential bubble." She took a neat bite of the cookie.

Nia nodded and chose her words to be careful, yet honest. Vidjas deserved honesty. "Idris agreed to try to extend some of the ironclad legal protections of Almaaz to him, for reasons it's best not to go into. If so, it would help my case."

"Ah-HA!"

"Aha?"

"Your style hasn't changed. Yes, counselor, my office will be at your service in receiving the bubble and getting it to you without delay."

There was an additional wait until the discovery meeting, when she would learn who the legalists on the other side, arguing for Val's intellectual property to go to his separated wife on Albion, would be, and who would be the presiding judge. Discovery would be brief and later today. She asked herself how a vagabond lawyer would wait. Spend some time in the common corridors, waiting rooms, refreshment corners—where kavva simmered all day and by now smelled far from fresh? Yes, the vagabond would wait like that. Help herself to one of the plush seats in the main waiting room, likely not.

Leaning against the wall of the main waitroom, she studied the crowd in here today. She recognized some familiar faces, and by now, she'd heard about a few long-familiar names. As always with those who graduated from law school, stratification set in after a decade or so. Some legalists settled into a lowly place in the field of law. Some selflessly took nonprofit or government work. And some became royalty in their field.

Someone she recognized occupied the plushest of the waitroom seats, surrounded by admirers and exuding an air of arrogant confidence. Her eyes narrowed. Kron Derriger had been a classmate of hers when she did the fieldwork that took her to Moira. He had led the chorus of scorn and disapproval when she returned from her pyrrhic victory there. He'd been a Faxen loyalist then. He would have been very likely to go into the field of Azurean-Faxen interplanetary law. Val's separated wife could have hired lawyers on Albion to argue her case on Azure, but would have been well advised not to do so, if she could find help on Azure that occupied the top rung of the legal establishment. Which Kron apparently did.

Besides Kron Derriger's entourage and other lawyers, there were uniformed policemen, court officials, reporters, and clerks in here today. One man walked through with an air of exceptional alertness. He saw Nia and veered to her side. "Waiting for the court?"

"Taffy!" A known and friendly face was a relief to her. "Yes." She glanced at the court-meeting display board. Her innocuously titled discovery meeting was listed but had just dropped five lines down. Either more urgent cases had cropped up, or the other side had asked for a bit more time to prepare. "And I'll be here a while longer."

"How about better kavva in a quieter place?"

She agreed instantly. They went out into the wide main street of the city. The day was as warm as Azure ever got, a mild afternoon provided you were out of the wind. She remembered the Parhelon Fair at the perihelion of the orbit of Wendis around its golden sun, less than two years ago. Hiro had been determined to talk her into playing the role of Europan Queen in the Fair. She'd been determined to stay out of it, but the day at the Fair had played out in ways no one expected, and it started the whole adventure she'd had since then. The adventure had finally brought her home again, and she was very glad of it all.

Taffy showed her the way down a side street, and then onto an even more minor street, and finally into a scruffy bar favored by policemen, artists, and students. At this hour of the day, it smelled like fresh kavva.

Several youngish patrons suddenly, and unobtrusively, departed. Law students, she guessed. She was recognizable enough if you knew who to look for, and she was in the good graces of the Dean, having been granted faculty-level privileges. The students might think it better for her not to see them here. But the kavva was excellent.

Over the rim of his cup, Taffy observed, "You're dressing down." Right. He'd seen her that night at the cathedral too. "Otherwise they wouldn't underestimate you like you want them to."

Smiling, she sipped her own kavva, then swirled the liquid in the cup, watching it behave in the perfectly ordinary way it should in real planetary gravity. In Wendis, an unwary swirl could send it out on the spinwise side of the cup. Kavva-swirling was a habit she'd had to break after she moved there. It helped her think. "You used to be an Azurean patriot, not a Unionist. It's not my business to criticize or even know, but are you still?"

"Yes," Taffy said firmly.

"Is that okay for you?"

He shrugged. "I'm a detective, not a politician. My politics haven't mattered yet. I hope they don't."

She could imagine a scenario where it would matter. She thought about Castle Courant, with room for Taffy and his wife and little Taffies too, if they ever needed a safe harbor—provided it wasn't the landing ground of an invasion. "Is Vidjas in danger?"

"That's still assessed as unlikely. But your father had an odd incident late at night with his clerk."

Right. Martan had succeeded in dialing the matter back to where it looked like just that, an odd, random incident. Edvard still had no idea what kind of protector he'd had that night.

"Your father may be too obsessed with building his tower to be vigilant in the street at night," Taffy said. "Lucky his clerk was."

"It was better than luck," Nia confided. "The man who was acting as his clerk at the time is my husband."

Taffy's face showed open surprise. "You married a clerk?"

"He's the Proctor at the university in Wendis. His background includes military service and a great deal of special operations training." She gave Taffy a wry smile. "And he knows how to understate himself too."

The court-case display board still showed the discovery meeting today. Now it had a firm time, at the very end of the day. Did someone think it would amount to an afterthought to the court's business? The board also proved her guesswork correct. Her legal adversary would be Kron Derriger.

Compact as Denevez was, it was easy for her to return to her office in her father's offices and put on the professional tunic she'd brought from Wendis. Not typical courtroom style here, it was well-tailored and becoming on her.

In the discovery meeting, she sized up the court and the judge. He was an older jurist, meaning he had a long track record. She could find out a great deal about him before the formal court date two weeks from now.

Derriger smoothly petitioned for the matter to be summarily decided because of the clear merits of the case. Nia skimmed the legal brief he provided. It was well done. He knew what he was doing.

She waived the right to make a decisive defense against Derriger's inheritance action. That clearly gratified him. Then she asked for that case to be mooted. She held up sealed depositions from the legal counsel of the university on Tellas and from Timm in his role of Val's department chair. "These depositions prove what I wish to advise the court."

"And what would that be?" the judge asked.

The court AI blinked readiness to record her statement.

Nia slowly and clearly said, "Vienradzis Al-Savre is alive and well at the University of Tellas."

Taken by surprise, Kron Derriger scowled.

There was real danger in announcing this in the Hall of Law. SECINTAG, if this news reached its higher levels, could decide to swoop down on Val. He'd already had enough charges leveled against him to be detained once, at the behest of a low-level SECINTAG operative. Somebody on a higher level would eventually add up the clues and decide to make a much more ironclad detention.

But it might not matter now. Val was already planning to disappear again, to go somewhere—else.

20

CONSPIRACY

Patrolling a university at night was second nature to Martan ever since he became the proctor for the university in Wendis. The main difference here was that the sky didn't consist of a curving sea. Tonight, stars shone in the clear night sky of Tellas. He identified the bright white star of Azure and missed Nia.

Oddly, he thought about her father too. He wanted to tell Edvard more about Delagua. Doing so had been good somehow, left him feeling less cold, clotted sorrow deep inside himself.

Val Savre was meeting with some of his confederates tonight. They were in the house of his Almaazan colleague—in the room where she had her mysterious hearth—making plans for Val to disappear again. Val's doctor would go with him. Maybe a few others would too, but at this point, Martan didn't need to know who they were. A conspiracy by definition operated on a need-to-know basis. He intended to make his way back to Azure as soon as Val was safely away; he didn't need to know about their plan. In a week, he might be back on Azure to be with Nia. Maybe they'd go back to that ice cream shop. He remembered how her blue eyes sparkled, and the wind blew strands of her hair across her face as she ate her ice cream that day, and how beautiful she was. He could hardly wait to return to her. He just had to make sure danger to Val didn't intrude through the university before Val made himself disappear again.

Val Savre was an interesting man, Martan thought. On the surface, he came across as a typical astronaut-descended Albioni: polite, methodical, conventional. From all the evidence surrounding him, that was a highly misleading persona.

Martan stopped by a tavern on the edge of the campus. It was the place where, he'd been told, Val got into a scuffle a few weeks ago. Martan drank something with more flavor than alcohol and used his unnaturally acute hearing to scan the conversations and undertones. Nobody seemed to be plotting to cause trouble. The main excitement was anticipating the arrival of new exchange students. A number of them were coming from different planets, and would straggle in as their low-level academic visas put them in long lines behind more highly credentialed visitors to Tellas.

Finally he visited the university hospital. Kam Far, the doctor, met him in the morgue. Martan asked the doctor. "Got a travel bag backed?"

"Yes, and I'm always keeping it with me. We Sleighters can travel light."

The doctor seemed different from how he'd been when Martan first met him. He had a jauntier attitude, hand movements more expressive. Maybe that meant he was letting himself come across as more Sleighter. Martan told him, "I'm coming to respect your people minding your own business on the underside of the Union without coming to the attention of the state."

Kam gave him a brief, bright smile. Then he explained what he'd learned about the hellhound whose attack had been so effectively foiled by the gate in Val Savre's mind.

Unlike Martan after the fatal accident which he'd used as cover to defect from Faxe, there was no way that Val's attacker could be repaired. The parts of the brain that controlled respiration and other bodily functions were too badly disrupted. Physically, though, he was intact. Kam listed the physiological modifications he'd discovered, showing keen interest in the catalog of details. Much of it Martan already knew about because he had it too.

The doctor pointed to a diagram on his tablet, touching the outline of a human body. "The long muscle physiology is baselined differently. He wouldn't have to train up to peak endurance. Like horses, he's there, by design."

That was new. "He could go run a marathon or march into combat without months of conditioning?"

"Exactly."

Martan wondered if the new generation of hellhounds might be made for fundamentally different missions from his. Hellhounds that were both soulless and tireless would be a fearsome force in any operations verging on war. "I need to touch him again. Maybe there's more memory I can salvage, if I go deeper."

Kam checked the outside hallway, flicked a switch to lock the door, then unzipped the seam in the body bag. "Deeper in his mind sounds dangerous. What do I do if you seem to get stuck in there?"

"Knock me backward to break the connection."

"Will do." Kam touched the pocket of his white medical coat. "I've got a psych-emergency kit with ampules of stimulant and sedative."

Martan gave a faint shrug. He doubted there was a booby trap in that blasted mind.

Even with Kam's shoulder to lean on, Martan walked unsteadily out of the morgue, crying uncontrollably. The late-night staff on the main floor looked over at him.

"S'OK," Kam whispered. "We're coming out of the morgue, and bereaved people can look like you do now."

Kam was right. The eyes of the staff were kind.

Idris answered the door of her house to let them in. She took a long look at Martan. He probably still looked stricken. She said, "They're by my hearth, in that room, having discussions I didn't need to hear. I don't need to hear what you have to say to him either. But I warn you, either speak the truth or keep silent, in the presence of my hearth."

It was a metal box with an open lid, exposing a low yellow flame. A hearth on Almaaz, according to what Martan had heard, could take up the entire end of a room. On one occasion a hearth like that had incinerated an intruding hellhound. At least that was hellhound lore in his day, and the upshot was, *don't go there*. Fine. He wasn't on Almaaz, he was in the same room with a small yellow flame. Incredibly tired and disoriented, he sagged into the nearest chair.

Val sat cross-legged on the floor. Lane leaned against him with her legs folded.

"How did it go?" Kam asked them.

"Plans are in place," Val answered.

"I'm ready." Kam gracefully lowered himself into a cross-legged position too, mirroring Val's. Sleighters didn't care for chairs? Fine.

Val had his arms crossed. "I hate being turfed out of my university, my work, my commitments to my students, and my friends like this. I understand that the Faxen secret intelligence agency is behind my trouble. I hate it."

Nia had told Martan that the flame in the hearth box could somehow register truth or falsehood in statements made in its vicinity. The flame had no reaction to what Val said. It didn't have to. The fury in Val's voice was plain.

"SECINTAG," Martan said. "It's definitely behind your problems."

With vehemence, Val said, "I want SECINTAG out of my life, I want its claws out of my family, and I don't want it to touch the results of my research. For that matter, besides whatever Nia can do legally to fend off its machinations, and I wish more power to her, I wish SECINTAG into the deepest pit of hell!"

"What about you, Martan?" Lane asked.

"I once believed in the ideals it professed. Since then I lost that faith. And now I understand how bad it is."

The flame reacted. For a few moments it burned higher and whiter.

Kam said, "Val, Martan went into your hellhound's mind and sifted the pieces at the bottom, taking a good look at the details. It shook him up. He told me what he found." Kam had pieced together what poured out of Martan's mouth in the morgue after touching the hellhound, and made sense of it. That was lucky, because Martan couldn't have done so even now. He stared at the hearth flame while Kam said, "SECINTAG once was primarily what it's called—an intelligence agency, designed to ferret out political undercurrents and threats of assassination or sabotage to leading figures in government and industry. It evolved into taking out dangerous and violent opponents of the regime. That's why hellhounds were designed. Surgically precise instruments of counterterrorism."

The flame sank back down. Fine. The origin of hellhounds wasn't being weighed on the scales of truth and falsehood. It was factual.

"A few hellhounds may have slipped out of the hand that held them—Martan, here, for one—and they decided that had to be prevented. They used to just juvenate candidates, make them psychologically susceptible to being reformed, and proceed to tailor their temperaments, leaving them with free will. Now juvenation is followed up with traumatic brainwashing that guarantees disobedience to orders isn't conceivable."

Martan grimaced. That was what shook him to the core—knowing how it was done, and the end result of it.

"The dirty work is done inside the Faxen moon, Varry?" Val asked.

"Yes." Martan remembered Varry, and his own juvenation and training inside the moon. The memories were crisp and clear—and not unhappy. It had been grueling yet felt like what he was born for. Near the center of the moon, working out in the low-g training field had felt like flying. The obstacle course winding through the moon had been a challenge that put him in the first aid station again and again, but he got better and better at running it. There had been sheer play too—the hellhound pack roughhousing with each other. The whole process had given him subtle powers that no other kind of human being ever had. In retrospect, there'd been dirty work back then too. Besides each other, he and his packmates had practiced telepathic interrogation on criminals. He hadn't minded interrogating and finally killing an incorrigible criminal whose mind was full of his ugly crimes.

What he'd found in the mind of the hellhound in the body bag was memory of juvenation, but layered on top of that, the brutal, thorough brainwashing. Execution of hellhound candidates who couldn't be totally brainwashed. And interrogation being practiced on terrified and innocent political prisoners. The end result was a hellhound never motivated by values—not even misguided values—only by orders. An order to interrogate or kill, torture or rape, was just another order, implicitly obeyed, no matter who the victim was. And repentance would never happen.

In a low voice, Val asked, "What would you do if there was a way to cut SECINTAG off at the root?"

Martan shook his head impatiently. "I don't deal with hypotheticals, you do."

"Some hypotheses end up validated," Val said primly. "Timm and I have investigated the halo gate model, especially regarding flickering gates—like the one in the free trade moon Stannto—and gates that may be inactive, but intact, like the one here, inside the fissure in the hills, turned off and looking just like the rock around it."

Martan was busy making some order in his mind, stacking unwelcome new ideas next to each other, finding a way to store them. "So?"

"One of the inactive gates seems to be inside that moon. Veritas," Val said.

For a split second Martan was so surprised that his mind went blank. "Impossible, there's nothing but—" He reconsidered. "There are natural caves inside the moon, besides some beam-carved tunnels, but nothing that doesn't look like natural planetary rock."

"That's what an inactive halo gate looks like. Superb camouflage. I might be able to open it from inside the halo gate system, and admit an attack through the gate, into the moon."

Martan said harshly, "Bad place to try a surprise attack. It's full of seasoned operatives and hellhounds spring-loaded to attack whoever they're pointed at."

"Understood. Specifically, I envision sending a demon chase through the gate."

"Demon chase?"

"An invasion of Dhal demons. The demons infest the Vere system. They'd be overjoyed to find a new active gate through which to rampage." Val Savre wasn't thinking like a scientist now. But according to Lane, he was an initiate into a fraternity of demon-slayers. He sounded like it. "I think I can goad them through the gate."

It was a stunning idea. Martan managed to ask, "You and who else?"

"I have allies on Stannto and I think I can collect a few here as well."

A conspiracy to use an almost inconceivable opportunity to cut SECINTAG off at the root? Martan heard himself say, "Explain more but count me in."

"I want to do exactly that. It would be best by far to have an ally inside Veritas. Could you take our damaged hellhound's place, and report back to Varry?"

Incredulous, Martan let the idea sink in.

Lane's eyes were wide and solemn. It looked as though she'd heard this idea already, finding it every bit as incredible as Martan did.

Martan glanced at the hearth flame. "Maybe I could do that. Hellhounds aren't usually identity-verified by their allies, in their home bases, because the chances of impersonation by outsiders are nil."

"In your case, it wouldn't be impersonation by someone not a hellhound. You have insider knowledge like no other," Val pointed out. "But could you do it and survive? I'd hate to have to explain to Nia that I sent you to certain death."

Beside him Lane nodded emphatically.

Martan thought out loud: "With the memories I got from the hellhound in the body bag, including the name he used. With the help of this university sharing with me his false resume and references. With what I can glean from operatives and agents on the way back to Varry. Yes. It's not certain death for me. Just as risky as nine hells."

"Do you want to do it badly enough to even try?" the doctor asked.

To stop SECINTAG from meddling in Wendis, and here, and Azure? Martan couldn't come up with an answer. The flame was a globe of yellow light again, but there was something watchful about it, unless he was imagining that.

Maybe picking up on Martan's tension, or everyone's, the dhalcat made a long, low warbling sound.

Lane told Val, "The Sleighters already call you a mage, but sending Dhal demons through that gate would be the greatest sleight anyone's ever done."

"I suppose so." Val sounded diffident again.

"Believe it." Kam looked starry-eyed at the prospect. But he was a good doctor, one who knew human nature. He asked Val, "Do you want revenge for being killed by the demons?"

"Revenge is pointless. I'd be happy to extract recompense for all the destruction they've wreaked though."

"Are you sure enough your ideas would work to send Martan, and others, into a peril like that?"

"No," Val said flatly. "I'm sure about the gate being there, and I feel fairly confident of arranging for a plague of Dhal demons to go through it, but I won't *send* anyone. I expect to put myself in as much danger as anyone else. For others, it has to be their own decision."

Decide to risk extreme danger to put an end to the manufacture of hellhounds like the one in the bag? Martan abruptly said, "Yes. I want it badly enough to try."

The flame flared so bright that it was almost blue.

21

THRESHOLD

The stars were so bright that Val and Lane could see the trail ahead of them in the rocky hills. There was some moonlight, but Telmoon wasn't the lighthouse that Earth's Moon had been. Meanwhile the stars in this region of the galaxy were denser, brighter, and more rife with mystery.

Val looked back the way the two of them had come uphill from the university campus. "I remember how I came here that one night through the halo gate to check my model."

The wind from the sea was cool in their faces, but that wasn't why Lane shivered. "I'm glad I'm with you here. Apart from that, though, I don't feel glad about anything."

"Uncertainty is no fun. Hopefully we can resolve it. I must do this, test the gate before sending Martan out into danger. My plan will be useless if I can't leave this way." Of course, not being able to use the gate would leave Val himself in a precarious position. It was time to make sure one way or another.

They turned back to continue upward on the trail, toward the cliffs.

Val said, "He's an interesting man. He fits in around here, in the university environment, like hand in glove. He can seem very ordinary." Val remembered Martan coming into his mind that day on Idris' porch. It had been a distinctive impression, another mind entering his by his own invitation. It would have been unnerving, except that he'd felt something like that before—which he now remembered quite clearly.

Lane said, "He's not ordinary at all. He's a nightwalker, the Sleighters would say. They mean somebody who walks on the dark side of danger, a spy or a double agent. They respect that, if the person isn't so warped that they can't be normal again. If they came back from it."

"Evidently he did, because my niece married him."

"She's even more reason to make sure the gate works before you ask him to take that hellhound's place and go back to Varry."

Val said drily, "Agreed. Speaking as someone killed by the demons, to me it sounds even worse to be found out as a defector and caught by SECINTAG."

With less foliage up here, the wind was keener. It was a relief to find the fissure where the halo gate was supposed to be and get out of the wind. And maybe see the way into unprecedented new trouble, of course, but that couldn't be helped. "All right. Let's make sure we ourselves are on the dark side." Val shook out the blanket and adhesives he'd brought. They rigged the blanket up where the fissure narrowed, so the blanket would block light from being seen outside of the fissure. Then he turned on his torch to study the rock face in front of them. He placed his hands on the rock.

Lane put her hands on his shoulders.

And the rock morphed. A ripple went across it, and the rock folded itself back, more malleable than the blanket. Where there had been solid rock was a lens-shaped opening with dark air behind it. The air pressure in there didn't equalize with the air pressure in here. The gate kept the two masses of air apart. All halo gates could do that—and a great deal else, including destroying intruders, if the wards were active.

Val stared at his hands for a few moments. *It recognized my touch, just like before. I can open the gate.* Relief shivered through him. "The wards aren't active. Turning into solid rock is ward enough, with no one suspecting it's here," he murmured.

He remembered what he'd long known about the halo gates. The colored lights weren't what killed anybody, more like a readout on the status of the gate. Different patterns in the light meant different conditions. Only some of the patterns meant active wards, which in turn meant that any attempt to enter the gate would be countered by destructive psychological forces. He remembered all of that, and his remembered knowledge felt whole, without gaps.

On the rim of the gate, the rock face had a flat pentagonal plate built into it. Val put his hands there, remembering how touch translated into action by the gate. Behind the gate, a long, narrow corridor became visible, illuminated by a single strip in the corridor's ceiling. "Oh yes. I remember this corridor. I don't remember the star man bringing me through for the last time."

"You were in a coma."

And his rescuers, Donalt and the other wargamers, had said that his clothes and his skin felt startlingly cold. He'd been brought out from the interior of an artificial intelligence that almost certainly operated by means of quantum computing, so its thoughts could only unfold in cold and dark deeper than most parts of space. It had brought him back from death.

The open gate tempted Val severely. Stannto was out there across the gate system, with his other home, Jack and his other friends, and his son Dikk. But going through now would be foolhardy. He didn't have a rifle as protection from dhalrats and he knew nothing about the recent movements of demons in the Vere passageways. He murmured, "If we all go through with my plan, I can recuperate a bit more at Stannto. The lower gravity there will help me. Are you sure you won't come with me when the time comes?"

"I've got a virus to design."

"Very well." She wasn't legally married to him, so there was no obvious connection between the two of them. Nonetheless, staying behind here, she'd live with Idris and retreat to Idris' house at any hint of danger. Breaching the home of an emissary of Almaaz was a diplomatic sin of such an order of magnitude as to be unthinkable in the Faxen Union. Not to mention what would happen to any intruder with a dhalcat guarding the house. He said, "I'll miss you terribly but you'll be safe here."

"The danger to you terrifies me, but I still have the feeling it'll be safer for you in there than for the nightwalker if he tries to meet you in Varry."

"I know that all too well. So my part has to work." He put his head down, reviewing his plan, and what it would take to make it work inside the Vere system.

"Val!" she whispered.

He looked up.

The star man came toward them in the corridor, a dark human shape full of stars, walking in a not quite human way. Val's breath caught in his chest. He'd hoped for this meeting, while knowing no way to make it happen. The star man was the avatar of an ancient AI made by a people who went extinct before anyone on Earth ever made any but the most primitive of machines. He remembered telepathic encounters with the star man, which had been like Martan coming into his mind, not invasive but—considerably weightier and somehow very alien.

Val stood up. From incredible experience he knew it would be most effective to speak aloud and as deliberately as though lecturing a class full of students. "Thank you for saving my life."

Lane scrambled up too and said shakenly, "Thank you for making me." She'd never seen the star man in real life, nor in dreams, only in an inexplicable painting made by their son. But the ancient artificial intelligence had designed the vector that made her ancestors and she herself Verian.

Val told the star man, "We may be back soon, with friends, hoping to cross your realm to Stannto, the moon where our friends live. Only with your permission."

Val's nerves were stretched taut. Beside him, Lane seemed struck dumb. This was an incredible thing to ask, incredible even to imagine. But Val felt sure that permission was absolutely necessary. Wandering through the Vere system in ignorant impunity was out of the question.

The star man nodded. It was such a human gesture that Val almost felt unbalanced. He managed to say, "Thank you."

Holding hands, Lane and Val backed away. The star man watched them until they reached the mouth of the fissure, and then he turned and walked away.

When they reached Idris' porch, Val was shaky from exertion and excitement. "It's ready," he told Martan. Lane helped him fold down onto a Sleighter-style cushion on the floor.

Lane asked Martan, "Are *you* ready?"

Martan's face changed, muscles tightening, and his stance altered. It unnerved Val how much he could resemble the hellhound that had attacked Val in the library and gotten an explosion in his brain in return. Before that, Val had taken the hellhound for a researcher, one with a hard face, but some people did have hard faces; at the time Val had thought nothing of it. Martan said, "I am."

Val let out an uneven breath. "It's nearly time for the others to arrive."

"I'll stay."

Lane asked, "Are you sure you should know who's involved in this?"

Martan answered, "If the worst is about to happen, I can self-destruct, and to protect the rest of you, I will. Otherwise I need to know who and what to expect."

"That makes sense," Val murmured.

Idris stayed closeted in the other end of her house. But the dhalcat slunk out and sat beside Val, it's eyes bright and its tail twitching with excitement.

Kam Far, the Sleighter doctor, was the first to arrive. He looked flushed with excitement. Then Donalt, the wargamer, tapped on the porch door. He looked more scared than excited, but his jaw was set with determination.

Martan looked at the group gathered on Idris' porch: Kam, Donalt, Lane, and Val himself. "No offense, but you look like a thin crew for this mission."

"The Vere passageways are narrow," Val pointed out. "There's no room for a phalanx. I'll ask some fighter friends at Stannto to join in."

"To make sure you get there, I want you to take reinforcements," Martan said.

"Eh?"

"The Wendisan starship captain who got Nia here and back in the university starship left a couple of her crew behind in case they might be needed. They're seasoned fighters in corridor work in ships and stations. Show them how you fight and they'll catch on."

It sounded like an offer too good to turn down, especially the part about seasoning in corridor fighting. "How will I know them?"

"They'll be exchange students."

"Eh?"

"Besides knowing how to get into trouble and back out of it, and how to recruit hellraisers who can be team players, our

Wendisan friend knows how to create false ID that holds up to scrutiny. You'll recognize them for certain because they'll know a tune called 'Moonlight Sings.'" Martan hummed a sad-sounding melody different from popular music. As he did, his face changed, from the hard mask of the enemy hellhound, back to a softer, more human being. Privately, Val marveled.

22

CONFESSION

Today was the last business day before Greening Eve and Greening Day. It was *possible* that something could get crammed into the docket at the Hall of Law. More like *probable* if the other side wanted a maneuver to go unnoticed. So it wasn't a good idea for Nia to alertly wait around the Hall of Law. Let Kron Derriger think she was inattentive! She stayed later than usual in the morning at Castle Courant. But she felt unsettled and wandered through the upper levels restlessly. As a last resort, she dared to go into the chapel.

It had once been her favorite place in Castle Courant. After Moira, estranged from her father and with her faith shattered, it had been impossible for her to spend any time here. Today, it was quiet, faintly scented of incense, and brightened by a compact chandelier. The shelf in the back held icons, some of them of great antiquity, left by ancestors all the way back to the astronauts. The icons were never removed, just dusted before holy holidays. The small Christa Terra window was dark blue, still in morning shadow. It felt safe enough in here.

She was carrying the hugwort. Ever since she came back

from Tellas, it seemed to have missed her and wanted to spend time with her. She put it down on the smooth bench and it proceeded to explore the chapel.

She thought Edvard had left for Denevez even earlier than usual. He had a great deal to prepare for in the Green Holy Days liturgies and the logistics of filling St. Venture's Cathedral with worshipers. To her surprise, though, Edvard entered the chapel. She moved over on the bench and he sat down beside her.

Edvard said, "This place is much older than my cathedral. It's as old as colonization on Azure. This entire world was a frozen wasteland, yet they carved this space out of the rock and named it Chapel of Hope." His voice, which could rivet a large crowd, was soft today.

Voice soft, shoulders slightly hunched, Edvard wasn't the impressive and even overbearing archbishop right now. He seemed approachable. And there was certainly something she wanted to approach him about. "Martan told me that you quoted Olav Zakeri in the Firstnight service."

"It was Zakeri's observation that we are much like any of the other greening species, invasive on Earth, but vigorous enough to claim a foothold on raw worlds being terraformed. We are all weeds. I did add that we are angelfish as well." He smiled slightly.

He had always quoted theologians of all stripes, from times all the way back to Medieval Earth, and especially Saint Bonaventure, the patron of his cathedral. Those ancient voices often sounded unorthodox to New Cathor ears and almost no one minded. It probably wasn't the words he'd quoted on the first night of the Green Holy Days, but rather the name of Olav Zakeri that had attracted unfavorable attention and even resulted in a hit man being hired to frighten him.

Edvard looked up at the chandelier. "Privately, in his letters, Zakeri has interesting thoughts. On Moira where he lived for so long—and where you saved his life—" Edvard paused significantly.

Nia felt deeply grateful. Edvard had really changed his mind about what she did on Moira. He hadn't just stored it in the bottom cistern of his memory never to be touched again, expecting her to do likewise.

He went on, "There remain the bones of the Old Moirans whose sun incinerated their home world. If for us God revealed Godself in our home world, Terra—and Zakeri doesn't doubt that; his branch of our faith just doesn't make that central the way we do—in the Old Moirans' home world, was God revealed to them just as surely? Zakeri believes it was so. Then what does it mean that their world died?"

That was more speculative than was Edvard's wont. Between that, and his body language, Nia wondered what he had weighing on his mind or his shoulders today. She answered, "Worlds die, and so do stars. Civilizations die. My friend Lana, who was here briefly, has studied ruins of at least ten alien civilizations, the one on Moira being one of them."

"I'm sorry I missed her," Edvard said, not knowing whereof he spoke. Nia still thought the two of them could find explosive differences of opinion and do so in record time.

She told him, "You've often said that Terra is Christa, but Christa is greater than Terra resurrected. Our colony worlds, and the ecosystems created with great effort in Wendis, even taken altogether, are less than what Earth was."

"Yes, and that remains true however much humanity overvalues the successes of our terraforming."

Nia found herself enjoying this conversation. "We don't know if the Old Moirans were as wildly destructive and self-destructive as humanity. *We* killed Christa Terra, our God-given home world. They didn't destroy theirs. Their star did."

"It's counterintuitive that a civilization be technologically advanced and not potentially destructive," Edvard said, with his argumentative nature showing. In her younger years they'd had many invigorating arguments. It had helped Nia become a lawyer. "Of course, we are the only living star-going civilization we've ever known."

"Not quite. Wendisan history records an encounter with starfarers called Starbirds, bipeds with feathers and digits at the joints of long wings. They were an exploration starship crew from another starflight space that we can't reach. They fell out of their own starflight space. That can happen with unstable starjump points. A brilliant human starflight tactician found temporary starjump points that they could use to return to their home planet, the name of which was Trillhome."

Edvard looked alert. "I've never heard of Starbirds. They must be a myth."

"No. Just secret. Wendis is very good at collecting, archiving, and comparing secrets." She remembered the matter of Almaazan citizenship, how Friday had told her about it, and she'd petitioned Idris to extend it to Val. She hoped to get news of a bubble confirming as much. Today would be the perfect day for it. She glanced at her identity bracelet. It showed no signal about that, or anything else.

"You've worked your way deep enough into Wendis to know some of the secrets."

Given how little they'd talked about her life in Wendis, that was perspicacious of him. She nodded. He gave her a long look, almost as though evaluating a stranger he'd never met.

And then, to Nia's surprise, Adriance Vale joined them. Remembering that Adriance was her father's confessor, Nia asked, "Should I leave?"

"No," Edvard said. "I can— should—share my concern with you both."

Serene as almost always, Adriance gave the blue Christa Terra window a reverent gesture, then settled onto the other bench, facing the two of them.

Edvard asked, "Has my reputation become an impediment to the faithful?"

Adriance countered, "Why would it be?"

"My intransigence about my daughter saving Zakeri's life was notorious, and I was on the wrong side of history. I hurt Nia and callously sent her into exile." Pain showed on his face.

Nia marveled. Here, in the chapel, he was saying that to Adriance and her both. She would have come back to Azure for this moment alone.

Adriance said, "Well, quoting Zakeri has done much to counter your notorious history. Attendance in the cathedral will be up on Greening Day, you know."

"I know. What about my anti-Unionism?"

"Publicly you affirm Azure's independence from the Faxen Union without a hint of disunionism. So do many of our politicians and civic leaders, including the best of them."

Nia thought about Vidjas Finndur, and nodded. Then she said, "Not everyone recognizes me as your daughter because I look like so many other Azureans in the Hall of Law. I've heard various opinions about you, your cathedral, and even your Firstnight homily, but nothing unanimous. It sounds just like the usual scattershot of opinion about any leader, short of a crisis that polarizes everyone."

"You've been discrete about your political views," Adriance assured Edvard.

He rubbed his hand across his forehead. "But I have to write a sermon for Greening Day, and I'm finding it hard."

That was highly unusual. He was a born communicator, and the larger the audience, the better. Knowing that as well as Nia did, Adriance asked, "What's different this year?"

"As always, in the Green Holy Days we remember Christa in her holy beauty, our Earth, and the collective crime of humanity in polluting, exploiting, and finally destroying the ecosystems of Earth. Then we remember the endless night of star travel that brought human colonists to Azure and other worlds. Finally we rejoice in Christa resurrected in the terraforming on every colony world and here. We give solemn thanks for having enough to eat, because ever since humanity left the generous cradle of Earth, it has been endless work to grow and provide enough food. As usual, I shall identify a few distorted versions of these foundational truths of our faith, and counter those distortions, since on Greening Day many people are paying attention for once." He spread his hands in frustration. "What am I missing?"

In Nia's mind a door swung open. *Oh—oh no!* She had a locked room in her mind. It held memories she usually couldn't afford to remember. It wasn't guarded by a formidable gate like Val's amnesia, just a door that could unlock itself and swing open on smooth silent hinges. What the locked room protected her from knowing was both awful and momentous. She felt herself paling. Edvard and Adriance both looked at her with sudden concern.

Nia gulped a breath, trying not to be overwhelmed by what she suddenly knew, yet trying not to be so afraid that the door would close to protect her. She needed to know this now. Here. "Father, do you remember that I told you about Shandy?" Her voice came out strained and uneven.

He emphatically said, "Yes."

Sensing her distress, the hugwort galloped from the other end of the chapel, climbed into her lap, and wrapped its tendrils around her. Its furry root mass was as big and warm as a house cat. Holding it calmed her just a bit and every bit helped.

She told Adriance, "Before the Church council, when I went missing from Starway, it was because of Shandy, the dark god, that his Angels and some drastically gene-changed groups of people worship as either God or Satan." Nia gulped another breath. "He is an ancient AI that was created by mankind to archive all the knowledge of Earth in orbit when Earth was dying and the starships were leaving. He created his Angels and with them followed the starships. Because of his spies and agents all across the stars, Shandy knew that as bishop of Moira, Zakeri had changed Moira from the dumping ground of the Faxen Union's prisoners and exiles into a world with beauty, peace, love, and reverent respect for the dead, even including the Old Moirans. And Shandy knew Zakeri was under consideration to be elevated to the role of patriarch of the Old Catholic Orthodox Church. And he didn't want that. He had his Angels kidnap me. He thought by making me disappear out of known space, Zakeri's case would be less credible at the Old Cathor Church council on Goya. Alive or dead I would be a miracle or a martyr. If I vanished without a trace, my absence would weaken the case for electing Zakeri as patriarch."

Edvard looked aghast. Adriance's voice came out uneven. "So it would have."

As though the past were present, Nia recalled being Shandy's prisoner, the cold, the hopelessness, and the shattering certainty that she would never see her home or anyone from her past again. The memory made her feel hot and cold, like the worst respiratory illness she'd ever had.

Edvard said, "Why did a counterfeit Satan care about a rising religious figure?"

"That's what you need to know." Her memories of talking to Shandy were like a fever dream with edges sharp enough to make her imagination bleed. "He hated me for being a descendant of astronauts. He said my—*our*—ancestors helped murder the Earth, plundered Earth to build and equip the starships, and left Earth dying. He called what happened to Earth *climax evil*. He said that what Faxe has become is climax evil again. He knew that as patriarch of the Old Cathor Church, Zakeri would use all the leverage he could command to call on Faxe to repent. The Old Cathor Church has a significant presence across the Union, so the patriarch's statements would really matter. Shandy said that Faxe repenting, mending its ways, and waxing great and good, would leave his worshippers less darkness in which to live and profit from disorder."

Adriance listened in stunned silence. Edvard said, "He called Faxe climax evil for the second time in human history, on a par with the pollution and final destruction of nature on Earth?"

"He called it the third instance, because there was the colony world, Terra Nova, that turned into Terror and tried to subjugate all of known space thousands of years ago. Yes."

Adriance managed to say, "Climax evil is an apt way to put it in the first two cases."

Edvard crossed his arms. "Not Faxe."

"Father, Gale-Eris told me the truth the last time I visited her on Faxe. Gale is an old friend of mine who is now an interstellar conciliator, Adriance. She's highly successful, highly enough placed to know what most people don't: that although lands and seas on Faxe are protected as nature reserves in theory, mineral extraction goes on below the surface day and night. The ruling class, the syndexecs, are fixated on profit beyond any need or reason—as it was on Earth before the Star Age. The syndexecs engage in life-extending therapies. They want the universe and immortality—as their kind did on Earth. Through corporate militia, the Faxen Union is turning into a conquering empire. All of that is why Shandy calls it climax evil."

"That is Shandy's opinion," Edvard said stubbornly. "He is not God."

"No, he's not God, because it was possible to change his mind. I did it by quoting Olav Zakeri." Nia marveled, darkly. "Zakeri once told me that anyone can accuse a villain of villainy and it may even make the villain feel exalted, strong, superior. But suppose you show a villain that his villainy is wretched and meaningless, and you offer him a better and happier way to live, if only he lets go of the villainy he's so proud of. The villain may repent. But more likely he will lash out with all the violence of which he is capable."

Remembering Zakeri made Nia feel hopeful momentarily. Remembering talking to Shandy undermined even being able to imagine hope. Yet as with Shandy, so here too. She could talk coherently, because years of training in law had made her able to speak and even argue regardless of how she felt inside. "I convinced Shandy that if Zakeri accuses Faxe of its evil in a way that rings across the stars, Faxe could possibly repent, but probably will reject the criticism, complete its transformation into a violent Empire, blaze with arrogance like a supernova, finally destroy itself and a lot else, and leave Shandy and his worshippers to salvage the ruins all across known space. That sounded good to Shandy. He let me go."

Adriance looked shaken. "You were not unscathed. At the council, we heard about a long and uncertain recuperation on your part."

"I heard the same from your colleagues in Wendis," Edvard said urgently.

Nia shuddered. "What was worst of all was the way the Angels fly. The Angels have strange little ships that don't go through normal starjump space but can go anywhere. Anywhere. That's why they can interfere with anything. They fly in a kind of nonspace, nontime, so irrational that being there makes non-Angels insane. They usually give ordinary humans like me a drug that wipes out their memory, if they've carried away or kidnapped somebody. I cut a deal with a renegade Angel to remember everything, because I'd learned secrets of Shandy that Wendis needed to know. Wendis is the only power that can counter the designs of Shandy and his Angels. But I ended up insane. A Wendisan doctor and—a telepathic specialist designed the locked room in my mind to protect me from my memories." With Lila Tsuda's advice, *Martan* was the one who construct a secret room in her mind with a door and a lock, and autonomous vigilance. She bit her tongue, not wanting to give Martan away. "Consider this confession. Tell no one about this. If Shandy knew I remember his secrets, he'd send his agents to assassinate me."

Speechless, they sat with her in silence. That gave her space to reflect. "Now I see. What happened on Moira, and then here, and then events in Wendis and on Moira again, put me in the position to change Shandy's mind. It may not matter in interstellar affairs. Or make an incalculable difference." She took a breath that was ragged, but deeper than before. "Christa was with me even there, and what happened fits into my life story. I may be able to open and close the locked room's door at will someday. Not yet." She felt shattered, holding herself together only because she was in this place with these people. "I won't remember I told you any of this and if you ask me about it, the door will lock tighter than ever." *Enough. Enough. Please, enough!*

The door smoothly closed and silently locked again.

Her identity bracelet pinged. Startled, she stood up, hugwort and all. "I need to go to the Hall of Law right away."

"The catamaran is waiting for me," Edvard said. His voice was unaccountably gentle. "Take it. I need to stay here for a while."

She felt strangely unsteady as she ran toward the Waydown Stairs. She left the hugwort in its favorite window, then took the elevator instead of the stairs, not knowing why she felt so unsteady.

23

ATONEMENT

Edvard Az-Courant put his head in his hands.

Adriance said, "Do you believe her?"

"Yes. It makes my blood run cold. I believe her."

"So do I. It squares with the more credible rumors that flew around the Church council on Goya."

Rumors about her, and news about him. "Not only is my mistake notorious, but consequences are falling like dominoes across the stars." Even more to his distress, consequences were falling across his soul.

Capable confessor that she was, Adriance said probingly, "Some people would say God made you intransigent to set Nia up to encounter Shandy and providentially change his mind."

He felt tempted to believe that himself.

"Well? Was it God's chess game?"

After Nia so startlingly told him about Shandy the first time, he'd researched that topic of Shandy and Shandy's Angels. It had left him with a strong sense of professional and personal affront. "Shandy, that counterfeit Satan, is the kind of god that callously manipulates everything he can touch."

"What about our God, the Star-maker, the Christa-father, Compassion-Spirit?"

He answered with thick reluctance. "No. God didn't play puppeteer with me. My errors were my own and stemmed from who I am."

Adriance nodded. "Arrogant, ambitious, wanting Nia to be your tool in your political endeavors, and judgmental when her faith led her to save Olav Zakeri's life on Moira by scandalous legal means."

"Yes." They'd been over this ground before.

"You're saying your sin and your errors are your own, as with each and all of us."

"Well, yes." Not that he liked identifying himself with the ordinary run of humanity. He disliked thinking of himself as *weedy*. He might have been putting it off for years too.

"And yet, Edvard Az-Courant, you raised a daughter who in terrible danger could face a counterfeit Satan and speak the truth to that power."

There was that to cherish. Not much else. But that.

"Do you think the counterfeit Satan told the truth regarding Faxe?"

"I don't know. Do you?"

"I'm more sure than you, but not certain. If you would come to the ecumenical council that begins today, I believe one or another of those who will be there can throw light on that."

He'd meant to give the ecumenical council short shrift, pleading an overfull agenda for the next three days. That agenda was almost meaningless to him now. "Who are they?"

"Several delegates from the Old Catholic Orthodox Church in the Faxen Union, an Old Cathor metropolitan and two Later Saints from Goya, an Old Catholic from Estrella, a deacon and a priest of our own church on Albion. And delegates representing other faiths—two Buddhim from Wendis, representatives of Hinduism and Islam from Goya, and several people who represent unpopular minority religions in the Faxen Union and who did not make their travel plans known in advance, lest they be denied permission to travel. Azure was chosen as the place for this council because it is independent from the Faxen Union, and not part of the Alliance of Starmark either."

"With the archbishop of Azure being neutral too, not known to favor or to disfavor the Union's aims," he said tonelessly. "I have indeed been discrete in making known my politics. If climax evil is manifest in our day, though, discretion may be cowardice."

She looked surprised. "Are you serious?"

"In the name of God, yes."

"Speaking truth about power could put you on the losing side of a political upheaval. Or worse yet, make a martyr of you."

He shrugged. "As were greater men and women than me before my time."

It was midmorning. The equatorial sun shone through the Christa Terra window and painted a disk of vivid blue light on the other wall of the chapel. He watched it while his mind circled around new and very uncomfortable ideas.

He said, "If something happens to me, the Bishop of Beyond can become archbishop. He has the capability to do the work and would have support from the greater Church. The faithful in the outer solar system would think their interests finally mattered to the rest of us, too, and rejoice."

Adriance objected, "But he has no ties to Denevez. He wouldn't know how to deal with the tangle of historical legacies, vested interests, and power struggles in Denevez, all thicker here than anyplace else on Azure."

With an unaccustomed sense of detachment, Edvard suggested, "You could become the Bishop of Denevez. You're respected near and far, and at the right place in your career to step up like that."

She threw up her hands. "And have to deal with the white elephant of your unfinished cathedral?"

If in doubt about history, talk to historians, Edvard decided. Two reputable ones lived in the beam-carved rooms of Castle Courant. Eirene was away for the day in Arrival, but Edvard found Vim in his greenhouse, sweeping the floor.

Vim heard Edvard's concerns with a grave face. "The Faxen Union going bad is our greatest fear, Eirene's and mine. We've talked about the earmarks you just named—the syndexec class becoming infatuated with immortality, their lust for unlimited wealth and territorial expansion, and the Union turning into empire, without the consent of the governed, much less the invaded. When the Union failed in attempting to invade Wendis, we were overjoyed, and not just because we have family from there—our Nia and Inanna Riga."

Vim gave a smile that made him look very much like his mother, Edvard's grandmother, Inanna Riga, who many years ago came from Wendis to visit Azure, and stayed when she fell in love with the Azurean man who became Vim's father. "If anyone had asked *her*, she might have said Wendis would not be easy to invade! Now, if it's on good authority you have it that Faxe is being mined under the surface parks and wilderness, violating the sanctions against resource extractions . . . ?"

"Good authority." Edvard didn't name Shandy or Nia's friend Gale. Discretion *could* be the better part of valor and good order.

"Then it's an extremely bad sign. There's also their society saturated with computational and communications technology. In the ancient days, an excess of digital connectivity had much to do with the insanity that led to the convulsive collapse of civilization on Earth. Most societies on every terraformed world ever since are cautious about that, maybe overcautious. But every wisdom teacher present and past insists that the present place and moment, living touch and spoken word, blade of grass and fur of cat, are what make life worth living. Only on Faxe is it otherwise. Some philosophers there say that their planet with its alien electrical foliage is not worth looking at."

With conviction that he didn't expect, Edvard said, "They are wrong. God, the Creator, lifted the worldwide ecosystem on Faxe out of the primal elements. The Creator's handiwork is everywhere an icon for us. If alien flora and fauna are harder to relate to, we should try harder." He listened to the words coming out of his mouth with surprise. It wasn't a matter he'd consciously thought about before this moment. But he recognized the truth of it.

"You are right," Vim said serenely.

Edvard sighed. "In the recent history of Faxe it's all been there for me to add up. And in honesty, I have added up. But only in my study at night. Not publicly. I have been discrete."

"That's how a politician has a long career," Vim pointed out.

For what? And wasn't he supposed to be theologian and pastor first, a politician somewhere lower in the list of his responsibilities? A builder of the Church, that too. The cathedral —overambitious and ill planned by generations before him— had needed to be made whole and finished. By dint of his political acumen, he'd gotten it almost done. There was that.

Walking downstairs toward the catamaran dock on the frozen lake, Edvard remembered how, in his early years, Inanna Riga had done much to raise him. What had Grandmama Inanna once said of him, that he took exception to then—? Oh yes. He recalled it clearly: *You are precocious, Eddy, with the intelligence, charm, and drive enough to go high in this world.* Wendisans were fond of nicknames for everyone. No one but her had called him Eddy. *Courage, though, is not what I see in you. If that comes it will come late.*

Early in the afternoon the ecumenical council convened in a freshly finished meeting room in the cathedral. Edvard remembered when Adriance had reserved the room for the purpose, saying she hoped that it would be finished in time. Edvard had made sure that it was.

The ceiling was made of embossed metal. The chandeliers were bright and clean. The stone floor was warm because it benefited from the geothermal heat sources under Denevez. At tables placed near the walls of the room, dialogue was waxing, passionate speakers addressing and actively listening to each other. It seemed to be off to a good start. Of course, the ecumenically minded were always among the most secure and open-minded in their respective faiths. Insecure and closed-minded clerics were the ones more likely to build fortifications against other faiths and stay away from encounters with them.

The first formal session was, paradoxically for a conclave that presupposed extensive dialogue, contemplative prayer. The representatives of their respective faiths all seemed at ease with that, some sitting in chairs, some sitting on rugs on the floor. Edvard certainly knew how to do contemplative prayer too, not that he often had the patience for it. Today, he seemed to go deeper into stillness and silence than usual. When the appointed time ended with a chime, he felt sorry to return to the surface world of work and worry.

Still feeling silence-minded, he gave the words of welcome he'd prepared ahead of time, just not all of them. The words he left out were those that had the effect of aggrandizing himself. They looked written in accusatory red in his mind's eye; so he omitted them.

Ordinarily he would have then returned to his holy day preparations. Instead he lingered as focus groups formed to conference on specific topics. Adriance was in her element here, greeting old friends and introducing him to them. She had organized this well, he thought. She really was bishop material.

Along with everything else she was seeing to, Adriance made sure to introduce him to an Old Cathor metropolitan. Her rank was approximately equal to Edvard's. Metropolitan Undine brought greetings to Edvard from Olav Zakeri.

Edvard said, "My regards to Zakeri as well, and good wishes for his work."

Undine said bluntly, "He needs your prayers also. Assassins are after him. The government of the Faxen Union has realized that what the patriarch of my church says can matter, to the disadvantage of the Union's scheming goals."

Edvard thought about his correspondence with Zakeri, the man's public writings—and what Nia had said about the opinions of the counterfeit Satan called Shandy. "What he says matters."

"Especially now. Inconveniently for the Faxen Union, he moved to Goya as patriarch just when the Union is meddling in politics and purveying propaganda to soften things up for a takeover of Pangoya."

Pangoya was the single large continent on Goya. As far as Edvard knew it was a wasteland of mountain and valley, sand and rock, with grasslands faintly sketched on some of the warmer and wetter parts of it. "As I understand it, the Faxen Union has a long-standing alliance with the government of Pangoya. That counterbalances the Archipelagoes being allied with the Alliance. Given the longstanding balance of forces, why would the Faxen Union now try a takeover?"

"That's been uncovered lately, thanks to our church having alert priests and secular agents in Pangoya," Undine said intensely. "Goya was once a world blooming with life, until a supernova laid it to waste. But one of the legacies of its ancient life is oil. Pangoya has petroleum oil, a substance rare in the universe, incredibly useful, best kept in the ground except at special need, indeed, sacred. As you believe."

"Yes. That is a tenet of my faith."

"The Union wants to take it—to extract and monetize it."

Edvard was jolted. "That would be sacrilege."

Frowning, Undine said, "The way the Union is going, sacrilege is just a cost of doing business. They do dislike it being called out as that by Olav Zakeri, because his convictions could change minds and hearts across Goya. And even across the Faxen Union."

Faxe might have been slower on the uptake about that possibility than the counterfeit Satan. Faxe might not be any less evil than Shandy, Edvard reflected bitterly. Indeed, the Faxen Union might be *more* evil than a lesser god who was zealously protecting the interests of his worshippers. In contrast, of all those who admired, served, or even unconsciously worshipped the Faxen Union, few were not disposable. In the eyes of the Union as it turned into Empire, everyone, and everything, everywhere, existed only to be exploited.

Undine said, "Olav's elevation made Faxe look at other clerical leaders, realizing what they say can matter. Some clergy and Church officials in Pangoya find themselves persecuted. You are another one that a populace might listen to. The agents of disorder may regard you with enmity."

Edvard said, "There's been an attempt with empty threats to scare me into resigning."

The metropolitan lowered her voice. "Olav told me to tell you that in the view of Faxe's strategists and syndexecs, and worst of all, its secret intelligence agency, clerics who are pocket pets are a plus. Until now, in light of your history, you have likely been taken for a pocket pet. If you prove otherwise, you will be in danger."

Having much on his mind did not get him off the barbed hook of having much to do.

The cathedral bustled with last-minute preparations for the series of services that started tonight. But his subordinates and staff, the deacons, acolytes, vergers, and the crew of sextons with their mops and brooms, all knew what they were doing. So did Edvard's personal assistant Byron, who had been mollified back into his position when Edvard apologized for having been cavalier about his own safety and Byron's. Several members of a newly formed diocesan security detail now shadowed Edvard everywhere he went in Denevez.

He paced the length and breadth of the cathedral, finding much to praise, and little to correct. The dome stood above it all, with its chandeliers. Below the chandeliers, deeply seated in the dome and extending all the way to the floor, the ring of tall narrow windows gave views of Azure. It would have been sacrilege to shut out the sight and light of the world. The mountains and sea and snow forests and blue sky were the icons of this cathedral.

The organ was built into the cathedral's structure. The organ was permeable, a fact highlighted when he saw feet sticking out behind its massive main console. The feet wore shoes he recognized. "Radzi?"

Radzi backed out of the organ. "This is a magnificent musical machine. Your organmaster explained how it works. With more study, I can help him fit and tune it." Radzi was positively radiant at the prospect.

Edvard only wished the fitting and tuning had been complete before Greening Eve. There were always some among the faithful who were tone-deaf to the voice of God except when God spoke with the voices of organs and choirs. The organ, as it was now, was not going to have a convincing voice. Edvard just nodded.

Dome and all, the cathedral resembled many Old Cathor

cathedrals. The metropolitan from Goya had noted as much, approvingly. A location subject to volcanic tremors and heaves of ice did not favor attenuated arches and other delicate structures. The spire that Edvard planned would have strong yet elegant feet, marking four vertices of a square around the dome. Putting on his coat, Edvard left the cathedral to go outside. One of his security guards followed him out and stood unobtrusively beside a wall.

Edvard stopped to touch the building's cool smooth exterior wall, look up, and visualize the spire. It would be slightly taller than the Denevez city towers. Unlike those with their blunt top floors, it would have a slender apex.

Stars were coming out, already brightening beyond the twilight. As he looked up into the star-rich sky, Edvard realized that at this time of Azure's year, the constellation called the Astronaut was at zenith. He'd long been approvingly aware of that. But only now did he make a more ominous connection: Those bright stars were the suns of the union that was rapidly turning into a ruthless empire. In the Green Holy Days, his cathedral's intended spire would point directly toward the Faxen Union.

Edvard felt cold. In his chest he felt an unaccustomed pain. It wasn't physical. It was emotional, and almost unbearable. It was his heart breaking.

24

GREEN HOLY DAYS

What just happened? Nia felt as though another one of the unwelcome cold thick waves of irrational fear had passed by—leaving her unsteady, shaken and disoriented—but she didn't remember it happening. As the ice catamaran accelerated toward Denevez, the cold air helped her focus on the here and now. Her bracelet had signaled a development in her case in the Hall of Law, but not what that development was, whether good or bad.

Well, she had time to deal with it today. She checked the catamaran's chronometer. *What?* She frowned. In the chapel, she'd had an interesting theological conversation with Edvard, and Edvard had made his change of heart about her long-ago actions on Moira clear. Remembering that warmed her from the inside.

But surely their conversation hadn't lasted long enough for the chronometer to be showing the time it was. Losing time was not a good sign. Maybe she wasn't in the best of shape. She missed Martan's steady support, his perfect watchfulness of their surroundings, his being here on Azure. With luck he'd be back soon. Not that luck was guaranteed. Her hand went to touch the cool Christa Terra medal in her pocket.

At the Hall of Law, she learned that Kron Derriger had filed a motion to revoke Val's Azurean citizenship, on the grounds of Val being accused of sabotage of a Tellan research installation, conspiracy to deprive the Faxen Union of advancements in research obtained in said installation, and disunion terrorism. Evidently, the scheme to have his separated wife inherit his intellectual property against his wishes hadn't been called off just because Val was alive. Swiftly reading the fine print, Nia saw that there was an extradition demand too. Tellas, the other Union worlds, and in addition, Azure, were asked to extradite him to Faxe to face the serious charges leveled against him.

Val had given up his Albion citizenship to become a citizen of Azure. If that was revoked, he'd be a stateless person. He'd be easy to legally extradite, or illegally make disappear.

The soft gloves had shredded off this matter to reveal a fist gloved in chain mail. It was no longer possible to make it look like a family feud. Kron Derriger was flying high on prosecuting an enemy of the Union. The good news was the Faxen authorities weren't sure where Val was. The even better news was that this matter had landed squarely in Nia's own territory: interstellar law as it related to academic researchers. Anger helped her focus as she filed a countermove just before the courts closed for the day.

There was no news about a bubble that could give her a decisive tool to use. Fortunately, the religious holiday here, when presumably no such holiday was happening on Almaaz, would buy her time. It was a long and involved holiday, too, with four days which brought all routine business to a standstill.

At sunset, she found herself in Denevez with no more legal moves to make. The holy days began where the starship from Earth first touched Azure. She set out for Memorial Park under a twilight sky filling with stars.

She looked back over her shoulder at the tower called Denevez One, the seat of law and government. The Hall of Law took up the wide first level of Denevez One, as though civilization were built on law. As indeed it was. Was anyone, anywhere, still saying that law and specific laws were given by God? Some fringe faiths might believe that. But Catholic Orthodoxy was clear: Law was the creation of humanity: imperfect at best, corrupted at worst. It was her vocation to improve the imperfection, and to oppose the corruption, so that interstellar civilization had a better foundation. She would not have wanted any other life's work.

As night fell, the wind from the sea became chillier by the minute. But an increasingly large crowd gathered around the Memorial. Edvard was there—approximately a hundred people away—but it was one of his deacons who led a service of solemn utterances and responses. She knew how it unfolded and didn't pay close attention with her distracted mind. When the processional to the cathedral started, an unexpected person fell into step with her. "That was a highly meaningful rite," commented the ambassador from Goya, Darko Thuler.

His coat was no heavier than that worn by everyone else, most of whom were eager for the geothermal heat of the cathedral, but Darko looked comfortable, with his coat collar open. She asked, "You don't find the weather here cold?"

"I'm from Thule," he smiled. "The arctic end of the Goyan Archipelagoes."

She should have guessed that from his surname, Thuler.

"My fellow diplomats from the balmy regions of the Archipelagoes find Azure objectionably chilly. I love being here."

Glad he felt that way, she herself appreciated the warmth in the cathedral when the procession entered it. Adriance Vale led this service, with a thoughtful homily and finally the ritual meal. Nia explained the ritual for the interested Darko. "Ah," he said. "Food is not taken for granted on this side of the stars."

"Nor should it ever have been taken for granted on Earth," she answered. He inclined his head in agreement.

When she took a scrap of flatbread from Adriance's hand, the woman priest looked glad to see Nia and whispered a surprisingly elaborate blessing. It made her feel truly blessed.

Irony was piled on irony here. For long years, she hadn't felt safe in the places of worship of her faith. Last year when Lila Tsuda on one single occasion dragged her to the only Cathor church in Wendis, the service, which had been an innocuous Avensong, scorched her nerves. But now she felt safer than she had all day, what with that unremembered cold wave this morning and the adversarial business in the Hall of Law. It still troubled her that on a deep level she felt as though she were made of shattered pieces only staying together because their jagged edges caught each other. Yet here felt like a safe place to be that way. For which she thanked Christa.

The next day, she had a great deal of legal research to do. Thanks to a remote connection to the law school library, and the small, specific law library she'd brought with her from Wendis in a data pod, she could do it at Castle Courant.

Her concentration was poor. There was still that sense of being shattered inside and only tenuously holding together. She got the legal work done anyway. Then she went to the church in Arrival, where her concentration was no better, but it mattered less.

This was the service in which the readings and prayers recounted the suffering and death of Earth. You were not supposed to feel happy. Therefore, most of Denevez would stay away from the cathedral tonight, and it would be a vast echoing space. The Arrival church wasn't full either, but it was more compact and human-sized. More like the church in Wendis, which Nia had been attending in recent weeks. Adriance, leading the service, seemed so kind and sure of herself that Nia was glad to be here.

On the third day of the holiday Nia did legal work into the early evening. Then she made her way to the cathedral. Delegates to the ecumenical council joined the worship, with Edvard's official approval and welcome. The ecumenical delegates actually seemed more reverent and interested than some of the local people. That probably made religious sense.

In the darkened cathedral, with chandeliers dimmed, everyone heard the history of the Star Age. Earth's minerals, and especially oil, had been wastefully extracted and used up. Earth's climate was wrecked by corruption and boundless greed. Efforts to terraform Mars ended in failure: Mars was too far from the sun, too cold, and without a magnetic field, too unprotected from radiation.

Martan liked to be called Martan, because it was similar to his real name from childhood, but since it was the third part of the name he used now, it could be taken for a family name, and sounded like he must be one of the irradiated, gene-changed descendants of the colonists who gave up on Mars. That concern was unfounded. He was genetically Earth-standard, as was all-important to Azurean society.

Nia hoped Martan, Val, and Lane were all somewhere safe. They probably were if Val had used his gate magic to get to Stannto, where he and Lane had friends. Martan could make his own way from Tellas to anywhere. But if home for him could be here, and she hoped that it was or would be, she wanted him to come home safe and soon.

The solemn history continued. *This* night commemorated the almost endless night of crossing the stars below the speed of light. For those slow starships, the journey took hundreds of years, with everyone and every seed and animal embryo in suspended animation more like death than life. The starships crossed to another arm of the Galaxy, richer in stars and planets. Then began the tremendous work of terraforming. On Goya, terraforming almost failed. The unexpected arrival of the first of all the starships ever sent from Earth, brought resources and knowledge enough to help the Goyans pull their world through to stable terraforming.

Darko, sitting beside her, whispered his appreciation for Goya's part of the story being recalled tonight.

Azure, along with Albion, and then Tellas, had benefited from all that had been heroically learned on Goya. On Azure, thousands of years of terraforming warmed the air, melted the ice, laid green bands of snow forest across the lowlands, and greened the seas with diatoms and kelp.

The chandeliers brightened. The organ emitted a series of plain, pure notes. It wasn't finished yet, but at least it could make a few distinct notes.

Edvard spoke briefly, and made it plain: On Goya, then on Azure, on Agraria—Faxe's farm world—and on Tellus, Albion, and Estrella, Christa was resurrected, giving life itself to all the humans and animals and plants in those places. It surprised Nia that he mentioned Estrella, the Union's poor tail-end world. But it was true. Christa was resurrected also in Wendis with intricately recreated ecosystems. Mentioning Wendis was new too, but altogether fitting.

What it all meant was the reconciliation of God with humankind.

The service ended with joy. Jubilant celebration followed, with desserts and sparkling water and wine. An Old Cathor metropolitan who worked with Olav Zakeri introduced herself to tell Nia, "Olav wishes he could have come."

"Maybe next year, God willing!" Nia replied.

"May peace in our time let it be so!" Metropolitan Undine said fervently.

In joy at all of it, Nia joined her family in the ice catamaran to go home. They didn't mind a detour by Arrival to drop off a couple of dozen Arrivaltowners. Arrival was strung with colored lights. Tomorrow was a festival day which, although it started in church or cathedral, would go on to be full of family, friends, and good food and drink.

A lightheartedness had come over Nia. Edvard put an arm around her, and they stood together on the deck of the catamaran, going home again almost as though for the first time.

Greening Day sermons tended to be hopeful and uplifting, and possibly forgettable. Nia knew Edvard had been having unusual trouble writing his. She had no idea what he'd come up with.

In subdued midmorning light under high gray clouds, the cathedral's great doors stood open. Its interior was adorned with fragrant evergreen boughs. Its ring of floor-to-ceiling windows showed a panorama of distant, sun-glazed mountains with snow forests like rumpled rugs on their feet; the iceberg-studded expanse of the sea; the cloud-gray sky; and on the south wall, the cathedral's garden greenhouse, full of greens and golds and touches of red ripe fruit.

High in the east wall, set into the dome higher than the ring of windows, the Christa Terra window glowed blue, green, white, and brown. Terra's continents slowly moved under the terminator between night and day. They were the ancient greener continents from before the seas rose. The lands were those of prehistory, before human-caused desertification.

Choirs sang. The congregation sang in response. The organ added a few notes as though it were singing along with everyone else. The organmaster was making the most of an unfinished situation.

Edvard arose to stand behind the high lectern. He looked beautiful and authoritative. Nia remembered how usual it was for a heterosexual daughter to fall in love with her father. Which set her up for excruciating pain if they were ever estranged. With that realization, and her mind still being scattered anyway, Nia only registered some of what he said.

She tuned in to hear Edvard say, "For reconciliation with God, the Earth did not have to die. She was beautiful and generous enough to speak God's grace with every blade of grass, drop of rain, and ear of corn, if humanity simply heard that."

Beside Nia, Undine, the metropolitan from Goya, nodded. Nia had found herself folded into the midst of the ecumenical delegates, along with Darko. It felt right for her to be in their midst. She was from Azure yet she'd been shaped by the stars ever since she left home.

"The holy blood of Christa was oil. In the fevered final centuries, it was extracted and made to flow freely, burned in such quantity that it heated the atmosphere. The flesh of Christa was the soil. It was raked in exploitative agriculture, turning forest into desert. None of that should have happened. Some later philosophers said the triumphs of civilization—medicine and architecture, space travel and starships—justified the ruin of the Earth. It did not," he concluded in a ringing voice.

Nia knew that some Faxens thought the glory of Faxe justified the even longer arc of civilization, from the Ascendance, through the Terror that Terra Nova became, to the present day. A Faxen historian at her university in Wendis thought that way. *No,* she silently agreed with Edvard—not just because he was as compelling as he'd always been, but because she knew this to be true. The long and violent, stumbling, wasteful arc of history was not justified simply because Faxe glorified itself at this end of it.

She missed the next statement or two, but it registered with her when Edvard said, "Yesterday in the long night history of terraformed worlds found and terraformed, Faxe was omitted. Today I will make amends for that."

An interested stir went through the cathedral.

"The planet had a highly evolved ecosystem when it was discovered—by an exploration starship called *Adventus*—and originally named Fiat Pax. That meant *let there be peace*. Then *Adventus* journeyed on, finally to become the singular, spinning star city in our day, Wendis."

The delegates from Wendis glowed with appreciation. Nia had heard that Edvard had been closeted with the ecumenical delegates for much of the last three days. Evidently, he'd learned the history of Wendis from some of them.

"On Fiat Pax as on Terra, God was incarnate in matter, in mystery, majesty, and salvation. Fiat Pax might as well have been named Fiat Christus, *let there be Christ*." That was a new angle for Edvard to bring out. His voice rang with conviction. "From the start, the ecosystems brimming with alien life on Fiat Pax were protected from exploitation; the lands and seas were set aside as nature reserves. The nearby planet Agraria was terraformed and turned into an Earthlike breadbasket for the planetary system. Christa was resurrected there too."

Just then, the light coming in through the windows dimmed. The clouds were lowering. Nia guessed that Edvard had carefully consulted the weather forecast and timed his remarks to match it. She guessed that now, having described Christa Terra in more universal and inclusive, more inspiring terms than usual, he'd exhort his hearers not to just know about Christa, but see and serve Christa all around them, guide each other in good ways, and guard Azure from indifference and moral failure.

"Over the centuries, Fiat Pax came to be known as Faxe. And Faxe has strayed far from its calling to peace."

That—was not what she had expected. Quicker on the uptake than many of the well-fed and complacent Denevezans, the ecumenical delegates all went alert.

"Faxe became the seat of power of a union of planets, not all of which volunteered for the unification or profited from it. Faxe has now made war on Wendis. Faxe is reliably reported to be exploiting minerals under the nature reserves and coveting the minerals on other worlds. If so, then that is the violent exploitation of Christa. If Faxe or any other terraformed world has oil, to extract and exploit it for the sake of wealth is shedding the blood of Christa again."

This had become a very atypical Greening Day sermon, and by now almost everyone knew it. The attention focused on Edvard was so complete that Nia would have heard a coin dropped on the other side of the nave.

"Two nights ago, I went outside to imagine the spire planned for this cathedral and see how it would point toward the stars," Edvard said. "I couldn't do that tonight if the snow continues." Flakes of snow swirled on the other side of the windows. Azure used to be like Antarctica, that white continent at the bottom of the Earth, so dry and cold that it almost never snowed. Terraforming had changed Azure. Would Edvard now pivot to the signs of the resurrected Christa on Azure?

"But there is no need for me to look up like that."

Nia could see him well enough to realize that he wasn't enjoying this as much as usual. She saw perspiration beaded on his forehead, and tense lines beside the corners of his eyes

"God is not waiting to be found out there in the stars. As much as God beyond us is in the stars, God is already in the stardust of which we are all made, together with all the rest of the creatures and things made of matter. Our ancestors reached the stars, but the stars are not heaven. Heaven is the stardust and electrical sparks within our bodies and brains. And the sparkling plant life of Faxe too. There is no need for a cathedral spire to point at the stars." His voice took on a flinty edge. "Least of all, on these holiest nights, does this cathedral need to point toward the Astronaut."

"Astronaut?" Darko's whisper was puzzled.

"That constellation is the stars of the Faxen Union," Nia breathed. She was lightheaded with surprise. Edvard's symbolism would be blazingly obvious to people hearing about it anywhere from here to Goya, Wendis, and Faxe. And thanks to the presence of the ecumenical delegates, it would soon be heard about in all those places.

With a catch in his voice, Edvard said, "There is no need for a future spire. The future is now. The Cathedral of Saint Bonaventure is complete. It joins the fellowship of monumental and enduring places of worship across the stars, back through history, and into the future. It is finished."

25

ROAD TO HELL

Martan took a walk into the dry hills east of the university. He made it look casual. Pretending to be a university researcher, he mentioned wanting to see more of the landscape before his research ended and he returned home. In reality, Martan had a laserlike purpose.

Not far from the stargate, Val and Lane were camping along with Gerry and his family. Martan had done intelligence modeling using the computer resources of Val's department. The intel model indicated that Gerry, his wife, his daughter, and his small son might be used by SECINTAG to apply pressure to Val. Gerry could be arrested. His innocent family members could be kidnapped by Telal operatives. Martan didn't want those risks. Neither did Val. When Val had to run for it, Gerry and his family would go with him. The first goal was to visit their old friend Jack on Stannto.

Gerry's son, too young to know anything about dire concerns, was happy to be camping, playing with rocks and trickles of water, and meeting interesting people. The campers included one of the war reenactors who'd found Val weeks ago.

Martan asked Val, "He's still determined to go?" Martan had a professional reluctance to count on unseasoned civilians joining a dangerous operation.

Val answered, "Donalt was there when the gate first opened, and he found me. He's Tellan and takes some ownership of the halo gate being here. He knows what could happen if the Dhal demons came through and threatened the university." Val looked up into the sky, seeming to see past it and out into the stars with his mind's eye. "I have reason to believe that exposure to a gate like that can imprint a young person with a determination to experience it. The gate may be pulling him."

Donalt was directing people to stand in different places. They all looked expectant. Martan was glad to recognize two of them, who were not unseasoned civilians. One female and one male, they looked Goyan and young enough to be university students. Martan asked Val, "How are those exchange students working out?"

"They sang the tune you told me to expect. You said your friend the starship captain knows how to find hellraisers who are value-added in a fight. These two do match that description! They're handy with weapons, familiar with several different fighting styles, and quick to obey orders. We're pretending a summer fight school." He pointed to a pile of dummy weapons. Any real weaponry was not in plain sight. "Nobody here but us wargamers," Val said with a glint in his eye.

Good idea, Martan thought, to vet the volunteers before folding them into an interstellar war party. "If things take a turn for the worse, I'll come back to warn you."

"You could call." Val pointed to a portable netnode on a table.

"I need to see the gate working, so I know what I'm looking at in the end."

"Fair enough. Tonight, you'll find us sheltering in the fissure in front of the gate." Val pointed to the wide deep crack in the cliff. Beyond it, on the horizon, dark gray clouds were building up. "That storm system is heading this way."

"A storm could help you cover your tracks, electronic and otherwise," Martan said. "Just be ready."

He went back downhill and finished his day. He had certain arrangements to complete. That involved erasing traces of his intelligence modeling and overwriting the last electronic and physical traces of the bagged hellhound's presence here with his own. Finally, he returned to the hospital morgue one last time.

Officially and to all appearances, Gyle Night Martan had returned to Wendis a few days ago. Creating that impression had involved an obvious trip to the transit tower, secretly doubling back, and returning to the university, where he assumed the identity of the bagged hellhound, moving into the temporary university housing unit where the latter had stayed. To cover up the days the hellhound had been in the body bag, he invented taking a field trip to the interior of the continent and back to a pursue hobby: Martan told a few people that he was an amateur geologist. A rockhound.

Nobody had noticed that his appearance was somewhat different from a few days ago. Either they didn't look past his brown skin and dark hair, or the hellhound hadn't socialized enough to make much of an impression on anyone. Martan's generation of hellhounds had been lone agents, but not lone wolves. He'd been trained in etiquette and small talk.

When Martan had gleaned the last useful traces from the all-but-dead hellhound's wrecked mind, he made eye contact with Kam Far, and nodded. Kam dialed the body bag's life support system off. Kam had figured out how to send the body to a cremation facility, forging paperwork that purported to be the wishes of the family of the deceased. The pretense wouldn't hold up under much scrutiny. It probably wouldn't attract much scrutiny either. But even if the ruse was exposed, putting Kam into serious professional trouble, it wasn't going to matter. Kam picked up a backpack he'd tucked away in a corner and headed for the dry hills with a spring in his step.

Before now, Martan had hardly ever heard of the Sleighters. He'd never conspired with any of them, or against any of them. The secret intelligence agency categorized them as a powerless and apolitical underclass ranked very low in the scale of threats to the Faxen Union. Martan and Val intended for SECINTAG to learn better in the most consequential way imaginable.

An invasion of Dhal demons was exactly what Varry deserved. The hellhound training inside Varry now took away the names of the new hellhounds, and then took away their souls. Martan had sifted the remains of the all-but-dead hellhound's memory looking for his real name. The name he found, Nome, was meaningless, although unique. There was only one hellhound named Nome. Whatever Nome's name had been before they turned him into a hellhound, it had been obliterated.

Martan remembered his own childhood name. He'd been Mikal-Martin. *Martan* sounded enough like it to feel right. Today, he secretly cherished his own name more than he ever had before.

The storm broke in the early evening.

Martan loped uphill with rain streaming off his rain jacket. Lightning flashed above him. Thunder crashed.

The campers had retreated into the fissure but not gone to sleep. Martan told them all, "There's an arrest warrant for Val as an enemy of the Union. Gerry is wanted as Val's confederate. Both of you will be extradited to Faxe if you're caught. Get the hell out of here."

People were already throwing on backpacks and gathering up lanterns and camp stoves, with Gerry's daughter scooping up her little brother. It was a well-planned departure. A fraction of Martan's attention approved of that.

The dummy weapons were thrown into a crevasse, one not too damningly nearby, by Donalt, who soon came back soaked to the skin. Everybody lined up, carrying backpacks and bags—and real weapons. The only problem registered by Martan's heightened senses was the war party being packed into a dead end, a cave that went nowhere. That made Martan's skin crawl. He approached the back of the cave. "It's here?"

Val indicated the dimensions of the gate by gesturing at the rock wall.

"Let me try something." Martan placed his hands on the rock where the gate was supposed to be. Both of his hands had neonerves, sensitive to ephemeral electrical impulses in the human nervous system. He could read minds with his hands. Could he read a machine buried behind a façade of rock? Unlikely, but he had nothing to lose by trying. Val had said that the entire halo gate system was the mind of the artificial intelligence called Vere.

Val caught on to what he was trying and watched with keen interest.

Martan's fingertips picked up a signal. It was vanishingly faint, but it had some kind of structure, not the mindless fizz of a mechanical circuit. "I can feel it." He stepped back.

"Something you might recognize elsewhere?"

"No two ways about that. Yes."

With Lane standing behind him, touching his shoulders, Val Savre placed both hands on the rough rock of the back wall of the cave.

Then Martan felt something he had no words for, a sensation like hearing powerful gears twist and turn, registered not on his ears, but on his entire nervous system. It made the hair on the nape of his neck stand up.

In front of Val the rough, hard rock became air full of bands of colored light. Behind the lights lay a long dim passage that very clearly went somewhere. Even knowing to expect it, the sight of it astounded Martan.

Evidently the war party had been prepared for what they'd see. Their eyes were wide, but no one flinched. Some of them even quivered with eagerness. The eager ones included Kam, Val, and Lane. They were looking toward some kind of heaven: for Val, his home and friends on Stannto. For Lane, the Vere mystery that had designed her genes and allured her all her life. For Kam, the extremes of adventure that his people loved.

Val turned toward Martan. "Last chance to take an easier road than what you have planned. Come with us, and we can figure out another way."

Martan shook his head. Not for him the gate to some kind of heaven. More like the road to hell. He ran back downhill with rain washing away his tracks.

He'd done his own packing earlier. He snatched up his luggage, checked out of the university temporary housing room, and caught the monorail to the transit tower. It was a quick ride, in which he attracted no particular attention. *Nobody here but a visiting scholar leaving for home.*

The space elevator took him up, along with the other passengers, riding in an inertia-stabilized cabin. A real view out would have been disorienting, brimming with too much disconcerting motion because the ride was so very, very fast, with the cabin constantly rotating to simulate a consistent sense of gravity. The view window was a computer screen with a synthetic representation of the limb of the planet and the starfield. Even so, Martan felt real relief to not be trapped at the bottom of a gravity well any longer.

Granted there were nice gravity wells in the universe, one of them being Azure, home to the silver-haired love of his life. She was in for an interesting legal challenge and probably finding out about it just about now. He knew she could handle it. He only hoped that he would survive the road ahead of him and end up alive enough, sane enough, and free enough, to hear about it from her.

She and her icy home world were at a star beyond the dark side of the planet. *That star. There.* In the vacuum of space, Azure's star looked bright and close. He could easily reach it, obtaining passage on one or more starships going that way. That was a far greater temptation to him than walking into Val Savre's iridescent stargate.

No, he told himself. Not with what Val intended to do with his war party. Martan had to do his own part even if he died trying, although he didn't relish that prospect. He had everything to live for—life itself, love, and even the icy planet that had started to feel like home to him.

Faxe's Grand Union Station was the center of the vast interstellar web of trade, travel, and planetary exploitation. When the commercial starliner brought him there, Martan wrapped his impersonation of Nome tighter around himself. He'd been here once before on a counterterrorism mission, and traveled through here twice in his role as proctor of Avendis University in Wendis, but this time the stakes were exponentially higher. This was the most risky impersonation of his life.

Union Station had plenty of unmarked doors. Like transportation hubs anywhere, no markings meant whoever didn't know what the door was for, wasn't welcome. Most such doors had a lock or a palm plate to prevent the public from wandering in. This one was no exception. But this palm plate was sensitive to the neonerves in a hellhound's hand: a unique physiology shared by no other humans.

For a moment he just stared at the door. Hellhounds didn't

have unique biometrics. Their biometrics could be altered depending on the mission. They didn't have impersonators either. Until now. He hoped to God they hadn't added a new level of identification since his day. He hadn't found that in the Nome's memory. But it could have been a detail that got lost in the general wreckage. With his nerves taut, spring-loaded for a perilous escape if another level of identification existed, a query to which he'd have no acceptable response, Martan touched the plate.

It admitted him into the secret level of Union Station controlled by the secret intelligence agency.

Martan remembered meeting his handler here before, being praised for succeeding in his mission and rewarded with a lavish meal, while other agents and hellhounds attended to their own business. This time it was almost deserted, except for a few people who worked in offices and looked like nothing more special than bureaucrats.

He was supposed to report to Nome's handler. So he did.

The man didn't even ask why he looked somewhat different from Nome. Martan had a good explanation: cosmetic alteration the better to complete the mission. He reported that, instead of interrogating the target, he'd identified allies and a plot, and let the target escape, knowing he had information that could expose a whole network of conspiracy. The part about a conspiracy happened to be true—just not true in the details he had concocted. Martan regulated his respiration and pulse, lest sensors detect that he was lying and desperately hoping not to be asked to prove too much too soon.

Nome's handler looked satisfied and told him to expect a complete debrief at Varry with the Senior Control Agent. Martan slid the unused explanation about his altered appearance back into a pocket in his mind.

Debrief at Varry after a mission was standard operating procedure now. He'd discovered that in Nome's memory. That was what this whole plan hung on. Otherwise he'd have had to improvise a way to get to Varry. But no, the plan hadn't changed.

So he reported to the dark shuttle.

This shuttle would take him and anything or anyone else who needed to get from Union Station to Varry, and it would do so invisibly, not apparent on any of the ship-tracking equipment elsewhere in the bustling station. It wouldn't appear on the charts and viewscreens of any other traffic, even though they would have been interested, or depending on its proximity, alarmed, to know about it. The dark shuttle's star route would weave across the loom of traffic without being seen.

He reached his assigned seat in a private compartment. He found a packaged meal waiting for him, hot food and chilled drink. In all of that, he registered his significance. As Nome, he had reported intelligence that SECINTAG wanted on the highest level. The intel analysts at Varry would deconstruct his story down to the atoms. If they got the chance.

As he shuttled darkly across the stars, Martan analyzed what had happened in the secret annex under Union Station. The annex had been less like the invisible hotbed of intrigue that it had once been, more like a characterless outpost of bureaucracy. That had been a poor excuse for a handler too. The bureaucrat had even called himself Nome's *control agent*. A bureaucratic synonym for handler.

Some fragments from Nome's mind fell together in Martan's awareness.

SECINTAG had centralized its operations since Martan's day. The brains of SECINTAG were at Varry. Nome's real handler was a high-level operative, relative to whom the bureaucrat in the annex was just a functionary.

In other words, the power-hungry factions of SECINTAG had seized control and centralized it in Varry. So much the better for the plans he'd made with Val.

He had a small viz window. What it showed him was generated by a computer and could have been a lie as easily as not. But he felt it when the dark shuttle finally flicked into realspace and stayed there. The window showed him Varry, visibly spinning, otherwise with nothing to reveal the structures and intrigues concealed inside it. He wrapped his impersonation tightly around himself so no light would show: no glimmer of the truth that he still had a name and a purpose other than to be a deadly tool wielded by SECINTAG.

26

OPERATION INROAD

On the other side of the halo gate, the long beam-carved passageway stretched long and silent. It was pentagonal, with the strip of light on the ceiling brightening in front of them, dimming behind them. Val breathed the cold still air deeply and led the way. Beside him walked Donalt the wargamer. Tense but resolute, Donalt had his bow and arrows. Val held a spear with a razor-sharp blade, and he was glad to have that weapon.

They were inside the cliff behind the fissure. They wouldn't remain here for long.

They reached a doorway, where the air in the passageway darkened for no apparent reason. Val led them all through the doorway. On the other side of it, the gravity suddenly changed. It became less. Even if someone expected that, it was easy to stumble. The Pastfinders seemed to have better variable gravity reflexes than most people, and barely broke their stride. They went by the names Loki and Kali, and were from the Goyan outsystem, so they had native familiarity with moonbases and spinning stations. They carried beam rifles. Now that he knew what they could do, Val was damned glad to have them. He put them at the rear of the war party, and told them to keep a sharp lookout for anything coming up behind them. He told Donalt to watch out for anything ahead and keep his bow ready. The civilians—Gerry's family and Kam Far—were safer in the middle of the party.

They'd reached the Tellas moon, which was honeycombed with passages unknown to human colonists. This sector of it had once been dark and in disrepair. But for years, Val had been busy repairing the Vere system, with help from Sleighters and Verians. Now the passageways in this sector were well lit and marked where Val had drawn directional signs.

He was very glad that he could clearly remember having drawn those signs. So far, his recovered memory had stayed recovered. He hoped it would last.

Halfway home, one of the Pastfinders in the rear shouted, "I saw one!"

Val shouldered his way back to the Pastfinders. "What did it look like?"

"Humanoid but it moved wrong. It stared at us. It's in there." Loki pointed to a darker passage, leading somewhere Val hadn't done repair work yet. Val's nose caught the acrid-sweet smell. Not enough smell to amount to more than a demon scout or maybe two. He stepped between the Pastfinders and the lurking Dhal demons. "Look at me!" he shouted. "Your queen ordered me killed. But I'm alive!"

The response was a long harsh hiss.

That was the last sign of demons before they reached the friendly territory near the Stannto doorway and gate. Two at a time, with Lane going first with him, Val led everyone through the doorway to Stannto. Everyone except the Pastfinders missed a step in the distinct change of gravity—suddenly more than in the moon, but less than on Tellas. Val sent them all ahead of him through the Stannto gate, where he saw a welcoming committee of friends waiting on the other side of the curtains of light. Val and Lane went through the gate last, holding hands.

His friends erupted in cheers when he came out of the gate.

"Val!" His old friend, Mayor, spread his muscular arms wide. "We got word you'd be coming! You're alive!"

"Alive!" cried Jack Gi. "And Lane with you! And—Gerry!" Jack swept his old friend Gerry and Gerry's family into a hug.

Spark, the fierce girl who'd picked Val up when he was dying in Hades, crowded close to him. She shyly stroked his arm. "You're alive. You're warm. Who are these?"

He told her, "Some are innocents who needed to get away from Tellas, and others are fighters who kept us safe getting here. And now I intend to recruit more volunteers for another fight."

"That too we heard about," said Mayor. "A Sleighter in the free trade ring at Tellas sent word telling us to expect you, and that you have a grand sleight planned. And that the timing of it is critical."

Val was glad that Emir had done his part. "Jack, do you still keep a galactic timepiece?"

Jack nodded over the heads of Gerry's wife and children.

Still wanting to touch him and hug Val—obviously his death had caused bitter grief for them, which touched him—his friends pulled him into the park under the dome of Stannto, sweeping his war party along with them. Mayor fell in step with him. "Can you clue us in to your plan for a grand sleight that involves a fight?"

"I want revenge for the Dhal demons killing me. And to use them to terrorize a place that needs it."

"What would that be?"

Everyone in earshot stared at him. "The capital tower of Faxe?" someone asked doubtfully.

"Moira?" someone else asked, but another Sleighter said,

"That is not the cesspool it used to be. A bishop cleaned it right up."

At his side, Spark said, "I don't care where, I'm coming with you."

A more astute guesser than the rest of them asked, "Could there be a demon gate on that farm world of Faxe, Grange?"

"There are no halo gates in Grange!" Lane said sharply. "And Grange doesn't need Dhal demons!"

Val said, "With your permission, Mayor, let me call a meeting tomorrow evening. A council of war. I'll explain everything then."

Home was this small, airy house, on a narrow road that wound between houses and irregular plots of vegetation and drainage ditches full of plant life, under the shiny blue sky of the Stannto dome. Home was Lane with him in this house. Most of all, home was the two of them and Dikk.

Val and Lane held each other and Dikk for a long time. Dikk was bigger than Val remembered. Small children grew up so quickly. Dikk's face was more expressive, but his manner was still dreamy and always would be. Their Verian child. Their impossible child. Crypto-Verians couldn't mate with normal humans and have children. But Lane and Val had done just that.

Vere, the intelligence of the Vere system, had telekinesis subtle and accurate enough to design the viral vector that changed a human population in heritable ways. And Vere had been able to make Dikk happen by rearranging the DNA strands of inheritance, undoing some of the same changes designed to control and limit the hereditability of the Vere vector in a human population. Vere had done it in response to Val having a vivid dream about being a paleolithic man who journeyed to the top of a mountain to ask a star god for a child with his mate from a different human race who could never interbreed with his people.

Val believed that the paleolithic dreams came from his racial memory, and that by means of the dreams Vere had learned much about mankind. Val still could hardly believe that he'd dreamed about asking a star god for a mate. That it had been answered meant more than he could easily imagine. It also suggested basic courtesy that was highly applicable now.

As they ate the dinner that Jack and Jill had sent them home with, Val said, "I'll have to ask Vere's permission for this war party of mine. Somehow I know where to go. I don't know what reception I'll get from him or if I can find him at all, though."

"You will and it's right to ask," Lane said. She sounded sure.

Val went alone. It wasn't far from the Stannto gate, in the safest, cleanest sector of the Vere system. Somehow, he knew to stop in front of a familiar piece of wall, which immediately turned invisible. It was a hologram. He walked through it, and then down a passageway that he had never seen in his waking life, and yet remembered. It brought him to an unusual intersection of tunnels.

Five passageways met in this singular intersection. It held a long low wide bench, designed for sturdy Meridian legs, in front of a low console containing pentagonal surfaces that were blank, now. They had surely been full of informative light eons ago. This was where the Meridian scientists and cybernetic engineers had brought Vere to consciousness, artificial intelligence that Vere was, in this control room within the Tellas moon.

This was where he'd been that night years ago when he sleepwalked into a dream about asking a star god for a child. It wasn't far from the old spaceship where he and Lane had been sheltering that night, five years ago. She'd woken up and seen him gone, gone looking for him, found him in a tunnel, and wondered why his clothes were icy cold.

Years later, this was where Vere had brought Val back to life. He'd lain on that bench, cocooned in a thick blanket of possibly alien origin. The blanket was still folded on the bench. It was very cold here, close to the cryogenics that maintained the optimal conditions for the electrical activity in the mind of Vere. Presumably the cryogenic equipment was self-repairing, but Val made a mental note to find an expert in that area to do an assessment of the ancient machinery, just in case it needed a tune-up.

Val wore his warmest coat, gloves, and hat. He still found it damned cold in here. Carefully because of his cold-stiffened fingers, he took out of an inner pocket a compact data reader. Inside the reader was a data cube of gigantic capacity. The data reader, loaded with the cube, had spent the last few days inside a wrapper that made it look like ordinary camping food. In truth it was food for thought. At least Val hoped so.

Into the utter stillness, Val said, "I've brought you all the data from the computer model of your system that I've had running for years. Into the model itself I recently introduced a deliberate error. If any of my enemies manage to view the model or copy or steal it, it won't be accurate. This is." His voice echoed. He wondered if he was just talking to himself. "It belongs to you." He placed the data recorder on the console.

The data would be of no use without massive computational power. Which the star man had, or more to the point, which the Vere intelligence *was*.

The man-shaped darkness full of stars didn't so much arrive as materialize in front of Val. The star man was Vere's simulacrum, a three-dimensional visualization. Knowing that to be the nature of it didn't make it any less awesome. Or Val less cold. He reached out for the blanket, wrapping it around himself.

With a hand full of stars, the star man pointed from the reader to one of the flat pentagons. Val placed the data recorder there. The recorder's play light came on. The star man's telekinesis was evidently more deft than his fingers. His arms were well defined. After all, he'd been able to carry Val bodily. His fingers were still blurry. No matter. He was playing the data. The light indicated play at ten times normal speed.

Val said, "I can't stay until you've played the whole recording; it's too cold for me here, but I hope that you understand it. Now I want to tell you what I hope to do and why. I have a plan that involves you closely. It may help you too. Do I need to be asleep, dreaming, for something I plan to be made known to you?"

The star man shook his head.

Val suddenly felt tongue-tied. Several years ago, he'd dreamed about encountering a star god. The dream might not have been far off the truth. This was a cohesive artificial intelligence, eons old, that had changed a strain of humans with an exquisitely designed viral vector. That had given him a child with Lane, and that had brought Val himself back to life from the dead. This was the closest thing to a god that Val could imagine. For all intents and purposes, this was a god. Val made himself say, "I propose to rid you of many of the Dhal demons by attracting them to a human place that deserves an invasion of them." He added, "Only with your permission." Then he explained the plan he'd devised with Martan, visualizing everything he said. Then he asked, "May I do this, Lord Vere?" That honorific sounded right under the circumstances.

Slowly, the star man nodded.

Part of his mind, in a panic, asked, *Will I trust this sentient alien AI to let us play out this wildly dangerous game inside its realm?*

Another part of his mind answered, *I might as well, because carelessly trusting my own kind means certain betrayal and death.*

And he knew that the star man heard both sides of that internal debate.

When he returned home, Lane embraced him and wrapped their warmest blanket around them both. After a while he stopped shivering. He asked her, "Are you going to ask me how it went?"

"I think I know." She showed him a picture that Dikk had drawn while he was away this time. It was unmistakably the star man. His face, like his fingers, had always seemed to lack fine motor control. Val had never seen any expression on the star man's face. But Dikk had drawn the star man smiling.

The room under Mayor's surplus and salvage store was electrified with excitement. The urgent bubble from Emir, clandestinely funded by Timm Far, that alerted the Sleighters to his arrival, hadn't spilled any secrets, but had made it clear enough that Val needed help with a fight. Most of the Sleighter fighters Val knew well in Stannto were here, along with two who had moved to Stannto after the joint demon chase that got Val killed. All of them were on the edges of whatever chairs, stools, or shelves they were sitting on as they listened in suspense to what he had to say.

With Lane beside him, and Dikk in his arms—Dikk wasn't articulate enough to spill secrets—Val said, "I mean to rid Vere of a good many Dhal demons by luring them where they'll do the most good. I'll say exactly where, once I decide who's in. This will be deadly dangerous. I mean to be in most danger of all, though I don't intend to be killed this time. If you can't put yourself in overwhelming danger, just step out. You're warmly welcome to stay on Stannto." He looked at Donalt. Shaking his head, Donalt stayed put.

Four Sleighters silently left the room. Another one bowed himself out, saying, "My father is dying."

"Tend your father," Mayor said. But when the man had left, Mayor said, "Pity. He's our best technologist."

"No he's not. I am," said the man named Enghel, who had not stood up to leave.

Val looked Enghel in the eye. "I was under the impression that you don't fight demons, lest one of them take the shape of your brother who died on Dhal."

The Dhal demons were shape-shifters. They liked to take human shapes, especially the shapes of young human victims after they ate them.

Enghel said, "You faced a demon queen with a human face and she had you killed and yet you're back. It's time for me to face the demons."

Mayor, grim-faced, nodded a fraction of an inch. Val took that to mean approval with major reservations. "You're in. And Vere is in too. I mean the artificial intelligence that the system of gates and doorways, chases and electronics comprises. I've been repairing the system for years now and in so doing, repairing his very being. He brought me back to life after I died fighting the demons. This morning, I told him of my plan. He agreed to it. I hope it may be something like an exorcism for him. I don't know how he will help us, but I think he will."

Interest rippled through the war party. Spark's eyes shone. "The star man!"

"Yes," said Val. "Now, my plan is to lead the demons to, and through, a gate into the lesser Faxen moon, Veritas. Which is the headquarters of the Faxen secret intelligence agency."

A gasp rippled across the room.

"SECINTAG!" Enghel's voice dripped with scorn. "Prying more and more boldly into the free trade rings, interfering with my business, and lately putting a bounty on my head. Anything to cripple SECINTAG is a boon to the universe!"

"Agreed! Let me mention that if all goes well, we'll have a very capable ally inside Veritas. He intends to lay groundwork for this. And he has more than enough incentive to do so."

Mayor said, "The idea is the demons will chase you to Veritas?"

"He taunted them on the way here," said Kam Far.

"We'd rather be the ones chasing *them*," Mayor said.

"You will be." Val looked them over. His seven fighters included Donalt, Spark, and the two Pastfinders, the Sleighter named Gauriz, and Mayor, plus Enghel. They all had the qualities he most wanted to see: intelligence, experience, dexterity, and motivation. "We don't have enough force to fight a horde of demons, but I think we can herd them, if I open and close the right gates. I'm going to call it Operation Inroad," he added.

"Does the secret intelligence agency know you open and close stargates?" Spark asked.

"Not yet. But they eventually will. I have a lawyer who's good at legal smoke and mirrors to keep SECINTAG away from me for a while." He thought about Nia, on Azure, summoning up all of her intelligence and consummate skill on his behalf.

If she could pull off legal work to save his hide, and protect his personal and intellectual secrets from the secret intelligence agency, it would be a miracle, he thought ruefully. Or—it would be a *sleight*. A sleight of the first order of magnitude. Like him, she hadn't been born a Sleighter, but turned into one, complete with scars.

He was glad and immensely proud to have her as one of his family.

27

LEGAL EAGLE

In the deep-set window of her bedroom in Castle Courant, the eastern sky showed the colors of dawn, yet visible stars still shone in the sky. This wasn't the future of Earth past. This was Azure, in a part of the galaxy thick with stars and planets. And she had a part to play in making the future here. Anxious anticipation felt like butterflies that fluttered inside her chest. It felt like some of the butterflies had thin metal wings, an uncomfortable sensation.

Eirene tapped on the door and entered.

"How do I look?" Nia had on the opal dress, her wedding gift from Robard and Theo. Over it she wore a thick tunic that had been expeditiously styled for her by Vidjas' own tailor. The layers of fabric would keep her warm, and an opal collar framed her throat, hopefully a becoming effect.

"You look first quality." A circle of smooth small stones dangled from Eirene's hand. In a time of stress and uncertainty, Eirene would always hold her prayer beads. "I'm sure you can succeed in court. But will I ever see my son again?"

Nia answered honestly, "I don't know. He may have to spend

years in hiding. But I intend to make sure he's free, with Christa's help."

Nodding, Eirene folded both hands around her prayer beads.

After the ferry ride, during which the sun stood low over the eastern horizon and threw the ferry's shadow halfway across the ice lake, Nia stopped by her office in her father's complex. She was sharply disappointed to have no word from Vidjas about a bubble from Almaaz. But a bubble for her had come from Tellas with the highest level of academic confidentiality. The message inside the bubble, from Timm Far, was very much to the point. *His friends on Stannto know to expect him.*

Some of the metal-winged butterflies in Nia's chest dissolved. She had options today that she couldn't have used if Val were trapped on Tellas.

The model is safe from meddling.

That was good to know. Val's monumental theoretical modeling of the halo gate system could be relevant today too. Not that she herself meant to bring it up.

I myself am in the clear so far.

Good too! Before she left Tellas, she'd generated a snowstorm of legal filings, protests, and complaints on Timm's behalf. These were calculated not only to stave off any legal proceedings against Timm, but to generate the impression that he was an unwitting and indignant player in the interstellar drama swirling around Val. That Timm had been estranged from his onetime mentor, even before Val made his first disappearance, worked in Timm's favor, making her snowstorm plausible. She wasn't the kind of lawyer who relied on excessive court filings in lieu of honest law. But she could play that game.

She remembered something Hiro always liked to tell her: A Twentieth-Century expression for a lawyer was *legal eagle*. On Azure, snow eagles were conspicuous birds who masterfully rode the tangled currents of air over the mountains. She hoped to fly in the highest currents of law today and end up with a good legal eagle story for Hiro.

Estrangement that had been notorious, with a subsequent reconciliation not so well known, had its uses, Nia thought. She'd never realized that before today, and today she was seeing it twice.

The Hall of Law was full of busy civil servants. This being the first day after the holiday, they had plenty to talk about, and that included what Edvard had said yesterday from the pulpit of St. Venture's Cathedral. Even if any of these staff recognized her today, her old estrangement from her father had been famous. It was far less well known that they had reconciled. Nobody seemed to bite their tongue in her hearing. She heard a great deal about Edvard in just the first half hour of being in the Hall of Law. What she heard wasn't uniformly approving or disapproving. A better description would have been *volatile surprise*. She suspected that the surprise was now washing from Denevez to the other side of Azure and out into the Beyond, and to the headquarters of the New Catholic Orthodox Church on Albion. God only knew what the upshot would be.

She touched the Christa Terra medal in her pocket. She settled into her intentions as firmly and closely as the heavy tunic rode on her shoulders, took a deep breath, and entered the planetary courtroom.

The courtroom had a high ceiling, a polished stone floor, and on one wall the emblem of Azure: a circle with white, blue, and green quadrants to signify ice, water, and ecosphere, plus a quadrant colored magenta for the highest of Azure's auroras. The first time she'd been here as a law student, she'd wanted to belong here, and set her sights on exactly that. Having experienced the high court in Star City in Wendis, it struck her that the seat of Azurean planetary law looked—provincial. Provincial it might well be, but it was still honest, as far as she knew.

Judge Gund had been appointed by the previous prime minister. He'd also been advisory faculty in the law school for years. His silver hair came not from his Azurean ancestry, but from age. In the vote to expel her years ago, he'd abstained. And that was after asking her in private, in his capacity as an advisor, what had happened on Moira. Then and now, he had the reputation of being a fair-minded, strict constructionist. She could have done much worse than have Gund presiding today.

She wasn't so fortunate in the character of her legal opponent. Kron Derriger was a Denevezan of similar stock to the judge, and for that matter, Taffy: descended not from the first astronauts but from the later ranks of colonists, those who had made the star journey in the passenger holds. Derriger had always carried a chip on his shoulder about it. He recognized her immediately. "Ready to play the Az and Al cards?" he asked her scornfully. He meant the astronaut lineage signified by the *Az* before her last name, and Val's Albioni astronaut ancestry that gave him the *Al* in his formal name. "That won't impress Judge Gund."

She kept a neutral face. She hadn't been able to do that when they were both law students.

Visitors filed into the courtroom to find a seat in the audience area. The visitors included law students, which was no surprise, with a law school blocks away and an unusual case in the docket. What did come as a surprise was that Vidjas Finndur entered too. Vidjas gestured Nia over and whispered, "It was stalled but I think I've pried it loose. That took until today when regular staff are on duty. The scanners took the writing on the document inside to be secretive code. It took a human to recognize it as Almaazan."

That didn't give Nia certainty, but it meant better hope than a minute ago. Nia fervently thanked Vidjas. Then she took her place to wait for the arrival of the judge, still thinking about a hoped-for bubble from Almaaz.

Famously reclusive, Almaazans did not permit their language to be studied, despite the yearnings of linguists everywhere. Almaazans kept not only their language, but their society, under tight wraps. Yet a few non-reclusive Almaazans turned up at every interstellar university. Every human place and race had its ways of throwing off misfits. Sending them to an interstellar university was not the worst way of doing that. Whether they were ordinary professional people like Val's friends Jack and Jill on Stannto, or someone with the rank of emissary like Idris, they might report back something of importance they'd learned about the outside world, including danger to Almaaz itself. Which Idris had done when Val told her about the gate on her world. Which would earn Val the reward of Almaazan citizenship, Nia hoped.

When the judge entered the courtroom from his private chambers, everyone stood up, including the prime minister of the planet. Judge Gund's glance flicked over them all. He announced, "The matter before the court today concerns the rightful citizenship of one Vienradzis Al-Savre, and in conjunction with that, the disposition of his intellectual property, in the event of his death. Whenever that happens in actuality."

Nia was all too aware that Val's death in actuality could happen at any time—and on purpose. If operatives of SECINTAG learned about his memory having a hole in it, but his intellectual property would be inherited by his separated wife on Albion and soon stolen by SECINTAG, it might be expedient to just kill him. She was glad Martan was protecting him.

Judge Gund seated himself behind his high desk. Everyone else in the courtroom took a seat too, except for Nia and

Derriger. The ritualism of this reminded Nia of the religious rituals of Cathordoxy.

Judge Gund said, "Counselors, state your names and your interest in the case." He indicated Derriger.

Derriger said, "I, Kron Derriger, represent Savre's separated wife on Albion, who wants to be assured of inheriting his intellectual property if and when his death is real. She contests any inheritance of his intellectual property by his mother, Eirene Savre, an Albion citizen who resides on Azure."

"And you, Counselor?"

Nia answered, "My name accords with my own citizenship, which is Wendisan. Let the record say that I am Nia Inanna Courant." She was intentionally keeping her Az card off the table. "I represent Val Savre."

"Mr. Derriger, what makes Azurean citizenship contestable?"

"Savre is wanted for destruction of Faxen Union government property, namely a research installation on the moon of Tellas, and in addition, he stands accused of disunion terrorism in that and subsequent acts." Derriger sat down.

"Serious matters," said the judge, in a neutral tone. "Do you have a rebuttal, Counselor?"

Nia said, "With all respect, I request that the court consider his intellectual property on its own merits apart from citizenship or inheritance."

Derriger stood up abruptly. "I object. That makes no sense."

The judge said, "The court would like to hear an explanation."

Nia took a slow, steadying breath. "Under interstellar law, there are protections for knowledge that is vital to mankind. The mistakes of Old Earth included corporatizing and privatizing knowledge. So there are articles of interstellar law that apply to this matter, ultimately being based on the ancient legal treaties that defined the floor of the sea, the continent of Antarctica, and outer space as commons of all humankind. In our day, there are treaties that name Wendis as the neutral repository of scientific knowledge of highest importance to all of humankind. Azure is a signatory to these treaties, as are Wendis and the Alliance of Starmark. The principle of the commons of knowledge was rigorously tested in the high court in Star City in Wendis, held valid, and there elaborated."

She'd submitted a detailed brief. The judge used his scanner to flip through it. He then consulted the court's AI which digested and summarized it all.

Tense, feeling those butterfly wings in her chest, she had a sense of the law being a fragile tissue across the stars. By contrast, the history and practice of law had lain thick on Old Earth. Not even that had saved the home planet from destruction wrought by humanity.

Judge Gund told her, "Describe the intellectual property in question."

She had to draw a fine and calculated line between saying too much and sounding too vague. "One part of it is the function of the ancient artifacts called halo gates, on the planet Meridian and elsewhere. Val Savre has advanced our scientific understanding of a technology that could be of both material and cautionary benefit to humankind. It fits the most stringent standards listed in the documents I reference in my statements."

In truth, Val had figured out how to use the gates like the seven-league boots of ancient Earth lore, to stride across the stars. It spectacularly met the standards of commons-of-knowledge treaties. She watched Derriger's expression. His supercilious frown hadn't changed. It didn't look as though he understood that what was at issue was stargates.

She continued, "In a related matter, Val Savre has come to understand the famous Vere vector that affected human colonists on Meridian by changing the unwitting human genome." It would have been far more accurate, but far less advisable, to state that he'd found a wild wife whose biomolecular knowledge, own identity, and telepathic dreams had opened up an unprecedented understanding of the Vere vector. "That this is, again, consequential in the terms set forth by the referenced treaties is a proposition that would be widely accepted across civilization." Not to mention, the integrity of the human genome was held to be very consequential on Azure. That could put an invisible finger on the impartial scales of law.

"Is that all?"

"Without going into technical details, yes, Your Honor, that characterizes the intellectual property in question." She wasn't going to breathe a word about Val's computational model of the halo gate system. Not unless Derriger introduced it. He might not: If he'd been fed information by a low-level SECINTAG operative on Albion, the operative might not know about the model or how consequential it was. She had the sense from Timm's bubble that something had been done for the model's safekeeping in case SECINTAG tried to get to it. She resisted the impulse to hold her breath in suspense.

Judge Gund said, "The legal precedent that you're referencing was achieved by you in your capacity as interstellar lawyer for the university in Wendis."

That surprised Derriger. His frown suddenly deepened. He might have failed to research her background as thoroughly as he should have. She hadn't counted on that, but she'd hoped for it, and helped it along by looking like a threadbare academic lawyer, until today. "That is correct, Your Honor. However, my authorship is of minor importance in this. Let me explain." She walked as she talked, until she stood in front of the emblem, knowing that the shifting color of her opal collar would complement the emblem, a subtle suggestion of power. "I was acting as an agent of the university there, and in consultation with Wendisan legal establishment, which has matchless prominence in interstellar law."

The judge nodded infinitesimally.

She sensed her own talent, skill and experience. Win or lose, she was playing interstellar law like a musical instrument. She could remember when that would have been hard. It wasn't hard now. "That case stemmed from research conducted into the geology of the planet Agraria, in the Faxen system, by a research team composed of Faxen, Wendisan, and Goyan scientists and technologists. The resulting discoveries were deemed best to consider as belonging to mankind rather than any of the institutions involved. As in what is before us today, it had to do with potentially powerful technological artifacts left by a long-gone civilization. In that way it parallels this case."

Judge Gund said, "The law stands. Unless you are prepared with a detailed rebuttal?" He looked at Derriger.

"I request a continuation," Derriger tried.

"Denied, because your unpreparedness does not constitute grounds to delay and distract this court."

Judge Gund was running true to form: an admirer of well-done law, no fan of legalistic delay and distraction.

Nia heard murmurs of surprise from the direction of the courtroom visitors.

Derriger's frown froze.

Judge Gund tapped his gavel on the top of his desk. "We will turn to the case for negation of citizenship."

To his credit, Derriger recovered. He introduced statements from personnel at the Tellas moon research station, detailing how Val's disappearance into the gate was followed by a destabilization of the mysterious wards, an explosion that damaged valuable equipment.

As Nia understood it, the station had gotten off lightly. The halo gate wards could wreak destruction on square kilometers of real estate, and would do so if any large-scale attempt was made to force a way in. What happened after Val and Lane entered the gate barely qualified as a hiccup for a halo gate. She suspected that the damaged equipment was overvalued in the statement submitted by Derriger. She could submit correcting evidence. If it mattered.

Derriger's plumage seemed to shine as he made his case. He liked doing law on behalf of the Faxen Union. If it ever came to an invasion or Faxen takeover here, he might angle for a high-level job, maybe even that of prime minister. Or he might try to go to Faxe to practice law. That would be an uncertain path to glory though. Nia knew about Faxen law from her old friend Gale-Eris. On Faxe, Derriger would be a small fish in big pond.

Derriger had depositions about Val's appearances and disappearances in the Telmoon station, including how the halo gate stopped working after the last time he appeared there.

While she was on Tellas, Val had told her that he'd turned the gate off, because SECINTAG was taking an unhealthy interest in the station. And he'd done it at the confidential request of the station's chief engineer, who was a trusted friend of his.

Derriger's deposition was too detailed to be the recollection of a random station worker. More like a SECINTAG agent on the scene. Derriger wasn't just working for Val's separated wife. He was working for the Faxen Union. If not on the payroll, he was a believer in Unionism, as he had been years ago in law school.

It was going to be hard to contradict the evidence about Val shutting down the gate. It might be necessary though. If followed to a logical conclusion, turning halo gate off might just suggest to someone that Val knew how to turn one on. She did not want things to go there. Nor did she want these proceedings to last days on end. It could end up that way.

Behind the seated visitors, two people entered through the tall doors and made a beeline to Vidjas. One of them she recognized as Vidjas' chief of staff. He was carrying a valise. The other one was a uniformed official government guard. After a quick, quiet consultation with them, Vidjas gave Nia a significant look and a beckoning gesture.

Checking the courtroom clock—yes, it was midmorning—Nia asked for a recess. Judge Gund, who missed nothing in his courtroom, nodded. Nia walked to Vidjas as decorously as she could. She felt like running.

Vidjas pulled a split bubble out of the valise. Inside it was a document, written in Almaazan with a mirror version in Starmark standard language. There was also a message to Nia from Idris: *This isn't what you asked for but may work better. This document grants Val Savre an emissary status parallel to mine. It means he need not live on Almaaz, as a citizen who has no ancestral holding there must, but can reside elsewhere, as I do, and as long as he keeps a hearth.*

Surprised, Nia quickly read those sentences again. She hadn't expected this. But it might work for Val. It implied that he worked for the interests of Almaaz. Which in understanding halo gates, and trying to make sure Dhal demons didn't spill out of the gate on Almaaz, he was certainly doing.

I'm sure you have found out what kind of legal protections an emissary has.

Nia had.

The elaborate signature is the seal of the High Holy Priestess of Almaaz. Trust me, it doesn't get more official than that.

Recess or no recess, neither Judge Gund nor Derriger had budged. They were both closely watching her. When the judge tapped his gavel to end the recess, Nia approached them both. "Your Honor, the issue of negating Azurean citizenship, as a precondition to extradition, is now irrelevant."

"Irrelevant?"

She showed him the Almaazan document. "Val Savre has been granted the status of emissary of Almaaz. There are ironclad legal protections for anyone with that status, protections that Faxe is very much signatory to, since it is a matter internal to their union. The same ironclad protections are recognized by Wendis and the Alliance, and apply anywhere in known space. He has diplomatic immunity with respect to all polities that exist now or *will* exist. If accused of even the most heinous acts, he can be extradited only to Almaaz."

With a victory more complete than she had dared hope for, though she'd been praying about it for days, Nia found herself swept into an upscale and decorous bar on a higher level of Denevez One, above the Hall of Law. With her were Vidjas, several senior legal students, and two law professors. She couldn't tell them exactly how she'd gotten diplomatic immunity for Val, but they didn't want that so much as to celebrate her.

Val was safe now. He needed to keep a low profile, but he was safe. And damn, she thought, it had been fun. When she admitted as much, her friends old and new clinked glasses approvingly.

Afterward, with a glass of fine wine in her system, she walked across the greenhouse bridge connecting Denevez One to Denevez Two. The bridge was bright and warm and the glass walls gave her sweeping views of the landscape and seascape beyond the city. This was her native world, and she loved it as much as ever, even now when she'd seen other worlds across the stars.

In his office suite, she found Edvard alone. He asked, "How did it go?"

"I won."

"I am proud of you." His expression was solemn, almost rigid, but she could tell by his voice that he meant the words.

Glad, she hugged him. He felt stiff. "Father, what's wrong?"

To her surprise, he asked, "Did you ever consider canon law?"

"I familiarized myself with Old Cathor canon law some months ago. I'm not well versed in ours. Why do you ask today?" Suddenly she had an uneasy feeling.

Edvard said, "The prelate of our Church, the Archbishop of Albion, has demanded my resignation. Because of my remarks yesterday. Or else that I retract what I said. I won't."

Indignation welled up in her. "I can fight it."

"No. Now is not the time for that." When Edvard spoke in short, hard sentences, he was truly upset. "The cathedral is done and so am I. Even though it and I are both unfinished."

Stunned, unable to reassure him, she wrapped her arms around him. After a while her embrace registered on him enough for him to close his hand around her upper arm.

She felt an abrasive sense of unfairness. Why did this have to happen? She had won her case in court today. Val, wherever he was, was safe like never before. Martan, because of who he was, was safe too. He was probably busy protecting Val from any and all threats, for that matter.

Today, the last thing she wanted was for the first man she'd loved, her father, to be in deep political trouble.

28

HELLHOLE

Varry, the smaller moon of Faxe, which had become an incubator and training ground for hellhounds, as Martan remembered with utter clarity and even with a kind of fondness from his own past, was not as bad as he had imagined it might be.

It was worse.

Varry had become the headquarters of the secret intelligence agency and a nerve center of intended conquest. That was the energy Martan sensed here now. Plans were being made to control all of civilized space by subversion, corruption, or outright conquest. In conquest, the Tellus-Albion Consortium would play the starring role. High-ranking Telal officers were permanently stationed in Varry now. Martan sensed that Telal expected to be well rewarded, like the plundering army it would be, as conquest unfolded.

The recent failed invasion of Wendis had created shock and outrage in Telal and SECINTAG. Some high-level planners had been precipitously demoted because of it. And there were rumors about a hellhound defector in Wendis. Assessing the rumors, Martan felt cold hard dread. He was that defector. Being discovered here would doom him more surely than anything he'd ever imagined.

He could still run away. The dark shuttle hadn't returned to Union Station yet. He could bluff his way aboard and turn his back on Varry and the evil festering inside it.

Instead, he went to his scheduled meeting with the senior control agent in charge of Nome.

Agent Holdur looked closely at Martan. "You look different."

Controlling his respiration in case of suspicious sensors, moderating his pulse for the same reason, Martan laid out the story he'd fabricated: He'd had cosmetic surgery the better to resemble a researcher known to Vienradzis Savre. Thus he'd wormed his way into Savre's confidence, often meeting in a favorite corner of the university library. He'd learned of Savre having co-conspirators in a disunionist plan to bomb the headquarters of Telal in the capital city of Tellas.

"Commendable initiative on your part," said Agent Holdur. "Of course, we will verify your information."

"Of course," Martan said in an even tone. "There may be details I misconstrued or that have changed, since I last met with Savre."

"For now, relax," said Holdur. "You've earned it."

Martan said casually, "I may go play with the cubs."

Agent Holdur smiled. It wasn't a nice smile.

Martan hoped that the verification of his story would take a while. If it didn't, he would be in serious trouble. He could still run away on the dark shuttle. In a familiar hallway, one that looked as it had ten years ago, while the atmosphere felt different and made it hard for him to breathe freely, he froze for a fraction of a second. Then he continued toward the nearest elevator. He hit the button, harder than he had to, for the elevator to take him down into the heart of Varry.

Decades ago, Varry had been tunneled through and through

and finally set spinning to give the interior of it spingravity. Varry was a smaller world than Wendis. The spingravity in the halls and rooms near the moon's surface was stronger than in Wendis, but it rapidly lessened on the way to the center of the moon. Halfway to the center, in a natural cavern, was the training ground of the hellhound cubs, where they learned how to handle themselves in spingravity. Around the edges of the cavern were the stages where cubs learned hand-to-hand combat and practiced with each other. They also learned how to interrogate, again starting with practicing on each other.

On the far side of the cavern was the high, wide training wall. Arms crossed, Martan studied it. He wondered if it contained the halo gate. Val Savre was certain such a gate existed here, and that it was dormant, not dead. Their plan hung on that crucial detail, like the sword of Damocles hanging over someone's head in ancient mythology. Martan wanted to make sure.

There were cubs training in barehanded fighting today, paired off in the stages as their trainer put them through their paces. Early hellhound training looked as though it hadn't changed since Martan's day. If so, the seven cubs in this pack had started out as adults in their twenties or thirties. They looked younger because they had been juvenated, made more ready and eager for physical training and skill acquisition than any adult human being could possibly have been otherwise. They were being put through a rigorous training regimen day and night. If they were like Martan's own pack of cubs had been, they loved it.

Playing the part of a senior hellhound on shore leave after a successful mission, he walked through the cavern, glancing at the action in the stages, his coordination adapting to the local spingravity in only a few steps. He stopped where he had a good view of the climbing wall. His eyes narrowed. He remembered that wall well. It had protrusions, ledges, and niches enough to make it climbable, although the spingravity made that challenging. If you lost your grip or your balance, you skidded down and across the wall collecting bruises until you finally hit the floor. The wall drove home the importance of not losing your grip or balance in spingee.

As Martan expected, when the hand-to-hand session ended, the cubs had to climb the wall, never mind anybody having collected a black eye or sprained wrist in the hand-to-hand. With a quick howl, the cubs all swarmed onto the wall. Two of them made it to the top. One of them tapped the goal, which lit up in approval. But on the way down, too triumphant, he got into an impossible position where he was stuck. The other one who surged to the top then lost his grip, slipped part of the way down, and barely saved himself from a fall. Four of the cubs just ended up stranded somewhere lower on the wall. One fell off part of the way up. He rolled when he hit the floor and got back on his feet, probably bruised.

These cubs had the eager early innocence, Martan thought. They might not have even been blooded yet. Not yet allowed to make their first kills.

The cubs' trainer approached him. "I think I recognize you, hellhound, but not completely."

Martan remembered this trainer from years ago. "I had to change my appearance for my last mission. My name is Nome."

"Nome. You were good enough at this. Show them how it's done."

Martan pivoted on the ball of his foot and ran to the wall. He remembered the solid and the treacherous footholds and handholds. And the Zoned Park in Wendis had been keeping him in tone for an effort like this. At the top, he tapped the goal. It lit up. Then he angled back down. On a narrow ledge near the bottom, he stopped, looking down at the cubs.

Here was his best guess for the location of the halo gate, if any. He casually pressed both hands against the wall behind him. Then he felt the ethereal quiver, like that rock wall on Tellas. Like the solid rock that had turned into light, space, and escape for Val and his war party. As the realization sank in, Martan's heartbeat elevated. Not even he could completely control it in this level of excitement. No matter. If there were suspicious sensors in the cavern, he'd just had a burst of exertion and now he was the object of adulation. Seven faces looked up at him, six still eager, the seventh, hurt and defensive.

Balanced on the balls of his feet, relaxed to all appearances, Martan told the cubs, "The main thing is never put a foot or hand anywhere without knowing the next two reaches or steps. That way you can backtrack." He pointed at the hurt one who'd painfully fallen off. "What's your name?"

"Phoron."

"You've spent almost all of your life active, athletic, on a planet, right?"

"Yes. No excuse." So that was still the rule when you made a mistake in here. *No excuse.* If the mistake was bad enough, it would result in *no mercy*. But Phoron wasn't at that point, yet.

"Climbing is different in spingee. But you can make it." Then Martan verbally walked Phoron to the top. Even with a bruised shoulder, the cub made it the whole way, up and back again. He had good musculature and coordination, and maybe the most recklessly willing attitude of anyone in this pack.

"Well done," said the trainer. By clapping his hands twice, he called the cubs off training. It was their mealtime. They turned toward the slide pole by which they'd get to the meal station that was two levels downspin. They ran toward the pole in a tumbling group, like the cubs they were.

Martan checked his internal time sense. The way for this corrupt little world to end was there, camouflaged, but there all right. The time for the end was near. And he still didn't know enough. He casually offered, "I'd like to discuss how that session went."

"Glad to," said the trainer. They companionably walked to his office. When the door closed, Martan raised his left hand. That hand shouldn't have had neonerves, because hellhounds were made with only one deadly hand that could be amputated if they went rogue. Thanks to the doctors in Wendis, Martan had neonerves in both hands. He surprised the trainer, who never saw the left-handed interrogation coming.

It was easy. Hellhound interrogations followed the tracks of guilt in a victim's mind. The trainer had tracks like that, and they were rutted deep. He was guilty of his life's work of training hellhounds. And in recent years that meant defacing their humanity like never before.

Learning what was worth knowing, Martan withdrew from the trainer's mind, covering up the memory of the interrogation with slight brain damage. After looking blank for a moment, the trainer nodded. "Yes, good idea, since there's two more with the same background as Phoron." He didn't register that the idea had just been planted in his mind in an interrogation too subtle to remember.

This was very good, Martan thought. The trainer hadn't been immune to interrogation. More to the point, he wasn't suspicious about it. After all, the hellhound training was as tightly protected as the training itself was programmed. No enemy should have been able to get into here, not without the kind of onslaught that would have resulted in Telal warships arriving on red alert. Evidently, it was unthinkable to have an interloper who fit in and could interrogate a trainer.

They returned to the cavern. Another pack was there now. Their alpha howled a brief command. The alpha and the four other hellhounds swarmed to the top of the wall without missing a grip or a step. All of them tapped the goal. And they did so with exactly the same gesture of their hands.

From the trainer, Martan had learned that for the last few years, cubs were put through more severe training than

Martan's own pack had ever been. That matched the memories he'd salvaged from Nome's ruined mind. Early on, they were given new names, with their former personal names erased from memory. Phoron was one such artificial name.

The training of the pack that easily climbed the wall took the training philosophy to its logical conclusion. Their souls had been stripped out. This matched Nome's memories about the hellhounds coming soon after his generation. Martan was seeing it with his own eyes here. A onetime pack of cubs had been given a group mind, blindly obedient to an alpha, who in turn unquestioningly obeyed a control agent. Unlike Martan's generation, and even Nome's, they'd never graduate from cub to solitary hellhound, anti-terror agent with agency and semi-autonomy. Instead what had started as a cub pack had become a *wolf pack*.

This wolf pack was almost ready to unleash on an unsuspecting civilization. Their psychological brainwashing and brain training were nearly complete. Their physical training hadn't been stinted on along the way. They all came back down the wall without missing a handhold or foothold.

Martan could see a major problem with the new kind of pack. What if their alpha made a bad call? They'd all obey. If one of them saw that they were making a mistake, he wouldn't be able to warn off the others. He'd either lack the free will to do so —or the rest of them would turn on him and kill him.

To look at it another way, if the wolf pack got into trouble, they'd drive themselves into complete destruction, and none of them would live to be apprehended and studied. The potential for collective suicide might not be a flaw in the training program so much as a feature.

From the trainer, Martan had learned that the wolf pack had once had ten members. The attrition rate was 50 percent. That was higher than anything Martan had heard about when he was here years ago. The ones who'd washed out had been destroyed, except one of them had died early by accident, and not been mourned.

The trainer hadn't gotten his position, and held on to it for years, by virtue of a tender heart, but on some level he knew how very wrong the process had become. Ironically, he did care about the cubs. He wouldn't have been as effective in training them if he didn't. On a deep level the trainer knew, and blocked the knowledge from his self-awareness, that the new wolf packs were less a brilliant innovation in counterterrorism, and more an intelligence bureaucrat's wet dream.

The training-ground cavern in the heart of Varry used to be called the Hellhole, with a punning kind of fondness, because it was the natural habitat of hellhounds. Now it was truly a hellhole. That night, Martan slept only because he knew how to make himself sleep, and knew that he would wake up at any hint of danger. The next morning, he was summoned to another conference with senior control agent, Holdur.

"Your account is promising, but some of the details don't add up. Let's go over it again," Holdur said, without his usual sly and hungry smile. In other words, Martan thought, there'd been a failure to verify. And his life was now on the line.

"Of course." Martan checked the universal time readout and then repeated his fabricated story. When the story got weak with groundless details, and Holdur started frowning, Martan moved his left hand like a striking snake. He interrogated Holdur.

The man was no more immune to telepathic interrogation than the trainer had been. But it was harder. A true sociopath, he felt no guilt about all he'd done. Martan had to use a destructive level of force. But what he found was worth knowing. He ended up dizzied, panting, and nearly sick to his stomach, not that Holdur noticed. Holdur lay on the floor, his brain flooded with blood from a major stroke that Martan had induced. Martan did not regret that.

Holdur's mind had been full of plans to send wolf packs out

with Telal Consortium attacks on Goya in near the future. Fully half a Telal fleet, heavy with officers, was now here at Varry, scheming with SECINTAG. That made it a fine time for Val to come through with an invasion of Dhal demons. Given that much military presence here, the demons would be turned back, but not before they put a dent in Telal's resources and SECINTAG's too. Martan regretted that some semi-innocent lives would likely be lost, but the military necessity was paramount. Otherwise truly innocent life would be forfeit, everywhere.

Innocent lives mattered. Martan left Holdur's office with long, apparently confident strides that he was too shaken to have simulated in heavier true gravity. Entering the elevator, he rode upspin and stopped the elevator in the detention level. Here convicted criminals were housed because their sentence was to be interrogated and killed by hellhound cubs. The process blooded the cubs, teaching them the darkest skill of their trade. The detention level looked and smelled like a prison anywhere, only with a high degree of sterility designed to keep victims from falling sick until their day came to die.

According to what Martan had found in Holdur's mind, one of these cells housed a man Martan had once met. Several years ago, he'd been sent to interrogate that man, who was a notable disunionist. But he didn't intend to foment terror against the government of Faxe. He wanted to overthrow it by political action. Martan had been ordered to interrogate him anyway. But when Martan found purely political aims and no intention to get there by wanton death and destruction, he ended the interrogation, sparing the man's life. Overcome with disillusionment, Martan had defected, ending up in Wendis.

What was the disunionist's name? Martan had buried the memory but not too deeply to locate. *Laurend-Pol Kain.* Although Martan had spared him, he hadn't been scared enough—or more likely, he'd been too principled—to run away from the disunion cause and hide somewhere safe. So he ended up here.

With a proximity key he'd taken from Holdur's pocket, Martan let himself into the disunionist's cell. Kain was gaunt and wary; his shadowed eyes told Martan that he knew he was doomed. There wasn't time to explain everything, not that verbal explanations would have been believed anyway after all that Kain had been through. For the second time in Kain's life, Martan cornered him and gripped his throat.

29

NIGHTWALKERS

Much like the last time he went to war, Val left Lane and Dikk behind in safety on Stannto, not knowing if and when he'd see them again. But this war felt different to Val than the last one. It was a good difference. He knew all of the relevant factors far better. Some of those factors he understood better than anyone else alive. He had a motley crew that he'd hand-picked and were fast becoming a team. As he walked through the cool passageways of the halo gate system this time, Mayor was beside him, Spark and Donalt behind them, along with Kali and Loki the Pastfinders, keeping watch to either side, and Gauriz, with his keen senses, keeping watch to the rear.

Val had learned that his Pastfinders' families were patriotic expatriates from Wendis. The recent war, with the Faxen Union's secret intelligence agency attempting to subvert Wendis, hand in hand with the Union's Telal Consortium attempting an outright invasion, had affected them deeply. Kali and Loki regretted that they hadn't been in Wendis to help defend it. Being on a warpath against the Faxen Union suited them perfectly well.

The doctor, Kam Far, was coming too. He had a basic

proficiency with weapons for self-defense, and they might need a doctor before this was all over. Val's seventh fighter was Enghel, the technologist. Unsmiling, he trudged on through what had to be the nerve-clawing dread of encountering a shape-shifted demon with the face of his dead brother.

Even wracked with dread, Enghel had already proven vital to the mission. Much of the Vere system had been salted with inconspicuous sensors since the last time Val was here. That was Enghel's idea. The sensors registered the movements of Dhal demons. Enghel had a tablet with which he monitored the movements, inside a more detailed map of the Vere system than Val had ever seen. Evidently Enghel had been very busy. Mayor had a tablet with the same information.

For Val, the best difference of all from last war was that this fundamentally was not a war. After the last time, he hated war with a passion. Rather than a war, this was basically a trick. As the Sleighters liked to say, it was a *sleight*, albeit a remarkably ambitious and perilous one. The demons—not technologically skilled—would be armed with spears, clubs and maybe stolen rifles; not that the demons were good marksmen, but a bullet didn't have to be well aimed to do damage. Val's fighters had various weapons and bulletproof vests. But victory would not consist of killing more of the enemy than they killed of his people. Rather, victory would be arranging for two separate sets of enemies to kill each other while getting through this sleight alive.

What mattered more than anything else to him was that now, just like when he started out on the way to the planet called Hades, where the demons killed him, he meant to protect his home and family and all else that was dear to him.

To confirm the situation depicted by the tablets, Val sent Gauriz out to scout with copies of the map on his own pocket tablets. Gauriz rejoined the rest of them at the intersection that had been marked on the map for him to do so. "Yes, the demons are stirred up, and they know which way we're going. They want nothing more than to catch and eat you, slowly."

Val swallowed hard at that ghastly prospect. Yet if he suffered that fate, he'd be just the last of many previous victims and the first of many more. Not just human victims. Millenia ago, the Dhal demons first preyed on the Meridianers, the peaceable scientists who'd uplifted the intelligence of the apex species on Dhal without realizing that conscience was not a necessary corollary of intelligence.

Donalt and Kam both looked scared, but neither they nor Enghel nor anyone else had frozen in fear yet. Val wasn't going to either.

He kept a close eye on the universal time readout on his own tablet. When he saw that some demons were in the way, the sensors revealing their presence, not enough of them to constitute a real threat, he made sure to step out in front of the war party to taunt them. They ran away, hissing. That should guarantee they ran to different nests of their kind spreading the word that Val was alive and in the gate system. It was exactly what Val wanted. At least up to a point. Too few demons and the mission might be pointless. Too many, and his war party could be wiped out before it was all over.

The tablets showed him the effects of his progress through the Vere system. More sensors registered more demons, converging this way—following the war party in increasing numbers, moving increasingly fast.

"Never not have a bolthole," said Mayor, at his side. "Even dhalrats know that."

Val just nodded. Sweating with tension, he navigated the way to a major intersection. The intersectionality of this place was masked by holographic walls. "Loki, that wall should be an illusion. Take a look into what's on the other side of it."

Loki waved an arm in the apparent wall then leaned into it. "A tunnel branches off. It looks the same as this. Lights work."

This part of the Vere system was cold and empty, but in good repair.

"That other wall should be the same. Kali, check it."

She found the same thing that Loki had.

Val spoke quietly. This air was so cold and still that his words reached every ear. "I want two of you in that tunnel, and three in the other one. Ahead is our destination, through the doorway that you can see from here. I want the demons to follow me there and then I'll open the gate. I'll run through the gate to get them to come after me. The rest of you, provided the demons don't notice you waiting in the tunnels behind the holograms, follow the demons, chase them all out of the gate, but don't go through the gate. I want to be the only one of us to go out through the gate. My ally will be there." Val anticipated, hoped, and all but prayed that Martan would be there. "He can get me back in, even past a pack of demons. I also need someone to flank me at the gate. Gauriz."

Gauriz nodded.

"Me too," said Spark.

He hesitated. But she had a right to take the part she wanted in this. The demons had made sport of nearly killing her brother. "Yes."

"Bolthole?' Mayor prompted.

Val answered, "Long ago you taught me how dhalrats only have one bolthole, that finding both ends of their dens is how we kill them. I'd rather have more than one. Both passages behind the holograms are likely safe. They don't connect with anything behind us so the rest of you shouldn't be ambushed in there."

Mayor crossed his arms. "That's not an answer for you and Gauriz and Spark."

Val checked the tablets. "There's more than just one doorway up ahead, in fact, several. I know which one should go to the Faxen moon Varry. With the other doorways, I have no idea what gates they lead to and where, but I think I and anyone with me can go through one of them, and I can shut the doorway behind us. If we give it a while for trouble to dissipate, we should come out again in one piece. But I want to go ahead now and check the gate we want."

"There are a lot of them coming," Enghel said urgently, gripping his tablet with both hands.

Loki and Kali, Donalt and Kam stepped through the holographic walls to wait as he'd ordered them to. Val ran up the tunnel. Spark and Gauriz ran with him. This tunnel ended in three doorways. He ducked into one of them. The gravity was suddenly heavy. But the air was breathable. It went to an unknown planet, not that he meant to go there any time soon, although the gate was very near. Several people could hide in this tunnel for a while. He checked the doorway opposite the first one. The air behind that doorway was hot. It probably ended in a gate somewhere too hot for human life. That made it an unattractive bolthole.

Finally, he went through the third doorway. The gravity on the other side of it was—strange. He waved his friends to follow.

"Spingee," said Gauriz.

"Yes. I think this is the Faxen moon."

At the end of the tunnel was a diagram. It told him what he wanted to know. He checked the universal time on his tablet. It was past invasion time but not far past it. He touched the pentagonal plate beside the gate. The plate woke up, colors chasing across the surface, colors that he read as a gate ready to be opened.

Gauriz went alert, his head tilted, listening and sniffing the air.

"Demons coming behind us?" Val asked Gauriz.

Gauriz gave a sharp nod.

Val took Spark's shoulders and pressed her against the wall

just inside the gate. "You're so slender you'll be invisible when the light show comes on. Just be ready to shoot if any of them are about to kill me."

She raised her rifle.

Gauriz mirrored her position on the other side of the gate. He was bigger than Spark, but lean, and like her, wearing light-colored clothes, the better to blend into the light of a halo gate.

Val was lean and wearing light clothing too. The lights spilling out on both sides of the gate could obscure him as well. But he didn't intend that. He could hear the demons now, their running feet and laughter that sounded inhuman. Terror lit his nerves. He touched the pentagonal plate, the movement of his fingers saying *Open*.

The gate began to open, the rock with a diagram drawn on it melting into bands of light. He tensed to step through the gate and be the last bait to make sure the demons went through the gate too. Shaking, he started to force himself to take that step.

Even above the clamor of the demons coming, he heard Spark's high-pitched gasp.

A figure stepped into the gate where Val had meant to go. The figure was dark, bipedal, too thick and stocky to be human, and full of stars. With a thick hand, it waved Val away.

Val pressed himself against the wall of the gate next to Spark.

"Star man?" Spark quavered into his ear.

"Taking the shape of a Meridian!" he whispered back. "Lane saw them in a dream and that's what she said they look like."

As a Meridianer, the star man looked more solid than he ever had as a human. Vere probably understood Meridian anatomy well enough to simulate it better. He looked at Val with large dark eyes. Val had never seen eyes in the star man's face before.

Dhal demons crowded through the doorway. They had thin, unhuman shapes, except several of them had shape-shifted to look human. They had shrill, unintelligible voices, except one that looked human and cried out, "A Meddler!" It pointed at the star man. The Meridian-shaped void in the rainbow light was highly conspicuous.

Two more of the human-looking ones had human-type vocal cords too. They chorused, "One of the Meddlers!"

The star man turned and ran through the gate.

The demons followed him, brandishing clubs and spears and gnashing their teeth.

Val pressed himself to the edge of the gate and looked past the demon horde. There were human beings out there. They had uniform coveralls, so it had to be some kind of installation. He hoped to God that his calculations had been accurate and it was the right installation. He desperately reviewed his memory of the diagram that had showed exactly what he expected.

The Dhal demons raised their voices in what sounded like glee. The human-shape-shifted ones chorused, "Look! New plunder! *New meat!*"

30

BREAKING STORM

Warming a planet was a gradual process, but not a gentle one. Glaciers melted and mineral-laden meltwater flowed into the sea, energizing the primitive ecosystem already there. The glaciers melted under rain warmer than the air above the ice. The rain came from storm systems that had not existed before the colony ship from Earth discovered Azure and began terraforming it. The storms unleashed wind strong enough to drive tides past the usual edges of the ocean, blow buildings over, and wreck ships carrying trade and travelers.

Sunset today was calm and bright, with a hundred stars shining through the sky before the sun completely set, but the forecast weather told of a major storm system bearing down on Denevez. High-tide warning signs already blazed. So did the flood warnings.

Taffy's house was in an old district prone to flooding. There was newer housing on the mountain foothills north of the oldest part of Denevez, but city policeman that he was, Taffy felt it important to live close in, and risk a flood every so often. Before Nia left Denevez on the day of the court case, she invited Taffy and his whole family to stay in Castle Courant during the coming storm.

She explained her reasoning to her grandparents the following morning at breakfast. "In the past, they've stayed with Adriance, but as Taffy's family gets bigger, they're a crowd for Adriance to house. And it seems to me that Castle Courant really needs more people."

"We'll have one less with Edvard away on business," Eirene said.

"On business," Vim echoed sadly.

Early this morning, Edvard had taken the ice ferry to Denevez, there to board a sailing ship that would take him along the edges of Azure's main equatorial continent. He would visit the main provinces of Azure-Tierre to personally explain his resignation. The Archbishop of Albion—the head of the New Catholic Orthodox Church—having demanded that Edvard resign, had further decreed that an archbishop must not resign remotely.

As a result, Edvard would have multiple opportunities to repeat his warning about the Faxen Empire. The Archbishop of Albion hadn't forbidden him to do so. That prelate might even find his message to ring true. Yet the Church on Albion had to maintain a détente with the power of the Faxen Union. But by forcing Edvard to resign in person in each province, the Archbishop of Albion had ensured that Edvard's warning reached every corner of Azure. Church politics were complex, with quicksand for the unwary and opportunity for the prophetic.

Being in the process of resigning should make Edvard a far less likely target for assassins. Nonetheless, two security guards would accompany him from Denevez, around Azure-Tierre, and back to Denevez.

Ideally, Edvard would have departed two days from now. The approaching storm system made it advisable for him to leave early. That might be good, Nia thought. Instead of two days to brood, maybe it could be like getting back on the horse that threw him off.

Radzi wasn't at breakfast either. He'd been spending long days and nights at the cathedral, working with the organmaster to finish and tune the great organ. He'd even developed an aptitude for the engineering that went into the organ. Lately Eirene had had some long and revealing talks with him, her grandson. It seemed that by being reconciled with his father, he'd let himself recognize technical talent he'd inherited from Val.

At breakfast, Nia also told her grandparents how her day in court went. She explained Val's Almaazan emissary status in general terms.

"Almaaz where people are all black and shiny and brilliant?" Vim asked.

"Could Val go to live on Almaaz?" Eirene asked shrewdly.

"Possibly," Nia answered. "There's a science institute that might welcome him." Oh yes, ever since the institute had learned about a halo gate on the Almaazan island called Toliman's Hearth, research into that was its highest priority, Idris had told her.

"Is the court business over?"

"It is for now, so I can stay here during the storm and rest." She glanced at the breakfast room window. Cirrus clouds were flying across the sky, precursors to the storm system. Harmless clouds in and of themselves, they struck a sudden nervousness into her. "I hope," she added.

"Do storms still give you nightmares?" Eirene asked gently.

"I don't know. There are no wild storms in Wendis." Even as a young, bold child, she had nightmares when a storm raged outside at night. Many such nights, she had stayed with her grandparents, sleeping on the spare bed in their apartment because she felt too alone and small in her own bedroom. Even when Castle Courant had more people living here, it had seemed too empty and dark-haunted during a midnight storm.

Eirene's eyes were thoughtful. "I'll make up the spare bed. If you're disturbed during the storm tonight, come see us."

The first flashes of lightning in the night sky, with wind and thunder loud enough to be audible inside Castle Courant, made up Nia's mind. She came to her grandparents' door with her pillow under her arm, and the hugwort trailing after her, because it had sensed her distress. Vim turned on the small gas-fed fire in their fireplace. The three of them sat in front of it as they had years ago. The small, warm, living light of a real fire had always fascinated Nia. She felt her overwrought nerves begin to relax. The hugwort climbed into her lap. Its furry root mass purred.

"Where's your love tonight?" Vim asked, with a fond look at his own life's love, Eirene.

Nia honestly answered, "I don't know. He's probably somewhere with Val, making sure Val stays safe."

"Who is he really?" Eirene asked.

Eirene was the one who had looked at Martan and seen a sharp saber in a shabby scabbard. Nia answered, with surprise that she could be so honest, "His past is darker than I would like to talk about tonight, but someday we'll tell you his whole story. Someday soon," she promised.

"Toasted marshmallows, anyone?" Vim had everything ready, with his long smooth sticks and fresh marshmallows from his favorite candy store in Arrival. He'd always liked toasted marshmallows at least as much as Nia did.

Nia surprised herself again. She was able to laugh. "Someday soon we'll tell you my whole story too. I met Martan at Parhelon Fair in Wendis. It was his first Fair since the university hired him as its proctor, and my first Fair to make a day of attending. One of the attractions in the Fair is called Camping Out. People spend a night on a grassy meadow in the middle of Wendis, and they toast marshmallows on real fire. I only heard about it later. I can't wait to tell my legal assistant about making up for the marshmallows I missed there by having some with you here!"

They laughed with her. In a few minutes the air had the scorched-sweet smell of the marshmallows. Nia's nerves relaxed even though the storm continued unabated.

The storm system consisted of bands. The next morning, the sky above the mountains was full of the trailing edges of the first storm band. The sky above the sea boiled with black clouds of the next band by midmorning, when Taffy and his two children stepped off the ferry from Denevez. Nia welcomed them all.

The little Taffies were Dino and Caro, boy and girl, age nine and five. They resembled their father, with dark hair, clear eyes, and plenty of curiosity. When she introduced them to the hugwort, they were fascinated by it. Apparently, it liked them too, lifting its leaves happily. It might have been getting a bit bored lately. Dino earnestly took on the responsibility of feeding Edvard's angelfish and, equally important, keeping the hugwort out of their tank.

While the children were busy exploring the upstairs, Nia showed Taffy the lower levels of Castle Courant. They decided that Dino could come down here even without an adult, but Caro should not venture down here alone. The spiraling Waydown Stairs only had minimal guardrails and there were ill-lit slick spots on the Cistern floor, and in either case a fall could be nasty. Nia checked the sea gate and saw that the recent repairs were holding up. Even after rain from the storm blew on gusty winds all night, no water had seeped in through the sea gate.

She remembered accounts from the past where an

approaching storm system dropped the atmospheric pressure to deep lows, and the sea gate was opened to equalize pressure inside and outside Castle Courant. It had to be done before the storm hit, or else rain and tide flooded into the sea gate. Nia didn't remember that being done in her lifetime. In bygone days the Castle might have been more tightly sealed than now.

She showed Taffy the repaired control room, with a new metal plate covering the fissure in the floor. Unlike the last time she was here, the gate controls looked dust-free. He knew how the controls worked—they'd opened the sea gate several times when they were young, always on nice days with low tide. She'd learned that lesson early, when Val opened the gate and hundreds of jellyfish washed in.

When they returned to the upper level, Nia heard young voices full of excitement and laughter. It was good to have the little Taffies here. Maybe one day there would be one or more little Martans too. The idea thrilled her. Maybe sooner than later, she told herself. Maybe even war or no war, even though bringing children into a world at war was taking a chance.

Taffy's wife, Carole, arrived soon after noon. Since she was an engineer for Denevez, she'd spent the morning in emergency planning. The ice ferry crew handed down her luggage, then set off at top speed to dock at home in Arrival and secure the craft ahead of the mounting wind.

Carole was everything Nia had hoped she'd be for Taffy's sake: intelligent, kind, and attractive as well, not with the sleek looks that Suzana would have praised, but with a rangy, active build and a distinctive face full of character. Nia took an immediate liking to her and made sure that Carole had everything needed for the family to be comfortable.

Late in the day, the news came on to view. For that, there was a vizwall in the family room. The news viewer was a small section of the wall, like a window, which was a good reminder of its purpose: not to invade every human living and thinking space, but simply to communicate what was going on in the outside world and universe.

In the Twentieth and Twenty-First Centuries on Earth, news and communications and entertainment had invaded every nook and corner of human space, filled the atmosphere, and contributed to the insanity that destroyed civilization and life on Earth. It was incredible to Nia that the ancients should have found artificial sights and sounds conveyed by electric signals so interesting when the whole, living Earth lay around them.

Wendis understood the lessons of history and rigorously controlled communications and news, legislating and enforcing that the former be limited and the latter carefully balanced. Meanwhile, the culture of Wendis prized physical and sensory experience, thoughtfully experiencing the world, and being out of doors even in the self-contained world that Wendis was. Edvard would almost certainly say that Wendisans practiced incarnation, which New Cathorism encouraged both in theology and practice. Nia made a mental note to talk to him about that.

The window on the world glowed, and all the adults in Castle Courant gathered around it for the single hour of news today. In its own way, this was like Vim's little fire last night, Nia thought, everyone gathering like their ancestors millennia ago with light shining on their faces, to hear news of the world and be with one another. Electronic signals were dangerous, like fire, and as addictive as any of the various chemical substances discovered over the millennia.

It might be cosmic justice that although Earth's ice caps had dwindled with disastrous consequences as the planet's climate warmed, now humanity on Azure was doing everything in its power to warm the planet and melt the ice. On a planet tipped toward warming, though, storms could be stronger and stronger. This one was like that. Its bands were reaching intensities never recorded before.

"Uh-oh, that'll bring out the storm chasers," Taffy said gloomily.

"Who?" Nia asked.

"Fools who walk or drive or even fly into storms for the thrill of it. Some of them make useful observations. Others get into trouble and first responders have to rescue them."

Carole said, "The key levees are sure to be overtopped before this is over. The city has boats in place for water rescue. But thank you for inviting us to wait it out here where it's high and dry."

Edvard, by taking the sailboat early, had stayed out of it. He'd called to say that he'd reached his first port of call, where the storm was only a distant darkness in the sky. Because Taffy's family was safe and warm here, and Edvard was safe, too, Nia felt glad. The intensifying storm still made her tense. Night fell early, with rain and sleet mixing on the way down, and lightning flashing incessantly.

Everyone in this part of Azure was intensely interested in the unfolding weather, so that took precedence in the news. Nia was glad that her court case hadn't become public. Judge Gund had decreed that it be kept confidential, and people were living up to that. Or else any leaks had been overshadowed by the storm.

Suddenly, though, the news took a more distant turn.

The Azurean news commentators said the interstellar news service reported a disunionist attack on the Faxen moon, Veritas. Even on Azure, not a part of the Union and a dozen stars away, this was a startling development. The adults and Caro listened to the news intently. Dino was downstairs exploring the Cistern.

News about the disunion attack was coming in fresh star bubbles full of unconfirmed and even contradictory reports. According to one report, the strange kind of alien artifact called a halo gate had opened on Veritas. Nia thought it unlikely in the extreme that a halo gate would be admitted by the secret intelligence agency that controlled the moon. But it turned out that sources in Telal Consortium starships, which were present for some reason at Veritas, had leaked news about a halo gate.

Every adult in the room knew that Val—Eirene's son, Nia's uncle—was a leading researcher in halo gates. And that Nia had just spent a day in court making sure his work didn't get appropriated by the Faxen Union. They all looked at her.

Someone in the interstellar news service had done enough research to find out that a halo gate opening on the planet called Dhal had been the doom of a research station there, letting in an invasion of malicious alien predators. The Azurean news commentators breathlessly relayed that news too.

Nia's mind suddenly added up clues she knew—Val's work, and Martan's past, and somebody's remark in the little house where Idris lived at the University of Tellas: *It would be good if Dhal demons invaded Veritas.* She remembered Val's model, churning for years in the computational depths of the university, finding out about halo gates where none had been known. She knew just how much Val resented SECINTAG's interference with his work, and she knew how much Martan hated how hellhounds were made inside Varry. With an intensity that felt like the bottom dropping out of the pit of her stomach, she could imagine the two of them teaming up to change all of that, taking terrible risk to do so.

Eirene said, "Nia, you're pale. You're shaking. What's wrong?"

Nia was too stricken with fear to answer.

The news commentators explained that all of this news had come via high-priority interstellar bubbles from the interstellar news service. The latest bubble—with news that was at least three hours old but so stunning that the open bubble was handed to a commentator while he was in the middle of a sentence—reported that the Faxen moon, Veritas, had broken apart.

31

EXODUS

The disunionist was gaunt but able-bodied and in his right mind, a mind that Martan touched and queried.

"I remember you." Kain was hoarse from tortures that had made him scream. Martan knew about that from Holdur's mind. "You're asking me if I want to risk a perilous rescue? I'm already a dead man here. Yes."

Martan took a set of handcuffs from a well-stocked board on the prison wall. He put the cuffs on Kain's wrists, unlocked, but completing the impression of a doomed prisoner. Then he led Kain to the Hellhole.

The cubs soon came from breakfast eager for the next day of training. They surrounded him.

He checked his time sense. There were ways to spin this out, if uninvited company arrived slightly later than scheduled. Much later, and he'd be in dire trouble. But probably not much more trouble than if the intended company actually arrived. "Cubs, I know you've interrogated each other."

They chorused affirmatives. They were so young, he thought, so eager, so ready to be formed. The training plan was to form them into a wolf pack. Between one moment and the next, Martan knew with rock-hard certainty that he didn't want that for them. Or for them to die in a demon attack either. "Today, you'll practice hand-to-hand fighting, fair rules, no broken bones, through ascending bouts, until the final winner gets the grand prize. This criminal to interrogate."

Kain grimaced. That was a realistic enough reaction.

The cubs were excited.

Martan handcuffed Kain to the interrogation post in the stage nearest the climbing wall, again, making the cuffs look locked without really locking them. He muttered to Kain, "Whatever else happens, that won't. No death by interrogation."

Kain looked glassy-eyed, but he nodded.

Martan named a skirmish order, pairing the cubs off, himself paired with Phoron, because he could favor Phoron's bruised shoulder better than the youngsters could.

The trainer walked over to them. He didn't question Martan. In yesterday's interrogation, Martan had made that impossible. Martan asked, "We have the Hellhole for another hour, right?"

The trainer nodded. "The wolf pack is doing calisthenics in the gym."

Martan's heartbeat and respiration were through the roof. Even if suspicious sensors picked up on that, he couldn't spare the attention to moderate them. He was now responsible for himself, a doomed prisoner, and a pack of cubs.

There would be only one way out.

If that.

Martan signaled the start of the fighting. He let Phoron win, with the help of points awarded to Phoron for his real aptitude for this kind of fighting. Phoron looked surprised and happy and turned toward his next opponent. The three cubs who lost their fights sat down on the floor cross-legged, watching the fighting continue in the stages nearest the gate.

Suddenly the wolf pack entered the cavern. They lined up

along one wall, watching. What he was doing with the cubs wasn't usual, even though the trainer had obediently scheduled it. Unlike any military squad Martan had ever seen, he couldn't read the mood of any of the young wolves. If their alpha became suspicious, and ordered them to attack, Martan was going to be at least as doomed as Kain.

Then he felt the same indescribable sound-sensation he'd felt on Tellas. The stargate star was opening. His muscles and nerves tensed, and readiness to react sang in his ears. He held up a hand, signaling a full stop to the fight. Then he gave the short howl and hand gesture that ordered the cubs up the wall.

They were used to training being interrupted by more training. They obeyed. Nobody fell off, not even Phoron. Martan hoisted Kain onto his back and followed the cubs up the wall with hellhound speed.

Below them, a section of the rock wall melted into colored light. Looking down over their shoulders, the cubs were puzzled by the light. Martan howled an order to freeze. In gravity, most people—and hopefully other sentient beings—didn't look up at anything that didn't draw attention to itself.

Waves of light flooded the Hellhole. Through the light, a stocky, dark humanoid shape came running out. Martan had never seen anything like it.

Behind the humanoid came a few of the creatures called Dhal demons. Martan hadn't seen any of them before either, but they fit the descriptions he'd heard. They were chasing the humanoid.

The humanoid vanished. More Dhal demons poured out of the gate, looking for it, and instead seeing the wolf pack. The demons had hands full of weapons and heads full of teeth. They showed the unholy glee that the few surviving witnesses of demon attacks on Dhal and other places had reported when the demons found new victims.

The wolf pack watched a few moments too long. When their

alpha howled an order to attack, the demons had already scattered. Better if the pack had closed in on the demons at once, which would have happened in an ordinary group of seasoned fighters, the most alert of them recognizing danger first.

The demons scattered far enough that the way into the gate was nearly clear. Martan howled orders backed up with gestures. *Down! Fight! Flight!* He pointed toward the gate.

A few demons got in the way. Phoron, already with a bruised shoulder, failed to block a blow from a demon's club to his stomach. Phoron doubled over. The demon opened its mouth impossibly wide to take a bite of the cub. Another cub kicked the demon aside and dragged Phoron to the gate.

At the gate, Martan and the cubs almost collided with human fighters chasing more demons out. Martan shoved the cubs and Kain into the gate. Just inside the gate, Val watched them all come in. "Who are these people?"

"Innocents!" Martan told him.

One of Val's fighters looked back. "It's blood and body parts out there." Red strobe lights, brighter even than the halo gate lights, flashed on his face.

Above rising pandemonium in the Hellhole, Martan heard an ululating siren. The all-out red alert had never been sounded in the training base in Varry for real, only as a drill. Real was what it was now. *Good luck with that.* More demons had poured into Varry than Val had anticipated. The invasion was looking wildly successful.

"This way, everyone! We've got to get home!" Val ordered. He set off down the long tunnel behind the gate. His people quickly followed.

Most of the cubs were already looking at Martan expectantly. He swatted the other two, getting their attention. He used commanding voice. "Follow them!"

Val said over his shoulder, "I won't close the gate, and some demons may get back in, except they're wild to kill and maraud first. The gate will keep any human intruders out."

If anybody in Varry realized what the halo gate was, Martan thought, they would know that halo gates resist intrusion by exploding outward. If nobody in Varry figured that it out, they might learn the hard way.

More demons came running through the long tunnel. Val shouted at them, "Fight us or follow your kind to meat and plunder!" He gestured with his thumb over his shoulder. His fighters pressed against the tunnel walls with their weapons raised. The demons either believed Val or heard their marauding fellows ahead. They ran by the fighters, hissing.

The cubs looked confused. Phoron was clutching his chest, with at least one broken rib.

In commanding voice, Martan said, "Your training is over. Your mission starts now."

They believed Martan. They trusted him because he was a senior hellhound and because of how malleable their rejuvenation had made them. It was too much trust. He would have to somehow guide them into more maturity than this, and more humanity than the wolves they'd been intended to become. He pointed at the one named Chiron, who so far had been the smartest of them. "You're Alpha now. Make sure no cub gets lost on the way to where we're going, and somebody helps Phoron."

Chiron listened with an intensity like cotton soaking up liquid, then saluted.

Together, Martan's cubs and Val's fighters followed the tunnel until they came to a strange place. The light changed and so did the gravity, becoming something more like the gravity of a good-sized moon that didn't spin.

Looking back, Martan could see that they'd come through a kind of discontinuity in the air. It had to be vastly more complicated than just light changing, really a kind of membrane

—on one side of it Varry, on the other side, this place. Martan recognized what Val had described in their meetings on Tellas as a *doorway*. Every gate had a doorway nearby. And the destination of the doorways could be changed. Val had managed that with one of them before, after prolonged study of it.

On this side of the doorway stood a man with a two-handed grip on a tablet. His eyes widened at the number of people with Val—with the cub pack and Kain, Val's party had more than doubled in size. The man with the tablet tensely said, "There are even more coming. They haven't reached the holograms yet. We can still shelter there."

"Run!" Val yelled.

The group ran. A Sleighter carried Kain. On orders from Chiron, two cubs made a sling out of their arms to carry Phoron.

A kilometer or so later, at a branch in the tunnels, a man-shaped darkness. The dark shape held up one hand in an unmistakable gesture that meant *come no further.*

The group skidded to a halt. Several of Val's fighters dropped to one knee. The man with the tablet checked it. He gasped, "The demons are moving so fast they're already past the holograms."

The man-shaped darkness pointed at a branch in the tunnel.

Someone asked, "Where does that go to?"

The man with the tablet said, "That sector is off the edges of my map."

The hair on the nape of Martan's neck stood up in apprehension. The Sleighters shuffled their feet nervously. The cubs looked at Martan. He kept his face and body language calm, and they imitated that.

Val said, "I trust him. Follow me, all of you."

They entered a long tunnel that stretched straight and featureless. Martan praised the cubs and advised them on how to keep a long loping stride going in low gravity. The Sleighter fighters got the idea and gave the cubs encouragement and good advice too. When Val called a rest, the Sleighters brought water out of backpacks to share. Nobody had much food in their packs, but some of what someone had was given to Kain. He stared at the offered nutrition bar. Then something in him turned over, deciding that he might live after all and wanted to. He took the bar and ate it.

Meanwhile the doctor, Kam Far, quickly checked Phoron and Kain, made sure no one else had a serious injury, and gave a grim nod that meant *keep going*. The group walked for hours, trading off who carried Kain and Phoron. Finally they came to a discontinuity in the air: a doorway to somewhere else.

One of the Pastfinders asked, "Where to?"

"I don't know," Val admitted.

"It's changing, because I hear it!" The speaker was the youngest Sleighter, a girl with a rifle. "Where it goes is changing!"

Val stared at the doorway. "Spark's right. Look at the colors around the edges. Wherever it went a moment ago, the destination is changed. He's making it go somewhere new."

The hair at the nape of Martan's neck stood up. Val meant that the artificial intelligence embedded in this network had just changed the destination of this doorway. Because for some reason it wanted them to go that way.

Val said, "Let me by!" He dashed ahead through the doorway and soon returned. "Everyone come along, careful, it goes to planetary gravity. Not a super-earth, but more than a moon. The air seems quite good."

Some people dragged their feet, reluctant, until the Sleighter called Gauriz said, "We've got demons following us, and a pack of dhalrats with them."

Then the group went through the doorway as fast as they could. The strip of light on top of the new tunnel came on for them. At the end of the tunnel was a rock face with a diagram drawn on it. Val stared at it. "I know where this is." He sounded like it was something he didn't dare believe.

"Habitable?" Martan demanded.

"Yes."

The oldest fighter, who Martan had heard being called Mayor, ordered, "Open it!"

Visibly shaking from hours of stress and responsibility, Val put his hand on a pentagonal plane beside the rock face.

Someone in the back yelled, "They're coming!"

Being ambushed between the doorway and the gate would be bad.

Martan pushed his way to the back of the party, shoving a cub on through the doorway as he did. He morphed to let his fangs come out. Now he had cubs and Kain to protect. And the adrenaline simmering in his system had a way out. He shouted, "Open the gate while I hold them off!"

32

STORM CHASE

Nia shook with dread and certainty that Martan and Val had something to do with what had happened to the moon Veritas. They both might be dead. They might have been dead for the hours it took news bubbles to fly from Faxe to Azure. Or they might have been dying for that long. And she was helpless to do anything about it.

Dino trotted into the room, stopped in front of her, and asked, "Why is there a rainbow down there?"

His father asked, "Do you mean a rainbow in the sky?"

"No, down there in the Cistern."

In an instant, more clues fell together in Nia's mind. Val's diary saying *The gate was full of halos and arcs and then I saw the star man.* She'd thought it meant that he looked out through the open sea gate and saw late afternoon solar arcs and the constellation of the Astronaut already shining through the sky. But it could be interpreted another way. And there had been that gleam in Lana's eye when Nia showed her the Cistern!

The clues set off an avalanche of realization. Nia launched

herself toward the Waydown Stairs. She raced to the stairs, torn between terror and hope.

On the stairs, she heard footfalls behind her. She looked over her shoulder to find Taffy following her. "Eirene said go with you," he said, and waved her on.

Near the bottom, she saw strange light shining on the Waydown Stairs, colors chasing each other across the slick stone. Her heart leaped. She ran the rest of the way down with her hand barely skimming the guardrail.

The Cistern was full of colored light. A section of the far wall had stopped being the rough rock she'd seen all of her life. It was a deep turbulent pool of colored lights.

In the light, she recognized an impossible but very familiar figure. Val was coming out of the light but staggering so badly that he might not make it. With her nervous system on fire with hope and fear, she told Taffy, "Don't follow me any further. Don't let anyone else follow me either. It could be deadly dangerous. Understand?!"

He retorted, "I do not understand this but I'll do what you say!"

She ran into the light and caught Val before he fell over. His weight made her reach for the rough rock wall beside the gate to steady both of them. The rock was still real and it scraped her palm. Supporting Val, she demanded, "Where is Martan?"

Val jerked his thumb over his shoulder. "Coming through a firefight."

People crowded through the gate. She didn't see Martan with them. She called, "Martan!!"

The answer was a ringing howl in a voice that she knew was his.

People kept coming through the gate. Through the gate's pulsing lights, she saw the last few of them fighting off something that wasn't human. Martan was in the middle of them. She screamed, *"Martan!"*

He grabbed a spear that one of the inhuman creatures thrust at him and pushed back so hard that his enemy fell backward. He ran through the gate telling Val, "Close it!" Then he howled again. The two young men behind him leaped after him through the gate just before the gate faded. It turned into solid rock again with Martan's howl still echoing in the Cistern.

Martan was here. Val was here. If she hadn't had to stay steady to support Val, she might have collapsed in shocked amazement. Val and Martan were here and so were a lot of other people. Those clustered around Val were all panting, and ragged-looking, with one sturdy man carrying another man who looked thin and hurt. She recognized Donalt the wargamer and Kam Far the doctor standing near Val. "These are your friends," she told Val. He nodded.

She had people with her too. Taffy was behind her, and Dino had run down the Waydown Stairs and was goggling at everything.

The rest of the new people stood near Martan, with one of them being carried by two others. These all looked the same youngish age and very fit, with identical coveralls. She pointed at them and asked Martan, "These are?"

"A pack of hellhound cubs that belong to me now." He glanced around, recognizing the Cistern. "We made it. I made it through hell to you!" He finally smiled and it was his radiant, end-of-eclipse smile.

She threw herself at him, wrapped her arms around him, and kissed him, feeling his strength and how real he was, sharp fangs and all. He kissed her back. Fear for him gave way to ecstatic joy that he was here and he was hers.

After a few moments, she remembered that they had an audience. A very interested audience. All eyes were on the two of them.

Not letting Martan go, she said in a voice intended to carry, "Listen, everyone. We've got to cover this up. All our lives will depend on it. Taffy, open the sea gate. Then close it." She turned toward Kam Far. "What do you need to care for the injured?"

Kam said, "Light and clean water, please!"

She told him, "Follow Taffy to the control room. Get the injured in there. There's clean water in the tap. Go with the doctor," she told a fighter who was clutching a bleeding arm. "Dino, run upstairs and bring blankets down from the linen closet, you know where that is now."

Dino ran up the stairs at top speed.

She took a deep breath. "Anybody got trash? Drop it! Somebody go to that big trash bin, over there, turn it over and empty it on the floor. We are going to pretend all of you are weather chasers who crashed. It's hell of a lot more ordinary for a plane-load of weather-chasers to land at Castle Courant's old sea-landing field than for a stargate to open in the basement!"

There were a few chuckles from those catching on faster than the rest of them.

With a deep mechanical groan, the sea gate started to roll upward. Seawater and rain surged onto the floor.

"Everybody move that way!" She and Martan got all of them onto the higher platform that was near the stairs and the entrance to the control room.

The gate opened fully. Water washed over the floor of the Cistern and wind galed in. It was impossible to talk and be heard.

Taffy closed the gate, then leaned out of the control room amazed at what he'd done. The Cistern was awash with water, with sodden trash that included metal debris looking plausibly like it came from a wrecked airplane.

Nia realized that she had been imperious, and everyone had jumped to do what she wanted. She might as well make the most of it. "The airplane sank but we rescued those who swam out of it. Now every one of you who can speak this language, repeat after me, 'We are weather-chasers and our airplane crashed in the sea'!"

She got a ragged chorus.

"Say it again! 'We are weather-chasers and our airplane crashed in the sea'!"

This time it sounded better. The hellhound cubs, in particular, answered in perfect unison. They were quick to catch on.

Eirene had joined the audience. She stood on the Waydown Stairs with fuzzy house slippers on her feet, and astonishment written on her face. She looked at Val, and then at the fighters, the hellhound cubs, and Martan, but her eyes went back to her son.

Nia's head was spinning. Had Vere, the artificial intelligence of the gate system, once opened the stargate into the Cistern level of Castle Courant? Had young Val seen it, met it then? She rounded on Val. "You have a LOT of explaining to do!"

He answered diffidently, "I will. Right now you're doing a fine job of taking things in hand." He looked up at his mother and shakily started up the Waydown Stairs. She ran down the stairs and wrapped her arms around him.

Kam and the injured had disappeared into the control room. Dino dashed down with his arms full of blankets and followed them. Val's ragged crew of friends started laughing with relief and reliving how they got here and praising the hellhound cubs for everything they'd done well.

Nia reclaimed Martan. "You came through hell to me."

"Are you hurt?" He turned her hand over. She had blood on her palm. He had a cut across his own palm from grabbing that spear at the end of the fighting.

She closed her hand around his. It was right for their blood to mingle. They were that close to each other, heart, mind, and spirit, for better and worse and ever. And even after hell coming between them, they were finally together again.

33

SAFE HARBOR

For the next several days Nia wondered what to do with a house full of Sleighter fighters and hellhound cubs, not to mention the other guests. To start with, several people had injuries, which Kam tended. The hurt hellhound cub soon started recovering. The gaunt, weak man carried on somebody else's back turned out to be a political prisoner rescued by Martan. The man's name was Kain. He benefited just as much from well-informed, intellectual conversation as food, water and medical care. Vim talked to him at length and came away very thoughtful.

But what in the name of High Heaven, as Wendisans would put it, could be done with everybody else, all of them revved up with victorious spirit and, in the case of the cubs, primed to learn blazingly fast and try themselves against challenges physical and intellectual?

It turned out that one thing to do was to have a war game. That activity was highly relevant, because the old Courant sea-landing field was where the Telal Consortium might start an invasion of Azure. Nia cautiously sounded Vidjas out about an invasion scenario. Vidjas and her advisors thought that Azure could hold out for a long time against an invasion, provided it didn't start with an overwhelming success on the part of the invaders. The people of Azure, once startled out of complacency, would resist long and hard. So being able to stop an invasion at the start of it was worth a lot.

There was also the possibility that the halo gate could open again, and Dhal demons come through it. Val thought that unlikely, since Vere, the intelligence, had regained more control over the system than had been the case for thousands of years, and could make sure the Azure gate didn't randomly open. Still, vigilance was in order.

That meant honing the fighting skill of everyone who would remain at Castle Courant and making certain that they could work together. Some of the guests intended to inconspicuously find their way home across the stars. But only after leaving Castle Courant adequately defended and in good repair.

The storm system blew away after three days. It left damage around the edges of Castle Courant. Energetic guests turned out to be an immediate plus. The Arrivaltowners who came to check on the Castle, wondering if they were needed when they had their own trouble with storm damage, were treated to the sight of the Cistern awash in water and jellyfish, plus the staged debris, and the story of how a plane of storm-chasers had crashed and been rescued and were now industriously helping with storm recovery. Not needed after all, the Arrivaltowners went home with a happily-ever-after story to tell their friends and neighbors.

Today, the sky was blue as glass and the sea smooth as a mirror. It was a good day for a war game. By now, Nia had decided that she hated war as much as Val did. But she agreed with him that being able to fight an unwelcome war was far better than being attacked without recourse.

Donalt had taught Nia how to use a bow and arrows. They'd

found good quality sports bows for sale in Denevez. Donalt determined the bow best suited for her. After a few days of hard practice, she knew how to use it. Her arrows were tipped with electronic sensors. The guest named Enghel devised the sensors. He was a restless, brilliant, ingenious man. Several malfunctioning electronic devices in Castle Courant had been repaired by him already.

The war game was hellhound cubs against Val's fighters. The cubs were so plastic that they learned blazingly fast. As Nia understood it, the biggest problem was to introduce them to the idea of dummy weapons to use for practice without intending injury, since it was a make-believe war.

The war game was designed in such a way that the Household took in any casualties and looked out for itself. Kain, the disunionist, had sharp eyes, so he was a human sensor at the Castle's windows. So were Dino and Caro. Taffy's children had stayed here because their house in Denevez was flooded. Enghel augmented what his mechanical sensors said with what the lookouts told him. The Household also included Vim, who was having great fun watching the excitement while he guarded his greenhouse.

During the morning of the war, both sides discovered that the plasglass walls of the greenhouse were highly resistant to impacts. The weak point of the greenhouse was the door. The hugwort quickly figured out to stretch itself across the door of the greenhouse and trip invaders. It took the same trick to a vulnerable set of outdoor stairs. By the time of the scheduled truce for lunch, the hugwort had accounted for two cubs out of action because they'd tripped over its taut tendrils and taken a bad fall. The hugwort was undamaged and having fun, with lifted leaves every time Nia caught sight of it.

Radzi was officially neutral: At Donalt's suggestion he'd taken up the role of a Bard, singing as the fighting went on. His impromptu songs managed to inspire, praise, and gently mock people on all sides. The other neutral individual was Svetlana Tai. Responding to the locator chip she'd given Martan, Lana had rushed back to Azure from the red star training base. Since her arrival she'd shared some of her expertise in fighting, with emphasis on the formation of ethical fighters for the benefit of the hellhound cubs. Today she wore a white vest to signal her role as a Wendis-style war game referee.

Nia and Val commanded the Household—Val indoors, and Nia outdoors. During the morning, she made use of her bow and discovered that getting her point across without actually hurting someone was something she found quite pleasing. Those she hit reverted to Household, joining the other real and imaginary injured to watch as the game played out. By time for the truce for lunch, she had put two cubs and a Sleighter among the imaginary injured. She reflected on being careful about what you wish. She had wished Castle Courant to be more full of people and livelier. That wish had certainly been granted.

After the lunch truce, Nia positioned herself where she could do the most good: hiding above the lake gate. As a child, she'd discovered that she could climb up there to watch for visitors from Denevez. Kneeling behind a tough little evergreen tree, she was well concealed, but had an excellent view of the fighting on the wide flat yard next to the lake gate. She also had her bow and arrows in case the fighting spilled too close to the gate.

If ever invasion was truly imminent, explosives tucked into the right places could tumble some of the rock of the Arc into the sea, making the sea-landing field unusable. Landing craft would be wrecked if they didn't sense the rocks soon enough to wave off the landing. If wrecked, the craft would disgorge wet, angry invaders. With the sea gate firmly closed, the invaders might try to swarm around the Castle. They'd find the land doors that opened onto the Arc to be sturdy, with no windows to break through, and narrow enough that invaders would have to go through in ones and twos and be easy to pick off by defenders inside. That made the lake gate behind its narrow dock a prime target. The yard off to one side, by the shore of the frozen lake, made for a likely battleground. So the war's afternoon bout was designed to test that scenario.

Nia closely watched the war game sides taking shape. Val's fighter friends, under the leadership of the grizzled Sleighter who went by the name Mayor, were highly resourceful fighters. Martan, putting the cubs through their paces, was a creative and effective captain of them. And the alpha of the cubs, Chiron, had turned out to be a talented strategist. It was ironic how the hellhound makers thought they'd made up a meaningless name for him. Their education in the classics had been deficient. Chiron was a legendary creature on ancient Earth, a centaur, and a good Wendisan-sounding name. Nia looked forward to telling Hiro about it.

Minutes into the afternoon war, Nia saw the ice ferry coming from Denevez. She hastily stood up waving a green flag. Lana Tai blew her shrill referee's whistle, and everyone froze where they were. Lana bounded up to Nia's perch. Nia pointed out the distant ferry, still aiming for Castle Courant. Lana regarded it with narrowed eyes. "Routine delivery?"

"I doubt it. There's a new storm system forming. Edvard may have cut short his tour for now. I think I see him."

Lana suddenly grinned. "Sooner or later he needs to know who's in his Castle." She raised her referee's whistle. Nia didn't move to stop her. Lana blew the whistle, and the game resumed.

People soon saw the ferry. Everyone hid.

Edvard disembarked by himself. He looked forlorn as he stood alone with his luggage as the ferry sped away. But then he noticed that he was being watched from behind the boulders, the trees, and the columns in front of the lake gate. Moreover, the watchers were strange people sneaking closer.

"No harm to the high-ranking hostage!" Lana called out from beside Nia. "Take him who can! Fight on!"

A flurry of fighting resumed where it had left off. Two Sleighters sidled toward Edvard.

Nia's arrow hit the first Sleighter squarely. "Next one stepping forward is down too!" Bow nocked, she nimbly climbed down to the dock and took Edvard by the elbow. "He's mine!" she shouted at the other war gamers. She steered Edvard into the Castle, shutting the lake gate door behind them.

Val arrived at a run from upstairs. "Dino saw the ferry coming and spotted Edvard aboard it."

Edvard stared at Val as though seeing a ghost. "What are you doing here?"

Val cleared his throat. "It's a rather long story."

"And what are those people doing outside?"

"Practicing how to protect Castle Courant when the Faxen Union invades Azure."

Edvard blinked. "My son-in-law is one of them."

"Right," Val said encouragingly.

"He gave orders to three young men who moved like lightning."

"Well, you see, they're baby hellhounds. He's a real one."

Nia could tell that Edvard was winding up to ask questions and demand answers. She crossed her arms. "Father, this is an awkward time to tell you this, but Martan is a hellhound of Wendis. He helped Val plan an attack against the Faxen secret intelligence agency by opening a stargate in the Faxen moon, Veritas."

Val asked, "Did you hear about Veritas splitting into pieces?"

Edvard managed to nod.

Val explained, "It was the headquarters of the intelligence agency. Opening the stargate let an invasion of the predatory alien creatures called Dhal demons into Varry. The Telal Consortium was there planning with the agency how to invade the rest of known space. They stormed the gate in force, I'm sorry to say. The force of the Telal assault was matched by the gate's response. The gate exploded outward with such force that it broke Varry apart. It made for loss of life greater than anything Martan and I intended," Val concluded ruefully.

Nia said, "Val and Martan and everyone else you just saw out there retreated from Varry to here through a stargate Val opened in our basement."

At that, Edvard looked too stunned to ask questions much less demand answers.

Nia finished, "With Varry destroyed, SECINTAG won't be making much of its usual mischief like sending assassins after Zakeri or you. The Telal Consortium could still invade Azure, and we think they intend to, by using our old sea-landing field. But they won't take Castle Courant, because everyone is training to stop any such invasion as soon as it starts. Let Telal put its jackbooted foot here, and its invasion will get no traction." Her voice sounded ringingly decisive in her own ears. She'd never heard herself use that tone before. She'd never spoken about turning an enemy force away from her ancestral home before either.

If not completely following her explanation, Edvard registered her tone. "I believe you."

Val took his stepbrother by the elbow. "Edvard, I'll take you to join the rest of the noncombatants. They have an enlightening conversation going on around a bottle of Aquarel."

34

DESTINIES

For the last time in wearing archbishop's regalia, Edvard came to the entrance of his cathedral. In a ceremony half as old as history, he rapped with his ceremonial staff on the tall, heavy door.

The door swung open to admit him. Just inside, he halted and lifted his gaze to the organ. Ranks of pipes rose high, gleaming, on both sides of the high altar. Taking a deep breath, Edvard sang a brief litany of inquiry. Thanks to the acoustics, his voice would be audible in every corner of the cathedral.

The organ answered with a single pure, perfect note.

Heartened by the sound of the organ, allured by it, he walked toward the front of the cathedral. On either side, there were quite a few attendees. He recognized most of them. Adriance Vale, the next Bishop of Denevez, had numerous family members with her. The prime minister of the planet, Vidjas Finndur, had honored the occasion with her presence. Less predictable attendees included several self-identified interstellar riffraff and the disunionist in exile, Kain. Also present today, and even looking interested, was the Wendisan star captain, Svetlana Tai, who by her own admission hadn't been in a church, temple, mosque, or any other house of worship since the age of nine.

The seven hellhound cubs sat in a neatly dressed, well-groomed row between Tai and Eirene. The cubs' heads all turned toward Edvard with lively curiosity. They were growing up fast, and in a far better way than what had been intended for them. Eirene and Tai had their hands full with those cubs, but they were making them human again.

Not present was a certain Val Savre. Ostensibly, Val had remained in Castle Courant in the peaceful and quiet absence of all the other guests. Edvard suspected that Val might be somewhere *else*. The thought made a shiver run down Edvard's back.

He halted again in the center of the cathedral under the apex of the great dome. He sang a longer liturgical call. The organ answered with fluid notes in perfect harmony. Edvard felt such relief that it almost made him dizzy. The organ was finished, thanks to the hard work of many, including Val's son Radzi, and Enghel, the technologist. With two organists, Radzi assisting them, and Enghel busy in the organ loft like a mother hen watching all the technology at once, the organ finally worked.

And the organ, in all of its power and beauty, was having a dialogue with Edvard. The lowest of the organ notes resonated in the wood of which the pews were made. Touching the top edge of a pew next to the center aisle, Edward felt a subtle shiver in it.

He walked forward again. Noticing a few couples holding hands, he sent a blessing their way with a gesture; he blessed Martan and Nia, Spark and the doctor named Kam, the Pastfinder named Loki and an Arrivaltown girl. The citizens of Arrivaltown had been delighted with new neighbors showing up as storm chasers.

Oh yes, chasing storms, all of them. Himself included. Before the high altar, he halted for the last time.

He would sorely miss having authority here. He would regret not wearing the regalia. He could return to simply attend the cathedral, after a mandatory absence of a year and a day for everything to take new shape without him. This cathedral would by the grace of Christa be a safe harbor in the storm of history for centuries to come.

Harbor is well and good, said an old sailor on the ship in which Edvard made his final, painful farewell journey, personally resigning as archbishop. The old sailor added, *But ships are meant to be at sea.* Those had been words Edvard needed to hear at this point in his life.

Taking a full breath, he sang again, his side of the longest litany yet. The organ answered at full volume. The deepest notes vibrated in his chest. Higher, brighter notes washed over him like a baptism of sound. The music reverberated, notes folding over each other without any dissonance. The organ was perfectly tuned to the cathedral.

With the mechanical heart and nerves of the organ embedded in the cathedral—this building made of planet, heated by underground steam, full of the light of the world shining through the tall windows that showed Christa resurrected in green forests and blue sky, soft clouds and greenhouse garden—the organ was seamless with the cathedral. In the form and voice of the organ, his cathedral had come alive. Edvard sang and it answered him with a great, grand, assured voice. Looking up at the gleaming pipes, his eyes blurred with tears of gratitude to have his cathedral finished.

He wasn't finished though. He intended to begin a new chapter of his life beyond the sky above Denevez.

On a rough hillside, not far from the fissure where he'd returned to Tellus twice before, Val Savre waited as the sun set while stars already shone. The university lay below him with its own constellations of lights coming on. He appreciated the warmth of the air, compared to the perpetual chill of Azure.

Lane came up the pathway at run. She had Dikk with her. "Dikk drew a picture of you, and I knew!" she said breathlessly.

He took his son in his arms. Dikk solemnly touched his father's face.

Lane embraced them both. "I am so glad to see you. Touch you. After that coded bubble came from Stannto, we knew you were safe on Azure, of all places, but I didn't know if you could ever come back this way, or if you'd dare."

"It's no longer about daring. The star man and I are friends now."

Dikk looked at him with understanding in his eyes. He knew what *star man* meant.

"He's taken back control of his gates, which he has every right to do. But when I asked him if some of our friends could return that way to Stannto, he agreed, and we opened the gate for them. The older Courants were shocked speechless to actually see the stargate open and close in the basement under that edifice of theirs. So Mayor and Gauriz are back on Stannto now. That archer of mine, Donalt, headed for home in a more conventional way, through the transit tower."

She smiled the warm beautiful smile he loved so much. "He made it back and he's already filled Idris and me in on all that happened on the way to Veritas and back and in the war game that Nia's father interrupted by coming home. I'm proud of Donalt—and everyone."

Val smiled back at her, infinitely grateful to look into her eyes and Dikk's and be with them here, if only for a while. "Today Lord Vere invited me through when I was by myself because everyone else went off to a church service."

He thought that church service would go well. Radzi and Enghel had both been optimistic about the organ working as it was meant to. Val was proud of his son showing technical aptitude, under the tutelage of a brilliant technologist, one who was becoming a good friend.

"I'll need to stay in hiding on Azure for a while longer. Martan and Nia send their greetings. Her father told me to give you his best regards as one of our family, whenever I saw you next. He's had some serious shocks, but he's going back to Wendis with Nia and Martan." Edvard had even confided that he had hopes of finding a love match in Wendis, like his great-grandfather had, and like Nia had too. Stranger things had happened, Val thought. "How is living with Idris working out?"

"Because this gravity is hard on her, she's glad to have my help in her house. I'm so glad Nia helped me get back here, with Dikk, and that we're together. Idris loves Dikk. He's made friends with that dhalcat of hers. The cat even lets him ride her."

Slightly shocked, Val imagined his little son on the back of the huge, sharp-fanged, long-clawed dhalcat.

Dikk said, "Tsaalith."

They both looked at their son. Most children first said *Dada*, a few said *Mama*. Their Verian child's first word was *Tsaalith*, the dhalcat's name, which he pronounced perfectly. It was an abundantly strange universe, but one with more than a few mercies. Val asked, "And your research?"

"It wasn't just a dream. Now I know it's going to work. I'm glad you eliminated so many demons though."

"There are still too many left. I saw one on the way here. It ran away from me as if from bad luck incarnate." Evidently, the Dhal demons now associated Val with doom and disaster. He didn't mind that at all.

"My virus will take care of them in time." She looked thoughtful. "That's a good way to put it—it will take care of them. Transmitted to the demons through the dhalrats, the virus will work to devolve them, undo the uplift to intelligence that the Meridianers did without understanding the disastrous consequences. That's better than eradication. It just takes more time."

"We have time now."

Past the first urgency of meeting, they held each other and their child. Above them the stars, beautiful and mysterious as ever, brightened in the early night sky.

Martan had a strong arm around her, and she could feel the perfect coordination in how he moved as he guided her up the narrow, precipitous trail. The air was cold and windy. He compensated for erratic gusts of wind almost effortlessly. When they reached the top of the Gnomon, he wasn't even breathing hard.

Arcs, halos, and tangents of prismatic light filled the sky around the rising sun. They were as beautiful as any Nia had ever seen in Azure's skies. She shivered partly from the cold, partly from awe. She said, "Welcome to my world."

Martan folded her in his arms. "I like it."

Grateful for Martan's warmth and for how secure she felt in his arms, she sighed. "I was convinced that I might never come home again. I found a new home in Wendis. But now part of me wants to stay on Azure. I want to enjoy it with you."

"Someday, we will," he promised. "Everyone here will make sure you have a home to come back to."

She nodded. A lot had happened in the weeks since Martan and Val arrived with Val's war party and Martan's pack of cubs. The cubs had turned into good and willing defenders who knew how to cooperate with the Sleighter fighters who were staying here too. Enghel, the technologist, had set up a perimeter of sensors, so nothing hostile was going to catch the Castle unaware. Let the Faxen Union's Telal mercenaries try to put a jackbooted heel here, Nia thought with a flare of anger, and it would turn into a misstep for them. Castle Courant was ready. So was Azure. Vidjas was making sure of that. Nia told Vidjas, in confidence, just how effectively the Castle could fend off an invasion here. A botched invasion could be turned into a political and practical liability for the invaders.

In the meantime, the Castle had become a lively and happy place. The Sleighters were teaching everyone else how to do magic tricks. Radzi had gotten people to sing whatever old songs they knew, and new ones. The cubs had been training on the Gnomon, enjoying throwing themselves at the challenge of it, which was why Martan knew the terrain of this peak like the back of his hand.

More startlingly, the hugwort had come all the way to the top with Vim. According to Vim, the hugwort had figured out how to be a kind of living guidewire on the dangerous trail. Vim had been thrilled to scale the Gnomon for the first time since his youth. Nia was glad she hadn't known about that adventure until it was over; she would have been terrified for Vim. He'd trusted the hugwort implicitly, because they were inseparable friends now.

Nia said, "When I arrived here that night weeks ago, for what I thought was going to be dealing with fallout from Val's death, I dreaded facing Edvard. The most I dared hope for was some kind of truce with him." She took a deep breath of the bracingly cold air. "I didn't imagine that we'd be reconciled, and that I'd return to Wendis without the hugwort but with my father."

It was mandatory that Edvard stay out of the business of the Church for a year. It was advisable that he get away from potential assassins and political intrigue, soon, and not in a direction that his enemies would anticipate. He was going to Wendis with them. He was even looking forward to it.

Martan said calmly, "He's gone through a lot and he's changed."

"So have we all. And it's not over." No, it was not nearly over. History was at a dangerous inflection point, balanced on a narrow margin of stability, buffeted by winds of war. Potential disaster lay in more than one direction.

Yet right now on the Gnomon, with Martan holding her, on this terrain that he knew well, she felt safe. She even felt safe at the prospect of crossing the stars to return to Wendis and resume her work there. Most of what could go wrong across the stars and even in Wendis was also familiar territory to Martan. He was her protector as well as her husband and her friend.

All around them, Azure's horizon encircled around greening mountains and warming seas. Her world, with the brilliant beauty of the halos in the sky, reassured her of the resurrection of Christa Terra.

– END –

MORE ADVENTURES

If you enjoyed *Revenant*, try the first novel in the series, *Witherspin*, to see how Nia and Martan meet in that spinning city, Wendis, and the first challenges they overcome together.

In *Starmaze,* they venture far away into interstellar space and encounter unexpected dangers and wonders.

In *Adversary*, Nia and Martan are caught up in a momentous attack on Wendis by the Faxen Union.

Meanwhile, elsewhere, Nia's uncle Val has explored the single greatest enigma of the interstellar age—and gotten into very serious trouble—in *Halo Gate*.

And that sets the stage for *Revenant*.

Many more adventures are happening too. The five novelettes in *Tomorrow's Mascots* involve some of the same people and other entities as *Revenant,* and more.

To sign up for my occasional Newsletter, go to alexisglynnlatner.com, or here: http://eepurl.com/bvm_Bv.

ABOUT THE AUTHOR

Alexis Glynn Latner writes romantic speculative fiction that touches readers' hearts as well as their minds. She also edits and mentors creative writing and works at Rice University's Fondren Library in Houston, Texas. Her science fiction and fantasy stories have appeared in *Analog Science Fiction and Fact*, *Amazing Stories*, and many print and online anthologies including the *USA Today* best-selling *Pets in Space®*. She's had stories in mystery anthologies too.

Her science fiction novel *Hurricane Moon* was published by Pyr (Prometheus Books) in 2007 and again by Avendis Press in 2014 with the sequels *Downfall Tide*, *Star Crossing*, and *Helldive*. A new romantic science fiction series began with *Witherspin* and the first sequel, *Starmaze*, followed by *Adversary* and now *Revenant*.

Find out more about Alexis' books and stories:

www.alexisglynnlatner.com

facebook.com/AuthorAlexisGlynnLatner

ALSO BY ALEXIS GLYNN LATNER

The Starways Series

Witherspin

Mascot*

Starway*

Winter's Prince*

Pastfinders*

Starmaze

Adversary

Revenant

My future history, with its arc of characters, crises, and events unfolding across the galaxy, began with my first series of books: **Aeon's Legacy**.

The Aeon's Legacy Series

Hurricane Moon

Downfall Tide

Star Crossing

"Spike"*

Helldive

Collections of Stories

*My stories that first appeared in the USA-Today best-selling **Pets in Space**® Anthology are collected!

Tomorrow's Mascots

I have two other collections of science fiction short stories. In *Ascendance*, ten novelettes and short stories span five thousand years of future history. *The Shape of Wings to Come* is a collection of my science fiction and fantasy stories that all center on sailplanes—the most beautiful machines on this and other planets.

Ascendance, Science Fiction Stories about Reaching for the Stars

The Shape of Wings to Come

Made in the USA
Coppell, TX
21 January 2026

66357605R10193